Fortune Favors the Frivolous

Matchmaking Mischief Makers, Book 2

Beverley Oakley

ARE YOU SIGNED UP FOR DRAGONBLADE'S BLOG?

You'll get the latest news and information on exclusive giveaways, exclusive excerpts, coming releases, sales, free books, cover reveals and more.

Check out our complete list of authors, too!

No spam, no junk. That's a promise!

Sign Up Here

www.dragonbladepublishing.com

Dearest Reader;

Thank you for your support of a small press. At Dragonblade Publishing, we strive to bring you the highest quality Historical Romance from some of the best authors in the business. Without your support, there is no 'us', so we sincerely hope you adore these stories and find some new favorite authors along the way.

Happy Reading!

CEO, Dragonblade Publishing

Chapter One

"M E? FRIVOLOUS?" MISS Caroline Weston's obvious objection to the term rang across Devonshire House's grand ballroom, which she immediately followed up with a peal of laughter that made several nearby dowagers turn with narrowed eyes.

Eugenia, Lady Townsend, winced as she watched the spectacle from her position beside a marble column.

"Yet another example of that chit's gross lack of decorum," Eugenia's friend, Lady Pendleton muttered from her seat opposite her, her crimson turban bobbing with disapproval. "That gel will never find a husband if she continues to behave like a hoyden."

"She will not," Eugenia agreed, albeit with grudging admiration as she watched Miss Weston cross the ballroom, golden ringlets escaping her elegant coiffure, blue eyes sparkling with mischief. Behind her trailed her friend Miss Venetia Playford, and it was this contrast that caught Eugenia's attention. While Caroline was all bright energy, the equally striking, golden-haired Miss Playford moved with the careful restraint of someone perpetually under scrutiny.

"Miss Playford seems subdued this evening," Eugenia observed. "Not at all like the spirited girl from your Ghostly

Gathering two years ago."

"She, at least, has learned how to behave," Lady Pendleton replied crisply. "Unlike her bosom friend." Her pointed look returned to Caroline, who was now attempting to engage a marble statue in conversation, to the horror of nearby matrons. "I hope her mama—Oh!"

Eugenia turned her gaze to that which had caused Lady Pendleton's now interested look, and then she, too, drew in her breath. Despite herself, her gloved fingers pressed to her throat where her pulse had begun to race.

"My, my, the adventurer returns. I did not know Lord Thornton was back in town." Lady Pendleton's remark was almost drowned out by the ripple of whispers that swept through the crowd.

For, indeed, Lord Thornton cut an impressive figure in evening black, framed in the entrance of the double doors that had just been opened to announce him.

"At last, the evening becomes interesting. I haven't seen Thornton since that hot-air balloon escapade of yours," Lady Pendleton went on, adding with evident satisfaction, "Ah, he is coming this way."

Eugenia, for her part, was tongue-tied and hoped her fiery blushes did not give her away as Thornton approached with that devastating smile Eugenia remembered from her debutante days. In all the decades since, it had never failed to make her heart race.

Now he stood before them, bowing gracefully, a little grayer at the temples but just as handsome. "My dear Eugenia. Lady Pendleton. You both look radiant."

"Flatterer," Lady Pendleton replied, though she preened. "So good to see you back in England. Sit and tell us of your adventures. We heard tales of elephants and exotic princesses."

"All greatly exaggerated, I assure you." His eyes twinkled as he accepted the seat Eugenia indicated. "Though I confess, after two years of diplomatic tedium, even London's drawing rooms seem thrilling."

Eugenia was about to respond when another burst of laughter drew their attention. Miss Weston had somehow procured a serving tray and was curtsying elaborately before a group of gentlemen, offering them imaginary delicacies with such theatrical flair that even the stiffest among them were smiling.

"That child will be the death of her poor mother," Lady Pendleton declared.

Lord Thornton raised his eyebrows. "I remember her as a spirited lass when she first drew our attention at your Ghostly Gathering, Lady Pendleton."

"However, her particular friend seems much altered." Eugenia nodded toward Miss Venetia Playford, who stood apart, accepting refreshments with downcast eyes while her aunt, Mrs. Pike, hovered nearby. As usual, the older woman radiated disapproval.

Lady Pendleton sniffed. "I was remarking earlier at how pleasing it is to see that Miss Playford, at least, has learned how to deport herself with proper ladylike grace. Mrs. Pike has been most successful in teaching her niece grace and refinement."

Eugenia studied the pair more closely. Was it good manners that accounted for Miss Playford's apparent grace and refinement?

Or was it fear?

She frowned. Mrs. Pike's watchfulness seemed less protective than predatory.

"Indeed, the girl appears greatly diminished from my memories of her from two years ago," Thornton observed.

"Nonsense." Lady Pendleton waved a dismissive hand. "She's simply learned to conduct herself as befits her station. One cannot be a penniless ward and expect to carry on like—" She gestured toward Caroline.

"Penniless?" Thornton's brow furrowed. "I thought the Playfords were well-situated."

"Not anymore," Lady Pendleton replied, with the satisfaction of one privy to insider knowledge. "The father gambled away the family fortune before his death. Poor Mrs. Pike has made great personal sacrifices to provide for her niece these past twelve years."

Eugenia watched Mrs. Pike's thin smile as she steered Venetia away from a group of laughing young people toward a corner where Lord Windermere waited. Something cold settled in her stomach.

"How fortunate then," she said carefully, "that Lord Windermere appears interested in Miss Playford's welfare."

"Indeed!" Lady Pendleton brightened. "Wouldn't that be a most advantageous match for a girl in her circumstances? Mrs. Pike is beside herself with joy that he has taken such a particular interest in her niece."

"And Miss Playford?" Eugenia asked. "Is she equally joyful?"

They all looked toward the corner where Windermere was bending over Venetia's hand with possessive attention. The girl's face was carefully blank, but Eugenia caught the almost imperceptible way she leaned away from him.

"She'll learn to be grateful," Lady Pendleton said firmly. "A girl with no dowry cannot afford to be particular."

Thornton's expression had grown thoughtful. "Windermere seems unusually determined in his pursuit. I confess I am surprised at his interest...given what I know of his character."

"And what is that supposed to mean?" Lady Pendleton enquired.

Thornton shrugged. "With no disrespect intended towards Miss Playford, I would have imagined he'd have set his sights higher."

Lady Pendleton considered this a moment. "Lord Windermere has one of the finest estates in Gloucestershire. No doubt he is in London because he wants a sweet, obedient chit of a girl to wed. And Miss Playford suits, because money is *not* a requirement."

Eugenia felt that cold sensation spread, but before she could probe further, Caroline's voice rang out again as she swept past their group in pursuit of some new amusement. This time, however, she wasn't alone—she'd collected Venetia along the way.

"Come, dearest Venetia," Caroline declared loudly enough for half the room to hear, "you simply must see Lady Harcourt's new necklace. The emeralds are nearly as large as turtle eggs!"

For the first time that evening, Venetia smiled—a real smile that transformed her pale features. But as they passed Mrs. Pike, the older woman stepped smoothly into their path.

"Venetia, dear." The honeyed tone was at odds with the look in her eye. "Lord Windermere wishes to escort you to the supper table."

"Actually," Venetia said, and Eugenia was pleased to hear a spark of defiance in her voice, "Caroline wishes me to visit her tomorrow so we are going to speak to her mama—"

"Impossible," Mrs. Pike cut her off with a sharp smile. "You are promised elsewhere tomorrow. Come along now."

With that, she steered Venetia firmly toward Windermere, who received them with the satisfaction of a hunter claiming his prize.

Eugenia watched Venetia's shoulders droop in defeat and felt something fierce kindle in her chest. This would not do. Not if she could help it.

"Thornton," she said suddenly, "what would you say to another wager?"

He turned to her with interest. "Upon what would you wager?"

"Miss Playford's future." Eugenia kept her voice light, but her resolve was iron. "I propose that true affection will triumph over mere convenience—regardless of pecuniary desperation."

Lady Pendleton gasped. "Eugenia! You cannot be serious! The girl is penniless and a charge upon Mrs. Pike's purse. She has no choice in the matter!"

"Everyone has a choice," Eugenia replied quietly. "Sometimes they simply need someone to help them see it."

Thornton smiled. "You want to see Miss Playford escape

Windermere's clutches? You truly believe she does not wish to wed a man with a title or have the opportunity to run a magnificent estate with no financial cares in the world?"

"I believe," Eugenia said carefully, watching as Venetia cast one longing glance toward Caroline before being steered away, "that young Venetia would wish to assert her right to wed a man who would make her *happy*."

"And you are confident that Miss Playford does not believe Lord Windermere is capable of making her happy?"

"I believe she *knows* he will not make her happy," replied Eugenia. "And I believe that she has enough strength of will to assert her desire to wed a man of her *choosing*… regardless of what scheming aunts and predatory lords might prefer."

Thornton's smile was admiring. "And if she doesn't? If Windermere claims his prize?"

Eugenia's heart skipped, but she kept her voice steady. "Then the Persephone is yours."

"Ah." His eyes gleamed. "The painting you've guarded so jealously. And if you're right?"

"Then you'll owe me a favor of my choosing."

From across the room, Caroline's laughter rang out again— irrepressible, joyful, free. And suddenly Eugenia knew exactly what favor she would ask for, should she win.

"Agreed. We will decide the terms at a later date," Thornton said, and the warmth in his voice sent shivers down her spine. "In the meantime, let the game begin."

But as Eugenia watched Venetia being led away like a lamb to slaughter, she knew this was no game. A young woman's happiness—perhaps her very life—hung in the balance.

And Eugenia intended to make sure that fortune and success, in this instance, favored not the powerful and predatory, but the weak and deserving.

Chapter Two

FOR THE FIRST time all evening, Caroline's smile slipped as she pretended to engage in idle conversion with her friend Venetia. The truth was, she was as concerned as Venetia was about Lord Windermere's malevolent interest.

"Is he still looking at me?" Venetia asked, while Caroline stole glances over her friend's shoulder, wishing Henry would return so he could help with some necessary bolstering of their mutual friend.

"He is." Caroline nodded in response to Venetia's worried question, noting how her friend's complexion had paled. Poor Venetia. The young woman seemed to shrink into herself whenever Lord Windermere's gaze fell upon her. And yet, Venetia hadn't always been this way.

"I know Henry thinks I'm being overdramatic," whispered Venetia, biting her lip, "but if he had only overheard what I heard my Aunt Pike say to Lord Windermere last night."

"You cannot be forced to wed against your will, Venetia," Caroline reassured her, though her stomach knotted with worry. She had known Mrs. Pike for years and recognized the woman's determination to be free of her guardianship responsibilities. "I know your aunt has not been the most indulgent, but I do not believe she would insist you wed Lord Windermere if you did not wish it."

Caroline reached for her friend's hand, giving it a gentle squeeze. As the daughter of Sir Frederick Weston—their late father after whom her brother had been named—she had been afforded freedoms Venetia could only dream of. The contrast between their situations had never felt so stark, nor so unfair.

"She would if it got me off her hands," Venetia said darkly. "You do not know how much my aunt has objected to being my custodian all these years, and if I had only managed to win even a half-suitable marriage offer these last two seasons, I would have gladly left her household. But the lack of a dowry means I am all but unmarriageable unless someone would take me out of charity—like Lord Windermere."

Venetia shivered, and Caroline felt the tremor through their still-joined hands. "Quite frankly, he is the last man on earth I would wish to marry."

"He's not *so* bad, surely?" Caroline said, forcing herself, now, to play the role Mrs. Pike had assigned her. The words tasted sour in her mouth, but she had promised to make an attempt at changing Venetia's mind. It was the only way Mrs. Pike would continue allowing their friendship, a connection Caroline cherished too much to risk. "I certainly would not recommend marriage if you do not like the gentleman; however, he is not unhandsome, and he does have a distinguished presence, and he is rich."

As she spoke, Caroline saw Lord Windermere turn his head towards Venetia once more. The predatory glint in his eye made her own skin crawl.

"I care for none of those things. Not when he makes me shudder every time he is near me. Is that not enough? Are you like my Aunt Pike, who thinks I should be so grateful that a man is prepared to take me with nothing?"

The hurt in Venetia's voice pierced Caroline's heart. "Oh no, my dear Venetia, of course, that is not what I think," she said. "To be quite honest, I was merely discharging the one thing your aunt asked of me, and that was to try to talk what she calls sense into you by making you see the advantages of being the wife of a baron with a grand estate."

Caroline leaned closer, lowering her voice. "I, too, find him deeply objectionable, but I had to say what I said so that I could report to her that I had done my best. Now there is nothing more to be said on that subject. You will not marry Lord Windermere, and nor could you be forced to do so. So please rest assured that you have my full backing, and I'm sure everyone else's, because we do not live in the dark ages, fortunately."

The relief in Venetia's eyes was worth any displeasure Mrs. Pike might direct at Caroline later. She would face far worse to protect her friend from an unwanted marriage.

"The dark ages, eh?" Henry's voice cut through her thoughts, rich and warm with barely suppressed amusement. He had returned with a footman bearing drinks, and Caroline found herself studying his profile as he handed Venetia a glass of orgeat. When had her childhood friend grown so devastatingly handsome? The candlelight caught in his hair, illuminating hints of gold among the reddish brown that she had never properly noticed before. Or perhaps she had noticed but never allowed herself to truly *see*.

This evening, she had—for the first time, it seemed. She couldn't remember having had so much fun.

Her breath caught as their eyes met briefly over Venetia's head, and something seemed to pass between them before he looked away with what seemed like deliberate effort.

"This is very serious talk for two such lovely ladies of this enlightened era," he continued, his voice taking on that teasing tone she knew so well. "What has prompted your frowns?"

"Lord Windermere," Caroline replied, rolling her eyes as she slanted a look across at the gentleman. She accepted a glass from Henry, their fingers brushing momentarily. Such a simple touch shouldn't have sent fire racing up her arm, yet it did. These new feelings for Henry were becoming increasingly difficult to ignore—and increasingly dangerous to her peace of mind.

She noticed Henry's fingers linger just a moment longer than necessary before he withdrew his hand and wondered if he felt it, too—this strange new awareness that seemed to shimmer in the air between them.

"Well, Venetia, as Caroline says, we do not live in the dark ages, and I do not think you need to worry," Henry said. "It's not as if he is going to whisk you off from beneath the noses of us all with you kicking and screaming and expect that he can get away with it. He will try to charm you as any gentleman would, but that is the worst he can do."

Caroline admired the easy way Henry reassured Venetia and felt a swell of affection so powerful it nearly stole her breath. How many times had he offered her the same steadfast support? He'd been there when she nearly made the catastrophic mistake of eloping with Mr. Greene, pulling her back from the brink of ruination with a mix of stern wisdom and gentle understanding that no one else could have managed. Why, he'd even disguised himself as a postilion in order to be on Mr. Greene's coach in case matters got quite out of hand during Lady Pendleton's infamous Ghostly Gathering two years earlier. Fortunately, Caroline had seen sense before then, but it just showed the extent of Henry's devotion.

Devotion. The word hung in her mind, taking on new meaning. Had it always been more than friendship? Had she been blind to what was right before her eyes?

Venetia glowered, oblivious to the charged undercurrent between her companions. "I have no choice but to accept him when he asks me to dance. Of course, Aunt Pike makes sure of that, if it weren't already the height of bad manners for a lady to refuse a gentleman's offer to be led onto the dance floor."

"Then cast your eye around this room and tell me which gentlemen you would consider marrying, and I shall do my best to facilitate it," said Henry with a wink that made Caroline's stomach flutter most inappropriately. "Put aside all your sensible considerations for once. After all, you heard Caroline say it: Fortune favors the frivolous."

"Oh Henry, you are such a card! Mama was telling me the opposite this evening!" said Caroline with a laugh that came out slightly breathless. "She says that until I learn that life is *not* all fun and frivolity, I will languish on the shelf, disregarded by all serious marital contenders. But Venetia, although Henry is only a bit more serious than me, he really is a hero. You'll always be safe if Henry is around."

The truth of her own words struck Caroline like a physical blow. Henry *had* always been her safe harbor, her constant companion. But now the thought of him playing that role for Venetia instead sent a sharp, unexpected pang through her chest that felt suspiciously like jealousy before good sense reasserted itself.

"But what if he is not?" Venetia closed her eyes, not looking reassured at all.

"Then you have to marry someone else, and quickly," said Caroline, forcing herself to focus on Venetia's predicament. "You've been saying you wanted to get away from your Aunt Pike—well, let us consider the options in this room. What about Mr. Benson? He is a pleasant, unobjectionable young man."

"Whose breath smells like onions," muttered Venetia.

"Sir Roland?" suggested Henry, stepping slightly closer to Caroline as he surveyed the room. The nearness made her skin tingle with awareness. "He belongs to my club and has a certain flair when it comes to tying a cravat. Now, I know that's not everything—"

"Indeed, it is not," said Venetia darkly. "I have heard he spends a great deal longer at his toilette than most ladies."

"Yes, and he uses blacking on his sideburns," Henry conceded with a grimace. "Ah!" he said, obviously alighting upon another candidate. "Sir Reggie Molesworth."

"Heaven help us," said Venetia. "He sneezes every time he gets nervous. Which is often."

"And he lives with his mother who interviews every young lady who crosses his orbit." Henry wrinkled his nose. "Maybe not, now I think of it."

Caroline scanned the room, still searching for a suitable candidate, before her eyes fell on a gentleman observing their group with obvious interest. "What about Mr. Edward Rothbury?" she suggested. "I hadn't noticed him before, but he's watching you now, Venetia."

As Venetia glanced in the gentleman's direction, Caroline noticed how quickly Mr. Rothbury averted his gaze. There was something refreshingly genuine about his interest, highlighted by the observable reddening above his cravat.

"Mr. Rothbury has a very pleasant face, and I have been struck by his smile," said Caroline, warming to her own suggestion. "I believe his grandmother was Italian—hence his magnificent eyes—and I have heard he is very considerate of his sisters, which I think a jolly good endorsement. Don't you, Henry?"

She smiled at her old friend. "I know you do because you are so very good to your sister Charlotte, who I see is dancing with Mr. Barnaby. I hear that marriage bells are in the wind."

"Quite possibly," said Henry. His eyes were dark in the candlelight, fixed on her face with an intensity that made her breath catch. "It's time for her to settle down—she's as flighty as you are, Caroline."

"You are terrible, Henry!" Caroline gave him a playful swat, her fingers lingering against the fine fabric of his sleeve longer than propriety dictated. The contact sent fire racing up her arm, and she found herself unable to pull away. Henry caught her hand, his thumb brushing across her knuckles in a caress so subtle she might have imagined it—except for the way his breathing seemed to deepen.

Their eyes met and held, the ballroom fading around them until there was nothing but the space between them, charged with possibility and longing. Caroline felt her lips part slightly, her pulse thundering so loudly she was certain he must hear it.

"Caroline," Henry said softly, her name sounding different on his lips somehow—intimate, precious.

The spell was broken by Venetia's sharp intake of breath as she repeated Mr. Rothbury's name. Caroline jerked her hand free, heat flooding her cheeks as she remembered where they were, while Henry stepped back, running a hand through his hair in obvious agitation.

"Well, it is decided," Caroline said with forced brightness, her voice only slightly unsteady. "Venetia will marry Mr. Rothbury, meaning there'll be no need to rescue her from Lord Windermere's evil clutches."

The words came out more breathless than she intended, and she saw Henry's jaw tighten at the reminder of the danger facing their friend. Or perhaps it was something else entirely that made his expression grow so dark.

Catching sight of Mr. Rothbury approaching, she put her hand to her mouth, saying with a sly smile, "Goodness gracious, Venetia! Mr. Rothbury is coming in our direction, and I don't think he is about to ask me to dance!"

Venetia steeled herself, straightening her shoulders with a determination Caroline admired, before suddenly observing Mrs. Pike through the press of dancers and the haze of candlelight. The woman's gaze was fixed on her niece, her fan tapping impatiently against her palm, and Caroline felt a fresh surge of protectiveness toward her friend.

"Smile," she whispered to Venetia. "I am sure Mr. Rothbury is very nice. Indeed, I have heard—"

She broke off as a tall figure cut through the crowd, moving with unsettling purpose. "Ah, Lord Windermere—" Caroline stepped forward instinctively, placing herself between the approaching baron and her friend. She was conscious of Henry close behind her, his presence both protective and distracting, while she attempted to draw Windermere's attention, pretending she assumed he had come to ask *her* to dance.

But with very little finesse, Lord Windermere all but ignored Caroline, bypassing her—indeed stepping in front of her—and bowing over Venetia's hand. The dismissal stung, not for her pride's sake but because it rendered her attempt to shield Venetia utterly ineffective.

"Miss Playford, I see you are alone and that Mr. Henry has claimed Miss Caroline as his partner in the next quadrille," Windermere said smoothly, his presumption breathtaking. "I cannot bear to see you left out. Would you do me the honor?"

Caroline sensed Henry stiffen as the baron's words registered. They had made no such arrangement, yet Windermere's bold fiction made refusal impossible without creating a scene. She caught Mr. Rothbury's troubled frown as he halted several paces away, clearly uncertain. The poor man looked as if he wanted to intervene but knew not how without causing a scandal.

"Actually," Henry said, his voice carrying a warning that made Caroline's pulse skip, "Miss Caroline and I—"

But it was too late. Caroline watched helplessly as Lord Windermere caged Venetia's hand upon his forearm and forcibly steered her away, cutting off Henry's objection. Their eyes met briefly, Venetia's panicked gaze seeking reassurance that Caroline wasn't sure she could honestly provide.

"We must do something," she whispered urgently to Henry, grasping his arm without thinking. The muscle beneath her fingers was rigid with suppressed anger. "I cannot bear to see her so distressed."

Henry covered her hand with his own. "We will," he promised, his voice low and fierce. "But we must be careful not to make matters worse."

Wordlessly, they watched Lord Windermere lead Venetia into the dance, Henry standing too close, but Caroline couldn't bring herself to move. Not when his thumb was tracing small, comforting circles on the back of her hand. Not when she could feel the warmth of his body even through the layers of fabric between them.

"Perhaps we should join them," she said reluctantly, nodding toward the forming sets. Her voice came out softer than intended, almost breathless.

"Perhaps we should." Henry's smile was strained but genuine and as he offered his arm with exaggerated formality, Caroline felt her heart do something complicated in her chest. This was Henry—her Henry—yet somehow he was suddenly a stranger, full of new mysteries and dangerous attractions she was only beginning to understand.

She placed her hand on his arm, acutely aware of the way his breath seemed to catch when she looked up at him through her lashes.

Whatever was happening between them was as thrilling as it was terrifying.

Chapter Three

T HE FOLLOWING AFTERNOON was drawing to a close and Caroline was preparing to dress for dinner when her maid appeared with a note, her usually composed face betraying obvious agitation.

"Please, miss. It's from Miss Venetia. Her abigail gave it to me and says she is very distressed and that I must wait for an answer."

Caroline took the note with raised eyebrows, her stomach clenching with foreboding. Venetia was not hysterical by nature—quite the opposite. She had matured greatly during the last couple of years, far more so than Caroline, she had to admit. But then, Caroline was given free rein to pretty much do as she chose, while Venetia…

Having reassured her brother, Sir Frederick, of her good sense by not eloping with Mr. Greene several years before—though that had been a near thing indeed—Frederick was now so caught up in marriage and fatherhood that as long as Caroline didn't cause a major scandal, he didn't interfere in her day-to-day dealings. It was a freedom she perhaps took for granted.

Of course, she did still live with her Mama who had, fortunately, made a miraculous recovery having been so ill during Caroline's debut, which had been brought forward for fear that

Lady Weston was indeed on her deathbed. But unfortunately, it now seemed her mama wanted to exert an even more rigid parental eye over her unmarried daughter to make up for her absence when, perhaps, Caroline's waywardness had frightened off any potential suitors.

Other than the duplicitous and now thoroughly disgraced Mr. Greene.

Venetia, by contrast, lived under the iron rule of her very exacting aunt, where every nuance of behavior was reported back to Mrs. Pike with the efficiency of a military intelligence network. The poor girl could scarcely sneeze without permission.

So Caroline now wondered whether Venetia's letter was merely the latest cry of distress due to her aunt's impossible strictures, or something more serious.

Quickly scanning the note, she felt the blood drain from her face. This was no mere complaint about social restrictions. Her hands trembling slightly, she hastily put aside the gown she was about to don before appearing for dinner in an hour and instead opted for a fashionable walking gown and a pair of sturdy half boots.

"Millie, you can tell whoever is waiting that I shall meet Venetia in the park in five minutes, but that I can't stay long if I'm to be home in time for dinner. I will meet you at the front gate as I'll need you to accompany me, obviously."

So, knowing that her message was going to be relayed in half that time, Caroline was able to make a more measured progress through the house in order not to attract attention and to arrive calm and unflustered at the gate of the park which Venetia had obviously had just unlocked.

Calm and unflustered was decidedly not how her friend appeared. Spying Caroline from beneath a plane tree, Venetia virtually flew toward her and threw her arms about her neck with such force that Caroline staggered backward.

"Aunt Pike has invited Lord Windermere to dinner!" she cried, her voice high with barely controlled panic.

"I'm sure that won't be so terrible," Caroline soothed, though her earlier confidence was rapidly evaporating in the face of Venetia's obvious terror. "Remember what I said. He can't force you to do anything you don't want to do."

"But that's the thing!" Venetia's grip on Caroline's arms was almost painful. "My maid told me she saw Aunt Pike packing some of my things in a traveling bag. When she asked her what she was doing, Aunt Pike looked a little red and reassured her it was for our visit to Bath next week. But Caroline—" Her voice dropped to a whisper. "I don't believe we are going away next week."

Venetia put her hands to her face, and Caroline was alarmed to see actual tears leaking through her fingers. "I think she means for Lord Windermere to take me away tonight. She knows how resistant I am to his overtures and so she means for him to take me forcibly."

At first Caroline was shocked by the audacity of such a suggestion, then she smiled as she put what she hoped was a reassuring hand on her friend's shoulder. "That is all rather dramatic. I'm sure there is quite a reasonable and rational explanation. Of course, your aunt was not packing a bag to give to Lord Windermere in preparation for his kidnapping you and forcing you to wed him. That is the stuff of sensation novels and this is ordinary life."

But even as she spoke the words, Caroline felt doubt creeping into her mind. Mrs. Pike's desperation to be rid of her ward was no secret, and Lord Windermere… well, he made her skin crawl.

Venetia shook her head violently. "You don't know my aunt as I do. You don't know—sometimes I think she is quite mad with resentment, and I truly believe Lord Windermere has persuaded her that he would be doing us both a favor by taking me off her hands." She shuddered so violently that Caroline instinctively drew her closer. "Maybe he's involved in something terrible— perhaps he means to sell me, or worse."

Coming from her normally sensible friend, Caroline almost

laughed before she quickly sobered. The fear in Venetia's voice was all too real. "Oh my, I truly thought you were being overly dramatic. But you aren't, are you?"

"I am not, because I know in my very bones that something terrible is about to happen to me, and I have no one in the world to help me except for you." Venetia grasped Caroline's hands with desperate strength. "You would help me, wouldn't you, Caroline?" she pleaded. "You would rescue me if it turned out I was not wrong?"

"Well, of course I would!" Caroline declared without hesitation, though her mind was already racing ahead to the practical impossibilities. "But my dear Venetia, I must return for dinner, otherwise Mama will send out a search party." With a final reassuring squeeze she added, "You only have to send me a note, and I will be there!"

But that did not seem to satisfy her friend. "Caroline, he will be here tonight. What if I am right and he tries to force me tonight? What if by tomorrow it's too late?"

Caroline thought for a moment, studying her friend's pale, frightened face. The idea that there was even a grain of truth in Venetia's fears seemed quite ludicrous, yet... "I will have someone on standby to respond at the earliest," she said finally. "Now I really must go."

Poor Venetia. As Caroline sat through dinner with her mama, mechanically responding to her remarks while her thoughts churned, she realized the girl really did need a champion. Someone like kind Mr. Rothbury—though he seemed far too mild to be of use in an actual crisis.

Though, if Venetia really were in danger, as she suggested, perhaps this would be a good test of the young man. He did appear rather dull and ineffectual, but perhaps learning that Venetia was at risk of being forced to marry against her will would prompt him into action.

Her thoughts kept circling back to Henry. He would know what to do. He always did. But Henry was dining at his club tonight, and even if she could reach him…

The pudding was just being cleared away when a tap on her shoulder by one of the serving maids was the precursor to a screwed up piece of paper being dropped in her lap. Caroline's heart began to pound even before she unfolded it.

"Caroline! Are you listening to me?" her mother snapped. "You have contributed very little all evening. And your attention is certainly not where it should be. Is there something I should know?"

"Not at all, Mama," Caroline reassured her, fighting to keep her voice steady as she glimpsed the desperate scrawl. "I beg your pardon. I had not meant to be rude, for you are generally more inclined to scold me when my tongue runs away from me rather than when I am quietly occupied by my thoughts."

She rose, for fortunately dinner appeared to be at an end. Regardless of her strictures, her mama appeared to be more occupied with a worsening megrim than with her daughter's behavior and wished to go immediately to her bed.

Back in her bedchamber, Caroline smoothed the crumpled note with shaking hands, her heart lurching as she read Venetia's desperate words: "He is here. The carriage waits. Aunt insists I travel with him tonight to his country estate. She says it's proper as we're to be married within the week. Help me, Caroline! I beg you—there is no one else!"

Caroline's mouth went dry, and her heart pounded even harder. Her earlier dismissal of Venetia's fears now felt not just foolish but potentially catastrophic. She rose and began to pace.

If this were truly happening—and clearly it was—there was no time to waste. Mr. Rothbury would be of no use now, even if she could locate him. This required immediate, decisive action.

But what? What could she, a mere girl of twenty with no experience beyond the drawing room, do to help her dearest friend?

And then, like a bolt of lightning, she remembered Henry's quick thinking during her own near-disaster. How he'd adopted the guise of a postilion in order to escape notice on the post chaise that Mr. Greene had ordered to whisk Caroline to the Scottish border. Henry had been prepared for anything, even willing to risk scandal and arrest to protect her.

The memory sent a stab of longing through her chest. If only Henry were here now! But he wasn't, and time was slipping away like sand through her fingers.

What did it matter that Caroline was a girl? Her slender frame might even be an advantage in disguise. And if Henry could transform himself for her sake, surely she could do the same for Venetia's.

Without dwelling on propriety—for there was no time for such niceties when a friend's life hung in the balance—she flew to the trunk at the foot of her bed and withdrew a bundle, hidden beneath her winter shawls. The breeches and jacket, discarded by one of their footmen years ago, had been trophies from a childish prank with Henry. She had kept them, partly from sentiment and partly from that rebellious spirit that had so often led her into trouble.

Now, perhaps, that same spirit might save her dearest friend.

The fabric was rough and unfamiliar against her skin as she hastily exchanged her dinner gown for the disguise, the masculine attire feeling both foreign and strangely liberating. She bound her chest tightly with a long strip of linen, wincing at the constriction but knowing it was necessary. The restriction made breathing difficult, but it flattened her feminine curves effectively.

Her abundance of hair presented the greatest challenge, but she twisted and pinned it mercilessly close to her head before securing a cap firmly over it. Several pins bit into her scalp, but she ignored the discomfort.

Studying her reflection in the candlelight, she was struck by the transformation. Her features, which she had always considered too delicate for true beauty, now appeared almost boyish— her high cheekbones and wide eyes lending her the appearance of a youth on the cusp of manhood. With a smudge of ash from the fireplace applied beneath her cheekbones and across her chin to simulate the shadow of a beard, the disguise might just pass a cursory inspection in poor light.

But would it be enough? Caroline gnawed her lower lip as she considered the daunting logistics of her rescue attempt. Lord Windermere would have arranged a carriage, likely with hired men rather than his own liveried servants, to avoid gossip. She would need to appear as though she belonged, to slip into their midst without raising suspicion.

She could claim to be a groom or stable boy from the posting inn, sent to assist with the horses for the journey. No—that might raise questions if they had already made their own arrangements. Perhaps it would be better to watch and wait, to follow the carriage at first and look for an opportunity when they stopped to change horses.

At the first posting house, she could slip into the stables and pose as one of the ostlers, volunteer to ride postilion for the next stage, citing some story about extra payment already arranged. In the confusion of a busy coaching inn at night, such impositions might go unquestioned. Men came and went, seeking work wherever they could find it.

Her mind raced through possibilities and pitfalls, each more dangerous than the last. What if she were discovered? The scandal would be immense, ruinous. Her reputation would be destroyed, her family's name dragged through the mud. Yet the alternative—abandoning Venetia to Lord Windermere's clutches—was unthinkable.

She remembered the terror in her friend's face, the desperation in the words she'd written. No, there was no choice to be made here. Some things were more important than reputation.

Her heart thundered in her chest, fear and determination warring within her like opposing armies. She had never done anything so daring, not even during the misguided near-elopement with Mr. Greene. Then, she had been swept along by romantic notions and youthful foolishness; now, she acted with clear-eyed purpose, despite her terror.

She slipped a small knife into her boot—a precaution learned from Henry during their childhood adventures when he'd insisted she learn to defend herself. The blade felt cold and reassuring against her ankle. She tucked a few coins into an inner pocket, along with her mother's smelling salts, purloined from her dressing table. The night would be cold, so she added a woolen muffler that could be pulled up to obscure the lower half of her face.

Catching sight of her reflection as she prepared to leave, Caroline was startled by the fierce resolve she saw in her own eyes. Gone was the frivolous society miss. This was someone she barely recognized.

But maybe this was the real Caroline.

The true, brave friend.

For this was no childish prank or impulsive folly. This was for Venetia, who had no one else to turn to. And perhaps, she admitted to herself with painful honesty, it was also for the girl she had once been, who had needed rescuing herself and found it in Henry's steadfast friendship.

If only she had time to send word to Henry! His steady presence and quick wit would be invaluable, not to mention his superior strength and knowledge of the world. But Venetia's note had been clear—there was no time to lose. By the time she could reach Henry and explain the situation, Venetia might be halfway to Gretna Green or locked away in Lord Windermere's estate, beyond all hope of rescue.

No, this task fell to her alone, at least initially. Later, perhaps, she could send word to Henry once she had ascertained Venetia's whereabouts and the route they were taking. Henry could follow with a proper rescue party while Caroline kept watch over her friend.

The thought of seeing Henry again—of having to explain this mad scheme—sent a flutter through her chest that had nothing to do with fear and everything to do with the way he'd looked at her at the ball. Would he be furious with her recklessness? Impressed by her courage? Or simply relieved when she was safe?

She pushed such thoughts aside. There would be time to worry about Henry's reaction once Venetia was safe.

Barely daring to breathe, Caroline tiptoed through the house and let herself out of the scullery, wondering, briefly, if she had finally gone too far. The shadowy garden seemed to whisper warnings, and every rustle of leaves sounded like her mother's voice cautioning restraint, propriety, common sense.

But the thought of Venetia, trapped and desperate and terrified, strengthened her resolve beyond all doubt. Caroline squared her shoulders beneath the rough jacket, feeling simultaneously vulnerable and powerful in her disguise. The weight of the knife against her ankle, the snug binding across her chest, the unfamiliar freedom of breeches—all of it served to remind her that she was no longer Miss Caroline Weston, sheltered daughter of Sir Frederick.

Tonight, she was someone else entirely. Someone brave enough to risk everything for friendship.

Chapter Four

"WHERE'S THE LITTLE varmint? Did you see where he went?"

Less than an hour later, Caroline held her breath in the suffocating darkness, sweating in the wooden trunk that had become both her refuge and her prison the moment she realized the coachman had discovered he had a stowaway. The rough wood pressed against her spine, and the musty smell of old leather and travel dust filled her nostrils.

"Have you looked there? In the trunk?"

She heard their heavy tread as they approached, both of them scrambling from the box up front where the coachman had been about to whip the horses into movement, to the rear where their passengers' luggage was stored. Their boots rang ominously against the wooden footboard.

The carriage was well sprung, and it swayed gently with their movement. No doubt Venetia was ensconced within the silk-lined interior, quailing with dread and wondering what was happening above her head—wondering if the strange sounds meant rescue or merely fresh disaster.

Wondering if she should flee if Caroline failed in the defiant act of bravery she'd so confidently assured her friend would save her from the fate that poor Venetia railed so desperately against.

Caroline hoped with every fiber of her being that she would.

She hoped Venetia would see that all was lost and simply throw open the carriage door and flee through the muddy streets of this little village where they'd stopped to change horses. If she could reach the woods beyond, she might find sanctuary until Caroline could find her. Surely Venetia would know it was her best—perhaps her only—means of escape, and that Caroline would move heaven and earth to find her as soon as she could.

To remain within the carriage would mean all was completely lost. Her future would no longer be hers to determine.

Trying desperately to steady her ragged breathing, Caroline pressed her fist against her mouth to muffle any sound. It was a terrible mistake. She gagged on her own knuckles, gasped for air, and—obviously hearing the telltale noise—the men stilled like hunting hounds catching a scent.

She heard a low, menacing chuckle and fully expected the lid to be thrown open and her disguise exposed to these rough men who smelled of ale and cruelty.

Thank the Lord she was dressed as a stable boy. Who knew what they'd do to a defenseless young woman discovered in such compromising circumstances? Like poor Venetia, who was just as defenseless and being taken advantage of this very moment in a deplorable manner that was completely condoned by society and orchestrated by her evil aunt.

But the lid wasn't thrown open. Instead, she heard the ominous sounds of squeaking leather and straining metal as they adjusted the straps that bound her wooden prison to the carriage. Confusion gave way to horror as understanding dawned.

"That'll teach 'im," came the coachman's gravelly voice, thick with malicious satisfaction. "Now, let's whip up these horses and we'll do a round of the village square, then pick up the poor old box that were set loose wiv all the commotion, eh? See what's left of our little spy."

Caroline's blood turned to ice water in her veins. The coachman had no intention of giving the "stowaway stable lad" a reprieve. He intended to dash her bones onto the cobblestones so he could have the pleasure of dragging her broken body out before horsewhipping whatever remained. These were not merely rough men—they were sadists who would take genuine pleasure in her suffering.

"Run, Venetia!" she cried out silently, willing desperately to hear the sound of the carriage door opening, but all remained ominously silent below until the lurching forward of the carriage and the sickening shift of her wooden box indicated that the moment for escape had been lost.

Hers included, although perhaps if she could force the box to tumble before the carriage gained dangerous speed, she'd have a better chance of survival.

Twisting her cramped body within the confined space, making short, jerky movements that set her bruised ribs screaming, she tried to rock the trunk toward the edge of its precarious perch. But it was nearly impossible. Despite the coachman's intention to lose the box over the side, the straps held firm, and the box was now shifting perilously from side to side with each turn of the wheels.

The best she could hope for now was for the straps to finally loosen, and a soft landing in mud once they'd left the village and cleared the murderous hard cobblestones.

And now, here it was—the moment of truth.

She sensed the weightlessness more by the sudden absence of the carriage's rumbling vibration than by any physical sensation. Her stomach dropped as gravity claimed her, and she tensed every muscle for the impact that would either save or destroy her.

She could imagine the morbid glee of her tormentors, two men reeking of beer and casual violence who clearly enjoyed their cruel sport. Bullies both, but ever so obsequious when Lord Windermere had given them their instructions. How different men could be when they thought themselves unobserved.

But now she was free of them all—if she could survive what

came next.

The impact drove the breath from her lungs and sent stars exploding behind her closed eyelids. But miraculously, she hadn't broken her neck. She'd been badly jolted, every bone in her body singing with pain, but thank goodness for soft young bones and the mercy of muddy ground.

And for the fact she was wearing breeches and a jacket, her hair still bound securely inside the old cap. At least she still had that protection—the disguise that might yet save her life. For if she had any hope of surviving, much less saving Venetia, she could not risk being exposed as a woman to any stranger who might happen upon her.

"Whoa there! Stop!"

Caroline, who had been about to emerge from the splintered remains of the box, now kept herself huddled in the wreckage and prayed fervently that the newcomer's sharp command related to something—anything—other than her predicament.

She forced herself to remain hidden, scarcely daring to breathe, waiting until all was silent and the coast was clear before she dared venture out. She was winded and shaken, her entire body a symphony of aches and pains, but she didn't think she'd suffered any permanent damage. She just needed to extract herself from this predicament before Venetia's sadistic coachman completed his circuit of the village square and returned to collect his victim for a proper horsewhipping.

"Barnaby! What do we have here?"

Caroline heard the distinctive sound of a gentleman's boot against splintered wood, followed by the jingle of a horse's bridle. She could also detect the approaching sound of wheels on the road—another carriage, perhaps, though the cultured tones of the speaker suggested he was either mounted or traveling on foot, unlikely though that seemed given his obvious breeding.

Yes, the voice was educated, refined. Surely a gentleman would be more merciful than common ruffians?

Three heartbeats. Two. One…

With a burst of desperate energy borne of pure survival instinct, Caroline launched herself from the wreckage, scrambled upright on unsteady legs, and took off across the muddy field like a hare bolting from hounds.

She expected whoever had discovered the box would simply let her go. What possible interest could a gentleman have in pursuing a bedraggled street urchin, for that was surely how she appeared in the darkness?

But she heard the commanding shout following her through the night air: "Get the little rascal!"

There was some good-natured laughter from his companion. So there were two of them, and they seemed to be treating this as sport rather than serious pursuit. Caroline's heart lifted slightly. If they were simply wealthy young men seeking amusement in this dull rural hamlet, they might be content to chase her briefly before losing interest.

That hope sustained her as she struck out determinedly across the plowed fields, her boots squelching in the soft earth.

If they were drunk or merely playing at pursuit, they'd not catch her. They'd not be inclined to muddy their expensive boots, much less their fancy pantaloons, she thought with growing confidence—perhaps too much confidence, for it made her careless, slowing her desperate stride just enough to prove fatal.

The next moment, she was sent flying by a tackle from one of the men, landing face-down in the cold mud with enough force to drive every bit of air from her lungs. Before she could recover, rough hands hauled her upright, and her wrists were pinioned behind her back with unnecessary force before she was marched back to where her captor's companion lounged with deceptive casualness against his horse.

"Boy in a box!" her attacker chuckled. "What shall we do with our mysterious foundling?"

"Let him go, naturally." The voice of the other carried an edge of impatience, as if this entire episode was an unwelcome distraction. "Come, Barnaby. We're late as it is."

"Let him go? He's obviously up to no good, Ashworth. Boys don't hide in boxes unless they're running from something—or someone."

Caroline's heart nearly stopped. Barnaby? …And Henry?

"How do we know that?" The gentleman who wasn't Barnaby—though surely he wasn't her Henry, either—seemed more interested in contemplating the moon than becoming involved in her predicament, for his face was turned skyward, revealing only a shadowed silhouette of classical features above a pristine white cravat. "He might have been stuffed in that box by someone else entirely—someone attempting to hide their own crime."

"Hey there, boy," he now said, "are you injured? Come now, Barnaby, loosen your grip on the lad. Poor fellow looks frightened half to death." There was a pause filled with genuine concern. "Are you hurt?"

Caroline might have nodded in response—perhaps she did—except that every coherent thought fled from her mind the instant the young man lowered his gaze from his celestial contemplation to focus on her upturned face.

She could scarcely believe it. But there was no mistaking those kind eyes, even though darkness all but swallowed him up.

She swallowed hard, her throat suddenly parched, and began to cough uncontrollably. The shock of seeing Henry here, of all places, combined with her recent ordeal, seemed to steal every bit of moisture from her mouth.

"Took quite a tumble, did you?" Henry's voice was warm with sympathy. "Barnaby won't harm you, lad. Come now, Barnaby, give the boy something to settle his nerves. He's had enough excitement for one evening."

"Give a street urchin my finest brandy?" Barnaby's tone dripped with disdain. "I think not, Ashworth."

"Consider it medicinal," Henry replied firmly, "and an act of Christian charity, of which there is far too little in this world."

The kinder of the two men—her dear, wonderful Henry—reached for the silver flask at his waist and extended it toward

Caroline.

He'd always been kind, had Henry, protective and generous to a fault. Never was Caroline more grateful that, of all the people who might have stumbled upon her in this desperate moment, it was her oldest and dearest friend.

But this Barnaby—Caroline studied him with growing unease. Yes, she knew him as the suitor of Henry's sister, and Caroline's friend Charlotte. Yet having had too much to drink, his true nature was on full display. The grip on her wrists had been unnecessarily brutal, and there was something cold and calculating in his eyes that suggested he was a man who enjoyed having power over those weaker than himself.

It seemed that he was not merely surly from drink, but genuinely cruel. She amended her assessment when he let out a harsh bark of laughter at her violent reaction to the strong spirits. The truth was, she'd never tried anything stronger than whatever had been used to flavor the Christmas cake, and the brandy burned her raw throat like liquid fire.

Her hands, mercifully released when Henry shot Barnaby a sharp look of disapproval, shook so badly that she had to brace them on her knees while she coughed and spluttered like a drowning woman.

Henry straightened suddenly, his entire demeanor shifting. "We must go," he said with startling abruptness. "Leave the lad to his own devices. He obviously belongs in these parts, and he's caused us no real trouble. Someone must've been playing a malicious prank."

Caroline stared in dismay. What? Henry was proposing to simply abandon her here? To leave her to fend for herself in the dark countryside? She glanced nervously at Barnaby, her instinctive dislike of his bullish neck and pugnacious expression intensifying. What was Henry doing in company with such a brute? Well, she supposed it was inevitable—if Barnaby was to marry Charlotte—that Henry would be obligated to accept him as family.

But with this bully at his side, Caroline dared not reveal her true identity. She had seen the cruel pleasure in Barnaby's eyes as she'd choked on the brandy, felt the unnecessary force with which his large hands had gripped her wrists, leaving them red and throbbing. There was something deeply unsettling in his manner that went far beyond mere drunkenness.

"Please, sir, is there sumfink I can do to be of service to the fine gennelmun?" Caroline had always been an accomplished mimic, able to reproduce accents and dialects with uncanny accuracy. She'd often had Henry in fits of helpless laughter with her cockney slang or her imitations of their stuffy dancing master. Surely she hadn't lost the skill, for he seemed completely taken in by her performance.

Thank the Lord for small mercies.

But he wasn't taking the bait.

"Nothing I can think of, lad. We'll leave you to find your own way home."

"But… but…" Caroline looked about her with growing panic, her eyes widening as she took in their surroundings. The village was now nothing more than a distant speck of golden light, while all around them loomed the dark shapes of trees and empty fields.

As for poor Venetia, she had vanished completely, spirited away in that accursed carriage to God only knew what fate. When the sadistic coachmen had spotted Caroline in company with two gentlemen, they had obviously abandoned their cruel game and headed off towards the north road at top speed.

Now darkness was falling in earnest, bringing with it all the dangers that lurked in the countryside for the unwary and unprotected.

Caroline could under no circumstances be left to her own devices in such a precarious position, but how could she explain without revealing everything?

She cast a desperate glance toward the fading lights of the village. Even if she somehow made it back there safely, what then? Venetia was being carried away to an unknown fate while she stood here, helpless and utterly alone. The enormity of her failure was crushing.

Caroline frantically considered her options. If she revealed her true identity to Henry, he would be horrified. Oh yes, he'd certainly help her—of that she had no doubt. But at what devastating cost? He would be honor-bound to escort her home immediately, and any hope of rescuing Venetia would be lost forever. Worse still, if she revealed herself to both Henry and Barnaby, her reputation would be destroyed beyond any hope of repair. A young lady discovered in men's clothing, unchaperoned in the night countryside with two bachelors… the scandal would be absolutely ruinous.

And Barnaby! The malicious pleasure she'd seen in his eyes when he'd bruised her wrists had confirmed every negative instinct she'd ever harbored about the man. In society, he managed to present a respectable facade, but here in the darkness, his true nature was emerging.

No, Caroline could never entrust Barnaby with such a dangerous secret. He seemed precisely the sort of man who would revel in holding such devastating power over a young lady of good family, and she shuddered to think what use he might make of the information.

Henry, however, was studying her more intently in the strengthening moonlight, his head tilted in that familiar way that meant his keen mind was working.

"Perhaps you are rather far from home," he observed, his tone shifting to one Caroline recognized with growing alarm. "And that accent of yours seems to slip when you're distressed."

Caroline's heart hammered against her ribs like a caged bird. She knew that particular tone all too well. It was the voice Henry used when he suspected mischief was afoot, the same one that had caught her out in countless childhood escapades. In all their years of friendship, he had always been the one to see through her schemes and stratagems.

Barnaby snorted with obvious impatience. "It's enough.

You're right. Let's leave the guttersnipe, Ashworth. We've miles yet to cover before we reach Gimley's gathering, and you know how Charlotte bristles when we arrive late. She'll have my head if I make her wait."

The casual mention of Charlotte's name steeled Caroline's resolve like nothing else could have. If Barnaby was soon to become Charlotte's husband, he would inevitably gain influence over Henry's beloved sister—and, by extension, over Henry himself. Caroline had witnessed firsthand how marriage could alter the dynamics between old friends. Her own brother Frederick had become so absorbed in his wife and growing family after his wedding that he now allowed Caroline freedoms that would have been unthinkable merely two years before.

Now, she could not risk providing Barnaby with such dangerous ammunition against her—information that might one day drive an irreparable wedge between herself and Henry. Or worse, be used to manipulate and control her.

"I—I need to follow that carriage, sir," she blurted out, desperation overriding caution. "The one that just departed. There's someone inside who desperately needs help."

Caroline held her breath, watching Henry's face carefully. She could see his natural curiosity kindling, his ingrained instinct to help those in need warring visibly with whatever social obligations were pulling him towards this mysterious gathering with Barnaby.

If only she could speak to Henry alone, perhaps find a way to hint at the truth without completely exposing herself to Barnaby's cruel scrutiny…

But the brute's looming presence beside her dearest friend created an impenetrable barrier to honest communication. Under other circumstances, she would have trusted Henry with her life without a moment's hesitation. But tonight, her beloved friend stood allied with a man she instinctively feared and despised. Until she could somehow separate them, her true identity must remain hidden at all costs.

Still, she could not—would not—remain here on this dark and dangerous country road, alone and utterly defenseless. Somehow, she had to find another way to appeal to Henry's better nature, to make him understand the gravity of the situation without revealing the full truth.

The fate of both herself and poor Venetia depended entirely upon her ability to convince him—and soon—before the trail to find Venetia went completely cold.

Chapter Five

AND SO SHE tried one more time.

"Please, kind sir, I don't know this area. I were… I were kidnapped and I wanna go home, but I were tryin' to help out in a desperate situation when I was caught by the men who put me in this box." Caroline stared fearfully—though hopefully—between Henry and Barnaby, her heart hammering as she waited for their response.

A cold wind swept across the fields, carrying the scent of approaching rain while the moon kept slipping behind scudding clouds, plunging them into moments of absolute darkness before emerging again to cast its silvery light over the scene.

"Kidnapped!" Barnaby's voice dripped with scorn. "Why'd anyone want to kidnap a scrap like you? What have you done, eh? Up to no good, I'll warrant."

"Where do you live then?" Henry narrowed his eyes, and Caroline thrust her face up, hoping desperately for some sign of dawning recognition without voicing this to his untrustworthy companion.

But once again, the moon disappeared behind clouds, casting Henry's beloved features in shadow just when she most needed to read his expression. Her most desperate mission was not yet lost. But, right now, only Henry could help her.

"I live back there—" She hooked her thumb to the south. "But me... me mistress were kidnapped and forced into a carriage. Lord Windermere is taking her to his hunting lodge. He's forcing her to marry him, and that's why I'm trying to stop them."

"Lord Windermere?" This got Henry's attention immediately. "I know Lord Windermere." The curl of his lip indicated he didn't think much of the man. "Who is the young lady?"

"Miss Venetia Playford." Caroline tensed, watching his face carefully.

"By God! I know Miss Playford. And her aunt, too." To Caroline's relief, the effects of drink were suddenly no longer in evidence. He appeared—miraculously—alert and ready for action.

Until Barnaby said in a bored tone, "He's playing you, Ashworth. Come, just leave him to his own business while we attend to ours."

"Which is?" Henry's tone had grown suddenly cold as he looked at his companion. "Mindless drinking at some tavern?"

"We've been invited to the Gimleys—your sister will be waiting for us. But here you are, about to be bamboozled when we could be enjoying ourselves at what promises to be a riotous house party."

Caroline put her hand to her mouth in horror. How could dear Charlotte be marrying this awful man?

But time was of the essence—her most important task was convincing Henry to help Venetia.

"Please, sir! Me mistress, Miss Venetia, is in danger. Unless someone stops Lord Windermere, her future will be in ruins."

"No one marries against their will," Barnaby scoffed.

"Do you know her?" Henry turned sharply. "Of course you do! I came to know Miss Playford very well during a house party at Pendleton Castle, where I formed a very high opinion of her." He vaulted into the saddle. "She certainly is no adventuress!"

"You're not about to do something crazy, are you, Ashworth?" Barnaby frowned. "Racing into the dark on a wild goose chase only to discover that this lad is parroting names of the gentry that he's only heard. Surely you don't really believe him?"

"It's true! And I do know where he's takin' her!" Caroline piped up. "That's why he put me in a box so I'd cause no trouble. Please, sir, you've got to help me!"

"What's your name, lad?" Henry leaned down to address her, ignoring Barnaby.

Caroline blinked. Lord, what was her name? She tried to think of something male and non-aristocratic and could only come up with her brother Frederick's horse.

"Flash, sir," she said, swallowing hard.

"Flash. Odd name," Henry observed, but he reached down his hand. "Well then, you'll have to come with me and tell me where they're going."

Caroline grabbed his hand, gasping as she was hauled into the saddle in front of him. The familiar strength of his arm around her waist made her breath catch. How many times had he steadied her thus during childhood riding lessons?

"You can either follow or go home, Barnaby," Henry said firmly. "Venetia is in danger, and I won't stand by and do nothing."

"The lad is lying!" Barnaby's face flushed dark. "Good God, man, he's simply repeating names he's heard. It's a trap!"

"How could this lad make up such stories with the right names if at least some of it weren't true?" Henry's voice was resolute. "Follow me if you will, otherwise I'll see you when next we meet."

Caroline didn't know if Barnaby followed, for it took all her strength just to keep from sliding off the galloping horse. The night air slashed at her face as they rode, but Henry's warmth at her back was both comfort and torment.

Poor Venetia. She didn't want this marriage, yet she was powerless against her aunt. This abduction had taken both girls completely by surprise.

"I see a light!" Henry pointed ahead.

Caroline's heart leaped as she spotted the distant glow of carriage lamps. "That'll be them, sir. Lord Windermere's coach."

Henry reined in behind a thick stand of oak trees. "There's an inn just ahead—the Red Lion. They'll need water for the horses before the next stretch."

The sound of approaching hoofbeats made Caroline stiffen. Barnaby had followed after all, his face mottled with exertion and anger as he drew alongside them.

"Ashworth, this is madness," he hissed. "You can't interfere with a private matter between a gentleman and his intended bride."

"Intended bride?" Henry's voice was sharp. "Miss Playford has made no such agreement. From what young Flash here says, this is abduction, not elopement."

Caroline felt Henry's arm tighten around her waist. "The coach is moving again," she whispered urgently.

"We'll follow at a distance," Henry decided. "Once they're past the crossroads, the only place they can be headed is Windermere's hunting lodge at Thornwood."

"And if you're wrong?" Barnaby challenged. "If this lying guttersnipe has sent us on a fool's errand and we discover we've been had? With knives at our throats?"

"I'm willing to take the risk. At worst, I believe I'll have lost nothing but a night's sleep if the lad is lying," Henry replied coolly. "But if I'm right, and I fail to act..." He left the implications hanging.

They set off again, maintaining distance while keeping the coach's lights in view. Caroline could feel the tension in Henry's body, so different from his usual easy manner.

"I know men of Windermere's ilk," Henry shouted to his friend over his shoulder as they slowed to round a bend. "Men who believe their position entitles them to whatever—and whomever—they desire. If there's even a chance Flash is telling the truth, I won't abandon Miss Playford."

The coach ahead began to slow as they approached a fork in the road—one path leading north toward Scotland, the other east toward Thornwood.

"Now we'll see," Barnaby said triumphantly. "If they turn north, it's to Gretna Green, a proper elopement. If east… well…" He shrugged.

Caroline held her breath as the coach's lamps illuminated the signpost. For a heart-stopping moment, it seemed to hover at the intersection. Then, decisively, it turned east, towards Thornwood. She let out a slow sigh. At least they were not pressing on towards the border.

"Well?" Henry's voice was grim. "Windermere's hunting lodge is this way."

Barnaby's face contorted with frustration. "Perhaps the lady is accompanying him willingly."

"Willingly? At this hour, without a proper chaperone, if what Flash says is true?" Henry shook his head. "You know what such an action would do to her reputation, willing or not."

"It's not our place to interfere," Barnaby insisted weakly. "Think of your sister, man! What will Charlotte say when she learns you've forced me to abandon her to chase after another woman?"

Henry's jaw tightened. "I'm forcing you to do nothing. And Charlotte would expect nothing less than that I act honorably. Honor demands I investigate this."

Barnaby wheeled his horse around, sending up sprays of mud. "Do what you want, Ashworth. I wash my hands of this foolishness. But don't expect me to explain to your sister why you've gone haring off after another woman when you were meant to be at Gimley's."

His voice dropped to a menacing hiss. "I will tell her exactly what her noble brother has been up to—racing about in the dark on the word of some filthy stable boy."

"Are you threatening me, Barnaby?"

"Merely stating facts. You've made your choice." Barnaby's

horse pranced sideways. "I'm returning to civilized society where I belong. Good luck with your... rescue." The last word dripped with derision.

His hoofbeats faded into the darkness, leaving them alone in the night. Caroline barely noticed. Her attention was fixed on the coach ahead and on Henry's reaction to Barnaby's threats.

Heavy drops of rain began to fall, cold and insistent. The road would soon turn treacherous, but the coach was picking up speed again, and Venetia's future hung in the balance.

"Hold tight, Flash," Henry murmured, urging their horse forward into the rainy darkness. "We've got a rescue to accomplish."

Caroline shivered, unable to respond over the wind and rain, but Henry's solid warmth and determination to do what was right gave her hope. Whatever came next, she was no longer alone in this desperate quest to save her dearest friend.

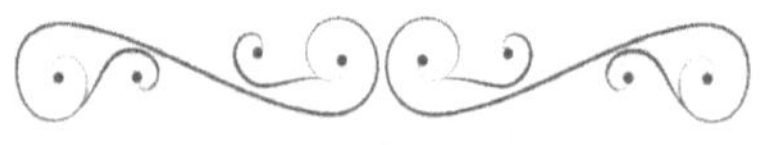

Chapter Six

THEY RODE IN tense silence for what felt like hours but could only have been minutes, keeping the coach's lights just in view. The terrain grew rougher as they moved deeper into Windermere's lands, the path narrowing between dark stands of ancient oak.

When the coach slowed to navigate a particularly steep incline, Henry seized the opportunity to gain ground and Caroline had to cling to the saddle as their mount surged forward, Henry's arm around her waist.

"When we reach them—" Henry raised his voice to compete with the thundering hoofbeats of his mount, his breath warm against her ear. "—I want you to stay back. Do you understand, Flash? These men won't hesitate to harm a boy."

Caroline nodded, though inwardly she bristled at the command. She had come this far for Venetia—she would not abandon her friend at the critical moment.

Through a break in the trees, she could now see the hunting lodge itself, a low stone building with light spilling from its windows. The coach had pulled up before it, and even from this distance, Caroline could make out the figure of Lord Windermere emerging from the carriage before extending an arm to help his prize out onto the gravel driveway.

Henry guided their horse off the main path, and Caroline squinted to see Venetia being ushered towards the stone steps to the hunting lodge, her posture rigid with resistance.

"Now, Miss Playford, there's no need for such theatrics," Lord Windermere's voice carried through the night air. "Your aunt has given her blessing, and by tomorrow evening, you'll be my wife and the envied mistress of one of Gloucestershire's finest estates."

Henry's jaw tightened at these words. "You wait here with the horse," he instructed, his voice leaving no room for argument.

"What are you going to do?" Caroline asked.

"I'll go in and demand that he release her."

Caroline screwed up her face, though he couldn't see her in the dark. "That don't sound a clever idea, beggin' yer pardon for being frank."

"And why not? What do you know about Lord Windermere that I don't, lad?" Henry asked. "I gathered you only had the misfortune of making his acquaintance this evening."

"Oh, I know him, all right!" Caroline burst out, adding as she warmed to her role and relishing the freedom to express her true feelings, "Begging your pardon, sir, but 'e's naught but a pudding-headed looby, if you ask me. Strutting about the stables like 'e owns every 'orse in England, but can't tell a fetlock from a forelock, if you take my meaning."

Then, fearing she was getting too carried away with this deliciously forbidden slang that was so necessary to remain credible right now, she added, "Er… that's what the other stable lads say, sir."

"Rather strong opinions for a stable boy." The amusement in his voice was plain, and Caroline, unable to resist, shot back, "You ain't seen 'im ordering the grooms about, sir. All airs and graces in 'is fancy coat, but we all know 'e's just a pudding-headed fop with more gilt than wit." She'd been storing this one up for months, wondering if she'd ever get an opportunity to use it—

much less in such a setting.

Oh, how she missed those days of pitting wits with Henry. There'd been many a time when they'd playfully sparred with words in the days following sticks as pretend swords. It occurred to her for a brief second that she could quit the pretense and reveal herself now, but realized that would only delay matters when time was of the essence.

Henry shook his head. "No, Flash, I intend to handle this like a gentleman. Windermere has got carried away, but he'll soon be made to see reason and, if I can arrange for Miss Playford to be returned to London before daylight, no reputations will be hurt, I trust."

Caroline shot him a dark look. Her view of the world might not really be as brutish as that of a stable lad confronting authoritative masters, but she had a fair idea that Henry's optimism was mightily misplaced.

"Oi! He's got her in the front room!" she whispered suddenly. "I'll make a noise to divert them, and when the servant comes to the door, you can knock 'im down. Or you can climb through the window."

It took a few seconds of silence for Caroline to realize he was laughing at her. "Flash, lad, that might be the way matters are conducted where you grew up, but I am a man of honor. And so is Lord Windermere. No, I shall knock on the door, wait to be admitted, and then calmly ask Miss Venetia if she wishes to remain with Lord Windermere, which is tantamount to agreeing to elope with him to Scotland, or if she wishes to come with me." Henry calmly dismounted, clearly expecting Flash to make his own way off the back of the enormous horse.

Lord, Caroline hadn't leaped from such a height since their tree-climbing days as children. And even then, Henry would have his arms outstretched and waiting to break her fall. Taking a deep breath, she closed her eyes and let herself slide, landing with a thud on her face when her legs buckled beneath her.

"Not very accomplished for a stable lad. No doubt you're glad there was only me to see your clumsiness. Now—" Henry took a few steps towards the front stairs, adding in a whisper over his shoulder, "I shall settle this in a civilized fashion, gentleman to gentleman. Just wait here in the meantime. I should only be gone a few minutes. I'm quite sure Venetia will be only too delighted to come with me."

Caroline wasn't sure what to say. It certainly seemed a waste of breath to dissuade him. Well, she knew it was. Could Henry truly believe this could be conducted in a civilized manner?

Fearfully, she tiptoed up the steps and put her face to the window. To her surprise and relief, there was a gap between the curtains, which afforded her a clear view of the interior.

And within a second, she observed the surprise on Lord Windermere's face as a servant announced his visitor.

She saw, too, the relief on Venetia's face, whom she was gratified to see sitting on a chair by the fireplace, her pale countenance suddenly filled with hope.

Poor Venetia. She was a bold young woman, and Caroline had taken to her enormously when they'd met at Lady Pendleton's Ghostly Gathering two years before, but the years after Venetia had left the ladies' seminary to return to her aunt's house to live had taken its toll. Aunt Pike had grown more erratic and cruel with the years, Caroline gathered, making Venetia increasingly subdued.

Mrs. Pike's obvious plan to rid herself of Venetia by allowing the much older Lord Windermere to elope with her had confirmed that Venetia had absolutely no say in her future.

Caroline pushed her shoulders back as she was assailed by the enormity of the plan in which she was currently embroiled. Yes, her reputation was at stake, but with no one else to help Venetia, Caroline simply had to step up and help her best friend.

Fortunately, in company with Henry. Caroline could always depend on her wonderful playmate to come to the rescue. The help he offered wasn't always what was needed, but his heart was good. Why, he didn't even know Flash was Caroline, and yet he'd treated the "stable lad" with far more respect than Barnaby treated his own horse.

And now he was playing the knight in shining armor because he knew Venetia and wanted to help her. In just a few minutes, surely Windermere would have no choice but to admit that the game was up and to let Venetia walk away with Henry.

Caroline had just glanced down at a scurrying noise near her foot when a piercing cry shattered her complacency that all was going to plan. Jerking up her head, she saw that Venetia had risen to her feet, a look of pure terror upon her face, and that Windermere was brandishing a pistol.

A pistol pointed right at Henry, who was unarmed.

Dear Lord, how had that happened? How had they underestimated Lord Windermere's determination to have his way? Surely he was not a murderer? After enjoying Aunt Pike's collusion, surely there was a point at which he would realize he had no other choice but to concede?

Like a gentleman?

The hackles rose on the back of Caroline's neck. Yes, that's what it felt like!

Holding a pistol at poor Henry, who'd walked in believing he could talk reasonably to the nobleman, was just not on.

Fury banished any hesitation as Caroline took in the scene. There was the servant standing impassively by the door, his face a blank mask as if it didn't surprise him in the least that his master was behaving lower than the murderous ruffians who slunk in and out of London's dankest, most dangerous slums. Not that Caroline had first-hand experience of that, but she'd heard whispers that life wasn't as genteel as her experience of it.

And Lord Windermere was speaking—snarling, actually, because when Caroline put her ear to the glass, she could just make out what was being said—to Henry, warning him that he really would put a ball through his chest if he tried to wrest his avowed bride-to-be from his tender care.

Yes, this really was too much! Once her brother Frederick got wind of this, he'd be outraged.

Unfortunately, Frederick wasn't here. He and Amelia were on a sojourn to one of his houses in the Cotswolds where he was looking at the tenant farms with a mind to making improvements. Her brother was a king among men. A gentleman and a war hero. His reputation might have suffered from his younger days when Caroline had heard whispers he'd been associated with several women who were married. But they must have tricked him into believing an untruth, for Caroline knew that her brother was the noblest of noblemen.

Not like that scoundrel Windermere.

Glancing about in her desperation to find some inspiration that might assist in the current dangerous impasse—for Henry really could do nothing while Lord Windermere had a pistol pointed at his chest—her eye alighted upon the stones bordering the nearby rose garden. Perfect!

Closer, and half-hidden in shadow, was a heavy iron boot scraper, though she wasn't sure she could easily wield that.

And, a short distance away, was a neat stack of firewood.

Caroline's heart thundered in her chest as she formed her plan. She'd have to time this perfectly.

Gathering her courage, and the other physical resources she needed, she first seized a nicely sized stone. The weight of it steadied her nerves. Inside, Windermere was still pontificating about his rights, his voice growing increasingly unhinged. As if he'd bought Venetia like a chattel and had already paid for her.

"Now!" Caroline whispered to herself, and with all her might, she hurled the stone through the window. The crash of breaking glass was spectacular, sending Windermere spinning toward the sound. In that split second of confusion, Caroline grabbed the boot scraper and sent it sailing through the new opening. Her aim was true—it struck Windermere's hand, sending the pistol flying.

But Caroline wasn't done. Seizing a log from the woodpile, she launched it through the window with a wild cry. The heavy piece of oak caught Windermere square in the chest, sending him stumbling backward into an ornate side table.

"Run, Venetia!" Caroline shouted in her natural voice, forgetting herself entirely in the chaos.

Henry didn't waste a moment. As Windermere wheezed and cursed, trying to regain his feet, Henry seized Venetia's hand and pulled her towards the door. The servant, showing his true colors, had already fled.

Caroline melted into the shadows as Henry and Venetia burst out of the house, her heart soaring to see them safe, even as something twisted painfully in her chest when Henry lifted Venetia onto his horse with such gentle care. This was what she'd wanted—Venetia's rescue—so why did watching Henry's protective tenderness towards her friend feel like a blade between her ribs?

"Flash!" Henry called out into the darkness. "Flash, where are you, lad? I owe you my life!"

Caroline stepped forward just enough for him to see her outline.

"I'm sorry, lad, but I must get Miss Playford to safety. Here—" He tossed something that glinted in the moonlight. Caroline caught it—a sovereign. "Get yourself home, Flash. I won't forget what you've done tonight."

Then they were gone, horse's hooves clattering down the drive, leaving Caroline alone with her sovereign, too triumphant at the success of their mission to rescue Venetia to fully comprehend her own dire situation. For the moment, she simply stood in the drive, staring after Henry and Venetia on horseback, disappearing into the darkness.

Behind her, she could hear Windermere bellowing for his men.

Dear Lord, so he wasn't going to give up without even more of a fight? Why did he want to wed Venetia so much? She wasn't an heiress, and she had made her dislike of the idea of marriage abundantly clear.

Caroline didn't have time to think any more about this, for

the next moment, the heavy studded oak doors to the lodge had been thrown open wide, and Lord Windermere, now dressed in a heavy black cloak and hat pulled down over his ears, was striding out, his big black boots clattering over the stones.

Hurrying towards a large elm tree, Caroline tried to melt into the shadows. Oh, why hadn't she taken cover deep within the gardens and allowed herself to be swallowed up by the dark?

Because she'd been too afraid of being swallowed up by the dark. Instead, she'd planned to slip into the house when, presumably, Lord Windermere departed and find refuge somewhere warm and safer than the great outdoors.

But of course, Lord Windermere would need to satisfy himself as to how three great heavy projectiles could have been flung into the room in quick succession.

"There he is! Get him!" his lordship barked, stabbing his thumb in Caroline's direction.

The baron didn't even bother to move, for his minions reacted so quickly and with such stealth that as Caroline sought to disappear into the shadows, one of them snatched her roughly by the arm before dragging her, struggling and whimpering in pain, to his master.

And as Caroline lay in a heap at Lord Windermere's feet, his shadow falling over her like a dark promise, she had to wonder how tonight's adventure—for her, at any rate—had gone so terribly, catastrophically wrong.

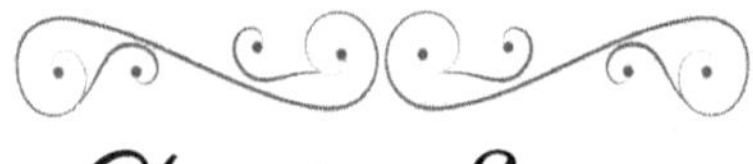

Chapter Seven

With the wind whipping through his hair and the cold biting at his cheeks, Henry could only imagine the discomfort Venetia was enduring. The night had grown bitter, and the earlier rain had left the air damp and penetrating, chilling them both to the bone.

She was barely clinging onto the horse's mane as they thundered over the rutted road, the animal's labored breathing creating plumes of vapor in the frigid air, visible whenever they passed beneath the scattered moonlight filtering through the racing clouds. But the fear of Windermere making enough ground to intercept them was greater than any worry about Venetia's comfort.

A murderous villain wanted to kidnap and make her forcibly his wife. If there had been any objection to Henry whisking her off like that, she'd have made it clear. No, she did not want to be Windermere's wife, and if Henry could only ensure she was safely under chaperonage before daylight, her reputation would be safe.

Lord, if he was caught with her in the middle of the night, her reputation would certainly not be safe, he thought with a stab of fear that twisted in his gut. Honor might require him to—

He forced the thought away, focusing instead on the road

ahead. In the distance, thunder rolled across the hills, promising more foul weather to come. The land around them seemed eerily empty, the occasional farmhouse dark and shuttered against the night.

He closed his eyes briefly as he went over the enormous risks he was taking. For a good cause, of course. And doing the only thing a gentleman would do.

But the thought of what might be required of him if they were discovered under such circumstances could not be dismissed. Granted, he liked the girl enormously. She was delightfully entertaining. Well, that's how he remembered her from Lady Pendleton's house party, though she had grown extremely subdued lately. And he remembered that they shared a sense of humor. But he did not want to marry her. He didn't want to marry anyone.

Well, maybe he'd make an exception if Caroline decided she wanted to make an experiment of it. But perhaps that would be making a grave error of judgment and confusing the easy camaraderie of youth with the more serious business of forging a life together.

There wasn't much time for thoughts like these in between avoiding the potholes and treacherous ruts while trying to put ground between them and Lord Windermere. A man as determined as he would have someone only a few minutes behind them as they saddled a horse and struck out in pursuit. Even now, Henry could almost feel their pursuers' presence like a shadow at their backs, driving them forward into the uncertain night.

Every few minutes, Henry twisted his head to look over his shoulder at the road behind them, the darkness seeming to shift and move with imagined threats. Each time, he was relieved to see it empty, though the moon's inconsistent light made it impossible to be certain. The open paddocks on either side were tempting in order to shear off into the woods in the distance, the dark silhouettes of trees offering the promise of concealment, but the danger of uneven ground in the poor light was too great a risk. One misstep could spell disaster.

"Argh!" Venetia screamed as the horse stumbled on the uneven ground, and she was nearly dashed out of Henry's protective arms. Her cry pierced the night, seeming to echo across the empty landscape, and Henry instinctively tightened his grip around her waist.

"Do you want me to stop?" Henry shouted, but couldn't hear her answer above the sound of thundering hooves and his own thundering heart. The wind carried her words away, leaving only the urgent rhythm of their flight.

So he kept going. And when he saw a wood to the north with a narrow path off the main road, shadowy and uninviting but promising secrecy, he changed course at the last minute, unsure if they were being observed but believing this the safest course. The horse balked momentarily at the sudden turn, sensing perhaps the uncertainty of the path ahead, before responding to Henry's firm guidance.

He wished Barnaby had decided to come after all. At least one of them could have got Flash to safety, but he supposed the lad was used to the dark and couldn't be too far from his home. He'd hitch a lift on a wagon if he were lucky.

Still, Henry did feel bad. There had been something about the boy—something oddly familiar that nagged at the edges of Henry's consciousness, though he couldn't quite place it.

Now that they were off the main road, the urgency didn't seem as great and, with an easing of his high tension, Henry slowed his mount. Tree branches reached overhead like grasping fingers, occasionally scraping against his shoulders as they passed beneath. He wasn't quite sure where they were, but from the top of a hill a little way back, he'd seen the lights of what he suspected was an inn or hostelry. If he could rouse someone, they'd have a comfortable bed for the night. Henry could ensure Venetia's safety while he scouted around for some solution to their plight.

As the horse's canter turned to an easy gambol, Venetia

straightened her position upon the pommel, twisting her body to look up at Henry. The moonlight caught the tear tracks on her face, silvering them against her pale skin. He thought she was about to ask him to set her down, but her face was twisted with anguish as she cried, "You've got to go back there, Henry!"

A terrible fear gutted him, cold and sudden as a blade. "You wanted to marry Windermere? You were really eloping?" The words tasted bitter on his tongue.

"No, no!" she cried, her voice trembling. "Nothing fills me with greater fear than that prospect, but—"

Her words were cut short by the sound of a pistol shot ringing through the night, the report echoing through the trees with frightening clarity. A rough voice cried, "Put the lady down or I will shoot your horse from under you!"

Venetia's scream nearly deafened him, her body tensing against his chest as if trying to make herself smaller. Henry's heart lurched painfully as a dark figure materialized on the path behind them, the moonlight glinting off what could only be the barrel of a pistol.

But there was no earthly way Henry was going to do what the villain demanded. He had to rely on his speed and agility together with the gamble that their pursuer was not going to risk putting a bullet through the lady's heart. If Windermere were so desperate to have her as his bride, he was not going to be too happy to have her dead before he got her down the aisle.

"Hold tight!" he shouted to Venetia, whipping up his horse once more when he'd assured himself she'd gripped the pommel tightly in preparation for another bracing race across the countryside. The animal responded magnificently, surging forward with renewed energy despite its earlier exertions.

His horse was fleet; he had to give him that. It wasn't his usual mount, and he'd only saddled up a borrowed horse on the spur of the moment that evening. He'd have expected it to have tired by now, but it appeared to relish the chance to have its head. It was a plucky beast.

Plucky, like Venetia. Lord, what other lady would have managed to hold on so long and so uncomplainingly? Her gown was surely ruined, her hair a nest of tangles from the wind, and yet she hadn't uttered a single complaint about her discomfort. Only concern—for what, he wasn't certain, as her words had been interrupted.

Perhaps anyone who knew that the alternative was a fate married to a monster would show similar fortitude.

After what seemed like an age, but which perhaps was only another ten or fifteen minutes cantering over hills and dales, the muddy road led them through a small valley. The sides rose steeply on either side, dark and imposing in the night, funneling them forward as if by design. At the bottom was nestled a small hamlet, its buildings huddled together as if for warmth against the encroaching darkness.

And there was a light burning bright. A hostelry where they would surely be able to seek shelter, its windows glowing with the promise of warmth and safety.

Henry just hoped they hadn't been seen. Though of course, if their pursuer came this way, they'd see it as the only alternative Henry could have taken. Perhaps it wasn't so wise.

But what else could they do? He couldn't put Venetia through any more. She mightn't have the strength besides. He could feel her trembling against him, whether from cold or fear or both, he couldn't tell.

"Is anyone awake?" Henry shouted as he trotted into the stables behind the hostelry. The smell of hay and horses was a welcome change from the damp night air. "A shilling for your pains."

That brought a sleepy-looking lad from amongst the hay bales in the loft. Climbing down the ladder, the lad lit a lantern, its golden glow illuminating the weathered beams and casting long shadows across the straw-strewn floor. He regarded them with heavy-lidded eyes which widened when he took in Venetia's finery, now sadly bedraggled but still unmistakably that of a lady of quality.

"Road to the north's that way," he said, stubbing his thumb in the direction of the road they'd left, his expression knowing and a little sly.

"We're not eloping," Henry said quickly, for clearly the lad assumed they were on their way to Gretna Green. "In fact, I'm rescuing the young lady from someone who is pursuing her for that purpose. That's why I need to find the young lady somewhere comfortable to sleep and would ask that if anyone comes after us, you could put them off the scent. You haven't seen us, all right?" Henry fished in his pocket for a couple of coins which he handed to the lad. "And you'll get double if you ensure that the villains who are after us are headed in the wrong direction."

The lad's eyes widened as he pocketed the coins, the silver gleaming briefly in the lantern light. He headed towards the inn as he said over his shoulder, "I'll find Mrs. Snicket. Sure, she has a room."

"Two rooms!" Henry called after him before he turned his attention to Venetia. She looked like a wilting flower, her golden hair flecked with mud, her face pale in the moonlight, her lips tinged with blue from the cold. Despite her disheveled appearance, there was a quiet dignity about her that he couldn't help but admire.

"Oh, Henry!" she all but wept. "You saved my life and I can't tell you how much I appreciate all you've done for me. But—"

"M'Lord! M'Lord! The lad just told me of the terrible trouble that's been visited upon you!" An outraged voice cut the still night as the door to the inn was flung open, a rectangle of warm light spilling out into the yard. "Elopement! Abduction! My, my, words cannot express—"

"Your kindness does you credit, Mrs. Snicket. I take it that is who I am addressing," Henry began as the large, voluble speaker surged down the stairs towards them, her words loud enough to wake the dead, her substantial form casting an equally substantial shadow. "But really, all we need is a couple of rooms for the night—"

"And you shall have them! My finest, for it is not every day that I am honored to accommodate guests of such high station as yourselves. Viscount Roxingham, to be sure!"

Confused, Henry glanced between the stable lad and the woman who was dabbing at her perspiring cheeks with her apron, clearly tied over her nightgown, her gray ringlets falling beneath her night cap, which sat askew on her head.

"I'm not the Viscount Roxingham."

"Not the Viscount Roxingham? Then his son," said Mrs. Snicket comfortably, sending a meaningful look at Henry's signet ring that caught the light as he helped Venetia down from the horse. "And a true hero, I'm told! Now, come this way, follow me, young things. Mrs. Snicket will take you to the most comfortable bedchamber in the village."

"Henry! We can't stay here!" Venetia said, gripping his sleeve then putting her hand to his cheek to make him attend. Her touch was ice cold against his skin, her eyes wide with some unnamed fear.

"Mrs. Snicket, we need two bedchambers," Henry said, understanding Venetia's concern and feeling his cheeks burn as he ushered Venetia ahead of him while he ducked to follow them inside the inn.

Ahead, her candlestick sent a feeble glow that barely illuminated the passage, casting grotesque shadows on the walls as they proceeded. The floorboards creaked beneath their feet, and somewhere in the darkness, a clock ticked. He saw Mrs. Snicket stop, turn the doorknob, and give Venetia a gentle push into the room, which he continued past as Mrs. Snicket said loudly, "And his lordship shall have the room two doors along. No one shall say Mrs. Snicket doesn't ensure propriety at all times with you young things in such fearful straits and not yet married."

"We're not eloping." Henry tried ineffectually to interrupt her, but she wasn't listening as she pushed open the door to his room, the hinges protesting with a long, low squeal.

"Breakfast is at your convenience."

Outside, the wind continued to moan around the eaves, and in the distance, another roll of thunder suggested the storm had not yet finished with them. Henry stood for a moment in the darkness, lit by a single candlestick, listening for any sound of pursuit, but heard nothing beyond the ordinary creaks and sighs of an old building settling for the night.

For now, at least, they were safe, but for how long?

And what of poor Flash, left behind in the darkness?

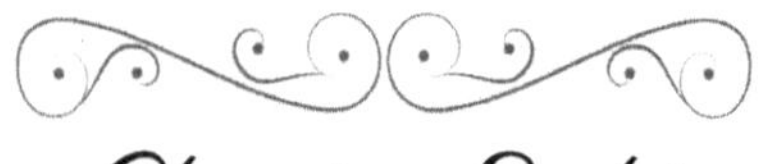

Chapter Eight

EXHAUSTION SUDDENLY FELLED him like a woodsman's axe, his limbs leaden, his mind clouded. The worn mattress embraced him, the rough linen sheets cool against his skin. In fact, sleep had claimed him, it seemed, before his head had even touched the pillow.

And then, jarringly, he felt a tapping. Yes, a tapping upon his brow at the same time as a gentle squeeze upon his arm. Like a persistent bird pecking at the edges of his slumber.

Frowning, he blinked open his eyes and was shocked to find Venetia standing over him. Venetia?

The single candle she held cast wavering shadows across her face, highlighting the worry etched into her features. Her golden hair, all but undone from its earlier styling, fell in disheveled waves around her shoulders. She had clearly made an attempt to restore order to her appearance, but the evidence of their desperate flight remained.

She was in his bedchamber? A myriad of possibilities warred for supremacy in his mind, flickering through his consciousness like the shadows on the wall.

She was in love with him and wished to enter his bed?

No, that did not at all make sense.

Lord Windermere had discovered her? She'd heard him in the

corridor, seeking her out? The floorboards outside his room creaked as if in answer to his thoughts, and he tensed, listening for approaching footsteps.

"Venetia! What is it?" Henry pushed himself up on his elbows, still groggy with sleep, the rough wool blanket falling to his waist. The chill night air prickled his skin, bringing with it the clarity of wakefulness.

"Oh, Henry! I've been trying to get your attention since the moment you threw me onto your horse and galloped away!" Her words were so fraught with emotion it was difficult to understand what she was trying to say. Her hands twisted the fabric of her skirts.

"What is it, Venetia? Is it Lord Windermere? Has he returned?" Henry's heart quickened its pace, fear washing away the last vestiges of sleep. "Are you afraid? I cannot stay with you. You do know that!" He glanced toward the door, half-expecting it to burst open at any moment.

"I know that, Henry, but this is too terrible, and I can barely believe it has happened." Her voice dropped to an urgent whisper, her eyes darting to the window where the wind still rattled the panes. "Do you not wonder why someone knew to throw those heavy things through the glass window to deflect Lord Windermere?"

The memory flashed in Henry's mind of the shattering glass, the shouts of confusion, the momentary chaos that had allowed them to escape. He had given it little thought in the frantic flight that followed.

"Of course I know who did. It was that brave stable lad, Flash, whom I discovered a short while earlier after he alerted me to the danger you were in." Henry ran a hand through his tousled hair, the events of the night replaying in his mind with new clarity. "Were it not for him, Lord Windermere would have had you halfway to the border now. Flash told me—"

"Flash?" she all but shrieked, then clapped a hand over her mouth, glancing fearfully at the door. When she spoke again, her voice was lower but no less intense. "You call the stable boy Flash?"

The candle flame jumped as she leaned closer, her shadow looming large against the peeling wallpaper.

"That's what he told me his name was." Henry frowned, puzzled by her reaction. Something cold and uneasy settled in the pit of his stomach.

A very brief second of thought preceded Venetia's next words, her breath catching before she spoke. "Flash is the name of her brother's horse—"

"Whose brother's horse?" Henry sat up fully now, his fatigue forgotten, swinging his legs over the side of the bed. The floorboards were cold beneath his stockinged feet. "Venetia, I'm very sorry this has happened, but I gave Flash a sovereign. A very great sum of money and amply deserved for his bravery."

The coin had gleamed in the moonlight before the young lad had caught it in his small hands. He remembered that now—how delicate those fingers had seemed for a stable lad.

"I wish I could have ensured his safety from Lord Windermere, but I suspect all will go well for him, as Lord Windermere would have been more concerned with finding you."

"But—" Venetia stepped closer, the candlelight illuminating the tears gathering in her eyes.

"Venetia, you really shouldn't be here, and I'm sorry I abandoned Flash—" The clock in the hallway struck the hour, each chime seeming to emphasize the impropriety of their situation.

"It wasn't Flash, Henry! That's what I'm trying to tell you!" Her voice cracked with emotion, a single tear spilling over to trace a path down her cheek.

Henry frowned. A faint drift of memory assailed him like a whisper from the past. The expression of the lad's eyes as he'd gazed briefly into Henry's before Barnaby had claimed his attention. There'd been something familiar about them, he'd thought at the time. A particular shade of blue, a certain tilt at the corners…

A lad working in his own employ who'd somehow been caught up in Lord Windermere's evil scheme?

"His name is not Flash?" Henry tried again to imagine what he had missed, the pieces of the puzzle refusing to align. The wind moaned around the eaves of the inn, an eerie counterpoint to the tension in the room. "Then who is he?"

"It's not a he, Henry. And not a stable lad or anyone you are likely to think of." Venetia's face was pale in the candlelight, her expression grave. "No, Henry!" She gave his sleeve a more forceful tug for emphasis, her eyes boring into his as she clearly sought to ensure she had his full attention.

The candle flame guttered in a draft, sending shadows dancing wildly across the walls.

He was silent, his body seeming to thrum still from the reverberation of all those seemingly endless hours of pounding hooves. Suddenly he didn't want to hear her response as that hauntingly familiar piercing gaze he'd dismissed at the time seemed to take on a greater import. A terrible suspicion began to form in his mind, too outlandish to be true.

"No, Henry, that was not Flash we abandoned at Lord Windermere's hunting lodge." She drew in a shuddering breath, the sound loud in the hushed room. "That was Caroline!"

Chapter Nine

"S O WHERE DO you suppose that whippersnapper scoundrel has taken my bride-to-be?" Lord Windermere snarled as Caroline looked up at him from her position on the cold ground.

The moonlight caught the gleam of malice in his eyes, turning them to chips of ice. He loomed above her, his broad shoulders blocking out the stars, a dark silhouette against the night sky. Somewhere in the distance, a fox barked, the sound sharp and unnerving in the stillness.

Poor Venetia. Was this what she would have been subjected to if Lord Windermere had succeeded in spiriting her away? That snarling voice, that barely contained violence, that absolute certainty that he owned whatever he desired? The thought made Caroline's skin crawl.

Yes, and didn't that mean the two of them had been justified in doing everything she could to ensure her escape? Caroline had no regrets about breaking the window of his lodge. Not when faced with this man's true nature, laid bare by his thwarted desires.

She turned her cheek and curled herself up into more of a ball at his feet. The gravel beneath her dug painfully into her side, and the chill of the ground seeped through her borrowed clothes, into her very bones. She didn't want to speak more than she had to, and she hoped that appearing pathetic and defenseless—which is what she was, really—he'd think she was nothing more than a stable lad who was of no use.

"Cat got your tongue, boy?" Windermere prodded her roughly with the toe of his polished boot.

"Please, sir, me ma will be lookin' for me," Caroline mumbled, trying to keep her voice low and gruff. Her throat ached from the effort of maintaining the deception. Maybe that would appeal to his better nature.

But, of course, he didn't have one.

"Then she'll find you locked up because the magistrate is where I'm taking you for affray and destroying property." His voice carried the casual cruelty of a man accustomed to wielding power over those he considered beneath him.

Caroline gasped as she rolled to avoid his boot, which she suspected, rightly, he was about to use on her. The movement sent sharp pain through her shoulder where she'd been manhandled by Windermere's servant.

"The magistrate? He'll hang me, sir! Please, no!" Real fear colored her voice. It wasn't difficult—the threat of discovery loomed as large as the threat of punishment. Her heart hammered so loudly in her chest she was certain he must hear it.

"Then tell me what you know of the young lady who has just made her escape." His voice softened. No, lowered with menace. That's how bullies operated. He crouched down, close enough that she could smell the brandy on his breath. "You know your mistress's habits. If you take me to her and help me finish what I started tonight, I'll spare you and you won't hang."

The night air seemed to grow colder around them. Caroline covered her face with her hands, partly for effect, partly to hide the feminine features that might give her away. The dirt on her palms smudged across her cheeks, providing an additional layer of disguise. "You want me to nab on me mistress? When I's gone to so much trouble to save her after she begged me to help her?"

"No doubt she paid you handsomely." His tone suggested he

found the loyalty of servants to be a commodity, something easily bought and sold.

Caroline nodded cautiously, careful to avoid looking at him directly. She didn't want to be scrutinized too closely, but they were in the dark, and she was lying in the dirt at his feet at the bottom of the steps. The shadows were her allies now, concealing what daylight would surely reveal. "Then arguably playing turncoat and working for me will be far more rewarding, since it'll mean you don't meet your death at the bottom of a hangman's noose." His teeth gleamed white in the darkness, like those of a predator about to strike.

"You want me to turn me mistress in?" Caroline clarified, her mind racing through possibilities. The bindings around her chest felt suddenly constricting, making it difficult to breathe. "And you promise you'll not turn me into the magistrate?"

Lord Windermere's expression twisted into something like amusement. "That's my stipulation. You accept it?"

Caroline drew in a shuddering breath while her mind spun. Perhaps this could play into the hands of justice. As long as he didn't know she was not a lowly servant, he'd think he had leverage over her. If he hauled her in front of the local magistrate and her identity as Miss Caroline Weston was revealed, Caroline's reputation would be in tatters, but she would argue he tried to kidnap her. That would certainly be a desirable outcome.

Then she remembered how men like Windermere could hoodwink others of their kind and, if the magistrate were not an honorable man of the law, Caroline would be in a worse position as Windermere exerted his superior standing. Her reputation would never recover. Frederick would be devastated, and even Henry might look at her differently. The thought made her heart twist painfully in her chest. She recalled the way Henry had looked at her—or rather, at "Flash"—with casual dismissal, never recognizing the eyes that had gazed at him across countless ballrooms.

No, better that she maintain her deception and try to lure

Windermere to where he'd be caught in the act of trying to kidnap Venetia. If she played her part well, she might yet turn this disaster to her advantage.

"Yes, sir," Caroline whispered, infusing her voice with defeat. "Can I go now, sir?"

Windermere laughed. "You're going nowhere. Black!" He barked, and a servant materialized like a specter, his face impassive. "Take this boy back to the stables and lock him into one of the stalls. In the morning, we'll get back onto the road. Miss Playford will be back home by then, but I don't foresee much trouble with her aunt. It's just a question of time."

So Mrs. Pike was as complicit as the girls had assumed, thought Caroline, frightened yet resigned as she was hauled, none too gently, to the stables behind the hunting lodge. The servant's grip on her arm was bruising, but she didn't dare protest. As they crossed the moonlit yard, Caroline glanced up at the night sky, wondering if Henry had realized yet whom he'd left behind.

The stables smelled of hay and horses, a familiar scent that should have been comforting. The leather of saddles and bridles, the earthy aroma of the animals themselves, the sweet musk of clean straw—all reminded her of happier times riding with Henry at her family's estate. But as Black thrust her into an empty stall and shot the bolt home with a resounding clang, the familiar environment became a prison.

"Don't try anything, boy," growled the servant. "His lordship ain't known for his patience." His heavy footsteps receded and when he was gone—and with him the light—Caroline sank onto a pile of straw, fighting back tears. What a fine mess she'd made of everything! Here she was, trapped in Lord Windermere's stables, dressed as a boy, while Henry rode off with Venetia, unaware of her true identity.

Yet despite her predicament, a small part of her thrilled at her own daring. She'd saved Venetia. She'd thrown objects at a lord of the realm. And for one glorious moment, she had been free of the constraints that bound ladies of quality. The memory of

Venetia's face as Henry had swept her onto his horse—a mixture of terror and relief—made it all worthwhile.

Now she just had to work out how to escape before Windermere realized who she really was. The sovereign Henry had tossed her was still in her pocket, warm from being pressed against her body. It would be useful—but only if she could find a way out of this stall, past the watchful eyes of Windermere's men, and back to civilization before dawn broke.

Perhaps all was not lost after all. She was Caroline Weston, after all—the girl who had nearly escaped to Gretna Green at seventeen, who had bested Frederick in chess more times than he cared to admit, and who'd helped save Venetia.

Surely, she could outwit Lord Windermere.

Chapter Ten

HENRY STARED, FROZEN, as Venetia's words sank in. The single candle in the room guttered in a draft. Shadows danced across Venetia's worried face while, outside, the wind had picked up, rattling the ill-fitted window in its frame.

"That was… Caroline? Flash was Caroline?" he repeated, his voice cracking, while Venetia tugged urgently at his arm. His mouth had gone dry, his heartbeat thundering in his ears like a galloping horse.

"Yes, and I've tried so hard to tell you, but you have to go back. Now," she said, her breath hitching.

Of course, he had no option, but his stomach roiled with horror and fear as to what might have happened to his dear friend in the meantime. The floorboards creaked beneath his weight as he paced the small confines of the room.

Caroline would surely not be where he left her, he thought as he went through all the alternatives, each worse than the last.

What if Windermere had discovered her? What if he'd discovered she was a woman? Or her real identity? Would that bode worse for her? After all, if he were so desperate to elope with Venetia, taking her by force, would he consider Caroline a second-best option? She obviously came with a handsome dowry. But he'd know he couldn't force her.

Wouldn't he?

A log shifted in the dying fire, sending up a shower of sparks. Windermere had powerful allies within government, while Caroline's brother Sir Frederick had alienated some in power with his progressive ideas and sometimes outspoken stance. Lord Windermere had friends in high places. Friends who might turn a blind eye to a noble's indiscretions.

"I'll go now." Already he was pulling on his boots, sitting on the bed, frowning while his mind raced over the best course of action. The leather was still damp from their earlier journey, cold and stiff against his skin.

He glanced up at Venetia, noting the strained pallor of her face in the candlelight. "What will you do, Venetia? You have to stay here. Alone and unchaperoned. Oh Lord." He sank his head in his hands a moment when the second boot was on, the weight of his dual responsibility pressing down on him. "What have I done to you and your reputation?"

"You were doing the only thing you could have done. It was the most miraculous coincidence that you crossed paths with Caroline when you were alone and could come after me," said Venetia, putting a comforting hand on his shoulder. "You know that she was hiding in a wooden trunk on the back of Lord Windermere's carriage when he pushed it off and her with it. He was going to fetch her when you arrived. You *saved* her—even though you didn't know it was her. And after that, you did everything in your power to save *me*. At her behest."

Grateful, Henry patted her hand. She was a plucky girl. Not the kind of girl who excited him from a romantic point of view. But she'd shown her true colors on this journey and instead of crumpling into a tearful heap, she'd persisted in trying to make things right.

"I wasn't alone when I came upon Caroline. Barnaby was with me, but he elected not to follow. He didn't believe Flash." He grimaced, the muscles in his jaw tightening painfully. "Caroline. Oh Lord, if Barnaby were only with me now."

"I don't know what your sister sees in that man," muttered Venetia. "I wouldn't say it to her face, but she could do much better. Granted, he's handsome and charming—when it suits him. But now you must go."

Together, they went to the door. Wincing as the rusty hinges protested, Henry eased it open, peering cautiously into the dimly lit corridor.

"You go back to your room, Venetia, and I'll return as soon as I can. Do you have money in case I'm delayed?"

She shook her head, and he dug in his pockets, handing her a gold coin as they stepped into the corridor.

"Good Lord! Miss Venetia Playford?"

Guiltily, they turned at the shocked aristocratic voice and found themselves looking into the scandalized eyes of Sir Gideon Gascoyne, a gentleman of advanced years who had served with Henry's father in Parliament and whose reputation for moral rectitude was legendary in their circles. His nightcap sat slightly askew on his balding head, and his dressing gown was belted tightly around his substantial middle.

"And Mr. Ashworth?" he went on, glancing up and down the corridor as if looking for someone who might lend legitimacy to the midnight disbursement from Henry's bedchamber and the public exchange of money in the corridor. His spectacles glinted in the low light, magnifying his disapproving gaze.

"Sir Gideon, this is not at all what it looks like," Henry said, striding forward, signaling over his shoulder that Venetia should go back into her room. "I have just been called away to fix a great miscarriage of justice. I can't explain more, but suffice to say that Miss Venetia has done nothing wrong."

"Cryptic, Ashworth, but my eyes did not deceive me." Sir Gideon's outraged tones carried loudly in the quiet corridor, despite his attempt at a whisper.

"Gideon? What is it, my dear?"

The door behind him opened with a soft creak, and the face of presumably his wife appeared, her forehead beneath her nightcap creased with curiosity. Her gray hair was plaited in a single braid that hung over one shoulder, and her eyes looked puffy as she rubbed them.

"I fear I have encountered a gross example of lax morals, and I am considering what is to be done," said her husband, still frowning at Henry, who shook his head and raised his hands.

"Please, Sir Gideon, I can't allow myself to be detained any further," said Henry, bowing at Lady Gascoyne. The seconds seemed to stretch into minutes as he contemplated Caroline's increasing peril. "I must make the most of this full moon before the clouds gather. I shall return as soon as I can—"

"Young man! I recognize this child, and I know you! What would your poor father say about such conduct?" Lady Gascoyne pulled her shawl more tightly about her and focused scandalized eyes upon them, for Venetia still stood guiltily in the half-open doorway.

Caught between his duty to Caroline and his duty towards Venetia, Henry felt like sinking into the ground with shame while simultaneously galvanized into being the rescuer he must be. Rain began to patter against the windows at the end of the corridor, a soft drumming that seemed to echo his racing heart. Windermere was dangerous. What would he do with Caroline if he caught her—and there was a very great chance that he would have in the several hours that would have elapsed before he could get back to her?

His mind conjured an image of Caroline at Windermere's mercy, and a cold dread settled in his chest, making it difficult to breathe. Windermere would not take kindly to discovering how he'd been deceived.

"My father… my father would fully endorse my conduct," he faltered. "Yes, it is late, but as you see, Miss Playford and I are by no means in a compromised position." He indicated their full dress and then realized that the disarray of Venetia's hair hardly bolstered this statement.

Lady Gascoyne scowled, the lines on her face deepening in

the shadows. "You're Mrs. Pike's niece, are you not?"

Venetia nodded while Lady Gascoyne contemplated the matter, her fingers worrying at the fringe of her shawl. "Penniless, are you not? Yes, I've heard Mrs. Pike lament the fact. She's been your guardian for many a year. She'd be outraged by this insult to her nurture."

As Venetia looked on the verge of tears, Henry interrupted, "With all due respect, Lady Gascoyne, Mrs. Pike is delighted by the state of affairs which is that I…" He cleared his throat, nearly paralyzed by fright at the ramification of what he was about to say. His collar suddenly felt too tight… Like a noose. But how else could he atone to Venetia?

One hurdle at a time, his father had always told him.

And that meant ensuring Venetia's good name held before he plunged headlong into clearing the next hurdle: rescuing Caroline.

"Have offered for the girl?" Sir Gascoyne broke in with clear relief, his bushy eyebrows lifting toward his nightcap. "That's what you're trying to say, young man, is it not? And Mrs. Pike is asleep and waiting for her niece to finish her farewell to her intended. Is that not so? So we'll lower our voices so as not to disturb her."

Henry blinked, his heart sinking even as he saw the path of least resistance open before him. The rain outside intensified. "Er… yes!"

And before he knew it, Sir Gideon was pumping his arm and Lady Gascoyne was twittering her own endorsement of the happy occasion, saying she'd be delighted to congratulate Mrs. Pike on the news when the two ladies could take tea in the parlor in the morning. The couple's voices seemed to come from far away, as if Henry were underwater, drowning in the consequences of his words.

"And now I must leave you all, for I do have an important mission to accomplish," he said, his desperation rising, taking a few steps backwards, and casting an imploring look of apology towards Venetia. "I shall be back as soon as I can to… to bear you and your aunt company home to London tomorrow."

Finally, he escaped down the corridor, the weight of what he'd just committed to weighing on his shoulders like a physical burden. He'd essentially agreed to marry Venetia to save her reputation. Yet Caroline—his Caroline—was in even more dire straits.

Yes, Caroline's rescue came first, he thought as he took the stairs two at a time. Then he would face the consequences of this tangle of honor and obligation that had suddenly ensnared him.

In the stables, he found the drowsy stable lad who, with the promise of another coin, quickly saddled a fresh horse. The boy's movements were slow with sleep, each second of delay an agony to Henry.

In one fluid moment, Henry mounted, his thoughts in disarray. He'd set out to rescue one lady in distress, only to find himself honor-bound to marry her while racing to save another—the one who, if he was honest with himself, had always held his heart in her hands, even when they were children crossing swords with sticks.

The memory of Caroline's laugh, bright and fearless, echoed in his mind, spurring him onward.

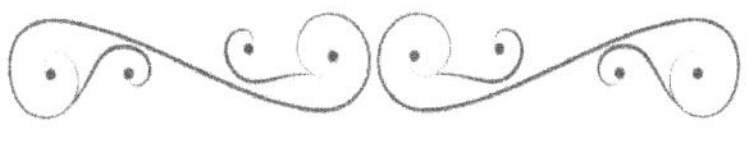

Chapter Eleven

LIGHTHEADED WITH HUNGER and the relief of having effected a miraculous escape, it was the smell of cooking food that made Caroline change direction, tacking away from the London road she saw in the distance. The tantalizing aroma drifted on the breeze, rich and savory, making her empty stomach clench painfully.

She didn't think she'd ever been hungrier. Some kind of delicious meat was being roasted over a crackling fire, and as she crested a hill and saw the colorful wagons and the cluster of people gathered in the dell below, she could not divert her path. The morning mist still clung to the hollows of the landscape, and the dew soaked through her worn boots as she made her way down the slope.

The scene that greeted her was like something from a dream. Brightly painted wagons formed a loose circle around a central fire, their sides decorated with theatrical masks, moons, and stars. A man with an impressive gray beard was juggling what appeared to be flaming torches while a woman in flowing emerald skirts practiced a dance, her movements graceful and precise. Children ran between the wagons, some walking on their hands, others practicing tumbling routines on the grass.

Near one wagon, a young man was rehearsing lines from

what sounded like Shakespeare, his voice carrying clearly across the camp, "But soft! What light through yonder window breaks? It is the east, and Juliet is the sun!"

A woman's voice called back from inside the wagon, "More passion, Edgar! You sound like you're ordering breakfast, not declaring undying love!"

The sound of laughter rippled through the camp, and Caroline realized these were traveling players—a theatrical company making their way between towns and villages, bringing entertainment to rural England.

Of course, they were suspicious when she appeared. A ragged boy approaching their camp could mean trouble—perhaps a spy sent by local magistrates who didn't appreciate traveling folk, or a thief looking for easy pickings. As she approached, the juggler caught his torches and set them aside, while several others paused in their activities to watch her warily.

"Well now," said the bearded juggler, who seemed to be their leader, "what have we here? A young patron of the arts, perhaps?" His voice carried the trained projection of an actor, rich and melodious even in casual conversation.

Caroline looked around at the group gathering near her. There was the woman in emerald skirts, now revealed to have intelligent gray eyes and prematurely silver hair pinned back with combs. The young man practicing Romeo had approached, along with a motherly woman holding a baby and several others whose clothing marked them as performers—bright colors, well-mended but dramatic in style.

"I… I was hoping you might spare some food," Caroline said, remembering to keep her voice gruff. "I can pay."

"Can you indeed?" The silver-haired woman studied her with the sharp gaze of someone accustomed to reading people. "And what brings a young lad to our humble troupe with gold in his pocket?"

Pure joy, Caroline thought as the savory meat—seasoned with herbs and cooked to perfection—filled her empty stomach.

The troupe had welcomed her to their fire once payment was established, and she found herself surrounded by the most fascinating collection of people she'd ever encountered.

There was Master Aldrich, the gray-bearded leader who was their manager and lead tragic actor. His wife, Constance, was the silver-haired woman who specialized in grande dame roles and seemed to run the practical side of their operation. Edgar, the young Romeo, was their romantic lead, while the motherly Rosalind played character parts and served as their seamstress and costume mistress.

"We're bound for the market town of Millford," Constance explained as she watched Caroline eat. "Three days of performances at their Harvest Fair, if the weather holds." She glanced at the sky, where clouds were beginning to gather.

"The boy has excellent table manners for a stable lad," observed Rosalind, bouncing her baby as she studied Caroline. "And such soft hands."

Caroline nearly choked on her food. Rosalind had moved closer, ostensibly to offer her more bread, but Caroline caught the knowing look in the woman's kind eyes.

"Come," Rosalind said gently, taking Caroline's arm. "Let me show you our costumes. Young Edgar here is nearly your size. Perhaps we have something that might... suit you better than those travel-stained clothes."

Inside the costume wagon, surrounded by an extraordinary collection of gowns, doublets, cloaks, and props, Rosalind turned to Caroline with a maternal smile.

"Now then, my dear," she said softly, "what's a young lady doing wandering the countryside dressed as a boy? And don't try to deny it. I've costume-fitted enough actors to know the difference."

Caroline's disguise crumbled under the woman's gentle but perceptive gaze. "I... there was a man trying to abduct my friend. I helped rescue her, but now he might be looking for me."

"Ah." Rosalind nodded as if this explained everything. "And

your friend is safe?"

"Yes, she's with… with someone who can protect her." The memory of Henry riding away with Venetia still stung, but Caroline pushed the feeling aside.

"But left you behind to fend for yourself?" Rosalind's tone sharpened with disapproval. "That doesn't speak well of your protectors."

"He didn't know it was me," Caroline said quickly, then realized she was revealing too much again. "I was disguised as a stable boy. He gave me this sovereign as payment and rode away with my friend. I…I can pay you for new clothes."

Rosalind's expression softened. "For now, you need to get home safely."

"To London," Caroline confirmed. "But I don't know how—"

She was interrupted by voices outside—harsh, demanding tones that made her blood run cold.

"Search every wagon! The boy came this way—someone must have seen him!"

Rosalind's eyes widened, then narrowed with determination. "Quickly," she whispered, pulling Caroline deeper into the wagon. "We must get you properly disguised."

Working with the swift efficiency of a professional, Rosalind stripped Caroline of her boy's clothes, rummaged in an old trunk, before dressing her in a simple gown of deep-blue wool. Over Caroline's golden hair, she placed a cap and veil in the style favored by young matrons, while Caroline rubbed at the dirt and smudges on her face with a damp cloth Rosalind had thrust into her hands.

"There," Rosalind said, stepping back to admire her work. "You're now my niece, visiting from the next county. Keep your eyes down and let me do the talking."

The wagon lurched as someone climbed the steps. Caroline's heart hammered as the curtain was thrust aside, revealing a rough-looking man in riding clothes.

"Who's in here?" he demanded, his eyes sweeping the interior.

"Myself and my niece," Rosalind replied calmly, shifting so that the baby in her arms was more visible. "Is there something you need?"

Behind the first man, Caroline glimpsed a familiar figure that made her blood freeze—Lord Windermere himself, his cold eyes scanning the wagon's interior.

"We're searching for a boy—a stable lad who's run off with something valuable," Windermere said, his gaze lingering on Caroline. "Small, slight build, fair hair."

"I've seen no such boy," Rosalind replied smoothly. "We've been rehearsing all morning. My niece here has been helping with costumes."

Windermere stepped closer, and Caroline fought the urge to shrink back. "Lift your head, girl," he commanded.

Caroline raised her eyes just enough to show her face, praying her disguise would hold. Windermere studied her for a long moment that felt like eternity.

"Pretty little thing," he murmured, and Caroline felt sick at the predatory gleam in his eyes. "If my business weren't so urgent, I might be inclined to become better acquainted."

"My niece is betrothed," Rosalind said firmly, "to a blacksmith in the next county. A man with a very protective nature and large fists."

Windermere laughed unpleasantly, but stepped back. "Search the rest of the wagons," he ordered his men. "The boy's here somewhere."

After what felt like hours but was probably only minutes, the men concluded their search and departed. Caroline remained frozen until she heard their horses' hoofbeats fading into the distance.

"There," Rosalind said, letting out a breath. "That's done. But you're not safe here, my dear. Men like that don't give up easily."

"Will you... can you help me get to London?" Caroline asked, hardly daring to hope.

Rosalind and Master Aldrich, who had appeared in the wagon's doorway, exchanged glances.

"We're heading in the opposite direction," Aldrich said slowly. "But..." He studied Caroline thoughtfully. "You've got a good ear for voices, haven't you? I noticed how you changed your accent when you spoke to that brute."

Caroline nodded, confused by the direction of his questioning.

"We're short a player for our Millford engagement," Constance said, appearing beside her husband. "Our ingénue ran off with a traveling merchant last week. Young Edgar here has been forced to play all the romantic scenes with himself, which is rather less than effective."

"You want me to... to act?" Caroline stared at them in amazement.

"Why not?" Edgar grinned, clearly delighted by the prospect. "You're the right size, you've got a lovely speaking voice, and after watching you fool those ruffians, I'd say you have a natural talent for performance."

"Three days in Millford," Aldrich mused, "then we head toward the London road for our winter engagements. We could have you back in town within the week."

"But I've never acted before," Caroline protested, though excitement was beginning to bubble up inside her.

"Nonsense," Constance said briskly. "You've been acting all morning. Besides, most of our audiences are more interested in the spectacle than the subtleties of performance. A pretty face and a clear voice will suffice."

Rosalind placed a gentle hand on Caroline's shoulder. "It would keep you safe," she said quietly.

Caroline thought of Henry, possibly even now making arrangements to marry Venetia to preserve her reputation. *Oh, dear Lord, no!* She thought of her mother, expecting her home for dinner and completely unaware of the adventure her daughter had undertaken. She thought of the conventional life waiting for her in London—balls and morning calls and eventual marriage to some suitable gentleman.

Then she looked around at these remarkable people who had taken her in, fed her, protected her, and were now offering her something she'd never dreamed possible: the chance to be someone completely different, if only for a few days.

"What sort of plays do you perform?" she asked.

Master Aldrich's smile was answer enough.

"Oh, my dear girl," he said, his voice warm with approval, "I do believe you're going to fit in perfectly."

Outside, she could hear Edgar beginning to rehearse again, his voice carrying on the morning air. "But soft! What light through yonder window breaks?"

For the first time since this whole adventure began, Caroline found herself smiling with genuine anticipation. Perhaps fortune really did favor the frivolous—or in this case, the theatrical.

Chapter Twelve

HENRY STARED UP at Windermere's hunting lodge, gray and forbidding in the cold light of morning. Mist clung to the stone walls like ghostly fingers, while a solitary raven perched on the chimney, watching his approach with predatory eyes.

He really didn't know where to start. He just knew that he could never live with himself if he did not do everything in his power to rescue Caroline.

How could he have not recognized his dearest friend? She'd been pressed close against him on his horse, her slight form fitting perfectly against his chest, and he'd spoken to her for miles. Yes, there'd been that jolt of familiarity—something that had made his pulse quicken in a way he hadn't understood. But she'd been dressed as a boy, playing her part with such conviction that even her voice had fooled him completely.

The foolishness of her quest. The breathtaking bravery of it.

That was so like Caroline—rushing headlong into danger for someone she loved—consequences be damned. If she were here right now, he'd shake her for taking such risks.

And then he'd probably kiss her senseless.

The thought struck him like a physical blow. He'd never kissed Caroline before, but suddenly the idea seemed not just appealing, but inevitable. When had his feelings for his childhood companion shifted into something so much deeper, so much more dangerous?

He'd never felt such overwhelming concern for anyone's safety before. The very thought of Caroline in Windermere's clutches made his blood boil.

Now he had to decide how to approach this carefully. Windermere had nearly put a ball through his chest last night and would probably shoot first and ask questions later if he recognized Henry on the premises again.

Which was why he'd found new clothes and borrowed a horse, intending to make his investigations without Windermere's knowledge. Hopefully, he'd not be recognized by anyone in the stables as the man who'd had an altercation with the master. Only the household staff would have seen him.

"You there, lad!" He hailed a groom who was leading a limping horse from the stables. Windermere's carriage was conspicuously absent, which suggested the master was not currently in residence. Still, Henry couldn't afford to be complacent.

The boy looked up, his expression sullen and wary. A large red welt across one cheek suggested a recent and violent encounter, and Henry's stomach tightened. "That looks painful. How did you come by it?"

The lad said nothing, pushing past Henry to lead the horse toward the mounting block. Henry followed, noting the careful way the boy moved. As if his ribs pained him.

"You should put some salve on that cheek before it festers," Henry said conversationally. "Trouble with the other stable hands?"

The lad stopped and turned, his eyes narrowed with the suspicious wariness of someone accustomed to harsh treatment. "I dunno what business brings you here, but the master ain't about, which is jest as well, since he's in a right foul temper."

Henry weighed his options. He needed information, but direct questions might make the boy clam up entirely. Still, he had to try.

"The truth is, I'm looking for someone." He pulled out a coin, watching the groom's eyes fix on it with hungry interest. "A stable lad who might have passed through here recently."

"No!" The response was so fierce it made Henry start.

"No?" he prompted gently.

The lad touched his swollen cheek gingerly. "You see this? That's what I got for letting the prisoner escape."

Henry's blood chilled. "Prisoner?"

"Aye. Master had a lad locked up in the tack room overnight. Said he was a spy what needed questioning. But I felt sorry for him—couldn't have been more than fifteen, though small as a child—so I brought him some water and bread." The boy's voice dropped. "Door weren't locked proper after that, if you take my meaning."

Relief flooded through Henry so intensely he nearly staggered. Caroline had escaped on her own. "And the boy got away?"

"No problems as soon as he realized the door would open. Headed across the fields toward the London road." The groom eyed the coin hopefully. "Master took off after him with half his men, but that were hours ago. Long gone by now, I'd wager."

Henry handed over the coin without hesitation. "You did the right thing, helping him."

The boy pocketed the money quickly. "Don't much matter now. Master'll probably dismiss me when he gets back, anyway."

"There's another shilling in it if you can tell me anything else," Henry said. "About the young lady who was here last night."

The groom's expression darkened. "Poor little miss. Crying and carrying on something fierce when they brought her in. Master kept saying she'd thank him later, that her aunt had arranged everything proper-like." He spat in the dirt. "Didn't look much like a willing bride to me."

"But she got away too?"

"Aye, the gentleman what came calling took her away safe.

Caused quite the commotion, he did. Master was ready to shoot him, but then someone started throwing things through the windows. Rocks and logs and such. In all the confusion, the gentleman got the lady to his horse and away they went."

Henry smiled grimly. "And Lord Windermere went after the stable boy instead?"

"Aye, that he did."

"Thank you," said Henry, tossing the boy another coin. "If anyone asks, you never saw me."

Henry rode hard toward the London road, his mind racing. He'd assumed Windermere's interest in Caroline was simply revenge for her interference, but what if there was more to it? What if Caroline was in even greater danger than he'd realized?

He questioned farmers and travelers along the way, following the trail of a "lad in rough clothes" who'd been spotted heading south.

With each mile that passed without finding her, his anxiety grew.

It was near midday when he spotted the traveling theater company's colorful wagons camped in a grove beside a stream. The sight of their painted sides and theatrical banners should have been cheerful, but something about the subdued activity around the camp set him on edge.

"Good day," he called to a silver-haired woman who appeared to be in charge. "I'm looking for someone. A young person who might have passed this way."

The woman's eyes sharpened with interest and wariness in equal measure. "And you are?"

"A friend," Henry said simply. "Someone who's very worried about a brave but foolish young person who may be in trouble."

"Ah." The woman—Constance, she introduced herself—studied him with the penetrating gaze of someone accustomed to reading character. "And this young person... would they be traveling in disguise, perhaps?"

Henry's heart leaped. "You've seen them?"

"We may have." Constance exchanged a meaningful look with a motherly woman holding a baby. "The question is, are you here to help or to harm?"

"To help," Henry said earnestly. "To take them somewhere safe. My name is Henry."

The motherly woman—Rosalind—stepped forward. "She spoke of you," she said quietly. "Henry, eh? Said you were a hero, always doing the right thing."

"She's here?" Henry looked around desperately.

"Was," Constance corrected. "We offered her work if she wanted to stay. But when she said she had to be back in London before she were missed, we helped her on her way after some unpleasant men came looking. But I'm afraid she may have fallen into other hands."

They told him about the farmer who'd offered Caroline a ride towards London, their suspicions about the man's true intentions which had filtered back to them, and the direction they'd headed.

Henry's blood ran cold as he learned Caroline might have escaped one danger only to fall into another.

He thanked the theater company and rode off like a man possessed, following their directions towards the main road, his horse's hooves thundering against the packed earth as he pushed both himself and his mount to their limits.

It was the sound that reached him first. A girl's cry of distress carried on the wind, and he spurred his horse toward it.

He crested a hill and saw them: a farmer's cart pulled to the side of the road, a young man pursuing a girl in colorful skirts who was running desperately across an open field. Even at this distance, there was something familiar about the way she moved, the set of her shoulders as she fled.

"Caroline," he breathed, and then he was thundering down the hill, his only thought to reach her before her pursuer did.

The young man was gaining on her, his longer legs eating up the ground between them. Caroline stumbled on the uneven terrain, her borrowed skirts hampering her progress, and Henry saw her glance back in terror.

He launched himself from his horse while still at full gallop, tackling the young man with enough force to send them both rolling across the grass. They fought viciously, Henry's gentleman's boxing skills pitted against the other man's brute strength and desperation.

"You'll not touch her," Henry snarled, landing a solid blow to the man's jaw.

"She owes me," the man spat back, wiping blood from his mouth.

Henry's fist connected with the man's solar plexus, doubling him over. "The lady owes you nothing."

The man scrambled away, apparently deciding Caroline wasn't worth a prolonged fight with an obviously superior opponent. Henry watched him retreat toward his cart, then turned to where Caroline stood watching, her chest heaving with exertion and relief.

"Caroline," he breathed.

She pushed back the loose curls that had escaped her headscarf, golden strands catching the light. "Henry." Her voice broke on his name, and he heard a world of emotion in that single word. Relief, gratitude, and something deeper that made his heart race.

"My dear girl, I've been searching everywhere for you," he said, drinking in the sight of her. The colorful clothes suited her somehow, bringing out the wild, adventurous spirit he'd always loved about her. "Venetia told me what you'd done, how you'd risked everything to save her. Dear Lord, and to think I didn't recognize you!"

"Venetia? Is she safe?" Caroline's first thought was still for her friend, and Henry felt his love for her deepen even further.

"Safe and sound at the Rose and Crown," he assured her. "Though she's worried sick about you."

Caroline's impish smile appeared. "I gave the theater company your sovereign. Seemed a fair trade for the clothes and safe passage."

The cart driver was shouting from the road, starting down the hill towards them with obvious hostile intent, so Henry whistled for his horse, which had stopped to graze nearby.

"We need to move," he said, helping Caroline mount. The feel of her waist beneath his hands, the way she fitted perfectly against him after he swung up behind her, all felt so right, so natural, that he wondered how he'd been blind to his feelings for so long.

And blind to the fact that Flash was, in fact, Caroline, the night before.

They rode hard for the better part of an hour, putting distance between themselves and any possible pursuit. But they couldn't make it to the Rose and Crown in one stint, so Henry found a small, respectable inn called the Fox and Fiddle, its thatched roof and welcoming windows promising safety and rest before they'd continue.

The innkeeper's wife took one look at Caroline's unconventional attire and Henry's protective stance and drew her own conclusions. "Eloping, are we, dears?" she said with a maternal smile. "Well, you'll find no judgment here. Love will find a way, as they say. Come along, miss, let's get you settled while your young man sees to the horses."

Caroline's cheeks flushed pink, but she didn't correct the assumption. Henry found himself equally tongue-tied, watching her follow the woman inside. When had Caroline become this woman who made his pulse race and his hands tremble? Who made him want to gather her close and never let go?

He saw to his horse with unsteady hands, his thoughts in complete turmoil. He'd known Caroline his entire life, had thought of her as a sister, a friend, a cherished companion. When had all of that changed?

He swallowed, his mouth dry as he acknowledged the depth of his feelings. When had she become the woman he couldn't bear to lose?

Inside, the innkeeper's wife had installed Caroline in a cozy private parlor with tea and fresh bread. And when Caroline looked up when Henry entered, something in her eyes—a new awareness, a shy uncertainty—made his breath catch in his throat.

"They really think we're to be married," she whispered.

"I daresay we should correct them," Henry replied. The words hung between them, charged with possibility.

"Probably." She studied her teacup. "Henry, thank you for coming after me. I know what I did was foolish—"

"It wasn't foolish," he interrupted, moving closer. "It was the bravest thing I've ever known anyone do. You risked everything for Venetia, without a thought for your own safety."

"I couldn't let Windermere force her into marriage," Caroline said fiercely. "She deserves better than a man who will treat her unkindly, no matter that she'd no longer want for material things."

"She does," Henry agreed. "And so do you."

A silence stretched between them, fragile and charged with unspoken meaning, until the sound of approaching horses made them both tense. Henry moved to the window, carefully peering out from behind the curtain.

"Just travelers," he said, relieved. "Not Windermere." He turned back to her, noting the exhaustion in her posture, the way she was trying so hard to appear strong. "We shouldn't linger too long, but you need rest."

"How far to the Rose and Crown?" Caroline asked.

"Another hour if we push hard," Henry said. "But you're exhausted, and Venetia..." He paused, remembering the complications awaiting them. "Venetia is safe with some kind people who are looking after her. There's no immediate danger... from a physical point of view." Still, he felt sick at the thought of how the Gascoynes might trumpet their exploits to the world.

As soon as Caroline and he had rested, he'd press on and plead his case to the elderly pair. Surely they'd be made to understand.

He crossed to her chair and took her hand. "You've been

through so many ordeals these last hours, Caroline. You need to rest."

Her gaze dropped to their joined hands, and he saw her breath hitch slightly.

His thumb traced small circles against her palm, a gesture that felt shockingly intimate. "I'll see to getting us some rooms and supper."

As he turned to leave, Caroline called after him, "Henry?"

He paused at the door, his heart hammering.

"I'm glad it was you who found me and… not anyone else." The simple words held a weight of meaning that made his chest tight with emotion.

"Always, Caroline," he said quietly. "I'll always come for you."

Outside in the corridor, Henry leaned against the wall and tried to steady his breathing. Everything had changed in the space of a day—his understanding of his feelings for Caroline, the danger she was in, the impossible situation they now found themselves in.

Because there was still the matter of Venetia to consider, and the assumptions people would make about Caroline's reputation after her adventures. There were social expectations and family obligations and a dozen other complications that stood between him and the woman he was only now realizing he'd loved for years.

But for now, she was safe. She was here, and she was safe, and that would have to be enough.

Chapter Thirteen

WHEN HENRY HAD gone, Caroline picked up her cup of tea but, this time, her hand was shaking so much that the teacup clattered into the dish, spilling liquid onto the cloth.

She put down her teacup and, resting her head in her hands, leaned forward and began to cry. The tears came silently at first, then in shuddering waves that left her breathless, releasing all the fear and tension she'd held inside during her ordeal.

"There, there, now lovey, I'm sure it ain't all that bad," the innkeeper's wife clucked some time later with a sympathetic smile. "It's not too late for regrets now. The border is a good few hours away and nothing is signed and sealed. If you want this young man to leave you alone, Mrs. Binns will help you get back to them what'll take care of you."

"Oh, he's been utterly wonderful!" Caroline protested. "There is no one better than my Henry, and he has risked his life to help me. Really, I'm just—" she hesitated, fingering the damp handkerchief in her hands "—overcome by how much has happened so suddenly."

"No regrets, then? Sure?" Mrs. Binns's kind eyes searched Caroline's face.

Caroline shook her head, a warmth spreading through her chest at the thought of Henry that had nothing to do with embarrassment.

"I think it's a fine thing when a grand gentleman will go to such lengths to be with the one he truly loves rather than break hearts—his own included—by doing his duty." Mrs. Binns's smile broadened. "Why, to think o' the lengths you young 'uns have gone to. You, miss, a lady by your refined voice and manners, disguising yourself as one of them theater people so that you could escape your family and follow your heart. Why, it's just like one of them lovely romances. Now, your young man, who has just arrived back, tells me you need to rest a few hours, so let me show you to your room. Yes, he has paid me handsomely for me trouble and so I have reserved the best room for your good selves. Up you get, miss, and come along with me. Ah, here's your young man now."

Caroline was too tired and overwhelmed to object. Or was she waiting for Henry to object as Mrs. Binns led them along the corridor? To a single room? The thought sent a flutter of anticipation through her that she wasn't entirely prepared to examine.

Really, she told herself, she just wanted to rest her head on a soft pillow and sink into blessed oblivion. And she wanted Henry's company. He'd always been her companion, and why should it be any different now? He'd just rescued her, and he'd shown the extent of his devotion. Why should that stop at the door to her bedchamber? Henry was a gentleman, and they were simply friends, after all.

And with everything she'd just gone through, she needed him. The thought of being alone, even in the safety of the inn, made her heart race with renewed anxiety.

Thank the Lord that Henry had arrived in time to save the day.

Wordlessly, the two of them followed Mrs. Binns up the creaking staircase to the "best" chamber she'd allocated them. Their shoulders brushed as they climbed, Henry's presence beside her, solid and reassuring.

Stooping beneath the low door frame, they stepped into a charming bedchamber with windows open to a lovely view across the woodland that surrounded the village. The calmness of the outlook was soothing to the soul.

But a look at the comfortable double bed in its carved wooden frame made her throat dry. The quilt was patched but clean, turned down invitingly at one corner. She darted a look at Henry, who looked equally awkward but who nevertheless smiled as he said to the innkeeper's wife, "My thanks for your good care of us. When we have rested for an hour or so, please have your best dinner ready for the lady and something for me to take on my journey."

And when Mrs. Binns had quit the room, the door closing with a soft click behind her, he said apologetically to Caroline, "Forgive me for not correcting her but, truly, I am so exhausted having not slept since rescuing Venetia last night that I think I will quite literally expire if I don't rest for an hour or two. Would you mind terribly if I lay on the bed with you, who must also be exhausted?" He put his hand to her cheek and murmured, "You have been so brave, Caro."

His touch was gentle, his fingertips brushing her skin with a tenderness that made her heart skip.

"Oh, Henry, you have been so much the hero. Of course, I don't mind!" Caroline cried, thinking what a blessed relief it would be to curl up next to her greatest friend and ally. Taking his hand, she led him to the bed.

Already she was yawning as she climbed up onto the mattress.

"And please, will you let me rest my head on your chest as I go to sleep? I have been so terribly frightened these last hours." The request came without thought, borne of a need for comfort that went beyond propriety.

"Of course! That's what I'm here for, Caroline!" he declared, smoothing her pillow and the mattress. "To make you feel you were not abandoned, as you must have felt when I carelessly tossed you a coin and told you to make your own way back to wherever you lived. You cannot imagine how I've tormented myself. First by not recognizing you and then by leaving you in the clutches of that terrible man who tried to abduct your best friend!"

"As long as Venetia is well… and unharmed," Caroline said, snuggling against him, feeling the steady rhythm of his heart beneath her cheek, "that's all that matters."

He hesitated, his arm coming around her shoulders to hold her close. "As well as can be expected. Fortunately, she suffered no ill treatment beyond the denial of her liberties."

"Dear God, that is a relief. But only because you, Henry, reached her in time. You did what you had to do. It was your most important duty because Lord Windermere was going to do all in his power to make her his bride." She sat up suddenly, her hair falling in a tangled curtain around her face. "I overheard the stable boys talking about some business that concerned Venetia, which is why Lord Windermere wanted her. But I could glean nothing specific."

"What did you hear?"

"A couple of stable boys repeated what they'd heard."

"And where had they heard it? Tell me everything."

Caroline forced her mind back, despite her weariness. "I couldn't make out the name or the circumstances. I just heard part of it: 'Bee.' A name that ends in 'Bee.' They said this man had been blackmailed by Lord Windermere and to get out of his difficulties, he'd passed on the knowledge of what he'd learned. Something that made Lord Windermere want Venetia."

Henry gave a low whistle and then, embarrassed, quickly put his hand over his mouth. "Hardly well mannered in the presence of a lady," he murmured, causing Caroline to slap him playfully on the chest.

"It's never stopped you before. And I dare say one could argue that it's hardly gentlemanly to be in the same bed with a lady you have no plans to wed." She grinned. "But needs must, as they say." She sobered. "We have always been the very best of friends, have we not, Henry?"

He nodded, his expression grave, something unreadable flickering in his eyes.

"And there is nothing we wouldn't do for each other, is there?" She made a gesture to encompass them and the room. "That's why we're here."

Again, he nodded, his gaze never leaving her face.

She was about to snuggle back into the bed, satisfied with his answers, when she suddenly wrinkled her nose.

"I didn't notice it in the midst of the drama of everything happening so fast, Henry, but do you not get the impression that this performer's clothing has been bundled up at the bottom of a musty trunk for a good long while?"

Henry gave a delicate sniff. "I think you may be right, Caroline, though I would be too much of a gentleman to say it, and truly it was not at the top of my concerns when I brought you here. Besides, you have no alternative, do you?"

"No, but I do not think I can sleep with the… mustiness filling my nostrils and I'm sure you could not either." She sat up again and wriggled, the movement drawing Henry's gaze. "Please, will you help me take it off?"

Henry blinked, his cheeks coloring. "I don't think—"

"Well, I can't even find some of these wretched fastenings, for the girl who helped me—Rosalind—just grabbed the gown and suddenly I was dressed."

"So your stable boy's clothing is beneath?"

Caroline blinked. "Oh, dear me, no. The breeches were in good condition. Rosalind would have liked them very much for one of the younger actors, I think." She sighed, wriggling again. "But Henry, I cannot bear to have to sleep in them and then wear them again after I've rested and without them being aired. Please find where the fastenings are."

With seeming reluctance, Henry began to explore the cumbersome clothing, finding a ribbon tie and a clasp that, when released, together with the buttons at the neck of the gown, had all falling away. His fingers worked with unexpected tenderness, careful not to touch her skin. "Oh, Caroline! You're not wearing a chemise!" he exclaimed, his voice strained.

And although Caroline felt a moment of heat curling through her at his discovery, she determinedly threw off her remaining clothing, saying, as she pulled on the nightgown Mrs. Binns had provided upon request, "How could I wear a chemise when I was in breeches and shirt and not to be exposed as not being a real stable boy? Now, just turn your head away." The cotton nightgown settled around her, soft against her skin. "You know, I think it's not very gentlemanlike to draw attention to something that, when a girl's been kidnapped, is therefore so unimportant, for I just want to sleep, and I hardly expect that my unladylike lack of a chemise should make any difference to you. Good night, Henry."

BUT IT DID make a difference to Henry, even though he knew it should not. A few minutes before, his eyelids had been as heavy as if two copper pennies lay upon them. And even as they had chatted, when Caroline had first rested her head against his chest, he'd felt the most wonderfully blissful sense of calm and peace with her safe beside him.

But after her sudden insistence that she remove her clothing, and even though he wasn't touching her, the fact of knowing that she lay wearing just a thin nightgown beside him had him tense and jittery and…

Dear Lord, hard like he'd never been before. His body thrummed with an awareness that was both thrilling and terrifying.

But Caroline was his friend. His childhood playmate. The sunlight caught in her hair, turning the tangled strands to gold against the white pillow.

Soon, her gentle breathing indicated that she was asleep. With her cheek resting on her clasped hands upon the pillow, she looked desperately vulnerable. But also exquisitely contented, as a small smile played about her lips. The curve of her shoulder peeked from beneath the nightgown, smooth and pale in the afternoon light.

Yes, she was the sister he must protect, he told himself severely. He'd rescued her, and now he must follow through on his pledge to see her safely back to London.

Swallowing, closing his eyes, and trying to tamp down his fearsome erection, he told himself that he would. He'd force himself to think pure thoughts, and to imagine that she was like his own dear sister, Charlotte. And that he'd behave accordingly.

Henry was exhausted. If he just closed his eyes and rolled to face the opposite direction, he'd wake up rejuvenated and with a new sense of duty… and honor.

And so that's what he did. The first part, at least.

He closed his eyes, and sleep felled him. But when he awoke, it wasn't from natural causes. Caroline was stroking his cheek and forehead, her touch featherlight yet burning against his skin. And her face was inches from his, her lips curved into a smile. Not suggestive—as would have been just cause for his instant, fearsome response—but deeply fond and sweet. Her eyes held a warmth he'd never noticed before, or perhaps had never allowed himself to see.

Like a sister, he told himself severely.

He only wished her words had been more sisterly. For instead, as she trailed her hand from cheek to chin, she murmured, "Who'd have thought you'd be so heroic, Henry? Why, if I were a queen in medieval times, you would be my knight in shining armor, and I'd wrap my favor around your arm as you went into battle for me. Because—" She leaned across to kiss him gently but briefly on the lips, the touch sending sparks through his entire body, "I couldn't think of anyone braver."

Henry blinked, both embarrassed but liking her words so very much he didn't know quite what to say. Her nearness was intoxicating, the scent of her skin—somehow still carrying traces of orange blossom beneath the earthy notes of her adventure—making his head swim.

Caroline laughed, the sound musical in the quiet room. "So speechless. That's not like you, Henry." She shifted a little to lie on her back and look up at the ceiling. Her hair was tangled and there were smudges on her cheeks. Henry thought he'd never seen her look so beautiful. Her very imperfections made her perfect to him.

He swallowed. "Those are the kind of words calculated to make a fellow feel rather a dunce."

"Oh, Henry, you look so darling when you say that. So bashful." Caroline leaned on one elbow to reach a hand around his neck and kiss him tenderly once more on the lips. But this time, with more calculated precision. Her lips lingered against his, soft and inviting.

Drawing back quickly, she looked at him suddenly wide-eyed as she put her hand to her mouth, saying, "I shouldn't have done that, should I... but I don't know why I never have before." A blush stained her cheeks, but her eyes remained steady on his.

"You don't?" He cleared his throat, swallowed again, and counseled himself not to respond to the invitation in her eye. Yet his body betrayed him, and he leaned closer.

"No." She shook her head, her voice wondering, a new awareness dawning in her expression.

Did she not remember that she was in only the thinnest of night gowns beneath the covers? Did she not recall that they had fled from a man who had threatened both her friend and herself? She should be shivering with fear, unable to concentrate on anything but returning to her safe, normal life.

Instead, she raised her hand to his cheek once more and said, wonderingly, "Do you not think that danger makes the blood in one's veins so much more... active? And one's body so much more… alive? Have you felt that, Henry? You're a man, so maybe you're used to feeling this way. But I…" She shrugged, the movement causing the nightgown to slip slightly from one shoulder. "I want to kiss you again, Henry, and you can refuse—and I shan't be the slightest bit offended—or maybe you can let me because there is something here, in my heart, that makes me want to feel even more alive. Is that strange?"

"No, not strange at all," Henry said, clearing his voice and shifting a little closer, the space between them charged with possibility. "And you can. I don't mind at all. In fact—"

But his words were truncated, for suddenly Caroline's lips were on his and his body was on fire and what had started off as the sweetest sensation imaginable was suddenly the most incendiary. Every nerve ending seemed alight, as if his body had been waiting for this moment without his conscious knowledge.

Their lips met again, and this time there was nothing sisterly about it. Caroline's mouth was soft, yielding, yet somehow demanding as she pressed closer. Henry's hand found its way to her hair, tangling in the blonde strands as he deepened the kiss. She tasted of honey from the tea earlier, and something uniquely Caroline that made his head spin.

She made a small sound in the back of her throat—half sigh, half moan—and Henry felt it resonate through his entire body. His other hand slid to her waist, pulling her closer, feeling the heat of her skin through the thin shift she wore.

Caroline's fingers traced patterns on his chest, each touch leaving trails of fire in their wake. Her fingertips crept beneath his shirt, slipping inside to caress the bare skin beneath, sending shivers of pleasure through him. When they broke apart for air, her eyes were dark, pupils dilated, and her lips were slightly swollen. Henry traced them with his thumb.

"I think," she whispered against his finger, her breath warm against his skin, "that I've wanted to do that for quite some time."

"Have you?" His voice was rough, unsteady, filled with wonder and desire in equal measure.

Instead of answering, she kissed him again, this time with more urgency as her hands roamed over his bare chest, and Henry groaned. He rolled them slightly, so she was beneath him, supporting his weight on his forearms as he explored her mouth with reverent thoroughness. The world beyond their bed ceased to exist; there was only Caroline, her warmth, her scent, the soft sounds she made as he kissed her.

When they finally parted, they were both breathing heavily. Caroline's hair was spread across the pillow like a halo, her cheeks flushed, eyes bright with something that looked very much like love.

"I think," Henry said carefully, his voice husky with emotion, "that we need to have a very serious discussion about our future when we reach London."

Caroline's answering smile was radiant, transforming her face. "I think you might be right."

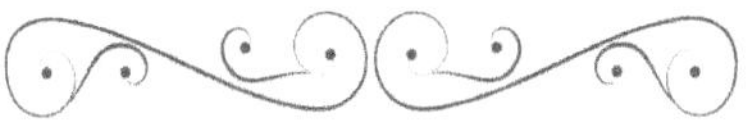

Chapter Fourteen

CAROLINE KNEW SHE'D slept some more. In fact, she was in the midst of the most exquisite dream when a gentle hand upon her shoulder roused her.

But she wasn't yet ready to open her eyes. In her dream, she was a lady of the court of King Arthur astride a white horse, and coming towards her was Henry, dressed in shining battle armor and balancing a lance. His smile was the same she remembered, but tinged with shy pride, for he'd just been victorious in battle and was coming to claim his reward. The pale-blue favor that she'd tied around his arm fluttered like a banner in the breeze.

He was just leaning across in the saddle to kiss her when someone else intruded from a different sphere, shaking her. Just as she was about to kiss her brave knight.

She frowned and tried to resist, but the shaking was insistent.

"Caro, it's time to wake up. I have to go." Henry's voice, gentle but urgent, pulled at the edges of her dream.

Doggedly, she kept her eyes closed. Let him kiss her again. She'd liked it too much the last time but had been left somehow unsatisfied, as if there were depths to kissing she had yet to discover. She wasn't sure why. She just knew she had to be allowed to breach the last distance between them so she could press her lips to his.

She was nearly there. The horse shifted slightly, and her lips touched only air. But he was leaning back towards her. He wanted their kiss as much as she did.

"Caro, please!"

This time his shake was more forceful and, with a gasp, Caroline sat up in bed, her dream knight dissolving into the golden afternoon light.

"What happened?" She glanced down at her thin nightgown, not immediately remembering the events of earlier, her mind still half lost in Arthurian romance.

"Nothing happened, Caroline, I promise! Well, nothing bad or serious, if that's what you mean—" Henry backed away, his hands raised as if to prove his innocence, though his eyes held a warmth that suggested he wasn't entirely sorry about their earlier intimacy.

"Oh, Henry! Of course! It's only you, and now I remember everything." Relieved, she pulled the covers up to her neck while a delicious warmth spread through her at the memory of his lips on hers, the way he'd held her as if she were something precious. Then she threw her arms wide and exclaimed, "I've had the most beautiful sleep after the most wonderful adventure. Of course, the first part of the adventure was truly terrifying, but then you came along and now I'm even glad it all happened because—"

She stopped, aware of the intensity in his gaze as he watched her, the way his breathing seemed to quicken at her enthusiasm.

Suddenly she remembered her friend and, horrified, straightened, her previous dreamy contentment evaporating like morning dew.

"Venetia! Where is Venetia? Is she safe? Oh, Henry, what have we done by staying here—?"

"Stay calm, Caro. Venetia is safe. She's ensconced at the Rose and Thorn, and we had to stay here for some rest because I'd not slept all night and nor had you."

His eyes were shadowed with exhaustion, his cravat loosened, and his hair disheveled in a way that made her want to smooth it back from his forehead.

"But Venetia is alone."

A wary look crossed his face. "She is safe with others, as I told you, Caroline. I made sure of that. And now that you are safe, I can organize suitable transport to discreetly ensure your return home is somehow explained." He ran a hand over the stubble darkening his jaw and shook his head. "I've been pondering it the past hour or more. In fact, I've just returned from trying to source a suitable carriage to take both of you girls to London, but right now, there isn't one."

Caroline wrinkled her nose, glancing at the aromatic heap of theatrical costume upon the floor beside the bed. "I'd be better off in this disguise for now, surely?" she asked, feeling heat steal across her body at the memory of how intimately he'd helped her remove those very garments. "If you can bear being so near to me, I'd be quite happy to ride the distance to where Venetia is right now." She cleared her throat, realizing how much she wanted to feel his closeness again, the solid warmth of him at her back. "We could worry about a suitable conveyance then. After all, Venetia is dressed as a lady. She'd need to go in a carriage. I'm just... Well, no one would cast me a second glance."

Suddenly, the freedom was exhilarating. To be free of the constraints of being a lady, even for a little while longer. To sit astride a horse rather than sidesaddle, to feel the wind in her hair without concern for propriety or reputation. It was a heady thought, almost as intoxicating as Henry's kisses.

But Henry's next words were dampening. "You'll get attention you don't want, Caroline. Your clothing marks you out as a theatrical performer, and some people view such folk with suspicion. You might be accused of theft, or worse, before you know it." His tone was gentle but firm, protective in a way that made her heart flutter.

"Well, that's very unfair, since I've never stolen anything in my life. And I'm sure most of them haven't, either." She lifted her chin defiantly, though she appreciated his concern.

"Except you did steal the apples from Mr. Wilson's orchard, so that's not quite true." A hint of a smile played at the corners of his mouth, the same teasing expression that had charmed her since childhood.

"I was seven!"

"Yes, but I was just reminding you that your claims were not quite accurate—"

"Because you can't help yourself, Henry, from saying exactly what you think about me and my behavior, which is one of the things I like most about you," Caroline said with a grin that felt almost flirtatious. "I never have to worry whether you're being truthful or not. All right, then I'm an untrustworthy performer, but I still want to travel to wherever Venetia is, sitting astride a horse and pressed close to you."

The words hung in the air between them, charged with new meaning after their earlier intimacy. She watched as a flush crept up Henry's neck.

He bit his lip. "You're not ashamed about what happened between us?"

"Should I be?" She raised herself on the pillows, and quickly he interrupted, "No, no! I didn't mean it like that at all! I thought it was wonderful too. I was just worried you'd be regretting what we did and maybe even angry with me."

Caroline suddenly felt the wind drop from her sails as a terrible thought assailed her. Slowly she asked, "It was just a kiss, was it not?" Her heart seemed to pause between beats as she waited for his answer, suddenly aware of how little she truly knew about such matters.

For a moment, the room was utterly silent. Caroline's heart hammered in her chest as she watched Henry's expression shift from confusion to understanding to something that looked remarkably like tenderness.

"Lord, Caroline! Do you think I'd be so ungentlemanly as to go any further than a kiss?" His voice was a mixture of shock and disappointment—or perhaps relief.

The relief that flooded through her was powerful enough to make her lightheaded. But underneath that relief was a curious sensation.

Yes, disappointment, though she would never admit it, even to herself. She twisted the edge of the sheet between her fingers, avoiding his gaze as warmth crept up her neck.

"You'd never be anything but a gentleman, Henry. And I don't really know what going any further than a kiss really means, but I'll take your word as a man of honor that my reputation is not going to be compromised if we can find some way of returning to London and my absence—and Venetia's—somehow explained to everyone's satisfaction. Which I am sure my brother Frederick will help with once he knows everything." She looked up at him through her lashes. "But to get to Venetia, I believe the quickest and best way is for me to ride in front of you on the same horse. I do not want to be sent on my way. Alone."

Henry's cheeks colored slightly, and he turned to look out the window as if the pastoral view held sudden fascination. "When I saw you on the back of that cart, and then the country lout pursuing you, I was angry enough thinking you were just a country lass in need of rescue… But when I discovered it was you." He shook his head, his hands clenching into fists at his sides. "Oh, Caroline—"

"You came to my rescue just in time, and that's all that's important." She leaned forward, wishing she could touch his hand, offer reassurance and perhaps feel that spark of connection again.

But Henry was not yet ready to let the matter lie. "When I finally saw through your disguise…" He turned back to her, his expression earnest, his eyes dark with an emotion that made her breath catch. "I've never been more frightened in my life. The thought of what might have happened to you—what could have happened if I hadn't arrived when I did—"

"But it didn't happen," she interrupted, not wanting to dwell on the dangers she'd faced when the present moment felt so much more compelling. "And now we must turn our minds to getting back to Venetia and then home to London without causing a scandal that would ruin us both."

He nodded. "You're right, of course. Very practical, as always."

"Not always," she said with a small smile. "After all, I did dress as a stable boy and leap onto the back of Lord Windermere's carriage. Hardly the action of a sensible young lady."

That earned her a reluctant laugh, the sound warming her more than she expected. "True enough. You've always had more daring than sense, Caroline Weston."

"And you've always had both, Henry. Which is why I trust you to get us all out of this predicament." The words were light, but the sentiment behind them was genuine. She did trust him. Completely. With her safety, her reputation, and—if she were being honest—her heart.

"Well… I'll wait outside while you dress," he said, his voice suddenly formal though his eyes lingered on her face. "And then, yes, we'll ride together to the Rose and Thorn. But we must be careful. Windermere's men could still be searching for you."

As he reached the door, Caroline called out, "Henry?"

He turned, his hand on the latch.

"About that kiss…" she began, unsure how to continue. Her fingertips unconsciously touched her lips, as if they could still feel the pressure of his, the warmth and surprising softness.

His expression softened, his gaze dropping to her mouth before meeting her eyes again. "What about it?"

"I'd like to remember it properly," she said, emboldened by their shared adventure and the new understanding blossoming between them like a flower unfurling in spring sunshine. "When I'm not half-asleep and confusing it with dreams about knights and ladies."

For a moment, something flickered in his eyes. Something warm and promising and decidedly ungentlemanly that made her pulse race. Then he shook his head slightly and smiled, a smile that reached his eyes and made them crinkle at the corners in the way she'd always loved.

"Let's get you and Venetia safely back to London first," he said, his voice slightly rough with an emotion she was beginning to recognize. "Then we can discuss… proper kisses."

The promise in his words sent a thrill through her that had nothing to do with fear and everything to do with the adventure that awaited them.

Not just the journey back to London, but the journey of discovery they'd begun in each other's arms.

Chapter Fifteen

"Y OUR AUNT IS keeping to her bed rather late, Miss Playford, is she not?"

Venetia kept her head down and her voice steady as she replied, "Aunt Pike does like to conserve her energy during long journeys." She stirred her tea with deliberate slowness, avoiding the piercing gaze directed at her from across the table.

"For she is, as I have known her, a generally busy, rather early-to-rise sort of woman. Would you not agree?"

Venetia raised her teacup and smiled at the abominable woman across the table from her. With an effort, she managed to keep the liquid in the porcelain cup from spilling.

How had she found herself in such a situation? She was exhausted, her traveling dress was crumpled from all those hours of close confinement in Lord Windermere's carriage, and she was sure she must smell of horse from her race across the countryside with Henry.

Mrs. Gascoyne didn't seem to notice. The sunlight streaming through the inn's windows caught the silver threads in her hair, giving her the deceptive appearance of a benevolent matron.

Did the woman believe her? Or did she suspect that Aunt Pike was not in the bedchamber from which Venetia exited with Henry into the passage, and now she was determined to trap

Venetia, like a cat toying with a cornered mouse?

"Aunt Pike did complain of a megrim when she went to bed," Venetia said artfully, smoothing an imaginary wrinkle from her sleeve. "Maybe I should check on her and see if she needs anything."

"Oh, I'm sure she'd have sent a message down if that were the case." Mrs. Gascoyne waved Venetia back into her chair, her bony fingers fluttering imperiously. "Or perhaps I could go up and lend a sympathetic ear if she's feeling so poorly."

"Oh, there's really no need," Venetia protested as sweetly as she could. She'd certainly learned a lot over the past three years when such an offer under such circumstances would have had her sweating and choking on her response. "Aunt Pike can get a little testy when she's not feeling up to snuff. I shall ask the innkeeper's wife if she could make up a soothing posset, perhaps."

"Yes, that would be a kind thing to do for a kind woman. Mrs. Pike is so very considerate to all others. A godly woman, wouldn't you say?" Mrs. Gascoyne's eyes narrowed slightly, her lips pursed in an expression that suggested she was already certain of the answer.

Venetia thought her aunt the last thing from a godly woman she could think of, but she managed a muted, "I believe people are always very different amongst their nearest—"

"And their dearest. And that is what you are, is that not so, my dear Miss Playford? You are your aunt's closest living relative and, having no children of her own, it must have been a great comfort to her to know she had you to look after her in her twilight years. I had supposed that a gel like you would not marry, having not been endowed with a fortune." She hesitated, her fingers drumming a slow rhythm on the tablecloth. "But then the events of last night. Well, I'd feared my husband had jumped to conclusions, having seen you in company with the young gentleman Mr. Ashworth—"

"Well, now, I'm afraid it *was* rather jumping to conclusions since I only met Mr. Ashworth here while Aunt Pike and I were already staying here. A great coincidence it was indeed, for his sister, Charlotte, is a very great friend of mine." Venetia smiled with what she hoped was convincing innocence, though her heart fluttered like a trapped bird against her ribs. "And as Mr. Ashworth was in such a hurry to expedite a very important personal matter, I'm not entirely sure he understood properly what was being insinuated."

"Oh, he certainly did. And if you want to keep it secret for now, then our lips are sealed until it's made public. But, my dear..." Mrs. Gascoyne leaned her whole body across the table. "I've no doubt your aunt is delighted you've won the interest of a man of such considerable prospects as Mr. Ashworth." She hesitated, and her eyes narrowed. "And I'm sure she sanctioned your meeting with him last night, as she was no doubt offering all the required chaperonage. But she has not been well, has she?" Mrs. Gascoyne cleared her throat and went on, haltingly. "What I mean to say is... Has your aunt warned you of the dangers of consorting with young men like Mr. Ashworth when she is not physically present?"

Venetia widened her eyes as if the suggestion of liberties was front of mind and something she was at great pains to avoid. "She has, *naturally*, but as I said, Mr. Ashworth's sister is a dear friend of mine. Really, it is not quite as it appears for Mr. Ashworth happened to be looking in on Aunt Pike when you saw us in the passage, for I had just come out to say goodbye... at Aunt Pike's request. I'm afraid... well, Mr. Ashworth is indeed a very eligible potential suitor, but he is not, in fact, *my* suitor. Really, he was simply doing a kindness to Aunt Pike, being coincidentally at the same inn." The lie tasted bitter on her tongue, but Venetia kept her expression placid.

Mrs. Gascoyne pushed back her chair suddenly, the legs scraping harshly against the wooden floor, and hailed one of the young serving girls who had been hovering near the doorway. "Enough of this talk about your poor aunt when I know she would be down if she were well. We will ask the kitchen to make a posset and we will take it up to Mrs. Pike and reassure both ourselves that she is well."

"Oh, really, Mrs. Gascoyne, that won't be necessary. Did your husband not say he wanted to be on the road shortly?" Venetia's voice took on a note of desperation that she couldn't quite disguise.

Mrs. Gascoyne shook her head, her look serene though her eyes were sharp with suspicion. "I do not believe he said anything of the sort, so I can't imagine where you got that from, my dear. No, let us go up together and see your poor Aunt Pike."

"But—"

"She will not mind when she sees it is her old friend, Mrs. Gascoyne. And my husband does like a ramble in the countryside when he has the chance. A great bird watcher, is Mr. Gascoyne. And a great upholder of virtue, too, so he will not think of us departing from this inn before we have satisfied ourselves that you are in safe hands, which means ensuring that your aunt is well enough to see that all is right with you, young lady." She rose, fixing a brook-no-argument look upon Venetia, her thin frame vibrating with moral conviction. "Come now, we're going to see your Aunt Pike and I won't hear another word."

"But the posset—" Venetia made one last, feeble attempt at delay.

"Yes, we'll organize for one to be brought up by and by. However, my concerns are rapidly rising that if your aunt truly was in sufficiently good health to look after you, she'd be well and truly up by now."

Miserably, Venetia trailed after the woman who'd taken on the self-appointed de facto role of moral arbiter in Venetia's affairs and who set up an interminable chatter all the way up the stairs about the godly works of the godly Mrs. Pike until Venetia feared she might scream. Her footsteps on the wooden stairs felt like a slow march to the gallows.

If Mrs. Gascoyne had only spent one week in Venetia's position, she'd know that Aunt Pike was mean-spirited and that she thrived on malicious gossip and anything that would diminish the respect and dignity of the underlings in her household, namely Venetia, but also of the cowed servants who lived there. The woman's thin smiles always preceded her cruelest remarks.

For three years, Venetia had been hoping to meet a nice gentleman who was able to discount the fact she came with no dowry and for whom she felt more than a faint feeling of affinity. There had been Mr. Bilby who had seemed promising in the beginning but who'd decided he really did need her to come with a dowry.

And then, just a few months later, she'd met the most charming and engaging Mr. Barnett during a provincial assembly she'd attended with her aunt. His warm brown eyes and gentle manner had made her heart skip when they'd danced. He, too, was not sufficiently plump in the pocket—Aunt Pike's words—to support Venetia in a manner that would not harm Aunt Pike's reputation, and the romance had consequently been nipped in the bud.

But he had been a very nice man and even just thinking about him made Venetia's heart beat a little more rapidly.

Just as it was now as, with heavy footsteps, she followed Mrs. Gascoyne up the stairs.

Soon her lie would be revealed, and then what would happen? Mrs. Gascoyne took almost as malicious a delight as her aunt in condemning moral transgressions. And she would most certainly see the fact that Venetia was alone at an inn as a moral transgression. In fact, not only was Venetia alone at an inn, but she'd been seen walking out of a bedchamber alone with a young gentleman. Her skin prickled with dread. Even if there had been talk of a betrothal between them, it was still a moral transgression for a young lady to be alone with a man.

"If I'd known your aunt was staying at the same inn as Mr. Gascoyne and myself, we could have arranged to have shared a saddle of beef downstairs in a private chamber rather than have ours in our chamber, as Mr. Gascoyne did not care for the idea of descending the stairs when, to be quite truthful, we were not entirely sure of the reputation of this lodging house. But for the necessity of changing horses and the late hour, we'd have continued to Marbury, where we know there is a very respectable inn. Of course, with your aunt under this same roof, our fears in that quarter are now put quite to rest. Now, I shall knock just a little loudly, for it is not too early that your Aunt Pike shouldn't be awake if not up already."

Mrs. Gascoyne rapped sharply on the door.

Bracing herself for the inevitable silence, Venetia stared stony-faced at the wooden floor, then at Mrs. Gascoyne, for she could not give up so easily when it was possible the woman could be reasonable. Though the set of the older woman's jaw suggested otherwise.

"She is sleeping, I am sure of it." Venetia gave an exaggerated sigh, twisting her hands in the folds of her dress. "Poor Aunt Pike. Her megrim must have been worse than I thought. And to think I have been downstairs all this time talking to you when I should have been attending to my dear aunt with cold compresses and soothing possets." Lordy, Venetia couldn't count the number of hours she'd had to do just that.

"I am worried." Mrs. Gascoyne frowned. "Deeply worried, as you should be, young lady! Yes, you must go in and ensure that she is not expired as we speak!" Her voice trembled. "And I shall follow you with the necessary fortitude should it be needed. Rarely a more uncomplaining, stouter woman than your Aunt Pike could be imagined. Open that door, my girl, and we will ensure that your poor aunt is still on this mortal earth."

Well, there was nothing for it, really, Venetia thought, adopting a phrase that Henry would have used; closing her eyes as she turned the door handle, almost willing her deplorable aunt to be lying, eyes closed and feverish upon the bed.

But, of course, she was not. The room was bare, the bed slightly crumpled with no other evidence of habitation—other than the fact that Venetia and Henry had emerged from it earlier… together and alone.

Damning, damning! Even though nothing untoward had occurred.

But of course, Mrs. Gascoyne, and people like her with fevered imaginations, always thought the worst, Venetia knew. She'd lived with "people like that" since she'd been eight years old and her aunt had taken her in.

In the gloom, Mrs. Gascoyne looked like a blind baby bird as she peered about, stretching out the silence, her frown growing deeper as she seemed to think she really might find Aunt Pike beneath the bed. She even bent to check, her stiff skirts rustling as she stooped.

Finally, turning with great deliberation towards Venetia, she said heavily, "Your Aunt Pike is not at this inn, is she, Miss Playford?"

Venetia shook her head, her stomach sinking with dread. The game was up.

"You and that young man emerged from this chamber… alone… before he… abandoned you." Each pause in Mrs. Gascoyne's speech felt weighted with judgment.

Just as Venetia had expected to have the woman's deep disapproval and disappointment unleashed upon her, Mrs. Gascoyne's severe frown suddenly crumpled and she put her hand on Venetia's shoulder, gripping it fiercely as she said, "That young man shall not succeed in ruining an innocent young girl like you if I have any say in it."

"Please, Mrs. Gascoyne, nothing happened. I promise—" Venetia's voice rose with desperation.

"But you were alone in a bedchamber with him, hours from London, alone and unchaperoned," the woman went on, her fingers digging painfully into Venetia's flesh. "Correct me if I'm wrong, but those are the facts of the matter—is that not correct?"

"Yes, but Mrs. Gascoyne, it was not my fault. I was… taken against my will." Venetia swallowed hard, trying to organize her thoughts into a coherent explanation.

"He abducted you!" Mrs. Gascoyne's wizened face took on a

horrified quality, her eyes widening until the whites showed all around.

"No, not Henry—" Venetia tried to interject, but Mrs. Gascoyne was not listening.

"Henry, is it? Got you cozy with Christian-naming so he could spirit you off to the country. Did you not suspect his evil intentions? Did your aunt not warn you—" Spittle gathered at the corners of her mouth as her indignation mounted.

"Henry rescued me. He didn't abduct me. No, that was—" Venetia's words tumbled over each other in her haste to explain.

"Did you sleep in that bed?" Mrs. Gascoyne stabbed her finger towards the offending object by the window, which clearly had been slept in, the sheets rumpled and bearing the indentation of two bodies.

"I slept, but… that is all. I slept because I'd been in a carriage all night and I was frightened and exhausted, and then Henry came—" Tears stung Venetia's eyelids.

"And your Henry will atone! Mr. Gascoyne!" Barking an order that carried into the passage where her husband had just appeared through the open door on his way to presumably their own chamber, Mrs. Gascoyne made it clear that escape was not an option. Her thin chest heaved with righteous fervor.

"Please, Mrs. Gascoyne, that is not at all the way matters were," Venetia protested, close to tears. But it seemed Mrs. Gascoyne had fashioned herself into Venetia's savior rather than critic, her narrow face alight with the pleasure of moral vindication.

"The poor dear girl has been hoodwinked by a libertine," she hissed as her husband entered the room, closing the door behind him at her command.

"I haven't," said Venetia. "Not by Henry. Of course I was by Lord—"

"And now the young man has abandoned her. He is not here, is he? He's left you, my dear Miss Playford, having spent the night in this room with you while pretending upon departure that he was a man of honor." Her eyes nearly bulged out of her head as she said it, her voice dropping to a scandalized whisper. "Oh, Mr. Gascoyne—" she gripped his arm, her lips pursed, "—that young man will have to do the right thing. Wherever he is, we will find him before any of this comes to light. It's the least I can do for my dear friend, Mrs. Pike, who is probably sick with worry about your whereabouts."

"No, she's not sick with worry." Venetia opened her mouth to say that her evil aunt had in fact facilitated the means by which Lord Windermere had kidnapped her, but Mrs. Gascoyne spoke over her as she entreated her husband. "You will speak to him, Mr. Gascoyne. Oh yes, you will tell that young man that if he is not to be pilloried, and his name blackened and every institution set against him—because you have power in high places, indeed you do—he will do the honorable thing and marry this poor innocent. This poor young lady who had no idea what was happening when he insinuated he'd be a gentleman and then fell so far short."

Mr. Gascoyne's eyes narrowed further with each of his wife's pronouncements and his jowls quivered with indignation. "If that young man I saw earlier has indeed been guilty of what you say he is, my dear, then I shall leave no stone unturned before I find him."

Mrs. Gascoyne clenched her bird-like hands into fists as she turned back to Venetia. "Your secret is safe with me, my dear. But of course, your fate depends upon us running this scoundrel to ground. If it is the last thing I do, it's to honor my friendship to your poor dear aunt, by ensuring your virtue is protected at all costs. Mark my words, when Mr. Gascoyne sets his mind to it, he can do anything. And finding Mr. Henry Ashworth is what he will do."

Her bosom heaved, and she looked fiercely at Venetia as if expecting gratitude, her thin nostrils flaring with each breath.

Venetia didn't know how to respond. She only knew that if being kidnapped by Lord Windermere had seemed the worst that could happen to her twenty-four hours earlier, this was a close second.

And then hurried footsteps sounded up the stairs in the distance, coming closer as they traversed the corridor, while Henry's cheerful voice called out as he opened the door to step into the room.

"Venetia! I'm back! And you'll never guess who I've brought with me!"

Venetia thought she would expire on the spot as she watched Henry's cheerful expression melt away while Caroline, dressed in some strange, colorful garb, appeared at his shoulder.

Then Mrs. Gascoyne drew herself up to her full, albeit modest, height and pointed an accusatory finger at Henry.

"Mr. Ashworth," she intoned, her voice quivering with righteous indignation, "we have been waiting for you."

"OH HENRY, WHAT will we do?" Caroline burst out as they watched the Gascoyne carriage disappear a short while later. "They talk of rescuing Venetia from evil influences—meaning you—but they're taking Venetia straight back to her aunt!"

Henry shook his head. Then, squaring his shoulders, he took her hand and squeezed it. Not with loving tenderness, but with the bolstering energy that reminded Caroline of when they were children. "We need proof of Lord Windermere's evil deeds," he said grimly. "And we will find it! We will discover why Windermere wishes so dearly to marry penniless Venetia and why her aunt is up to her neck in skullduggery." Then, with a sigh, and a touch less heroism, he added, "Though, truth be told, I don't know where we'd begin. Mrs. Pike is Venetia's only relative. Her father and mother are dead. And so is anyone who knew them, it seems."

Caroline caught her breath. "Oh, Henry! I've just remembered. Just before I left home, my maid made mention of Mr. Rothbury, saying she'd been told by another of the servants that Mr. Rothbury's father had been bailiff to the Playford family. Of course, Mr. Rothbury would have only been a boy—"

"Capital!" With admiration written across his face, Henry dipped his head to kiss Caroline on the lips. "There has to be something about Venetia that makes Lord Windermere want her, and if Mr. Rothbury can throw any light upon the matter, then we've got a start. You never were one to miss an opportunity, my clever girl. We made a fearsome duo when we were children. Imagine how unstoppable we'll be when we're married!"

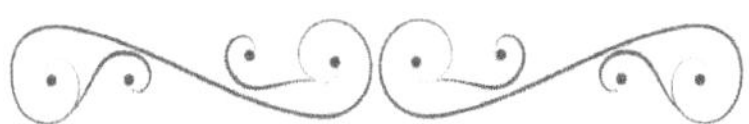

Chapter Sixteen

CAROLINE WAS EXHAUSTED by the time she and Henry arrived back in London, yet joy and elation were her primary emotions as she stepped out of the hired carriage and hurried up the front steps to her brother's home.

They had been delayed by necessity. First by Henry's insistence that they formulate a proper plan before confronting the web of lies surrounding Venetia, and then by Caroline's need to change out of her theatrical costume once they had reached Henry's home and entreated Charlotte's help in the matter of a change of clothes.

When Caroline had assumed Henry would accompany her to explain matters to Frederick, he had suggested that his presence after so long an absence on Caroline's part might prove a liability.

"Remember, your mama is likely to be tearing her hair out with anguish and no doubt will have relayed all her fears and suspicions to Frederick. Thanks to my sister, we hopefully will have provided you with an alibi. Charlotte was very ready to say, if asked, that you had spent the night with her, having hurt your ankle after you slipped away to supposedly visit her. My presence will simply muddy the waters."

Accepting Henry's wise counsel and buoyed by the fact that during their final hour of planning they had settled upon a strategy to discover Windermere's motivations, Caroline was not expecting all hell to break loose the moment she walked through the front door.

"Where have you been these last twenty-four hours, Caroline!" Her brother Frederick emerged from his study before the butler had even closed the front door. "I thought you had grown up, but it appears you are as wayward and thoughtless as you ever were. Do you ever think of anyone other than yourself?" he raged.

"Please, Frederick, I—"

"I don't have time to hear it! Poor Amelia has been sending discreet notes to anyone who might be able to throw some light on your unconscionable behavior—or should I say disappearance. In her condition, she has better things to worry about than my thoughtless little sister, who thinks only of her own pleasure!"

Caroline's heart constricted at the accusation. To think that Frederick—who had always been her champion—viewed her as nothing more than a selfish child was almost unbearable. "Please, Frederick, it wasn't like that at all!" Finally, Caroline managed to interject as she was propelled down the corridor and out of hearing of the servants. "I was trying to help Venetia. A terrible thing happened—she was kidnapped by Lord Windermere, who wants to marry her for reasons unknown."

"Caroline, are you feverish?" Amelia had appeared in the doorway, shadows under her eyes making her look pale and wan. "Frederick, please don't shout," she entreated, running the back of her hand across her forehead before sinking into a seat by the fireplace. "I know you are out of your mind with worry, as we all are, but surely Caroline has some acceptable answer for what has happened."

"Yes, I just told you," Caroline began, but her brother rounded on her.

"Do you really expect us to believe such nonsense? Why, you must have sucked this out of your thumb, my girl."

"No! Venetia's Aunt Pike is an evil woman, and she conspired with Lord Windermere to kidnap Venetia. I tried to rescue her—in fact, I did rescue her—"

Frederick laughed, the sound harsh and mocking. "Well, that excuse is the lamest I ever heard. Venetia is in no danger whatsoever." He turned to his wife. "Perhaps, my dear, you would like to tell Caroline what you learned in the course of your frantic investigations."

Caroline looked between them, her chest tight with dread. Her brother truly believed she was a liar? And Amelia supposedly had proof Caroline had fabricated everything? Her throat burned with unshed tears, and her hands trembled as she realized how completely she had miscalculated this homecoming.

"Your friend Venetia is in no danger from Lord Windermere," Frederick went on, for it appeared Amelia had not the energy to speak. She was leaning back in the chair, a pained look on her face, one hand placed gently on her swollen belly.

"Oh no, your Venetia is in fine hands, for word is all over town that she is to marry Henry Ashworth."

Caroline blinked stupidly. "But I saw Henry only—" She stopped herself and went on carefully, "I saw him very recently, and he made no mention of it."

"No?" Frederick cocked an eyebrow. "It appears his behavior has left something to be desired. A certain Mr. and Mrs. Gascoyne discovered the pair of them in a compromising situation. Of course, Mrs. Pike is trying to put the best face on it that she can, but she has ever been disappointed in that girl, as she is so ready to tell us all—"

Amelia finally seemed to find the energy to speak. "Venetia is a lovely girl. I am sure there has been a terrible misunderstanding to see her name maligned as it appears to be."

"That's only because Lord Windermere—"

"Will you stop this nonsense regarding Lord Windermere!" Her brother all but shouted, causing Amelia to put out her hand and say in soothing tones, "Please, Frederick darling, I know you have been worried to death about Caroline and that you're shocked to hear the news about Venetia. I think perhaps we should let Caroline go to her room. There is plenty of time to talk about this later."

"But there is no time to talk about it later!" Caroline cried, desperation making her voice crack. "Henry cannot marry Venetia because…"

This time, she was not cut off, but rather let her words trail into silence as Frederick and Amelia looked at her inquiringly. She took a deep breath and swallowed. This was not the time to tell them that she had, in fact, spent the previous hours in Henry's company and that he was going to marry *her*. Not Venetia.

No, Caroline needed to make them understand that Venetia was the victim of a grave plot by Lord Windermere and that she and Henry greatly feared he would not rest until he had made her his wife.

But when she opened her mouth for one final attempt to be heard, Frederick simply put up his hand. Closing his eyes in the attitude of one whose patience has been tried beyond endurance, he said, "Do as Amelia says and go to the blue room where you can reflect on what has been said, Caroline. I have no more patience with you and your childish flights of fancy. We will talk about what you have *really* been up to later. Thank goodness your sister-in-law has managed to mitigate the severest of damage to your reputation."

Caroline gasped, but remained silent. She turned toward the stairs, her vision blurred with tears she refused to let fall.

So! She and Henry really were on their own in this fight to save Venetia.

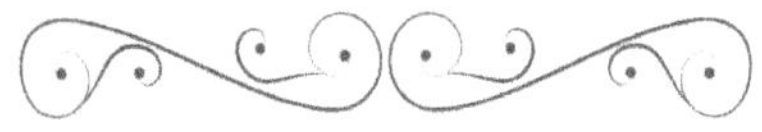

Chapter Seventeen

IT WAS AN unseasonably warm summer night as Lady Townsend idly fanned herself, seated in her usual corner of Lady Huntington's ballroom.

Had it been the previous season, she would not have found the enthusiasm or fortitude to have bestirred herself sufficiently to attend, knowing her chief companion would have been Lady Pendleton.

However, now, with Lord Thornton's return, a whole new world of excitement beckoned.

And the fact that she had all but won her wager was as good a reason as any for her to look forward—with heightened anticipation—to the arrival of the gentleman who had made her heart race for the past thirty years.

So, when Lord Thornton did indeed stride through the doors that led from the card room before turning, with a smile, in Eugenia's direction, Eugenia's heart gave more than just a little lurch.

Lady Pendleton had been absent for several minutes. Hopefully she'd be delayed, returning from the ladies' mending room.

Eugenia sighed, for, out of the corner of her eye, she could see her friend gliding through the ballroom, her crimson turban bobbing among the crowd like a warning flag.

But with a quickening of her pulse, she calculated that Lord Thornton would arrive seconds before. All she could hope for was that Lady Pendleton's love of gossip might see her waylaid as some juicy *on dit* was relayed to her en route. There had been no shortage of that lately.

But her hopes were in vain, for Lady Pendleton arrived at the very same moment as Lord Thornton, who immediately offered congratulations on Eugenia's acuity in correctly determining what neither he nor Lady Pendleton had observed—despite it being right in front of their noses.

"I cannot believe it! Miss Venetia Playford and Mr. Henry Ashworth? The latest match?" Lady Pendleton exclaimed, sinking into a chair at right angles to Eugenia. Quickly, she added with a frown, "However, a betrothal is not a marriage."

Eugenia knew how much her friend disliked not being right in all matters. As she had also not been the one to predict the match, she'd naturally do all in her power to throw cold water on Eugenia's excitement.

Still, Lady Pendleton did allow herself a small smile when Lord Thornton said mildly, "But it generally does lead to one. One of the parties would either have to renege, and if that was young Henry, the fear of being sued for breach of contract would be very real, especially given the fact that Miss Venetia could hardly do better given her own parlous situation in life. But if Miss Venetia were to renege, then her reputation would probably not withstand such damage. Indeed, being penniless, she might find she had just squandered her last opportunity for marriage. So I will give credit where credit is due and say congratulations, Eugenia. Your prediction has all but earned you your heart's desire."

"Her heart's desire, indeed!" scoffed Lady Pendleton. "I don't think we progressed beyond the ridiculous notion Eugenia put forward when wagers were last discussed. Permission to accompany Lord Thornton on one of his diplomatic missions disguised as his secretary, indeed? I have never heard of anything more preposterous."

Eugenia smiled. Of course she'd not been serious at the time they'd discussed wagers and heart's desires, but Lord Thornton had responded with a twinkling in his eye. She'd definitely felt a fizzle of connection before Lord Admiral Bennett had claimed his attention. The terms had not been discussed since.

Now Eugenia—with a shrug of her shoulders, and another smile for Thornton—said teasingly, "I think I should make an excellent secretary. However, perhaps it won't be possible since you claim that your diplomatic days are over, Thornton."

"It won't be possible because you are not a man," said Lady Pendleton. She frowned as she stared across the room towards the young couple in question.

Eugenia sighed. How delightfully demure Miss Venetia looked this evening, dressed in pale cream silk that complemented her fair coloring. A world away from the giggly debutante in her first season out. But those impulses were now well restrained. She was the perfect example of maidenliness.

And how much more sober young Henry appeared, she observed as she studied the young man who was standing with his sweetheart, both of them holding refreshments. His usually animated features were composed into a mask of propriety.

Obviously, the matching of their hearts had instilled a recognition of the sanctity of their union. Her heart soared. Yes, she had all but won her wager. In a few weeks, young Henry would walk his bride down the aisle, and then Eugenia could claim her prize from Lord Thornton.

"They don't look very happy, do they?" Lady Pendleton remarked in dampening tones. "Venetia looks as if she's attending a funeral, while Henry looks as if he has swallowed a lemon. No, Eugenia, I think you have made a mistake. I do not believe this pair will make it to the altar. Knowing both of them as I do, albeit not well, I don't believe they are at all well matched."

Eugenia shrugged. "I think they make the perfect match." And she truly did. "Time will prove it."

LANGUIDLY, CAROLINE FANNED herself on this hot summer's evening as she stared miserably about the room. How extraordinary to think that less than three days ago, she'd been dressed as a boy and hiding in a trunk on the back of Lord Windermere's carriage.

Knowing that he was here this evening was terrifying, so she was glad that any signs of fear she might exhibit—such as excessive sweating or too-rapid breathing—could be put down to the oppressive heat.

She hadn't wanted to come out this evening. She'd wanted to exercise her mind with every single possibility she could tease out regarding Lord Windermere's motivations for wanting Venetia. However, her mama had insisted.

And, besides, Henry was here.

"You claimed a megrim yesterday and the day before that, yet I have seen no real evidence that anything other than sullenness afflicts you," her mama snapped. Caroline noticed that her mama appeared to be enjoying herself this evening. She often appeared bored when accompanying Caroline, but now she suddenly said, "I must say, I am not one for gossip, but there is plenty of it this season. Lord Windermere has bought a grand estate thanks to his success on the Stock Exchange. Of course, we'd all heard rumors that he'd cast his eye in the direction of your friend Venetia— prepared to overlook the fact she is penniless—but of course, Henry proposed before Lord Windermere had an opportunity to make Venetia the richest young lady in this room." She paused, fixed a gimlet eye on her daughter, then said, "Perhaps you, Caroline, might be his chosen bride if you play your cards right."

"Mama, can you even be serious?" Caroline shuddered, and her face must have shown the extent of her horror and disgust, for Lady Weston said with mild disapproval, "You are in public, Caroline. I was just beginning to congratulate myself on a daughter who was not the tearaway Society has called her these last two years that you have been out. I had thought that, without Henry's bad influence, you had found the decorum which I have spent my life trying to instill in you."

"Henry has never been a bad influence," muttered Caroline, turning away to see her old friend at the very moment he, too, turned from speaking to Venetia. A flash of something difficult to interpret crossed Henry's face, but even from this distance, it reflected the pain in Caroline's heart—and in the misery reflected in Venetia's countenance as well.

"And there is Henry! Doesn't he look serious for a change? Come, let us go over and speak to them. I don't believe you've even congratulated Miss Playford since her betrothal to Mr. Ashworth was announced."

"You want to speak to Henry after you were so rude about him, Mama?" demanded Caroline, with a mutinous tilt to her chin.

Her mother looked surprised. "My tone has hardly changed about the young man. He was forever getting into scrapes as a boy, but now he is maturing, as I had hoped you were until you gave me that filthy look after suggesting Windermere might make a suitable husband. But I have always had a soft spot for young Henry, as you know. Now, come along, Caroline. I don't know what has got into you this evening."

Caroline was lost for words. How could she ever begin to tell her mother of Lord Windermere's crimes without compromising herself?

"Ah, Henry, Venetia, how delightful to see you this evening," said Lady Weston, having sailed up to the pair, forcing her daughter along in her wake. "Only three weeks until the happy day. Your aunt was telling me how delighted she was to see her only relative so well situated. And your sister, Charlotte, is over the moon to call you her new sister, my dear Venetia. What a happy state of affairs all round."

Caroline stared gloomily at Henry, who stared gloomily back, managing a weak smile that failed to reach his eyes.

Nevertheless, she made a brave attempt to keep her voice light. "Are you well, Henry?" she asked as they stood at the edges of the ballroom, watching the dancers perform their steps while Venetia was claimed in conversation by Caroline's mama. "You do look rather… preoccupied."

"Oh, and you think I would not when the woman I love appears to have blindly accepted that I wed another," he ground out, his voice low but intense.

Caroline swallowed and sent a nervous glance over her shoulder. "Of course that is not true! But what else can we do but accept the situation until we uncover what's at the heart of Lord Windermere's crimes, past and, no doubt, present. We agreed that we—"

"No, you said that we would have to be silent until Mr. Rothbury returns to London and we can hopefully learn something about Venetia's family history. But inaction is not natural to me, Caroline. As it is not natural to you." He shrugged helplessly, his fingers tightening around his glass. "Of course I appear distracted. I am nearly wrung out with distraction." He lowered his voice. "I love you, Caroline. I cannot act as if my heart belongs to another."

"No, well, you're not doing a very good job at it, I'm pleased to note." Caroline managed a wry smile while it took all her willpower not to cup his clenched jaw in the palm of her hand. "But in the meantime, you can't renege, and neither can Venetia, without a scandal. We just have to wait until we've spoken to Mr. Rothbury."

"Of all the inconvenient times to leave London," Henry muttered before sending Caroline an almost desperate look. "Do you think there really might be truth in your maid's claims that Mr. Rothbury was bailiff to Venetia's father and grandfather? And that he might know something that would help? As you yourself said, Mr. Rothbury would have been but a boy. What would he know after all this time?"

Caroline drew in a difficult breath. "He's the best hope we have."

"And are you sure it's a good idea not to tell Venetia about… us?"

Caroline closed her eyes. The conundrum was very real. "Poor Venetia seems almost numbed by shock. I don't know if it would register. Or, if it would make a difference," she finally admitted. "Anyone is better than Windermere, and she likes you which perhaps, for her, is enough."

"Oh, Caroline, you know your friend could never wed me if she knew you and I were in love," Henry said with renewed energy. "I think you should tell her."

"Or you should," said Caroline, just as Venetia turned her head in her direction and took a step closer as Caroline's mother engaged another in conversation.

"Are you enjoying the evening, Caroline?" Venetia asked. "You don't seem to be." Her own expression was hardly joyful. Not for one who was betrothed to the most wonderful man in the entire world.

"Of course. Are you?"

"Am I enjoying the evening?" Venetia repeated slowly, as if she truly were teasing out the question. "Why, I have so much to be grateful for. For a start, the most wonderful friends a young lady could have." Her eyes were moist as she put her hand on Caroline's arm. "You and Henry have risked reputations and lives for my sake. And—"

Before she could finish, a disturbance near the entrance rippled through the room. Heads turned, the buzz of conversation faltering momentarily.

"My, look at that young lady. How very how odd," Venetia murmured as she frowned towards the doorway.

Caroline, too, was trying to make sense of the growing volume of murmurs but could discern nothing due to the crowd.

When a nearby group dispersed, she saw that a young lady, unaccompanied, and striking in pale-blue sarsenet with pearls threaded through her dark hair, had just crossed the threshold into the ballroom.

But, of course, the reason everyone was murmuring in scandalized whispers was that the young lady appeared to be unchaperoned and in clear distress.

"Who is that?" asked Venetia, turning first to Caroline and then her mother.

"I've never seen her in my life," said Lady Weston.

"What did she say?" Caroline put her head closer to Venetia's, who answered with a frown, "She appears to be looking for someone."

The fact that Caroline had never laid eyes upon her was somewhat unusual. Really, there were very few people she did not recognize these days at the endless dreary balls she was forced to attend.

It hadn't always been like that. Not so long ago, she was filled with eager anticipation prior to every event where she might see Henry. She hadn't thought the reason was that she loved him. No, she thought only of the fun they would have together. Of the way he excited her senses as they whispered foolishly disparaging comments about their fellow dancers when engaged in a cotillion together.

Now Henry was to wed another. Except that Caroline and Henry *would* uncover the mystery surrounding Windermere's villainy before a wedding took place. All would be made clear, and once the pieces fell into place, Lord Windermere would be exposed for the villain he was.

Caroline slanted a look at Lord Windermere from over her mama's shoulder and saw that he was eyeing Venetia. Still! His predatory gaze made her skin crawl.

For the tiniest fraction of a second, it occurred to her that if he did indeed succeed in whisking Venetia off with him a second time—and marrying her—then Henry and Caroline could marry one another after all.

But the moment she acknowledged the thought, she angrily

dismissed it. What kind of friend would that make her? And after all she'd done already. Events, she acknowledged, which had shown her how much she loved Henry… without knowing it.

No, if she and Henry weren't able to learn the truth about Lord Windermere, then somehow Henry must find a way to graciously withdraw from their betrothal so they could all be happy.

Though, she acknowledged, it wouldn't really make Venetia happy to be without a husband with a fourth season looming, which would make her an old maid and condemn her to being handmaiden to Aunt Pike.

"Miss Caroline, I do beg your pardon." It was Mr. Rothbury, apologizing for having bumped against her as he passed by.

"Mr. Rothbury! You're back!"

It was little wonder he looked at her with as much shock as if Caroline had suggested that they take a moonlit walk by the lake. Alone. For Caroline's words had carried a warmth that clearly had taken her own mama by surprise.

Blushing furiously, the young gentleman first acknowledged Lady Weston before saying, cautiously, "I returned from Bedfordshire this morning."

Suddenly Caroline did not know what to say, though her mind churned feverishly. She could hardly demand if her maid was correct in her claims that Mr. Rothbury's father had once dealt with the financial affairs of the late Mr. Playford.

Mr. Rothbury cleared his throat, sent a cautious look at Caroline's mama, then said, "I hope you are enjoying this evening. I am not often at such events."

Caroline considered this statement. She'd certainly not noticed him at many previous such events. Mr. Rothbury was such a quiet, charming, unexceptional gentleman, he was easy to overlook with his pleasant face and pleasant manners.

Unexceptional? She thought quickly. He had a modest income, but it was sufficient to keep a wife. And the reason he did *sometimes* appear at such events was, surely, to *find* a wife.

Yet, he'd certainly not be looking for an heiress.

No, surely a sweet, pretty wife who would manage the finances with good sense and who had no reputation for vanity or obvious fondness for show and fripperies would answer to his needs?

Suddenly, Mr. Rothbury appeared the answer to her dreams in more ways than one. Hopefully, he had information about Venetia's father's finances…

But wouldn't he make the perfect husband for Venetia? He'd certainly shown interest before.

"I wonder if you enjoyed the performance of *Much Ado About Nothing* on Thursday last?" Caroline ventured, keeping her voice light.

His eyebrows shot up. Yes, it was indeed an unladylike gambit that suggested Caroline's potential interest in him, which of course must be debunked, so hurriedly she went on, "Oh, I wasn't there, but my dear friend Venetia mentioned she'd seen you there."

In fact, it was Caroline and not Venetia who had attended the Shakespeare comedy in company with her mama and brother and sister-in-law, but he'd never know that.

"She did?" he asked, blushing hotly—a very good sign. He glanced across at Venetia, who was standing by Henry's side, silent and looking as she usually did. Deeply unhappy.

"Oh yes, she spoke so highly of you after making your acquaintance last week at Lady Montague's ball." Caroline hesitated, glanced at Henry, then added in a whisper, "Poor Venetia is my dearest friend, and it is so sad to see how her aunt dictates her life."

Mr. Rothbury frowned, and sent an uncertain look at Caroline's mother, now in conversation with Mrs. Pike. Caroline took a step away, hoping Mr. Rothbury would follow. She was treading on dangerous ground and dared not risk either the older women overhearing her conversation with Mr. Rothbury.

"She does?" he asked, his expression troubled.

Caroline nodded, then dropped her voice even lower. "It is Venetia's third season out and her aunt insists that she accept the first marriage offer that comes her way."

Of course, this was the point at which Caroline knew she needed to find a way to gracefully end the discussion before Mr. Rothbury quizzed too deeply, and too close to the older women.

It was also the point at which fate conspired to aid her.

"Henry?"

The plaintive voice cut through the conversation, and all eyes turned towards the young lady in blue who was now making her way uncertainly across the ballroom floor.

"Henry, is that really you?" Flicking open her little ivory fan, the combination of hope, fear, and desperation in the strange woman's expression was quite shocking.

"Why, Henry, at last!" The young lady's voice was just a little louder than acceptable, and her English slightly accented.

Rooted to the spot, Caroline observed the exchange with the same uncertainty, it appeared, as Venetia. And everyone else.

The room seemed to hold its collective breath.

"My dear madam, I think you have me mistaken with someone else," Henry replied, his smile bland.

By this stage, everyone in the local vicinity was gawping at the scene.

"Henry, why did you leave me after—" She broke off upon a sob. "Finally, I was told I would find you here."

Caroline bit her lip and a sudden flare of rage lit her from within as she glanced from Henry and the young lady towards…

Towards whoever had set Henry up. It took all her willpower not to hurl herself at Lord Windermere when she saw his satisfied countenance. A satisfaction Mrs. Pike clearly shared. No, Caroline was not imagining it. This was all part of some grand design to further their ends, she was sure of it.

Across the room, Charlotte broke away from Barnaby and hurried over, joining their small group as the orchestra struck up another dance, their attempt to restore normalcy failing as dancers hesitated to take their places.

"Henry, what is Barnaby talking about? He says—" She stopped, biting her lip, her eyes darting nervously between her brother and the mysterious woman.

"I've never laid eyes on her in my life!" Henry muttered, taking a step back from the young lady who was clearly hellbent on making a scene.

Caroline put her hand on Charlotte's forearm and drew her slightly away. "I wouldn't put much store in anything Barnaby says on the matter," she said, without thinking.

"How dare you malign my betrothed!" gasped Charlotte before adding in a whisper that was unhelpfully loud, "Barnaby says he'd heard Henry had made payments to this woman's *brother*."

Another surge of frustrated fury coursed through Caroline as she responded. "Hush, Charlotte, people are listening! You are maligning *your* own brother in public! Without proof!"

Charlotte reddened. "I'm sorry, Caroline. That was ill done of me," she whispered. "But it's what Barnaby just told me."

"Then you'd do well to remember what a decent, upstanding man Henry is, and that such charges should be thoroughly scrutinized *in private* before you start airing them for all the world to hear!" Caroline hissed before turning on her heel and heading towards her dearest friend, Henry.

Just as the young lady in blue went on in plaintive tones, "Mr. Ashworth, you have wounded me more than you will ever know."

Caroline watched in horror as the color drained from Henry's face, while Venetia drew in her breath.

"My dear Miss Playford," came Lord Windermere's smooth voice as he appeared beside Venetia. "Your fiancé appears rather occupied at present. Might I suggest some air? You look quite pale." His tone was solicitous, but his eyes gleamed with calculating triumph.

Caroline took a step forward to intervene, just as Mrs. Pike materialized. "Come away, Venetia! I don't know what your fiancé has been up to. You must go with Lord Windermere."

"No, Venetia—" Caroline tried to take her friend's arm, but Mrs. Pike was already ushering her niece away.

"Henry! Lord Windermere has taken Venetia!" Caroline cried as she pushed her way between the woman in blue and her beloved. "Through the French doors and into the garden. You must go after her."

But Henry was the center of a hub of interest and activity, and Mrs. Pike, who'd returned, was all but hedging him in as she and now Ladies Pendleton and Townsend rallied around the now sobbing young lady in blue.

Frantically, Caroline cast about for another savior. Her gaze fell upon a familiar face.

"Mr. Rothbury!"

He had obviously gone in search of refreshment, for he was returning with a glass of orgeat and looked deeply reluctant to approach. Who could blame him with such a scene going on?

"My friend Venetia has been taken into the garden by Lord Windermere. You must go after them!" Caroline pleaded as she reached his side.

He stepped back. "I cannot do that." His gaze darted nervously to the spectacle unfolding around Henry.

"She did not go willingly!"

"She has danced many times with him, Miss Weston." Mr. Rothbury adjusted his cravat, clearly uncomfortable. "And, as she is betrothed to Mr. Ashworth, I believe it is his duty to intervene."

"Please, Mr. Rothbury, I beg of you." Caroline lowered her voice, hoping Mrs. Pike hadn't heard her, for that woman was uncomfortably near. "You don't understand what is happening. At least step into the garden so you can reassure me that all is well. Is that too much to ask?"

His eyes widened at her tone. However, her tone was hardly the most scandalous of what was happening.

Caroline would have gone to Venetia's aid, if only she could have done so without censure. She'd have taken Mr. Rothbury's arm for a turn about the gardens, but that would be risking her own reputation.

"Please—" Her voice broke with desperation.

"Of course I will do it," he said, taking a step towards the doors, just as Mrs. Pike moved out of the gathering, her eyes sorrowful as she looked at Henry and said, "Have you broken my niece's heart, Mr. Ashworth?"

And now Caroline stood alone and seemingly friendless while scandal swirled about them. Henry was being forced to answer questions from the elders in the room—namely Caroline's mother and Mrs. Pike, though Lady Pendleton was having a field day piling on the questions herself.

What could she do to save him?

She'd disguised herself as a stable lad to pry Venetia away from Lord Windermere, but still she had failed.

She wracked her brains. A young woman had so few resources to hand. And in this crowded ballroom, it appeared she had none.

Unless…

It had been a long time since Caroline had tried this trick. In the schoolroom, she'd perfected it—to the hilarity of those with whom she shared her lessons.

But she'd never tried it in public. After all, what well-brought-up young lady would go to such scandalous lengths to create a scene?

But if ever there were a time to put her skills into action, it was now.

Taking a deep breath, Caroline glanced about her, catching Henry's eye, and raising one eyebrow—their signal whenever they were about to do something wicked.

She gave him a couple of seconds to turn in her direction and to extricate himself from the young lady in blue who now had a posse of concerned matrons fussing over her, in between scowling at Henry.

Then, putting her hand to her forehead, and breathing out on a small, low—but very audible—wail of distress, Caroline commandeered the attention… and swooned.

The room spun around her as she let herself fall, aware of gasps and cries as she descended in a graceful arc towards the polished floor.

Chapter Eighteen

"CAROLINE!" SHOCKED, AND more motivated to help his beloved than make sense of what else was happening, Henry rushed forward, scooping Caroline up before she reached the ground. The crowd parted, a chorus of gasps and murmurs rising around them.

"Henry," Caroline murmured, her eyes fluttering open for just a moment as he reveled in the unexpected closeness. Her weight in his arms felt so right—familiar, wicked, and thrilling in equal measure.

He knew this was not the reason she'd resorted to such actions but with his arms about her and her wonderful, familiar scent of orange blossom intoxicating him, he was in paradise. For a moment, all the other strange awfulness could be forgotten. For the softness of her silk gown against his hands, the warmth of her body against his chest helped create a moment of perfection amid the chaos.

Except that her time in his arms would be short. Not for the first time did he curse himself for squandering all those other opportunities he'd had in the past for progressing their relationship beyond friendship. How blind he had been to what was right before him all along.

She was still half in his arms when he heard movement by the door and realized Venetia was returning. Glancing over his shoulder, he recognized Mr. Rothbury and saw that Venetia was flanked on the other side by Lord Windermere, his tall figure looming possessively near her. Mrs. Pike hurried forward, her face pinched with righteous indignation, her steps quick and determined on the polished floor.

"Venetia...?" Still holding Caroline, Henry made a half-hearted attempt at sounding as he should: concerned? Was he supposed to sound contrite, as the recriminatory looks seemed to imply?

No. Not when that would be tacitly admitting to something he hadn't done.

Venetia had halted momentarily near the doorway, her face pale, while Caroline remained in his arms, her weight and dependence upon him in this moment not to drop her a glorious reminder of what he wanted from the future. Her face was turned slightly into his chest, hidden from the prying eyes of society.

"Henry, don't abandon me," Caroline whispered, drawing his head down as he made a move to set her on her feet so he could go to his betrothed—as duty required. Her breath was warm against his ear, sending a shiver down his spine. "Venetia is too upset to notice us and... and if this is as close to you as I'll get for the rest of my life, I'm not about to release you too soon."

Henry sent a wary glance about him, but it seemed most people's attention was centered on either Venetia and her coterie, or the lady in blue who was just out of the periphery of his vision.

But it was Sir Frederick who arrived at that juncture, his expression stormy. It appeared Charlotte had summoned him, for she was at his side as he strode purposefully over to Henry, gripped Caroline by the upper arms, and muttered, "I don't know what you're playing at, Caro, but I think it's time you went home." His voice was low but carried an edge of steel.

"I don't want to go home," Caroline whispered back. "Please, Frederick. You don't understand what's happening. Venetia is—"

"Venetia is betrothed to Henry, and you're creating a scandal." His tone was sharp, brooking no argument. "Let him go at once. Come with me now." His fingers tightened on her arms, not enough to hurt but enough to make his determination clear.

As soon as Caroline had been reluctantly dragged from Henry's arms, Charlotte filled the void, her normally cheerful face distressed. The candles from the nearby sconce illuminated the tears gathering in her eyes.

"Henry, what have you done?" she hissed. "Barnaby has told me so many terrible things, I don't know what to believe!" She twisted her gloved hands together.

Henry squared his shoulders as he straightened, feeling suddenly bereft without Caroline's warmth. "I had thought Barnaby an ally," he said, feeling wounded. The betrayal stung more than he would have expected.

"It's difficult to be an ally when one knows someone is guilty of wrongdoing." Her large eyes were tear-filled, glistening in the candlelight. "What is happening tonight? First you're accused by that lady over there—" She looked about, but the lady in blue had gone, vanished as mysteriously as she had appeared. "And now these other terrible things Barnaby is telling me."

The horror in Charlotte's expression was worse than the bewilderment Henry felt at being implicated in a liaison with a woman he'd never seen in his life.

Could his sweet, gentle sister really be siding with Barnaby over her own brother? Before she'd even heard Henry's defense?

"Do you deny that what Barnaby says is true?" she demanded, her chin lifting slightly in challenge.

Henry saw over her shoulder that Barnaby was looking in his direction. He was frowning, but there was something else there, too. Something more insidious. A gleam of satisfaction, perhaps, lingering at the corners of his mouth despite his concerned expression.

"I have no idea about anything that has been happening... or said... this evening. By Barnaby or anyone else. And I certainly deny any wrongdoing if that is what you are insinuating." He swallowed, his throat dry, then ground out, "Or what he is insinuating."

He looked about for Caroline, but she was already being led away, her brother firmly guiding her toward the exit. She stopped to look over her shoulder, and for a moment their eyes met across the crowded ballroom.

Unlike Charlotte, he saw in her expression not accusation, but something that gave him strength. Yes, there was concern, but also trust. She didn't believe for a moment what others clearly did.

Her blue eyes held his, steady and unwavering, a silent promise of support.

At least he had one ally in this room.

Chapter Nineteen

B Y THE NEXT morning, Henry was very aware of what Barnaby had been insinuating. No, more than insinuating. The accusations hung over him like a storm cloud, dark and threatening.

And in another townhouse, the same insinuations were being strongly countered by Henry's staunchest ally if he but knew it.

Pacing before the window with its sunny view onto the street below, Caroline wrung her hands as she said to her friend, "But, Venetia, that's preposterous! Are you telling me that your Aunt Pike has said all this to you before you'd even finished breakfast?"

Venetia leaned down to offer Caroline's little pug an almond wafer beneath the table, unable to look Caroline in the eye. "Yes! She told me what I believe to be the most outrageous lies! She says the lady in blue is an Austro-Hungarian princess Henry met in London last year and that he led her to believe that if she escaped her husband and came back to London, they would run away together." There were tears in Venetia's eyes when she straightened, adding in a low voice, "And as if that weren't bad enough, she said something about Henry having secrets and scandals that are about to bring all hell down upon his shoulders. Yes, those were her exact words!" Venetia took a deep breath, unable to go on until Caroline took a seat by her side and, taking her friend's hand in hers, said bolsteringly, "Tell me exactly what else she said for we both know they were just lies! We know your Aunt Pike can in no way be trusted to look after your interests. And she's trying to blacken Henry's name. That's what this is, you know."

Venetia nodded miserably before going on. "She accused Henry of secretly purloining money from his father's accounts to give to this woman's brother. She said someone had whispered they had proof of it but she refused to say who."

Unable to keep her agitation contained, Caroline rose and began to pace, her skirts swishing against the carpet with each turn. "That is absolutely absurd. I've known Henry all my life. He would never do such a thing and, as I said, we know—"

"Yes, I know," Venetia said quietly. "But everyone is talking. Lord Windermere called this morning—"

"Lord Windermere?" Caroline couldn't keep the alarm from her voice. The mere mention of his name had the propensity to make her tremble like a blancmange.

Venetia shuddered. "I didn't know what to do when suddenly he was in our drawing room. It was shocking enough to see him at the ball last night. And when he led me away, I thought I should scream. Except that Mr. Rothbury suddenly appeared. But there was Aunt Pike, pretending that all was quite normal. As if she didn't know of the horrors he'd visited upon me for I *told* her he'd taken me against my will. I told her *everything!*" Her voice rose with each word.

"Did you tell her what Henry had done to be your savior?" Caroline nibbled at her lip, exhaling with worry, when Venetia nodded.

"But only when Mr. and Mrs. Gascoyne laid out their side of the story, for I could hardly keep Henry out of it."

"And what did Lord Windermere say?" Caroline's voice was steady despite the churning in her stomach.

"That he was concerned for my welfare, given the… circumstances." Venetia's lip curled in disgust. Clearly trying to find an outlet for her outrage, she leaned down to feed Pug another wafer, adding as she rose, "When Aunt Pike invited him to stay for tea, I thought I would fall out of my chair in a complete faint. I wish I had, now." The pug snuffled contentedly, oblivious to the tension in the room.

Caroline stood up and resumed her pacing, her mind working rapidly. The pieces were easy to fit together, and the picture they formed was horrifying. "We know this is all too convenient. A mysterious, supposedly foreign noblewoman appears from nowhere, Barnaby suddenly has evidence of financial wrongdoing, and Lord Windermere is hovering about, playing the concerned friend."

Venetia looked up, her expression uncertain. "Of course it is! And I am completely outmaneuvered. Lord Windermere is orchestrating this entire affair in collusion with my aunt."

"Yes, of course we know that, dearest," said Caroline, taking a deep breath as she readied herself to reveal the truth about Henry and herself. "But there's something else you should know—"

"Yes!" cried Venetia, rising suddenly, her expression suddenly clearing. "Only Henry can save me." She closed her eyes briefly as she clasped her hands to her breast. "Knowing that I have Henry to look after me is all that stands between evil Lord Windermere and… and utter despair!"

MEANWHILE, HENRY FACED his own inquisition. His sister, normally his staunchest ally, sat across from him in the morning room, her expression troubled as she refused to countenance his side of the story.

"Charlotte! Surely you understand these are all elaborate fabrications designed to blacken my name? There is not a jot of truth to any of it!"

Charlotte hesitated, her spoon clinking against her teacup as she stirred in a spoonful of sugar. "Are you *sure* you've never seen that woman?"

"Of course not!"

"But she spoke as if you'd... disappointed her—" Charlotte's eyes were shadowed with doubt.

"Lord, Charlotte, do you not believe me? First of all, this strange, unaccompanied young woman blows in here and makes straight for me and barely have you drawn breath before you're quizzing me about gambling or investments or... I don't even know what you think I've done." He swallowed, his throat dry despite the tea at his elbow. "Or what Barnaby thinks I've done."

Charlotte, normally so placid, reddened. Glancing about the breakfast room, its cheerful yellow walls now seeming to mock the gravity of their conversation, she lowered her head to whisper, "I told you that he said he'd found evidence of wrongdoing on your part, Henry." She hesitated, close to tears, a droplet trembling on her lashes.

"Then what form, exactly, did this apparent wrongdoing of mine take?" Henry asked, fighting to keep his voice level. Outside the window, a sparrow alighted on the sill.

But Charlotte just shook her head, unable to go on.

"And you would believe Barnaby's nebulous, unsatisfactory claim without citing evidence, over my word that I am blameless of his charges—on both counts, Charlotte?" Henry's voice was quiet but there was steel beneath the softness.

Charlotte sighed, her breath stirring the steam from her untouched tea. "Henry, I don't know what to believe. Barnaby is not a liar—"

"Oh, so if he's not, then by inference, I am?"

Charlotte looked pained. "Why would Barnaby lie, Henry? He's your friend, and he's my betrothed."

"And he's told you I'm a cheat and you believe him?" Henry pushed his plate away, his appetite vanished.

"He... he says he's found evidence—"

"But won't state exactly what evidence that is. He just expects you to believe I've done something wrong and won't believe your own brother when he says he hasn't." A servant passed by the doorway, slowing momentarily before discreetly continuing, no doubt sensing the tension.

Charlotte put her hands to her face. "I don't know, Henry. But Barnaby deals with the accounts of Lord Chartley. There was a sum there… paid to the brother of this foreign princess, but coming from our father's account. That's what Barnaby says." She hesitated, lowering her voice even further. "But father has no knowledge of that. He says the only person other than himself who has access to his accounts is… you."

Henry sat back, stunned. "Absurd!" The sunlight that had bathed the room in warmth suddenly seemed harsh and revealing.

"Is it?" Charlotte's tone was pleading, desperate. "Because if it is you, and you are in a scrape, you must tell me so I can ask father's help on your behalf."

"This is all fabricated!" Henry repeated firmly. "I have never made any such payment. I don't know any foreign princess or her brother. And I certainly haven't taken money from Father's accounts, and I've never been involved in a transaction with Lord Chartley." He leaned forward, taking his sister's hands across the table. "Charlotte, I give you my word. Whatever Barnaby thinks he's found, it wasn't done by me."

The doubt in her eyes wavered, then slowly cleared, like clouds parting after a storm. "Then you must discover who did," she said quietly.

Henry held her eye for a long time, contemplating whether to speak what was in his heart.

That Barnaby might not be the trustworthy party among them.

But he refrained. Charlotte was clearly in love with the man and would defend him to the grave.

Perhaps with more energy than she would Henry.

He thought of Caroline and his heart did a little lurch. The memory of her in his arms last night, the scent of orange blossom clinging to her skin, was both comfort and torment.

Love did strange things to a person.

IN YET ANOTHER townhouse, Caroline paced in front of the large windows that looked into the street as she tried to make sense of the night before. The gentle tap of her slippers on the polished floor marked the rhythm of her thoughts. Her sister-in-law, Amelia, sat comfortably in an armchair in the corner, her hands to her belly, for she was expecting their second child. The soft glow of impending motherhood seemed to surround her, making her appear almost serene despite the troubling subject of their conversation.

Perhaps that was why she was more receptive and understanding of Caroline's distress than Caroline's brother, Sir Frederick, had been.

"Frederick thinks Henry did something as wicked as he did when he went to the Continent last year." Caroline's hands twisted together as she spoke.

"What wicked thing did your brother supposedly do when he went to the Continent?" Amelia asked with a smile, her needle pausing mid-stitch. "Rumors do have a habit of taking on a life of their own when left unchecked."

"Everyone says Frederick was quite the man about town before he settled down with you," Caroline said, surprised. "And I can't believe that of Henry."

"I can't either, but what do you really know?" Amelia asked. "About either of them, for that matter. And what if Frederick was a man about town? It's not like he misbehaved after I met him. So, if Henry behaved in a way that occasions embarrassment, I maintain the same thing. This was all before he was betrothed to

Venetia." She bent her head to study her embroidery, teasing out a stitch that had snagged. "I've no doubt Venetia will forgive him. I'm sure it was all just a misunderstanding." She leaned back, her smile expansive. "Those two are made for one another. Anyone can see it. Henry's so vibrant and Venetia's so sweet." She resumed her stitching. "I'm sure it'll all blow over before their wedding."

Venetia. Again.

But then her sister-in-law hesitated, her hand poised in the air, holding the needle above the hardanger as if it were a weapon, ready to strike.

"Except that it does appear a little more serious," Amelia went on in quite a different tone, as if she'd not just spent the past few minutes reassuring Caroline. "I'm hearing it from various quarters now, even though I don't go about as much as before." Gently putting her embroidery aside, she reached out a hand. "I know how fond you are of Henry, but this must be especially painful for Venetia. The integrity of the man she is to marry is being questioned."

Caroline jerked back. She really didn't know what to say. Integrity? Henry was a man of the highest integrity. Surely Amelia was not questioning that?

Then another thought intruded. Cautiously, she asked, "Do you refer to… his sudden betrothal to Venetia and how that might have compromised people's belief in Henry's… integrity?"

Amelia shrugged. "Well, there is that, though of course, he acted honorably in a timely enough manner to satisfy all parties." She twitched the fabric of her skirts as if the topic made her uncomfortable, then went on, "I know how you've always championed Henry. Frederick has spoken often of the childhood bonds you two have, so I understand that you are very anxious to ensure that Henry and Venetia's marriage go ahead without the further scandal of what happened last night with this… strange noblewoman from abroad."

Caroline swallowed with difficulty. In fact, it took all her willpower to prevent herself from revealing her true thoughts on her feelings regarding Henry and Venetia's supposedly happy union. "I don't believe this story about a foreign princess," she said stolidly. "I think it's a fabrication to harm Henry."

"Good lord, Caroline, your sentiments echo mine, of course!" Amelia raised an eyebrow. "And your loyalty commends you, but where there's smoke, there's fire. I'm not suggesting Henry did anything wrong. But clearly this stems from something he *has* done." She sighed. "I think the sooner Henry and Venetia wed and go on a Continental honeymoon while this all blows over, the better."

Caroline rose. What could she say to Amelia that didn't compromise herself?

At the doorway, she paused, her hand resting on the polished wood. "Would you do one kindness for me, Amelia?" she asked.

"I would do a hundred if they were not unreasonable," Amelia said with a smile. "You are my favorite sister-in-law, after all."

"And the only one, so cultivating my good heart is a wise tactic," Caroline said, grinning. She took a deep breath, gathering her courage. "Please, would you speak to this supposed mysterious noblewoman?"

"Why, Caroline, I wouldn't know where to begin to find her." Amelia's eyes widened with surprise.

"She obviously could not leave last night without an escort and my guess is that Mrs. Pike might know something about where to take her home." Caroline's tone dripped scorn and Amelia nodded, her expression thoughtful.

"Of course," she said. "It is hardly an unreasonable request and, now that you've laid it out plainly, it should not be difficult to ascertain at least something of the motivations of this young lady."

"Or those who contrived for her to do as she did last night," Caroline's voice hardened.

Amelia smiled. "You really do believe in the grand conspiracy, do you not, my dear?"

Caroline nodded. "And you, with your greater years and wisdom, are just the one to reassure me. I look forward to hearing your opinion on the matter, after you consider this woman's responses."

So, WHILE CAROLINE waited for Amelia to do her investigative work, she needed to find Henry and reassure him.

And, although it took some effort and subterfuge, Caroline was becoming increasingly adept at what it took to make secret investigations.

She'd sent her maid, Beth, to enquire of one of the maids at Henry's London residence where he would be that day.

So, now Caroline was adjusting her bonnet, using the movement to scan the crowded Great Room at Somerset House. The exhibition hall buzzed with conversation, the air heavy with perfume and the smell of wool dampened by the light rain outside. Her companion, Mrs. Watts, was already engrossed in studying a particularly florid portrait hung at eye level while consulting her exhibition catalog with great concentration.

Finally, Caroline spotted Henry's tall figure near Turner's *Temple of Jupiter Panellenius*, which hung well above the line. He stood alone, hands clasped behind his back, neck craned as he studied the artist's dramatic use of light and shadow. Perfect. Even from a distance, she could see the tension in his shoulders. Poor Henry was under pressure from all sides these days.

Caroline hesitated, weighing up the best approach. Her mama, who had agreed that morning to accompany Caroline to see the exhibition at Somerset House, had cried off at the last moment claiming another megrim. For a tense half an hour, Caroline had feared this vital opportunity to apprise Henry of developments was about to be swept away from her.

Her final gambit, however, had succeeded. When Caroline

had declared that her painting master had strongly encouraged her to study a range of Constables to assist her with her work in progress, her mama had reluctantly agreed that Caroline could go.

But with Mrs. Watts as chaperone.

Painting was the one accomplishment her mama seemed happy to indulge more than usual.

Now, Mrs. Watts, who was a friend of her mama's, loved gossip.

In fact, she reveled so much in every little *on dit* that Caroline was prepared to bet that Mrs. Watts would be willing to set propriety aside—to a degree—in order to be the first one in the know.

Keeping Henry's beloved form in her sights, Caroline maneuvered herself between her chaperone and a group of chattering young ladies. "Why, there is Mr. Ashworth!" she said casually, her heart beating faster despite her calm exterior. "You know he and I are childhood friends. I really must demand that he enlighten me regarding that peculiar business last night with the Hungarian princess—or whoever she really is."

Mrs. Watts's eyes widened with interest, her mouth forming a perfect *o* of surprise. "Such a scandal! And that poor Miss Playford to whom he is betrothed." She cast Caroline a dubious look as her charge took a step towards the young man under discussion, her bonnet ribbons quivering with indecision.

Caroline sent her an artful smile. As all London was buzzing with the scandal, her mother would never have allowed Caroline anywhere near Henry. But Caroline knew her chaperone's weakness. She sighed heavily, the picture of concerned friendship. "Yes, poor Venetia. Mr. Ashworth's betrothed is one of my dearest friends, and she knows there must be some misunderstanding." Time was slipping away, but Caroline tried not to let her agitation show. Henry did not know she was here, and she was very much afraid he'd leave the building before she had a chance to speak to him. The crowd shifted around them, constantly threatening to obscure her view.

"You are also acquainted with his betrothed?" Mrs. Watts looked interested, leaning closer. "Where is the young lady?"

"I do not know," Caroline said. "I think I must ask Mr. Ashworth." And without waiting for final permission, she nodded at Mrs. Watts and slipped into the crowd.

She'd find some sop to appease the woman later.

Quickly, Caroline made her way through the crush, careful to keep her pace measured despite her urgency. As she drew closer, she saw the moment Henry sensed her presence. His shoulders tensed, but he didn't turn, his profile sharp against the brightly lit painting.

"I must say, Mr. Ashworth," she said, pitching her voice to carry just far enough, "Turner's technique is incomparable. Such dramatic light effects."

He turned then, and she saw the flash of pleasure in his eyes before he schooled his features into polite interest. The strain of recent events had left shadows beneath his eyes, but his smile was genuine. "Miss Weston. How unexpected. Are you enjoying the exhibition?"

"Indeed." She moved to stand beside him, tilting her head back to study the painting. Their shoulders nearly touched, the proximity sending a flutter through her stomach. From the corner of her eye, she saw Mrs. Watts had found a companion of her own—Mrs. Bellworth, another determined art enthusiast. They were deep in discussion over their catalogs, heads bent together like conspirators.

"The way Turner uses light here," Caroline continued, keeping her voice low, "creates the most wonderful illusion. Just like what happened last night. I suspect your mysterious lady in blue is not a foreign princess, after all." The murmur of the surrounding crowd provided a shield for their conversation.

Henry's hand tightened on his catalog. "Is that what you think?" He swallowed, his throat working. "Just as long as you don't think she is anything to me, Caroline."

"Indeed not, Henry. No, I believe last night was someone's very concerted attempt to embroil you in scandal." Caroline pretended to consult her catalog, the printed words swimming before her eyes. "And, of course, Lord Windermere is behind this entire charade. He means to destroy your reputation so he can step in as Venetia's savior."

"But where do I find proof? And why does he want to wed penniless Venetia?" Henry's voice was tight with suppressed anger. Then he sighed, his breath warm against her cheek as he leaned closer. "And why tell me this when surely you'd *prefer* my engagement to Venetia be broken?"

"Not at the expense of your good name." Caroline turned a page, though her eyes saw nothing. "Last night I studied the man when he didn't think he was being watched. I saw who he spoke to—Mrs. Pike, amongst others—and I saw how Windermere looked at Venetia. Like a predator eyeing prey. Venetia is my dearest friend. I would not sacrifice her only to save you. Both must be achieved. You who are caught in the middle of this horror which unfolded so recently must be reeling. But I have more distance and the time to consider the matter. Yes, Lord Windermere is behind this—with Mrs. Pike's collusion—and we must find a way to expose him while preserving your reputation and ensuring Venetia's safety."

"The difficulty being that any attempt I make to defend my-self will look like exactly that—mere defense against truth." A muscle twitched in his jaw, betraying his frustration.

They moved to the next painting, maintaining their facade of artistic appreciation. The canvas before them depicted a stormy seascape, the turbulent waters mirroring their own tumultuous circumstances. Caroline noticed Mrs. Watts glancing their way and dutifully raised her catalog, pointing to a detail in the corner.

"What we need," she said, "is for the false princess herself to confess," she whispered.

"And how would we do that?" Henry asked. "If, as you sus-pect, Windermere is backing her, he's paying her." A gentleman nodded to Henry as he passed, and Henry returned the greeting with admirable composure.

"Then offer her more." Caroline smiled, a plan forming in her mind. "I've petitioned my sister-in-law to pay the woman a visit. She will first need to seek out Mrs. Pike, who, I am sure, would like to deny all knowledge, but I suspect she cannot." She shrugged. "If Amelia can locate her, then surely we can discover who is putting her up to this. And why? And then we still have to speak to Mr. Rothbury."

"And then there's Barnaby." Henry's voice dropped even lower. "His claims about financial irregularities trouble me deeply. Charlotte is torn between us. I truly cannot believe it."

"One step at a time," Caroline murmured. "First the actress, then we follow the money. That talk of you taking money from your father's accounts to pay this woman's brother was surely just that... Talk!"

"Caroline—" Henry checked himself, because they were still in public. "Miss Weston. I don't know how to thank you." His eyes held hers for a moment longer than propriety allowed, conveying what words could not.

"Then don't. Just be careful. Windermere is dangerous, and Mrs. Pike is firmly in his pocket, though we *will* discover why." She closed her catalog. "I should rejoin Mrs. Watts before she notices our conversation has lasted rather longer than a proper discussion of Turner's technique might warrant."

"Of course." He bowed slightly, the gesture bringing him momentarily closer. "I thank you for your artistic insights, Miss Weston. They've been most... illuminating."

Chapter Twenty

CAROLINE PACED BEFORE the drawing room fireplace in her brother's house, her mind racing. "And this mysterious woman in blue? Once you ran her to ground, she admitted it? Just like that?"

Amelia reclined on the chaise, watching her sister-in-law with amused patience. "Not 'just like that.' I had to employ considerable tact and a small measure of... persuasion."

"Persuasion?" Caroline stopped pacing, her eyes widening. Amelia was so good, and transparent, she couldn't imagine her doing anything underhand.

"Nothing improper, I assure you. Merely a suggestion that Mr. Barnaby might not be as stalwart as Miss Barrett believes him to be. That he might, in fact, be preparing to depart for the Continent should the schemes in which she is a key player be discovered, leaving her to face the consequences of her falsehoods alone." Amelia's tone was light, but her eyes held a calculating gleam.

Caroline gasped. "Is that true? What do you know about Barnaby's role in this?"

"Only that—after speaking to Miss Barrett—I give you far more credence than I did before that something havey-cavey is going on, and that Henry is being maligned for reasons as yet unknown."

"So do you believe me now about Venetia being kidnapped—?"

Amelia held up her hand to stop her. "I believe that everything you say, while entirely possible, should never be discussed *in public* if either you, or she, are to hold your heads up high." She made a noise of disapproval, her hands resting protectively over her slightly rounded belly. "I'm not saying that is right. I'm just cautioning you to be discreet until the evidence is irrefutable. Now, back to Barnaby and why he should wish to blacken Henry's name. You suggest a possible connection with Lord Windermere, to whom no whiff of scandal has, as yet, been attached. So, you must, again, keep silent until someone *else* points a finger." She shrugged, then added, "And maybe Barnaby will take the bait and manage what I do not believe you or Venetia are capable. Barnaby, and men of his sort, rarely stand firm when confronted. In any case, my polite questioning had the desired effect. This *actress*, Miss Barrett, became quite agitated and admitted that Barnaby had approached her at the theater where she is performing *The Taming of the Shrew*. She was to come to the ball, play the part of a jilted lover and create a public scene to smear Henry."

"And did she say what reason Barnaby had given her?" Caroline could barely contain her agitation. She moved to the window, watching as a carriage rattled past on the street below.

"Only that he promised her five pounds for her performance and assured her it was merely a jest between friends." Amelia's expression grew serious as Caroline swung round. "However, I believe she knows more than she's saying."

Caroline resumed her pacing. "It's all connected somehow. We know that. Barnaby's accusations about Henry's financial improprieties, this false princess, Lord Windermere's persistent interest in Venetia, Mrs. Pike's complicity… but what's the link?" She pressed her fingers to her temples, as if the physical pressure might bring clarity to her thoughts.

"Perhaps it's money." Amelia adjusted a cushion behind her.

"It usually is, in cases like these."

"But Venetia has none. That's why her aunt was so desperate to marry her off."

Amelia raised an eyebrow. "People's financial situations can be more complex than they appear."

Caroline stopped abruptly. "So… you are beginning to think what I've been suggesting all this time?"

"I certainly believe far more of what you *have* been saying." Amelia rose gracefully, smoothing her gown. "But now, as you said yourself, we have to find a motive. In any case, I've done as you asked. I found your mysterious lady and confirmed she's no foreign princess. Now—" She hesitated. "You'll be at the Masquerade Ball tomorrow night?"

Caroline nodded fiercely. "I need to be wherever Lord Windermere and Barnaby are if I'm to discover what's… rotten in the state of Denmark."

Amelia's burst of laughter transformed her grim expression. "My dear Caroline, your mother would be impressed with your knowledge of Shakespeare."

Caroline shook her head sadly. "My mother is only interested in my making the most advantageous match. Just like Aunt Pike, only at least I have you and Frederick to look to my interests." She sighed, her responsibility weighing ever more heavily upon her. "Poor Venetia has only me to protect her."

Chapter Twenty-One

VENETIA SAT QUIETLY at her dressing table as her maid arranged her hair for the ball. In the mirror, she watched her aunt inspecting the gown laid out for the masquerade. Good lord, Venetia had no idea what her aunt had been thinking when she'd directed the dressmaker. For the gown was a confection of bold red silk with black embroidery.

"Lord Windermere is looking forward to seeing you at Lord and Lady Ridgeway's Masquerade tonight," Mrs. Pike said, fingering the fabric.

Venetia's stomach clenched as she glanced up at her aunt, meeting her sharp gaze in the mirror's reflection. "I thought Mr. Ashworth would be escorting me."

"Oh, he will be, of course." Mrs. Pike's smile didn't reach her eyes. "But Lord Windermere has been so kind, offering his support during this… difficult time. Such a gentleman."

"A gentleman wouldn't pursue another man's betrothed," Venetia said quietly.

Mrs. Pike's expression hardened, the lines around her mouth deepening into crevices. "Watch your tone, girl. Lord Windermere has shown remarkable patience with your ingratitude. Mr. Ashworth's reputation is somewhat tarnished and, unless he can redeem himself, you may find yourself thanking Providence that such a distinguished gentleman as Lord Windermere still shows an interest in you."

"I would rather remain unmarried." Venetia lifted her chin slightly.

"That is not an option." Mrs. Pike's voice was cold.

Venetia turned to her aunt. "Aunt Pike," she said, steeling herself to betray no emotion but to sound, rather, businesslike. "I have no dowry. Mr. Ashworth's offer is a generous one that benefits him nothing other than ensuring honor is maintained after—" she hesitated, "—after you know what happened when the Gascoynes misconstrued matters." She drew in a shaking breath, afraid that she was going to fail in her bid to show Aunt Pike that she was not a feeble girl whom she could crush so easily. "You know this was after Lord Windermere took me away in his carriage. I tried to tell you what happened. But you have dismissed it. You, who are my guardian? My own mother's sister?"

Now her voice really was trembling, as was she—from head to toe, like a jelly. Would her aunt really show no shame, no remorse?

It seemed not, for Aunt Pike merely shrugged one shoulder as she continued to finger the silk gown. "I don't know what you're talking about, Venetia," she said crisply. "You disappeared the other evening and my considerable alarm was hardly reassured by your return in ignominious circumstances by the Gascoynes before the opportunistic Mr. Ashworth stepped forward, pressured by them to propose. How do you suppose your ingratitude was felt by Lord Windermere who had showered his esteem upon you? Who feels such affection for you that he is prepared to take you without a penny."

Venetia's mouth dropped open, her lips parting in shock. "You truly intend to force me—?" She broke off as she sent her aunt a challenging look, daring her to go on. The maid, sensing the tension, quietly stepped back, becoming nearly invisible against the bedroom wall.

"You made your bed, Venetia, now you must lie in it… just like your mother." Aunt Pike's voice carried a chill that seemed to freeze the very air between them. A portrait of Venetia's mother hung on the opposite wall, her painted eyes seeming to watch the scene with silent sorrow.

"And what is that supposed to mean?" Venetia flung back with the most defiance she had shown to date, her hands gripping the edge of her dressing table until her knuckles whitened.

"Your mother was a wanton creature who didn't know how to resist the lures of a man. And you are just like her!" Her aunt's face contorted with a bitterness long harbored, like poison finally released after years of festering. The shadows deepened the lines around her mouth, making her appear almost grotesque in her anger.

"What?" exclaimed Venetia. "My mother and my father made a perfectly respectable match. Why, if you want to split hairs, my mother made an excellent match—you have said it before! She married above her, and isn't that what you aspire to for me? Money and status are everything in your eyes."

Venetia tried to quiet her outraged breathing, so loud in the silent room.

"I would not normally encourage, much less countenance, such impertinence from you, but since you brought up the subject, you might as well hear the truth." Aunt Pike took a step forward, her eyes narrowed, her mouth a thin line. "Your mother set her sights on a man far superior, and she made sure he was forced to marry her. Do you not wonder why you have no contact with your father's family? Why they have shown no interest in you? No? Well, it's because they were scandalized when their dear son was forced to give up the woman he truly loved in order to marry the one who had trapped him. The one who was carrying his child."

Heat burned Venetia's skin, and she put her hands to her ears. "Stop! I don't believe any of it! You are just jealous of my mama because she was younger and more beautiful than you." Venetia did not care that she was treading a dangerous line. How dare her aunt speak of her beloved parents like this?

"More beautiful, yes, but not like-minded as your Papa and I were." Aunt Pike's voice softened to a dangerous purr. "Yes, you may well look at me like that, but what I speak is the truth. Your father wished to marry me. He *was going* to marry me before your conniving mama insinuated herself—" Each word was delivered with precision, designed to wound and shatter.

"Into his affections? I can well imagine he would prefer my kind, sweet mama over a woman as cold and calculating as you." Venetia rose to her feet, trembling with emotion.

"If you would let me finish, it was actually his bed, not his affections, into which she insinuated herself. The scandal was something neither could live down when they were discovered." Aunt Pike's lips curled into a cruel smile. "Do you think he wished to marry your mama? No, he did not, and I can show you proof in the letters—such tender letters he wrote me." Her hand moved to her throat, where a cameo hung on a velvet ribbon, as if she were touching a talisman.

Venetia stared, transfixed by this revelation. Now she truly was lost for words. Could her aunt really have been a contender for her father's affections?

"Then show me the letters," she whispered, her voice barely audible over the crackling of the fire. "Show me the letters if you want me to believe you."

Aunt Pike laughed softly. "You will not want to see them, but I will show them to you. Later. For now, you must ready yourself for tonight's masquerade ball." She held up the masquerade gown Venetia was to wear. "Lord Windermere knows you will be dressed as a scarlet cardinal bird. Yes, how we did laugh to think you would venture forth so altered from what you parade to the world, yet so true to the wicked heart that beats within you." Her aunt took a few steps towards the door. "He is very much looking forward to explaining what a terrible mistake you are making if you persist in rejecting his interest." With a short laugh, she added over her shoulder, "Almost as terrible a mistake as your mama made all those years ago. And you certainly don't want to follow in her footsteps."

The door closed behind her with a decisive click, leaving Venetia alone and digesting these ominous words, and the cardinal costume laid out on the bed like a splash of blood. Its symbolism was not lost on Venetia. The costume would mark her as both a temptress and potentially a woman with secrets to hide. It would draw all eyes to her and make her a target for the gossips.

Venetia sat down on the bed and stared up at the portrait of her mother.

Did her mother really have secrets that had the potential to damn her child if they were unearthed?

Is that what her aunt was threatening? Defy her, and Venetia would rue the day she unleashed the scandals of the past?

Chapter Twenty-Two

EUGENIA TOOK A nervous sip of champagne, the bubbles tickling her nose as she gazed about the room. Candles blazed in crystal chandeliers overhead, casting a warm glow across the assembled revelers while musicians played a lively quadrille in the far corner.

What would Thornton think of her costume? More to the point, what would Lady Pendleton think? She, after all, was the arbiter of Eugenia's fashion choices, with the ability to crush her with a single derisive comment.

After thirty years of friendship, Eugenia should know better how to stand up for her decisions, yet her preliminary boldness always seemed to result in crushed feelings. Hers, that is. She smoothed a hand over her gown, the golden silk shimmering beneath her nervous touch.

"My dear Eugenia, surely that is not another champagne you are drinking?" Lady Pendleton had approached from behind, her eye trained on Eugenia's glass. But now she took in her friend's masquerade costume and gasped, her fan snapping open. "What were you thinking?"

She sank into her seat as her gaze traveled from the golden feathery headdress with its curved black beak down the line of shimmering luster. "You told me nothing of your plans to appear in such a scandalous rig-out. Oh, my dear, you will regret tonight, for you are not the decorous woman of advancing years society expects." She leaned forward and gripped Eugenia's wrist. "You are trying far too hard. Who is it you wish to impress? You knew what I would say, didn't you? That's why you kept your costume secret."

By contrast, Lady Pendleton's elaborate gown in deep royal blue and emerald green struck just the right note. The peacock feathers in her headdress quivered with each movement, catching the light like living jewels.

"Why, Lady Pendleton, your peacock costume suits you wonderfully," Eugenia replied. She did not add that thoughts of a royal peacock immediately conjured images of overbearing vanity—exactly what Lady Pendleton projected, though in masquerade it was exacerbated to a fine point. "Never before have I seen you look so regal."

Lady Pendleton preened, stroking her overskirt that mimicked a peacock's tail, adorned with embroidered "eyes" in shimmering thread and beadwork. "Do you really think so? Pendleton said I looked especially fine, but his opinion is hardly one I value."

"Then you have gone to great lengths to entrance someone else?" Eugenia caught herself up. The champagne was definitely affecting her. She never spoke so boldly to her friend.

To her surprise, Lady Pendleton appeared intrigued rather than offended. Her dark eyes flashed with excitement. "One is never too old to enjoy a flirtation." A smile played at the corners of her mouth, transforming her usually severe countenance.

Eugenia felt genuine shock. Lady Pendleton, though unhappily wed, was the last person who would court censure by allowing her eyes to wander.

"Oh, Eugenia, do not look at me like that. You cannot be so innocent," Lady Pendleton said, running a hand down her heavily beaded bodice. She accepted a glass of Madeira from a passing waiter. "Of course, you have never been married, so know nothing of the tumults of the heart. However, when a very handsome gentleman takes notable interest, it matters not how old one is. It simply demonstrates the power we women exert over the unfair sex."

"And what handsome gentleman do you speak of?" Eugenia asked, trying to modulate her shock.

"You really don't expect me to answer that, do you?" Lady Pendleton leaned back with a sly look, fanning herself with studied languor.

Something was different about her friend, and it wasn't merely the dramatic peacock feathers. Lady Pendleton appeared transformed. So… a man was involved. A man who was not her henpecked husband.

She glanced about the ballroom, filled with fabulously garbed guests in outrageous costumes. There was Bacchus draped in grape vines, Diana the Huntress in silver tunic and quiver.

And, now, Lord Thornton, sauntering through the crowd in a midnight-blue domino cloak over formal attire, his simple black half mask doing nothing to disguise his commanding presence.

To Eugenia, he looked the most arresting man in the room. As ever, her heart lurched, and she took a long draught of champagne to steady herself.

"I believe I shall seek some fresh air on the terrace," she said. "The heat in here is quite overwhelming."

"Yes, why not do that?" Lady Pendleton said, just as Lord Thornton arrived and urged Eugenia to stay.

"I don't think I have ever seen you appear so daring, Eugenia," he said admiringly. "A phoenix rising from the ashes and a magnificent peacock. I am quite cast into the shade by you two beauties."

And that was when Eugenia realized the truth. The fiery blush stealing across Lady Pendleton's cheek told her everything. Oh, dear Lord—Lady Pendleton's flirtation was with Lord Thornton.

Lord Thornton, the man who had set Eugenia's heart on fire

thirty years before. A fire that had never been extinguished.

She drained her champagne, and Lord Thornton immediately relieved her of the empty glass. The brush of his fingers against hers sent a familiar thrill through her body. He smiled, and though Eugenia knew there was no collusion in its depths, she felt as if her world was suddenly both full and utterly empty.

Lady Pendleton, with her status and confidence, would always triumph over the Eugenias of this world. If she had set her sights on widowed Lord Thornton, her ineffectual husband would be no impediment, while Eugenia would again be cast into the shadows of her friend's brilliance. The thought turned the champagne sour in her stomach.

"Why, there is our perfect match," Lady Pendleton remarked, nodding toward a couple passing nearby.

"Miss Playford and Mr. Ashworth?" Eugenia replied, fighting to hide her disordered feelings. She squinted at the betrothed pair through the crowd—Miss Venetia in fiery-red-and-black cardinal costume, Mr. Ashworth as a highwayman with pistol and tricorn hat.

"Only two weeks remain before their nuptials," Lady Pendleton observed. "Will you be successful in your second wager, my dear Eugenia? Though I wonder if this terrible scandal might give Miss Playford cause to cry off. She hardly looks joyful."

Eugenia's stomach twisted. Could Lady Pendleton and Lord Thornton truly be conducting an affair? The man with whom she had flown over London in a hot-air balloon after winning her first wager two years ago?

She straightened with as much dignity as she could muster. "Miss Playford could not ask for a more noble husband. This scandal has taken on ridiculous proportions. The lady in blue was clearly addled. I am confident there was no impropriety on Mr. Ashworth's part."

"Another balloon trip, Eugenia?" Lord Thornton's eyes twinkled behind his mask. "Did you enjoy it so much?"

"I did," she murmured, reliving those marvelous hours.

His scrutiny made her hand move self-consciously to her throat—still graceful, not like Lady Pendleton's turkey neck. A new determination rose within her, befitting her phoenix costume.

"Balloon rides are perhaps an occupation for young lovers rather than those in their dotage," Lady Pendleton said with a gimlet look. "Too much excitement might wear out one's heart."

"Just when I thought I was ready to retire with my pipe and slippers," Lord Thornton chuckled, tapping his chest, "you, Eugenia, made me realize there was still a lot happening here."

Eugenia nearly swooned at the gesture's implication.

"Have you ever spoken to them both?" Lord Thornton asked unexpectedly, nodding toward the engaged couple.

Eugenia had to admit she had not. "But I spoke to Miss Playford frequently during Lady Pendleton's Ghostly Gathering, and I know Mr. Ashworth by reputation. All reports confirm he is charming and congenial. I am confident my matchmaking has found its mark."

"Then perhaps you should confirm your instincts," Lord Thornton suggested, indicating where Miss Playford stood alone by a column.

Eugenia took a sip of her champagne as she considered this. And when Lady Pendleton leaned forward to command his attention, offering Eugenia her back, it was decided.

Approaching the young woman who stood a little apart from her aunt, now watching the dancers, Eugenia was struck by her melancholy expression as she watched the dancers. And more than a little troubled.

"My dear Miss Playford, how splendid you look. The cardinal bird suits you admirably."

"Thank you, Lady Townsend," came the lackluster reply.

"Your wedding approaches rapidly. Are the preparations proceeding nicely?"

Miss Playford's fingers tightened around her fan. "Yes. My aunt has seen to everything." Her voice was utterly flat.

"And Mr. Ashworth? He must be counting the days."

At mention of her betrothed, the girl's eyes grew suspiciously bright. "He says so, yes." A tear threatened to spill.

"Forgive me, but you do not seem as happy as a bride-to-be should be. Is anything troubling you?"

Miss Playford's composure nearly cracked. "It is nothing. Pre-wedding nerves, I suppose."

"I have lived long enough to recognize true distress," Eugenia said slowly. "I wonder if there has been adequate opportunity for you and Mr. Ashworth to truly know one another's hearts? The most illuminating conversation I ever had was high above London, with nothing but air between myself and the truth."

"I beg your pardon?"

"In a hot-air balloon, my dear. The most liberating experience. One feels both removed from the world and somehow more connected to what truly matters. Oh—!" Eugenia patted the girl's hand, excitement suddenly coursing through her. "Please excuse me. I believe I've just had an inspiration."

She hurried back across the ballroom, golden feathers quivering.

"I have it!" she announced breathlessly. "I must organize for Miss Venetia Playford and Henry Ashworth to be alone in a hot-air balloon. It will enable them to discover the true love I am certain exists between them."

Although Thornton raised his eyebrows with interested amusement, Lady Pendleton's mouth opened in shock. "That, my dear Eugenia," she said, "is the most outlandish proposition I have heard you make all year."

Chapter Twenty-Three

CAROLINE TUGGED NERVOUSLY at the ribbons of her shepherd-ess costume as she scanned the ballroom for Henry's distinctive tricorn hat. The crowd seemed determined to obscure her view at every turn, dancers and masqueraders swirling beneath the flickering chandeliers.

"Caroline, do stand still," her mother hissed. "Lord Winder-mere has been attempting to catch your eye these past ten minutes. It is the height of rudeness to pretend not to notice."

"I wasn't pretending, Mama. I simply didn't see him."

"As you didn't see Mr. Ashworth, I suppose?" Lady Weston's mouth thinned. "I have warned you repeatedly about the dangers of associating with that young man in the current climate. Yes, you might have been childhood friends, but—he is now mired in scandal and you are looking for a husband."

Caroline bit her lip. The injustice burned. If only her mother knew what Amelia had discovered. She wished Amelia had been able to better communicate with the gossips that the mysterious lady had been an actress paid by Barnaby to create precisely this scandal. But Amelia did not go about in public—or private—due to her delicate situation.

"I'm feeling rather warm, Mama," Caroline said, fanning herself vigorously. "Might I step onto the terrace for just a moment of fresh air?"

Her mother glanced dubiously at Caroline's flushed cheeks. "Very well, but only for a moment. I shall accompany you."

"Oh, but look—isn't that Lady Ferguson beckoning to you?" Caroline nodded toward a portly woman in peacock blue who was merely adjusting her gloves. "She did mention something to me earlier about intending to speak with you about the subscription for St. George's Hospital."

Her mother's attention swiveled instantly. "Well, you may take your air, but remain in full view of the terrace doors and return within five minutes. Not a second more."

"Yes, Mama," Caroline promised, already edging away.

She made her way through the crush, her heart beating rapidly. There, by the stone balustrade, his highwayman's cape lifting in the evening breeze, Henry stood alone, gazing over the darkened gardens.

Caroline glanced back to ensure her mother was engaged with Lady Ferguson, then stepped onto the terrace and moved swiftly to Henry's side.

"I've been searching everywhere for you," she whispered.

He turned, surprise evident behind his mask, then smiled with genuine pleasure. "Miss Weston. Or should I say, the most enchanting shepherdess in all England?"

"Oh, you!" she said with pretend coyness. How she wanted to grip his hand—but anyone observing might instantly learn the truth. "I have only a few minutes. I must tell you what Amelia has discovered."

Henry sobered, drawing her toward a secluded corner. "About the lady in blue?"

Caroline nodded. "She is an actress called Miss Barrett, who received payment from Barnaby."

Henry's jaw tightened.

"There's more. The payment was five pounds, and Amelia thinks—as do I—that this was no prank, despite what Miss Barrett claims."

"Barnaby? Why, I thought our main adversary was Windermere. With help from Mrs. Pike." Henry said grimly. "But Barnaby? He is to marry my sister. I thought he was my friend."

"Caroline!" Her mother's voice cut through the night air but fortunately Caroline was out of view. "I expressly told you five minutes!"

Caroline stepped back into view hastily, whispering over her shoulder, "I must go. But be careful, Henry. If Barnaby and Windermere are working together—"

"Tomorrow, meet me at the lending library at two," Henry responded urgently.

With a quick nod, Caroline hurried towards her mother, composing her features into innocent enjoyment as she located Venetia amid the throng.

"Do you know if Windermere is here this evening? Or what costume he is wearing?" Caroline asked her friend, glancing about. "Perhaps he is with Barnaby. It appears the two of them are thick as thieves."

Venetia's brow furrowed. "Barnaby and Windermere? You're not suggesting they're in this together?" Then, at Caroline's nod, she added on a gasp of outrage, "How can Barnaby have anything to do with this when he is Charlotte's betrothed and therefore Henry's future brother-in-law? He would be the last person to wish Henry harm."

Caroline shrugged. "You would think so. And yet when Amelia discovered this mysterious lady in blue, she was told that Barnaby had *paid* her to approach Henry and create that terrible scene."

Noticing her mother's gimlet eye upon her, Caroline assumed an innocent expression, smiling as she gazed about the room. To an outsider, she was merely admiring costumes. A stout gentleman dressed as King Midas wobbled past, deep in his cups. The Duchess of Pembroke swept by in an elaborate swan costume.

And then, with a shock that felt like ice water in her veins,

Caroline spotted a tall figure in a wolf's costume, the silvery mask covering the upper portion of his face, eyes glinting coldly as he conversed with Aunt Pike.

Lord Windermere. It could be no other.

As their gazes locked for a second through his mask, a shiver ran down her spine. What a malevolent creature he was. But there was no return flare of recognition—thank the Lord, he did not connect her with the stable lad he'd incarcerated.

What a ghastly experience that had been. And yet, she had to acknowledge it was through this ordeal that she had discovered her feelings for Henry—feelings which had translated into such joy as she had ever known. That had to be worth something.

And yet here they were, with only two weeks before Henry and Venetia were to marry. Time was running out to publicly expose the association between Windermere's evil designs and the false accusations surrounding Henry.

Caroline's mind worked feverishly. How could she achieve what no one else had? They still were no closer to discerning the motivation—Aunt Pike's for selling her niece to Windermere, Windermere's for wanting to marry penniless Venetia, and Barnaby's for bribing an actress.

She turned back to Venetia, whose fingers worried at the beaded trim of her costume. "There must be something deeper at work here. Something that connects all of them." She paused, damping down the impulse to reveal that Mr. Rothbury's father had once worked for Venetia's father and might be able to help, for the young man had not been seen these past few days.

But struck by a sudden thought, she asked, "Venetia, is there anything in your family's past—any connection to Windermere that might explain his persistence in pursuing you, despite your lack of fortune?"

Venetia's eyes widened behind her mask. "I—I don't believe so. Though..." Her voice faltered. "My aunt said something—" She gulped on a sob, unable to continue.

Horrified, Caroline bent to comfort her while shielding her

from prying eyes. Tears would be seized upon as gossip. "What did your aunt say?" she whispered, drawing Venetia toward a quiet alcove behind a potted palm.

Venetia dabbed at her eyes with her handkerchief. "She said my father was in love with *her*. With Aunt Pike, and that my mother stole him from her." Venetia gulped again. "She said I was the reason my mother tricked my father." Raising her chin, she asked in a whisper, "Can you imagine hearing anything more dreadful?"

Caroline was lost for words. Then her questioning mind had her asking with a frown, "What evidence did your aunt have to support such a claim?"

"She said she had letters to prove it. But I suppose I have only her word."

Caroline clapped her hands. "Letters? If your father truly was in love with your Aunt Pike—which I can't possibly imagine— then those tender missives must be shown to prove this."

Putting her head closer to Venetia's, she asked hurriedly—for her mother was bound to claim her soon—"Does your aunt have a secret compartment in her desk? Do you know where she might keep something as valuable as a love letter?"

Venetia shook her head. "My aunt is very secretive about everything."

Caroline smoothed her shepherdess's crook thoughtfully. "I would imagine the library or a locked box in her bedroom. I'm sure it won't be too hard to find."

Her friend's eyes grew wide. "What are you suggesting? That I rummage among my aunt's private things? Dear Lord, she'd flay me alive if she caught me."

"Which is all the more reason she mustn't catch you."

Caroline saw the wolf turn his head slowly in their direction. "You must find those letters, Venetia, or at least some written evidence that makes sense of Windermere's interest in you and his vendetta against Henry," she whispered, watching as Lord Windermere began making his way through the crowd towards them.

Venetia shook her head. "No, Caroline, I cannot. The servants will find out—they are my aunt's spies. It's not possible. If you only knew how close an eye she keeps on me."

Caroline made a noise of frustration. She wanted to shake her friend, then tried to remember how terror could make one immobile.

As Lord Windermere's malignant presence bore down upon them, she made one last attempt. "Unless this is the future you want," she hissed, flicking a glance at the gentleman in wolf's clothing, "I truly think you should."

Chapter Twenty-Four

"MISS PLAYFORD."

Caroline saw by Venetia's violent start that she had not connected the wolf traveling in their direction with Lord Windermere.

"Lord Windermere," Caroline answered for her friend with a curt nod. "You look very... dangerous... tonight." Desperately, she scanned the room for escape routes, but her mother had positioned herself strategically by the nearest exit.

"I certainly hope Miss Playford does not think me too dangerous to honor me with this dance." The voice emerging from behind the silver wolf's mask was silken, yet chilling.

Venetia's fingers trembled in Caroline's grasp. "Lord Windermere, indeed... I had not recognized you."

The wolf inclined his head slightly. "I had hoped the costume might conceal my identity from most—but not from you, of course."

"I'm afraid I'm rather fatigued—" Venetia began, but Windermere had already claimed her hand.

"Nonsense. One dance cannot possibly exhaust a young lady of your vigor." His eyes glinted through the mask's eyeholes. "Especially not when we have so much to discuss."

Where was Henry?

And how could Mrs. Pike sanction this?

Caroline could only watch helplessly as Windermere led Venetia onto the dance floor. The orchestra began another waltz, the intimate three-quarter time seeming to close the world around the reluctant partners.

Venetia held herself rigid, maintaining the maximum distance propriety would allow.

"You look positively enchanting," Windermere remarked, his gloved hand pressing slightly firmer against her waist than was strictly necessary. "In fact, dangerously daring in that almost scandalous costume. My, my, what an enigma you are. I really didn't credit you with so much spirit. And I do love a young lady with spirit." He sighed. "But spirit does not make up for the fact that you, Miss Playford, are penniless and without family."

"I have my Aunt Pike," Venetia said without thinking; and didn't wonder that Lord Windermere let out a snide laugh.

"Yes, but unlike you, your Aunt Pike understands that you are being needlessly obstinate in resisting my handsome overtures to give you everything your heart could desire."

"Except my right to choose my own husband, my lord," Venetia replied.

Windermere's laugh was low and unsettling as he guided her through a turn. "Tell me, how is your beleaguered fiancé faring amid the current… unpleasantness?"

"Mr. Ashworth's reputation is above reproach. The malicious rumors will soon be quashed when the truth becomes public."

"Rumors?" Windermere's eyes narrowed behind his mask. "I think we both know they're rather more than that. Though I suppose a woman in love would want to blind herself to another's… indiscretions."

"There have been no indiscretions," Venetia insisted, though she heard her voice waver.

"My dear Miss Playford," Windermere said, drawing her fractionally closer as they moved between other couples, "you are wasting yourself on a scoundrel. Henry Ashworth will never be more than what he is—a charming boy of moderate means and questionable judgment. He lacks the power to protect you, the connections to elevate you, and now, I fear, even the reputation to preserve you from scandal."

Venetia attempted to increase the distance between them, but his grip was unyielding. "I have no need for elevation, my lord. I am perfectly content with Mr. Ashworth's situation."

"Are you? Even knowing what awaits you?" His voice dropped to a dangerous whisper. "Your aunt has been most forthcoming about the family's... financial challenges. Did you know she can no longer afford to maintain you after the wedding? Ashworth has a modest income, but *I* can ensure you enjoy the lifestyle to which you've become accustomed."

"I do not aspire to luxury."

"Noble sentiments from one who has never truly known want." The wolf's mask seemed to grin in the candlelight. "But I wonder how noble you'll feel when you learn what else your aunt has shared with me."

Venetia faltered slightly. "I don't understand."

"Your father's letters, my dear. The ones that reveal the true circumstances of your birth." His eyes flashed. "Oh yes, I know everything—how your mother trapped him, how your very existence destroyed the match that should have been. Your aunt was most explicit."

"That's—I don't believe you!" Venetia could barely speak.

"I have seen the letters myself. As will all of society, should I choose to make them public." The threat hung between them like an ugly, tangible thing. Venetia tried to turn her head away, but he pressed his forefinger to her chin to force her head up and look him in the eye. "Imagine the scandal—far worse than anything poor Henry is facing. Your reputation would be beyond salvation."

The music swelled around them as Venetia struggled to maintain her composure. "You have no proof. You're just saying it—"

He shrugged. "Are you prepared to take the chance I'm lying? Foolish girl! Accept my suit, and not only will those letters remain our secret, but I shall also ensure that the rumors surrounding Henry mysteriously disappear. If you care for him as much as you lead me to believe, then... you have the power to restore his reputation and career."

"I will never marry you!" With enormous bravery, she added, "You failed once, and you will do so again." It was the first time she'd publicly alluded to his kidnap and the dreadful hours she'd spent as his prisoner. But here on the dance floor, surely it was safer to air what must be said? Nevertheless, she was trembling so much she could not go on.

The wolf's smile widened behind his mask. "You really are making this difficult for me, Miss Playford, when there are so few options open to you. Marry me, and Henry goes free, his future secure. Refuse me..." He let the sentence hang unfinished.

Trembling, she whispered, "And if I were to tell Henry of this blackmail?"

"Well, then, I daresay it wouldn't be long before the Ashworth family bank would face immediate scrutiny regarding certain... irregularities in their accounts. Irregularities that, while entirely fabricated, would nonetheless prove devastating. Banking, after all, is built on trust." His voice hardened. "Your Henry would not only lose his reputation, but his family would be ruined and possibly imprisoned. Is that the future you wish for him?"

The music was drawing to a close. Venetia's face felt frozen with horror beneath her mask.

"You have two weeks until your wedding day, Miss Playford. I suggest you use that time wisely." Windermere's final words were delivered with chilling finality. "Oh, and one more thing— your aunt has arranged a delightful musical afternoon in the coming days. I look forward to continuing our conversation there. In fact, I look forward to concluding our mutually beneficial arrangements."

SHE WAS SAVED by Henry, who was suddenly by her side, saying, "I would like to claim the next dance with my fiancée." His voice was tight with barely suppressed fury.

Windermere released Venetia with exaggerated courtesy. "Of course. I wouldn't dream of monopolizing the lovely bride-to-be." He turned to Caroline with a slight bow. "Perhaps Miss Weston would honor me instead?"

"I fear Miss Weston is promised to me," came a new voice, and Barnaby materialized beside them, resplendent in a Harlequin costume of black and white diamonds.

Caroline reared back in alarm, and Henry stepped smoothly between them. "Actually, since Miss Playford looks rather pale, perhaps she should have a moment of air on the terrace with her friend Miss Jackson while Miss Weston honors me with this dance?"

Before either Windermere or Barnaby could object, Henry had swept Caroline onto the dance floor, while Venetia seized the opportunity to slip away towards the terrace doors.

"They're toying with us!" Caroline whispered once they were safely beyond earshot. "And all the while, they're plotting and planning. Have you learned anything? Like… when is Mr. Rothbury back in town? I made it clear I wanted to talk to him, but he is nowhere to be found."

"I think your desire to speak to him might have been over-shadowed by the tumult caused by that mysterious woman in blue. No wonder Mr. Rothbury's mind was elsewhere." Henry raised an eyebrow. "And now Barnaby has supposed evidence he claims could ruin my family."

"I refuse to believe it!"

"That is what I am hearing. Meanwhile, Venetia's aunt claims she has evidence that could ruin her reputation—if she refuses to wed Windermere."

"I refuse to believe *any* of it!" Caroline declared. "These are empty threats to make Venetia too frightened to do anything but renege on marriage to you and then pliantly accept Windermere." She resisted the urge to brush her hand across Henry's cheek but her voice softened and her heart did a little somersault in her chest at the way he looked at her when she said, "While nothing would make me happier than for you to no longer be betrothed to Venetia, that doesn't solve the other evil that is about."

"No," Henry agreed, giving her waist a gentle squeeze. "Because unless we find out, we are all doomed to unhappiness."

Chapter Twenty-Five

VENETIA'S FIRST INSTINCT upon reaching her room, following the worst ball of her life, was to throw herself onto her bed and sob. She felt utterly powerless.

Indeed, she was powerless. Her twenty-first birthday was only three weeks away—in fact, a couple of days after her wedding—but her majority would change nothing. How she wished for the safety of marriage to Henry, even though she did not love him. He was kind and would protect her.

But what of Windermere's threats? No, she could not take them at face value and simply accede to marriage with him.

Which meant she had to find proof. Proof of what Windermere had said. Proof of what her aunt claimed.

Which meant she had to do what she had declared impossible: make a secret investigation of her aunt's locked room. This was a room at the rear of their London townhouse to which Venetia and all staff were denied access, save for weekly cleaning. The door was always locked.

Perhaps this was where Aunt Pike kept her valuables. And her secrets.

This might be where Venetia would most likely find the letters that would bear up her aunt's claims, though her aunt's bedchamber was another option. Of course, if Venetia found nothing, she'd be no closer to verifying if Aunt Pike's terrible revelations were true.

Lord, she certainly hoped she would not find the letters her aunt claimed proved a secret love affair between herself and Venetia's father. Even the thought made her feel ill.

But she had to look.

After succumbing to those tears, Venetia sat up on the bed, rubbing her swollen eyes, and tried to grasp the courage that had once been in far greater abundance before her aunt had sapped her of seemingly all spirit.

With a great sigh, she contemplated the worst that could happen. As a child, it had been a night locked in a dark, musty cupboard for a rude or sullen response.

Now it was marriage to Windermere.

There was only one way to find out what he and her aunt knew.

Venetia rose slowly, forcing courage into her veins. Her aunt was sleeping, having gone straight to bed after the ball. It was perhaps the best time to begin her search.

Caroline had risked her life to prevent Venetia from the very fate which Venetia was now sleepwalking towards... unless Venetia forced steel into her backbone.

Picking up the candlestick from the dresser, she did not even stop to change her clothes. For that might give her time to change her mind.

If she could not do this to save herself, then she needed to do it to prove her gratitude to Caroline for all her dear friend had done.

The corridor outside her bedchamber was silent and dark. Venetia held her breath as she eased her door closed, wincing at the slight creak of the hinges. Her candle cast eerie shadows on the wall as she made her way towards her aunt's study— hopefully the more likely place to begin her search than her aunt's bedchamber.

Her slippers made no sound on the carpet as she approached

the study door. It was locked, of course, but Venetia had been prepared for this. From her pocket, she withdrew a hairpin bent into the crude shape of a lock pick, a skill learned long ago from an unlikely quarter: one of her school friends from the Ladies Seminary.

Those had been among the happiest years of her life, she reflected, thinking back to her first season when she and the Misses P had attended the London round of balls and recitals in search of a husband. After her parents' early deaths, she'd experienced only a few months of her aunt's coldness before being sent off to school.

What a fool she'd been to imagine her aunt would be any kinder when she was an adult.

After several tense minutes, during which Venetia was certain the thundering of her heart would wake the entire household, the lock finally yielded with a soft click. She slipped inside, closing the door quietly behind her.

The study was illuminated only by faint moonlight filtering through the curtains and the weak glow of her candle. Aunt Pike's massive mahogany desk dominated the room, its polished surface gleaming in the dim light. Venetia approached it with trepidation, setting her candle down carefully.

The drawers were locked as well, but Venetia was determined now. One by one, she worked through them with her improvised lock pick until she reached the bottom right drawer—the only one that resisted her efforts. This had to be where the most sensitive documents were kept.

It took longer than the others, but finally, the lock surrendered. Inside was a small wooden box, ornately carved with a pattern of intertwined roses. Venetia's hands trembled as she lifted it out and placed it on the desk.

The box itself was locked with a tiny brass padlock and she worked at it feverishly. Her aunt was asleep, but with Aunt Pike, one could never be too careful.

At last, the padlock sprang open, and Venetia raised the lid with bated breath.

Letters.

Well, at least she'd found correspondence. It was a start, but it did not mean she'd find what her aunt had taunted her with: letters from her father.

Carefully, she withdrew a stack of letters and began to rifle through them. Correspondence with female friends, accounts of visits to the country. The dates began more than thirty years previously when her aunt had been a young woman. Nothing mentioned a man. Nothing from a man.

Until—

Venetia gasped, and her heart rate increased.

Nothing from any man other than her father, for she certainly recognized his handwriting with its distinctive slanted style. The last letter he'd ever written to Venetia when he knew he was dying was something she treasured and gazed upon often.

Now, here was his handwriting—in fact, a bundle of letters in his handwriting—amidst a pile of faded letters tied with pink ribbon.

With trembling fingers, she untied the bow and began to read the first letter.

"My dearest Eliza," it began. Venetia's breath caught—Eliza was her aunt's Christian name. "Not a day passes when I do not think of you and the moments we have shared…"

With a great sob, Venetia dropped the pile of letters onto the desk, swinging round to cover her eyes, and inadvertently sweeping a paperweight to the floor.

The noise reverberated through the house, but Venetia could not leave what she had begun. She had to read that letter.

"My Dearest Eliza—" she read once again, tears welling in her eyes as she continued.

It didn't get any better. The letter continued in the same vein, full of passionate declarations and plans for the future. Dull misery churned in her breast. This was exactly what both

Windermere and her aunt had claimed—proof that her father had loved Aunt Pike first. She hastily moved to the next letter, and the next, each one confirming the love affair that had preceded her parents' marriage.

"I see you've found what you were looking for."

With a gasp, Venetia swung round. Aunt Pike was standing in the doorway, a cold smile on her face. She wore a dressing gown of dark burgundy that made her look like a figure of vengeance in the dim light.

"I-I'm sorry, I—" Venetia stammered, but her aunt cut her off with a sharp gesture.

"I've been expecting this. You, who are never satisfied. You, who wouldn't have believed me otherwise? So I am glad that now you see how charitable I have been to you all these years." Aunt Pike stepped into the room, closing the door behind her. "Well? Are you satisfied? Have you found your answers?"

Venetia bit her lip, barely able to answer. "My father—he loved you first?"

"Loved me?" Aunt Pike laughed harshly. "Oh, he did more than love me, child. As I told you, we were to be married. All was arranged, all was perfect." Her face contorted with bitter remembrance. "And then your mother—my own sister—ensnared him."

"No," Venetia whispered, but her aunt continued relentlessly.

"You think she was so innocent? So pure? Let me show you the truth." Aunt Pike reached into the desk drawer and withdrew another packet of letters, these tied with black ribbon. "These arrived after their hasty marriage. Your father, confessing all to me."

She thrust a letter into Venetia's hands. The paper crackled as she unfolded it, her eyes scanning the damning words:

"Dearest Eliza, I write to you in the deepest shame. Your sister has informed me she carries my child—the result of a moment of weakness for which I shall never forgive myself. Honor demands I marry her, though my heart remains with you.

Forgive me, if you can…"

"No!" Venetia's tears fell onto the page, smudging the ink. "This cannot be true," she choked out.

"But it is true. Every word." Aunt Pike's voice was triumphant. "You were the reason he married her. You destroyed what should have been. And now you sit there, with his eyes looking out at me, a constant reminder of what was stolen from me."

"I-I didn't know." Venetia could barely speak. Everything she had believed about her parents, about herself, was crumbling around her.

With a bitter laugh, Aunt Pike gathered up the letters and replaced them in the box. "And there's something else you don't know which might just help you in your choice of future husband."

Venetia shook her head. On this, she was determined, and not even this discovery would change her mind.

"I will not wed Lord Windermere," she whispered. "Not on any account."

Her aunt appeared to consider this a moment. Slowly she walked to the window where she rested an elbow upon the sill as she carefully went through all the letters, one by one, as if committing them to memory.

Then, apparently finding what she was looking for, she glanced up at her niece. "There is one secret that I have been keeping, Venetia. One secret that no one else knows because to disclose it would destroy all your future prospects."

Venetia clasped her hands to stop them trembling, but it was fruitless. Her whole body felt as if it was succumbing to the ague. She couldn't even speak to ask what it might be.

Her aunt looked as if she relished the opportunity to tell her.

And of course, the telling was delivered with all the venom of which her aunt was capable.

"Your father did not marry your mother until after you were born."

Venetia blinked, frozen, as she processed the ramifications.

When she said nothing, her aunt put her head on one side and asked, "Do you realize what I'm saying, Venetia?"

Still, Venetia couldn't answer. Her tongue felt swollen in her throat, while tears of shame stung her eyes.

"I'm telling you that you are illegitimate. Technically, you are a bastard. And you know how bastards are treated by society?"

"But my parents were married!" Finally, Venetia was able to burst out her defense. "I know that's true! How else could they have been received in society?"

"Oh, you are correct, my dear. They were married." Her aunt gave another of her bitter little laughs. "But not in time to legitimize you. No, they were married abroad, and they brought home their little bundle of joy with all the world assuming they had eloped and were joyfully returning."

Her aunt began to pace. "Naturally, my sister Cassandra and I were estranged after they returned. Your father had no contact with me." She tapped the bundle of letters. "These are what I existed on. The fine, noble sentiments he'd poured out before Cassandra, four years younger, threw herself at him, seducing him, before running away in shame when she discovered she was with child. He did not want to marry her. Why would he have waited so long—all those months—before he followed her?" Aunt Pike sighed, and her shoulders sagged. "When the newlyweds returned to London and set up home, they entertained as if I had never existed. And you became their world. Why, I believe your father even doted on you. As if he'd forgotten you were the reason he'd had to give up his true love—me!"

Venetia cast her mind back to her eight-year-old self, to the days when she and her parents had lived happily together under the same roof. Just like any other family.

They had been happy. Hadn't they?

She lifted her head. Her aunt was speaking again, and the name that dropped from her lips made her tremble.

"Lord Windermere will call tomorrow. You will receive him properly, and you will accept his suit."

Venetia gazed at the glittering ruby ring upon her aunt's finger that tapped impatiently upon the desktop. Like a drop of blood, it looked in the dim light. "Yes, you will wed Lord Windermere, who will take you off my hands. It's time you paid the debt your mother incurred."

"I cannot—" Venetia began, but her aunt seized her arm, fingers digging painfully into her flesh.

"You have no choice. Unless you wish your illegitimacy to become common knowledge! Imagine the scandal—your saintly mother revealed as a scheming harlot who trapped a man into marriage." Her eyes glittered with malice. "Lord Windermere knows everything, and he is still willing to marry you. You should be grateful."

Still gripping Venetia's arm so that Venetia cried out in pain, she propelled her towards the door. "The choice is simple: marriage to Windermere, or complete social ruin."

"But I'm promised to Henry Ashworth—"

"You love him so much that you would risk everything? Even his good name?" There was skepticism in her aunt's tone.

"I would marry anyone rather than Lord Windermere."

"But no one else will have you. Well, they certainly will not once it is known that not only are you penniless, you are a bastard. Granted, Mr. Ashworth is fond of you, just as you are fond of him. But no passion burns in his breast. He did the honorable thing after the Gascoynes discovered the two of you alone and unchaperoned at an inn. No, I do not think that Mr. Ashworth will cross a thousand oceans to be with you, Venetia, though he is the kind of passionate young man who would do that for a woman he truly loved. But that is not you." She took a slow breath, then asked softly, "Is it, Venetia?"

Venetia stumbled back to her room, her aunt following close behind. Once inside, she threw herself onto the bed, bringing her hands to her ears as her aunt turned the key in the lock.

"You will remain here until Lord Windermere calls," Aunt Pike's voice came through the door. "And you will receive him with the gratitude his generosity deserves."

After a long silence, she added ominously, "Within the next two days, I expect you to call off your marriage to Mr. Ashworth."

Chapter Twenty-Six

EUGENIA FROWNED AS her protégé made her entrance at Lady Henderson's ball the following evening, looking pale but composed in a gown of dove gray that did nothing to flatter her complexion.

She had so hoped Miss Playford would be radiating joy with so few days left before her nuptials. Ten, to be exact.

"The poor child looks positively wretched," Eugenia murmured to Lord Thornton, who stood beside her.

"She does," he agreed, following her gaze. "And see how closely Mrs. Pike hovers. As if she fears the girl will bolt at the first opportunity."

"Which is precisely what any sensible young woman would do when Lord Windermere enters a room." Eugenia did not hide her distaste. "The way he looked at her at the masquerade—like a wolf eyeing a lamb. It quite chilled me to the bone."

Thornton's eyebrow rose slightly. "You've grown quite protective of Miss Playford."

"As is rational," Eugenia countered. "I have wagered that she and Henry Ashworth are the perfect match, and I do not intend to lose. Last night, it was made clear how much Mrs. Pike favors Windermere over young Henry. And with these absurd rumors circulating about the young man, I fear that she may prevail." She shook her head in frustration. "Indeed! Someone must intervene before the girl is pushed to renege on her current arrangement and enter into a most unsuitable alliance with the arrogant Windermere."

"And that someone is you, naturally," Thornton remarked, amusement playing at the corners of his mouth.

"Well, I can't see anyone else stepping forward. Henry and Venetia complement each other beautifully and I gravely fear that they will be parted by Mrs. Pike before they make it down the aisle." Eugenia's eyes narrowed as she observed Mrs. Pike guiding Venetia towards a circle that included Windermere and several of his closest associates. "What they need is time alone together, away from her aunt's interference and society's gossip so that they will fight with all their might against Mrs. Pike's machinations."

"My dear Eugenia, you make this sound like a Shakespearean tragedy," said Thornton with a smile.

"True love is not to be trifled with," Eugenia said severely, and with a lurch in the region of her heart. After a short pause, she added, daringly, "I know what it is to yearn for lost opportunities."

For a long moment, Thornton gazed at her. And just when she thought he might quiz her further, a very interesting gentleman obviously crossed his line of vision, for he started visibly.

"What captures your attention?"

"Rothbury," Thornton replied, nodding toward a tall, serious-looking gentleman engaged in conversation with Caroline Weston. "Hadn't thought about his father for years, but I knew him when he was bailiff to the Playford family. To Miss Venetia's grandfather, in fact." He frowned. "Thornbury left England to serve on the high seas when he was very young. And then I met him in Italy briefly."

"You never said!"

"I met a lot of people in Italy." Thornton smiled. "But none who then returned to England, and who clearly evince a very great interest in a young lady who is, to all intents and purposes, quite insignificant. Yes, I'm talking about Miss Venetia Playford."

"Miss Playford is a beauty if she would only but smile," Eugenia objected.

"I'm talking about her friendless, penniless state." Thornton narrowed his eyes as he continued his observation. "Have you not thought to wonder why Windermere is so overbearing in his attentions to penniless Miss Playford? He should be after an heiress, given the rumors I've heard of his financial affairs. And now, see how Mr. Rothbury keeps glancing at Miss Playford. I observed it on the last two occasions they were both in public."

"What an unusually perceptive observation. Men do not, in general, notice—" Eugenia swallowed, her throat dry. "—yearning glances across a ballroom." Her mind flashed back to when she'd gazed upon Thornton with surely unabashed yearning, to the balls and soirees of thirty years before. But then he'd married her best friend.

"I wonder if Rothbury knew Miss Playford before this season," Thornton responded, clearly not having registered her previous comment. "Young Rothbury was only fourteen, or thereabouts, when he went to sea. It's possible he may not even realize the extent of the connection between his and Miss Playford's families." Thornton frowned. "Yet his keen but quiet observation of Miss Playford has me curious. That is, in view of Windermere's interest, also, which I find unaccountable."

"Goodness, Thornton, you are suddenly quite the sleuth," Eugenia remarked as she turned to study Mr. Rothbury with renewed interest.

"Old Rothbury was known for his impeccable honesty—saved the Playford family from financial ruin during the '98 crisis, I recall hearing. The son inherited his father's integrity, by all accounts, for I have heard only praise for young Rothbury."

"A pity integrity doesn't pay dividends," Eugenia remarked. "And clearly Miss Playford's father still managed to drown himself in debt, since the poor girl is penniless. But this Mr. Rothbury is a man of excellent character, you say?"

"The very best. Steady, intelligent, principled to a fault." Thornton grinned. "He garnered great respect during his naval career, though I have no idea of his financial situation. Perhaps you will have to keep him in reserve for your next wedding wager, Eugenia." Thornton quirked a brow at Eugenia, who said, raising her lorgnette to peer at Rothbury once again, "The man has a very pleasant face. Very fine eyes. Part Italian, you say? Well, if he is so principled yet also penniless, I think I shall find him an heiress." Her smile broadened. "That is, once I have my current wagered pair happily married. Only ten more days. I am sure Windermere can't do anything too interfering in the meantime."

"My dear Lady Townsend! Lord Thornton!" It was Lady Henderson, fanning herself vigorously as she fluttered with excitement. "Have you heard the extraordinary news? The Astronomical Society has identified a new comet that will be visible next week! Only for three nights, they say, before it passes beyond our view, perhaps forever."

"How fascinating," Eugenia replied, though her attention was drawn to the serious, dark-haired young man who had wandered alone towards the supper table. However, when Mr. Rothbury was drawn into conversation with Rear Admiral Buccleigh, she gave Lady Henderson her full attention.

"Indeed! My husband is quite beside himself with excitement," Lady Henderson continued. "He's invited half of London to view it from our roof garden, but I fear we'll be dreadfully crowded."

Lady Henderson really was a dreadful bore, Eugenia thought, before a sudden inspiration struck. But seeing a comet from the roof of their townhouse would indeed be spectacular. That is, if she were one of the select to be invited.

And then inspiration struck as she was reminded of Lady Pendleton's dampening remarks to her previous ideas of hot-air ballooning as a strategy to bind Venetia and Henry's hearts closer.

"Why, Lady Henderson, all of society will want to view such a spectacle if the weather holds—which it appears it will. So, of course, more room is what is wanted, is it not?" she went on, receiving confused looks from Thornton and Lady Henderson.

"I mean, what we need is a grand celebration worthy of such a celestial event—a Comet Viewing Gala—where everyone can see the magnificent spectacle," Eugenia declared, adding quickly, "That is, everyone who is not fortunate enough to be one of the select few invited to your superior event." For Eugenia was recalling how popular Lady Pendleton's Ghoulish Gathering at Pendleton Castle had been, and how her friend had been feted and admired for her inventiveness—even though it was Eugenia who had devised most of the entertainments, such as the secret letters that had helped unite lovely Miss Amelia Fairchild with Sir Frederick Weston, Caroline's brother.

Her mind spun with possibilities. Pendleton Castle had provided the close proximity needed for Miss Amelia Fairchild and Sir Frederick's romance to flourish.

And wasn't a similar entertainment needed to ensure Henry and Venetia understood the fact they were made for each other? Certainly, to the point that Windermere posed no threat.

"A Comet Viewing Gala?" Thornton repeated with clear amusement. "How do you propose to arrange such a thing in time for the comet, which is only two days hence?"

"The weather promises warm and fine, and the novelty of short notice will not be lost on those who wish to attend," Eugenia said, refusing to allow practicalities to impede her enthusiasm.

"So you plan to arrange tents along the river's edge and serve champagne while your guests view the comet?" Lord Thornton said in dampening tones. "Perhaps you have forgotten that it is also Lady Mudge's August Ball that evening, in addition to Lady Henderson's just proposed event."

"Oh, I do not intend to diminish either of those," Eugenia

quickly assured the now frowning Lady Henderson. "I suggested it purely because I know so many people will be disappointed by not receiving an invitation to either and I—trading on the vagaries of age and… eccentricity… supposed it would be rather novel to organize something considering I have the funds but, alas, no husband who can tell me how I use them." Her mouth quirked as she watched Lady Henderson and Thornton grapple with how to frame a response.

But without waiting, she went on, her enthusiasm growing, "Why, I believe that, not only will I organize tents and refreshments along the river, I shall arrange for a hot air balloon. Perhaps even two! Imagine witnessing this once-in-a-lifetime astronomical wonder while floating among the clouds."

"My dear Lady Townsend, this is quite… an undertaking," Lady Henderson said, dubiously.

"And quite extravagant," Thornton added.

Eugenia shrugged. "I can't take my fortune to the grave, and I have no one to leave it to." Eugenia could barely contain her excitement. "Two days hence, when the comet first appears— what could be more magnificent? We shall have champagne, music, and the most spectacular view in all of London."

Lady Henderson's eyes widened. "But where would one even procure such a thing as a hot-air balloon on such short notice?"

"Oh, I can work miracles when I am so inspired," Eugenia assured her. "And as good fortune has it, I happen to be well acquainted with London's foremost aeronaut."

"My, my… A Comet Viewing Gala? From a hot-air balloon?" Thornton regarded Eugenia with undisguised amusement after Lady Henderson had left to spread the news that either Eugenia Lady Townsend had quite lost her senses or else was about to stage the most talked-about event of the year.

"Why not?" Eugenia sent him a playful smile.

"What if Lady Henderson is misinformed and there is no comet?"

Eugenia shrugged. "What does it matter, so long as everyone

believes there is?" Eugenia waved a dismissive hand while Thornton said, lowering his voice, "So you have not given up on your rather outlandish plan to force young Miss Venetia and Henry into close proximity high above the earth?"

Eugenia nodded. "I am tired of Lady Pendleton… sucking the air from any proposal which fuels my enthusiasm."

Lord Thornton's understanding smile was the sweetest thing she'd seen all night.

"So, I'm pressing ahead. Our evening together in the basket of a hot-air balloon, gazing over the great city of London, was the most miraculous and awe-inspiring spectacle of my life, Thornton." She drew back her shoulders. "And I want to do it again. I also want to provide it as an opportunity for young Henry and Venetia to be alone, together, in the majesty of nature, so they can know what is truly in their hearts. I want to provide them with a chance to reaffirm their attachment without Mrs. Pike or Windermere hovering nearby."

"And how do you propose to ensure that they—and only they—are the ones who ascend in this balloon? They will need a chaperone, and no doubt that will be Mrs. Pike."

"I shall manage the details," Eugenia replied with a dismissive wave, though she had not quite gone so far as to work out what these would be. "The important thing is to counter Windermere's growing influence. Look at him now, encompassing Mrs. Pike and her poor niece in his orbit like a hunter who's found his prey."

It was impossible not to see the very real fear in Miss Playford's expression.

"It's quite clear where her preferences lie," Eugenia remarked bitterly. "As for all these rumors surrounding Henry's supposed indiscretion with that woman in blue, and the whispers about financial improprieties… Even though I know them to be untrue, it takes time to wash away the mud and, in the meantime, Mrs. Pike has all the ammunition she needs to pressure Venetia into breaking the engagement."

"A balloon ride will not solve these problems."

"Not solve, perhaps, but certainly provide a respite. There's something about being suspended between heaven and earth that makes one see things more clearly." Her voice softened with remembrance. "As we discovered ourselves, not so long ago."

Thornton's expression grew thoughtful. "That was indeed a memorable experience."

"One that changed your plans considerably," Eugenia added. "One moment you were talking of graceful retirement to the country, the next you were in diplomatic service."

"Speaking of which," Thornton said, his voice taking on a more serious tone, "despite my earlier claims that my roving days are behind me, I've been offered a new posting in Budapest. The stipend is modest, but the work would be satisfying."

"Budapest," Eugenia echoed, unable to keep the dismay from her voice. "So far away." She hesitated, blinking back tears before saying with an attempt at levity, "Then if I win my wager, I can stow away in disguise as your secretary, like I warned I would."

Thornton laughed softly. They both knew there was no real seriousness in the proposal.

"The odd thing is that I find myself strangely reluctant to accept." Thornton studied her face. "I wonder if you might understand why."

For a long time, there was silence as the noise of chatter and music swirled around them.

Eugenia looked down while she struggled for a response. What was Thornton not saying? He surely couldn't mean what she thought for one painful, hopeful moment, he did.

That he would miss her?

The music came to a dramatic finale and then faded away.

Finally, Eugenia opened her mouth, finding at last the courage to speak. This was her moment.

But she was too late.

With a light shrug, as if Thornton had waited long enough and found his answer in her silence, he went on, "I rather think you are a little too fond of a challenge. Well, here's one for you, who have never known a day's worry over finances."

"I beg your pardon?" Eugenia blinked at the sudden change of subject.

"A modest diplomatic stipend would seem like poverty to someone accustomed to your level of comfort."

"What an absurd remark." Eugenia felt her cheeks warm with sudden hope. Was he suggesting she accompany him after all? "I am not some pampered princess incapable of living simply," she said with what she hoped was the right combination of mild indignation and arch suggestiveness.

"Aren't you?" His voice held a note of curiosity and teasing. "I wager you could not live six months on a modest income."

"And I wager that you, sir, could not survive six months without your clubs and comforts," she retorted.

"Then perhaps we should both find out," he suggested, his expression unreadable. "Six months of simple living, away from London society."

"In Budapest?" she asked, obviously getting too far ahead of herself, for he replied with devastating calm, "I had not initially thought of it but—"

"Ah Thornton, I've been looking for you everywhere."

It was Lady Pendleton, smoothing her gloves as she insinuated herself between them. She peered through her lorgnette at Eugenia. "Why, you've dropped something from the supper table on your dress, you clumsy thing. There! I've just removed it for you!"

Before Eugenia could discern whether concern or malice was behind her friend's quick action, Lady Pendleton had commandeered Thornton's attention, leaving Eugenia once more in the cold.

In the distance, she saw Windermere cage Miss Playford's hand upon his forearm as he led her towards the dance floor, while Mrs. Pike looked on with satisfaction.

And Mr. Ashworth looked utterly forlorn.

Well! Eugenia had a plan, so he must not despair. Since she was now superfluous following Lady Pendleton's arrival, she smoothly joined Mr. Ashworth, drawing him away so that he was out of earshot of Mrs. Pike.

"Mr. Ashworth, if I might prevail upon your superior knowledge, I wonder if you could tell me what you know about the arrival of the celestial comet in two nights' time that has Lady Henderson in transports of excitement."

"The celestial comet?" he repeated. It seemed he was reluctant to draw his eyes from the dance floor, and Eugenia didn't wonder. Windermere was dancing with his betrothed.

"Or perhaps it's simply a comet and there's nothing celestial about it at all," she amended.

"I did not know we were to be visited by a comet," he said, clearly distracted.

Well, she would soon give him something to be hopeful about.

"We are, and I plan to honor this rare event in the most stupendous way I can."

"You do?"

Of course, Mr. Ashworth did not know Eugenia well, but he certainly knew her, and he knew that his mama was on good terms with her. Still, it was dispiriting that he was barely attending, as if she were little more than a vaguely addled old woman rather than his fairy godmother.

Well, she would get his attention.

"I have secured London's most famous aeronaut, and in two nights' time he will ascend from the river in his hot-air balloon, taking several of my chosen guests high into the sky to see this celestial comet." She paused. "I want you and Miss Playford to be my guests."

"Me and Miss Playford?"

This got his attention, for he'd swung around and was now staring at her with the first real interest he'd shown.

"Yes, you and Miss Playford. I do not know if you know, but I took a balloon ride several years ago and have again secured the services of that excellent aeronaut who was responsible for me experiencing the unparalleled ecstasy of looking down upon London as few people have."

She had not secured this aeronaut's services, but Eugenia knew where to find him and, since money was no object, she was certain she could arrange it.

"And why should you honor Miss Playford and myself?"

Eugenia hadn't considered how she'd answer that question. She'd been too caught up in not feeling old and discarded.

"Why, because I believe you've been unfairly maligned, and even though the rumors have been all but quashed, I see how Lord Windermere is attempting to undermine you." She pressed her lips together, uncertain if she should go on since it might be too revealing of her interest in Venetia and Henry.

But as he had not responded and was still directing a look of perplexity at her, she went on, "But as I believe no more deserving a pair than you and Miss Playford exists, I want to do whatever I can to facilitate your happy union." She smiled. "And because I was very fond of your late grandmother, whom you greatly resemble. So call it the vagaries of a foolish, nostalgic old woman and do me the great honor of indulging me."

Chapter Twenty-Seven

CAROLINE FOUND VENETIA in the gated park, where they had arranged to meet. The secluded spot was shielded from the row of townhouses by a copse of elm trees, and as Caroline approached, she was both excited and concerned to see her friend.

Excited because any tidbits about Henry sustained her, and concerned because Venetia sat with hunched shoulders, hands clasped tightly in her lap, staring fixedly at nothing.

"Venetia?" Caroline called softly.

Venetia's head jerked up, her face a mask of misery. "You came," she whispered, as if she had doubted it.

"Of course I came." Caroline settled beside her on the bench, taking one of Venetia's cold hands. "Your note sounded urgent and ever since you were unable to finish telling me last night of your momentous discovery, I have been unable to think of anything else. What has happened?"

Venetia drew a shuddering breath. "I cannot marry Henry," she finally said, her voice barely audible.

Caroline felt her heart skip—a treacherous flicker of hope immediately smothered by concern. "What do you mean? The wedding is little more than a week away."

"I must call it off. Tomorrow." A tear slipped down Venetia's cheek. "I have no choice."

"Who has been threatening you?" Caroline didn't try to keep the anger from her voice.

"My aunt." Venetia finally met Caroline's gaze. "I found the letters from my father, Caroline. Yes! They exist and they were bad enough. And then Aunt Pike showed me more."

"Love letters?"

Venetia nodded miserably. "They *were* to be married, it seems. Until my mother... until she..." She faltered, then continued in a rush, "My mother fled to the Continent with child—with me. My father followed out of duty, but they did not marry until after my birth."

Caroline's mind raced to comprehend the implications. "You mean—"

"I am illegitimate," Venetia whispered, the words seeming to physically pain her. "My parents returned from abroad, pretending they had married before my birth. But it was a lie."

Caroline squeezed Venetia's hand, barely able to grasp the terrible enormity of such a discovery.

"My aunt has threatened to tell everyone the sordid truth if I do not break my engagement to Henry tomorrow. She says no respectable family would want such a connection." Venetia's voice hardened with certainty. "Windermere said the same on the dance floor last night. And, of course, I know that to be true."

"Yet Windermere is willing to marry you? Despite... such a revelation?" Caroline asked.

"He says that although he knows the truth, he is willing to marry me despite it." Venetia gave a bitter laugh. "How magnanimous of him."

Caroline toyed with her bonnet ribbons, mind whirling with conflicting emotions. Part of her—a part she despised—felt that quiver of hope at the thought of Venetia breaking her engagement. But she had risked too much to protect Venetia from Windermere.

"There must be some way to verify these claims," she said.

"Did your aunt show you proof beyond the letters?"

"What more proof do I need? The letters are in my father's hand."

"Love letters, yes, but what of the rest? Where is the proof that your parents were not married before your birth?"

Venetia looked up, a flicker of something—not quite hope—in her eyes. "I… I don't know. She has only shown me the letters between her and my father."

"Then we cannot be certain of anything else she claims," Caroline declared firmly. "Your aunt has always wanted you to marry Windermere. This could be an elaborate deception."

"But why would she fabricate such a thing?" Venetia gulped. "And how do I tell Henry? Of course, he won't want to marry me when he knows the truth."

"But *is* it the truth?" Caroline shrugged, then shook her head. "Do not, I implore you, break off your betrothal to Henry just because your aunt has been feeding you these… unfounded stories."

"The rumors are damning enough. We know how mud sticks," Venetia went on despairingly. "I don't know how much longer I can resist my aunt and Lord Windermere."

"Please, Venetia, stay strong a little longer," Caroline implored her as her friend began to cry. And then, even though it wasn't quite true, she added bolsteringly, "Henry and I think we have nearly discovered the reason Windermere wishes to marry a penniless girl." Oh, dear Lord, she did hope they had. "And then everything will be revealed."

"You and Henry?" Venetia frowned, then her face lit up. "I cannot believe what wonderful friends you both have been to me. Why, if you truly can discover Windermere's motivation, I think I shall just have to marry Henry out of gratitude… even though I don't love him."

Caroline shifted awkwardly. "Just as long as you don't marry Windermere. Believe me, Venetia, there is some mysterious reason your aunt and Windermere are working together." She rose, giving Venetia's hand one last squeeze. "And I believe we are nearly at the bottom of it."

CAROLINE LEFT THE park feeling more despondent than when she'd arrived. What had she been hoping for? Unless she discovered information that remained aggravatingly elusive, her dearest friend really was on course to marry the man Caroline loved.

Or would be forced to marry Windermere?

She was so deeply engrossed in these thoughts as she trudged the pavements with her maid beside her that she would have missed Henry entirely had he not called out from across the street, "My dear Miss Weston! What a coincidence!"

"Henry!" she called out, not hiding her pleasure. As they were passing a small park, Caroline indicated they step inside the open gates.

"Mary, you can take a gentle stroll to those bushes. Henry and I have much to say to one another."

To Caroline's surprise, Mary said diffidently, "'S'cuse me, miss, but your mama were most particular that I do not leave your side if you happened to talk to any gentleman."

"Good Lord, Mary, Henry is not just any gentleman—"

"Your mama said it was Mister Henry that I was not to leave you alone with," Mary interrupted miserably. "She was quite particular."

Caroline could not believe her ears. Henry blushed hotly. "I am sorry your mother does not consider me a proper gentleman, even though she has known me from the cradle."

"Henry, I am so sorry." Caroline drew him out of Mary's earshot. "I know your greatest burden is being so unfairly tarnished—"

"My greatest burden is that I cannot be with you, and that

honor will dictate I must marry your best friend rather than you… the only woman I love, the only woman I will ever love."

He said it matter-of-factly, which conveyed more than passion and poetry would have done.

"Oh, Henry, I would do anything to be with you," Caroline declared, gripping his hand. "I want to marry you, too, more than anything. But we both know we cannot do that if it leaves Venetia vulnerable to that evil man."

"The only way we are to be married is if a kind and honorable gentleman offered for Venetia," Henry said, his arm partially shielding her as if his greatest desire was to enfold her in his arms. "A man prepared to accept her without a dowry. A man who would accept her, knowing that she—"

"It's all lies!" Caroline declared hotly before realizing she'd nearly revealed Venetia's confidence regarding her aunt's declaration of her illegitimacy.

"That she does not love him?" Henry asked.

"Oh, that is not a lie. No, Henry, everything else swirling around is a lie, and I am in despair that she will accept either Windermere, or follow through with marriage to you."

Henry looked as grim as she felt. "If only some unknown gentleman, madly in love with her but unable to declare himself, would present himself. But with Venetia's family so disconnected from anyone of influence, and with her lack of dowry, I'd say that was well nigh impossible." He made a noise of frustration. "We haven't even been able to ask Mr. Rothbury about the vague possibility he knows something about Venetia's family that might throw light on the matter. The man has been most elusive."

Mary, who had edged closer despite Caroline's request, cleared her throat nervously. "Beggin' your pardon, miss, sir, but I couldn't help overhearin'…" She twisted her apron. "It's just that my cousin Betsy, who works for the Rothburys, says her master—Mr. Edward Rothbury—he has a likeness of Miss Playford in his study. Don't know why it's there but in view of yer mentioning the gentleman, just thought I'd bring it up."

Caroline and Henry turned to stare at her, momentarily speechless.

"And Betsy says," Mary continued, emboldened by their attention, "that old Mr. Rothbury, before he met his maker, was thick as thieves with Miss Playford's father and that Miss Playford's father was as rich as Croesus. Mr. Rothbury managed his accounts or some such. Betsy says the young Mr. Rothbury's as honorable a gentleman as ever lived, and all them what works for him says so. Never raises his voice, pays fair wages, and keeps to himself mostly." She dropped her eyes. "Not that I were eavesdropping, but I just thought his interest in Miss Playford might be worth knowin', is all."

Caroline put her hands to her cheeks as she turned glowing eyes towards Henry.

"Why did I not insist that my sister-in-law accompany me to Mr. Rothbury's residence to quiz him when we first heard of the connection?" she asked.

"Because there really didn't seem much that he could help us with, considering he was only a lad who probably knew nothing since he joined the navy when he was fourteen," said Henry. And although his tone was measured, Caroline could see he was growing excited.

"But, if what Mary tells us is true," he said, turning to smile at Caroline's maid, "it would appear that Mr. Rothbury has a great deal more interest in Venetia than would be expected on such minimal acquaintance."

Caroline squeezed his hands, then, after a quick look about to ensure they were unobserved, launched herself into his arms.

"Oh, my darling Henry, we are on the cusp of discovery, I truly believe it!" she cried.

"I think we are far from the cusp, dear girl, but we are considerably closer," Henry cautiously agreed. "And I think the sooner you can persuade Amelia—who really is a good sort—to take you with her to visit Mr. Rothbury, the sooner we can get to the bottom of all this. Now, Mary—" He motioned to the little maid.

"Please turn your head away for just five seconds and promise you won't tell Caroline's mama you've seen me with her. Not that it'll matter since we'll be married within the month, come hell or high water!"

And with that marvelously earth-shatteringly wonderful promise ringing in her ears, Caroline happily succumbed as Henry kissed her deeply and thoroughly upon the lips.

Chapter Twenty-Eight

T O CAROLINE'S RELIEF, Amelia was easily persuaded. It seemed she was just as concerned by the rumors swirling around Henry, and held Lord Windermere in equally strong dislike.

Whatever the reason, the very next morning Caroline and Amelia were received by young Mr. Edward Rothbury, who, it appeared, had been reviewing the family ledgers which were spread on the desk before him. Though modest compared to the abodes of his wealthier acquaintances, the room reflected its owner's character—orderly, unpretentious, but tasteful.

At least, this was how Caroline regarded young Mr. Edward Rothbury, who'd inherited his London townhouse from his father, she'd recently learned. They were a family whose members had distinguished themselves through service to Crown and country, most notably on the sea. Oh yes, Caroline had worked hard to discover all she could about Mr. Rothbury in a very short time.

"Miss Weston, Lady Weston," the young man greeted them with a bow, rising as the maid announced them. "This is an unexpected pleasure."

"Mr. Rothbury, it was kind of you to agree to see us," Caroline replied as she and Amelia sank into the two chairs he indicated in his study, Amelia taking the most comfortable.

Of course, a married man would have ushered them into the drawing room, but Mr. Rothbury was a bachelor and Caroline suspected his study was the most respectable—and guest-ready—room available at such short notice.

Most people she knew would not have accepted such an impromptu visit at such an unfashionable hour. Caroline knew very little of Mr. Rothbury, personally, other than the brief encounters in ballrooms. No doubt he assumed that Amelia—respectable and married Lady Weston—was the one who had matters to discuss with him and that Caroline had merely tagged along.

"And no doubt you are curious as to the reasons we are here, when our acquaintance is so very limited," Amelia spoke smoothly. She was, of course, the elder, and a married woman. Caroline was merely a debutante, not able to speak for herself if convention were to be followed.

In an unusually subdued tone that quite betrayed her nerves, Caroline whispered, "Yes, you are very kind to receive us like this, Mr. Rothbury."

She knew decorum required that Amelia lead the conversation, but it was so very hard to keep her agitation at bay and not blurt out everything that that led to this visit.

"And how can I help you today?" Rothbury smiled, though a flicker of concern crossed his features. "Since you have intimated this is not just a social visit."

"No, I am here to speak to you about the Playford family and your father's dealings with Miss Playford's father," said Amelia, coming straight to the point. "I recently learned your father was Mr. Playford's financial advisor many years ago, and I have some questions."

Mr. Playford sent them an enquiring look. "It is true that my father served Mr. Playford a great many years ago but I went to sea when I was very young, so I am afraid I have little knowledge of the years of which you speak."

Amelia flicked a glance at Caroline. Clearly, she was unsure how to proceed.

"Did you ever meet Mr. Playford and his wife? Venetia's parents? Venetia herself, in fact?" Caroline asked, boldly using her friend's Christian name to see if it elicited any reaction.

To her astonishment she saw the color burn his cheek before he looked away briefly, resuming his quiet contemplation of the question before he went on, "I did meet Mr. Playford and his wife on a number of occasions before I went to sea, yes."

"What do you remember of Miss Playford, then?" Caroline asked. Yes, she was onto something, she was sure of it. "She'd have been a child, wouldn't she?"

"Yes, a child of eight. Very sweet disposition." Mr. Rothbury smiled. "Very talkative, I remember. She told me many tales of her dolls' imaginary adventures, though, as a boy of fourteen, I was perhaps not as attentive as she would have liked." He cleared his throat. "Clearly, she does not recognize me from those days, and why would she? Her parents died just after I went to sea, and I did not see her again until this season."

"But you remembered her." Caroline couldn't keep the excitement from her voice, eliciting curious expressions from the other two.

"Of course."

"And has she changed?"

Mr. Rothbury blinked at the oddness of her question. "She is not as... lively as I remember. But she has grown into the beauty I would have expected. Like her mother." He rose. "In fact, I have a likeness of the late Mrs. Playford amongst my late father's papers."

Caroline twisted her head, expecting to see him rifle through files of paperwork. Instead, the likeness was at hand upon his desk.

It was Amelia who said, mildly, "Perhaps you might make a gift of it to Miss Playford if it has no value to you?"

He reddened again as he resumed his seat. "Oh, it has value. But I had, in fact, planned to do as you suggest though... was unsure of when it might be appropriate to approach her."

"Why? Because she is to be married?" cried Caroline. "Why should that prevent you? She would want to receive it from *you*."

Again, Caroline realized her passions were somewhat inexplicable to Mr. Rothbury, and she put her hand to her mouth as she murmured an apology for her outburst, finally throwing caution to the wind and saying, "I'm sure she'd be very appreciative since her aunt kept all mementos of her parents from her on the grounds that Venetia has been nothing but a drain on her finances since she first took her in."

"I beg your pardon?"

This last had the effect of making Mr. Rothbury lean forward and Caroline, thinking he was grieved to learn of Venetia's ill treatment, went on, "Yes! Her aunt wants to coerce her into breaking her engagement to Henry Ashworth in favor of Lord Windermere for reasons that cannot be fathomed and which she explains only as that Lord Windermere is prepared to accept her without a dowry."

"Please, Caroline, I think that was a little too much information," Amelia admonished in an undertone. "Mr. Rothbury will not appreciate your wild talk."

"But it is not true."

Ignoring Caroline, Mr. Rothbury, clearly too agitated to remain seated, rose and again went to his papers, shaking his head as he said, "Miss Playford was well provided for when her parents died."

It was as if a great wall of snow had suddenly doused Caroline. For a moment, she was too shocked to speak.

Then, both Caroline and Amelia burst out in unison, "What?"

And Caroline went on, "How can you know this?"

"It was mentioned in writing by my father. I came across his letter after his death when I was going through his correspondence."

"Your father was *executor* of the Playford estate?" Caroline asked with a gasp, but Mr. Rothbury shook his head.

"No, his cousin was, and he had an understanding of the financial transfer that occurred upon Venetia's father's death." He shook his head. "A very reasonable annuity was settled upon Miss Playford. Her aunt was adequately provisioned to ensure the care and upkeep of her niece. It's all laid out here in conversation between him and his cousin, who was executor."

He handed Amelia several letters before returning to his seat.

Caroline leaned over Amelia's shoulder, scanning the angled, sloping writing while Amelia clicked her tongue, saying in tones of wonder, "It does indeed indicate that Miss Playford was far from penniless." She hesitated before sending Caroline an incisive look. "Are you sure you have properly interpreted your friend, and that Venetia was not representing her aunt as more… miserly than she was?"

"Venetia has *not* misrepresented the situation!" Caroline responded hotly. "I've known her since schooldays which were a reprieve to her since she didn't have to live under her aunt's roof. But since she was a child, her Aunt Pike has locked her up alone in a cupboard whenever she says a word out of place. Mrs. Pike constantly taunts Venetia for being penniless, which is why Venetia did not wed in her first season out. And yesterday I saw the bruises on her arm when—"

"Bruises?" Mr. Rothbury interrupted.

"Are you sure it wasn't some innocent accident?" Amelia asked. "That is a very serious charge you're making, Caroline."

Caroline was not going to walk this back. Mulishly, she said, "Her aunt has often been violent, and she was particularly so when she found Venetia in her study looking for letters from her father to Aunt Pike." Caroline was too deep into the situation to concern herself with the fact that she was speaking far more candidly than Amelia or any other lady of respectability would countenance. But something in Mr. Rothbury's eye, and his tone, suggested she *ought* to speak thus.

"Perhaps Mrs. Pike believed Venetia had no right to go through her aunt's drawers when her back was turned," Amelia suggested mildly.

Caroline drew herself up. She hadn't been going to say it, but now she just had to reveal the terrible confidence Venetia had relayed to her. She prayed it was a terrible lie, but since Mr. Rothbury knew so much about Venetia and her parents, perhaps he'd be able to refute it. It was a dangerous risk and perhaps Venetia would have begged her to remain silent, but Caroline could not.

Drawing in a deep breath, she burst out, "Mrs. Pike told Venetia that her parents were not married at the time of her birth. She said Venetia's father had been in love with *her*, but that Venetia's mother had enticed him away. Of course, Venetia needed to find these letters. Especially when her aunt told her that if she didn't renege on her marriage to Henry, Mrs. Pike would tell Henry that Venetia was—" she drew in a difficult breath, before whispering, "—illegitimate."

"What!?" cried Amelia, clearly outraged.

"Yes, and her Aunt Pike threatens to make this public knowledge if Venetia does not comply with her wishes and... marry Lord Windermere."

"Dear Lord!"

Caroline wasn't sure what part of her torrent of words elicited such shock from Mr. Rothbury, but he quickly shook his head. "I am sure that is quite untrue!"

Eagerly, Caroline leaned forward. "You have proof?"

Rothbury was silent for a moment. "Not proof. But it makes no sense with what I know of her father's financial affairs and everything else mentioned in my own father's correspondence."

Distracted by the arrival of the tea, he finally said, when the maid had deposited the tray upon the table and Amelia was pouring, "These letters that... Miss Playford discovered that were written by Mr. Playford to Mrs. Pike," he finally said. "Have you seen them yourself?"

Caroline, disappointed that Mr. Rothbury had not magically produced evidence of either Venetia's parents' marriage, or her birth, shook her head. "No, only Venetia has. They were in her father's hand, and she was dismayed to find that they really were letters from her father conveying affection towards her aunt prior to his marriage to Venetia's mother, who was Mrs. Pike's younger sister."

"So you have seen no other letters to either prove or disprove what Mrs. Pike says?" asked Mr. Rothbury. He reddened, then added, "Regarding the circumstances of her birth."

Caroline shook her head. Suddenly, she felt deflated. How could there be a solution to the conundrum which faced not just Venetia, but Henry and herself, before it was too late?

"I see." Mr. Rothbury rose and moved to the window, his back to Caroline as he gazed out at the garden. "And you believe Mrs. Pike would follow through on such a threat?"

How strange to be talking on such intimate terms, regarding such revealing matters, about Venetia, Caroline thought suddenly.

And how deeply invested in her situation he appeared to be.

"Without hesitation. She is utterly determined to see Venetia married to Windermere," said Caroline. "In fact, Mrs. Pike sent her off in a carriage with him, against her will."

"Against her will?" Mr. Rothbury turned, frowning, while Amelia blushed fiercely, murmuring, "Caroline, that should, perhaps, not be made public."

"No, it's a scandal!" Caroline cried, clenching her hands together to hold back the tears as she recalled her own horrors. She closed her eyes, refraining from mentioning the full extent of her own involvement as she said, "I prevailed upon Henry to go after her and stop him. Windermere threatened Henry with a pistol, but he managed to rescue her, and it was when they were at an inn that Mr. and Mrs. Gascoyne discovered them and insisted that Henry was honor bound to marry Venetia." Caroline put her face in her hands.

"Oh, Caroline," whispered Amelia, putting her hand on her shoulder. "I am sorry if Frederick and I did not offer the support that was needed at the time. I had no idea of the extent of Windermere's villainy." She hesitated. "For I think you were perhaps too close to the drama to relay it in all its awfulness."

"It is indeed awful," said Mr. Rothbury grimly. "Lord Windermere is not recognized for his kindness and charity, but I had no idea he represented such a threat."

"But what can be done, Mr. Rothbury?" Caroline entreated.

His look was pained. "You came here to ask what I knew of Miss Playford's father and his affairs. I've told you what I know: That the late Mr. Playford was a man of integrity, despite certain... indiscretions in his youth. Yes, I have to include that, although, from what I can tell, his marriage to Miss Playford's mother reformed him." He raked a hand through his hair in a gesture of frustration. "As for the current situation, surely Miss Playford, if she is soon to marry Mr. Ashworth, will be quite safe from the threat Lord Windermere poses?"

Frustrated, Caroline leaned back. "Her aunt threatens that if Venetia does *not* break off her betrothal to Mr. Ashworth, then she will reveal the truth of..."

She trailed off, and Mr. Rothbury sent her a sympathetic look. "I do not believe there is any truth to the woman's threats. So your friend, I therefore believe, is in no danger."

Amelia, who had been thoughtful for a while, interjected. "So you believe Mrs. Pike may have... embezzled funds that were set aside for her niece? Including her dowry?"

It did not escape Caroline's notice that Mr. Rothbury seemed to redden considerably at this. But his tone was calm when he said, "I do believe that to be the case and when Miss Playford is safely married and her husband, Mr. Ashworth, can investigate the matter, I shall do whatever I can to provide evidence to support Miss Playford's claim."

Caroline felt the blood fizzing in her veins, and she tried her best to remain unaffected. But not only Venetia's future hung precariously in the balance, so did Caroline's. Unable to hold back, she cried out, "I...I don't believe Venetia wants to marry

Mr. Ashworth. I don't believe he can save her, either. Please, Mr. Rothbury, she needs your help. Can't *you* offer for her? I know you admire her greatly. I've seen you all these weeks watching her—"

"Caroline! Enough!" Shocked, Amelia put her hand on Caroline's knee. "What can you be thinking? I do apologize, Mr. Rothbury." She rose. "We have detained you long enough, and you certainly did not expect a morning full of such disclosures and—" she fixed Caroline with a hard stare "—hysteria."

But Caroline was not to be deflected so easily, and she remained uncontrite. Her entire future rested on Venetia finding someone to wed who was not Henry or Lord Windermere. "Are you not looking for a wife, Mr. Rothbury? I heard it was so."

The corners of Mr. Rothbury's mouth tugged slightly, but his smile was rueful. "You heard correctly—"

"Then is Miss Playford not the ideal candidate? She is bright and quite lovely—"

"Caroline!" Amelia cried, trying to draw her away.

"She is all those things, I agree," said Mr. Rothbury, "but she is also betrothed to another man."

"But if she weren't, would you ask her?"

"Caroline!" Amelia gripped her sister-in-law's arm and tried to drag her towards the door and, although Caroline followed reluctantly, she stared over her shoulder for an answer.

Mr. Rothbury's expression was surprisingly conflicted.

"I would be honor-bound not to do so," he said.

"Even if she were unattached?"

"Even if she were unattached," he confirmed.

Caroline gasped. "Then it's true, after all, what her aunt said? About her parents not being married when she was born."

Mr. Rothbury shook his head, his eyes flaring with distress as he replied, "No, indeed, that would not be my reason! I very much doubt anyone would find evidence to bear up Mrs. Pike's scurrilous allegations surrounding the legitimacy of her niece. So, Venetia's aunt has no grounds on which to make her break her attachment to Mr. Ashworth. You can rely upon that, Miss Weston."

"But of course, if you have no feeling for her—"

"That is not true, either, Miss Weston."

"Then why?"

He shook his head, and there was sadness in his eyes. "That," he said, "I am honor bound not to tell you."

Chapter Twenty-Nine

CAROLINE ARRIVED AT Mrs. Pike's townhouse via the scullery, but the urgency of the situation overrode social niceties. The housemaid who admitted her and her maid sent a worried look up the corridor before pointing her directly to Venetia's bedchamber.

She found her friend sitting motionless at her dressing table, staring blankly at her reflection. Venetia's face brightened momentarily upon seeing Caroline, before misery reasserted itself.

"You shouldn't have come," Venetia whispered, glancing nervously at the door. "Aunt Pike has forbidden all visitors... especially you. I'm surprised Lottie let you in."

"Oh, Venetia, surely you know how cunning I can be. And don't worry, I shall be quick," Caroline replied, taking Venetia's cold hands in her own before sitting on the edge of the bed. "I *had* to see you before this evening's event."

"I shan't be attending." Venetia's voice was flat. "I've told Aunt Pike I'm unwell." She sighed. "Not that Aunt Pike took any account of that. I fear she will drag me there."

"But you must attend!" Caroline squeezed her friend's hands urgently. "But first of all, listen to me, Venetia. Whatever your aunt has threatened, whatever you fear about your parents, you mustn't throw Henry over publicly today."

Venetia's eyes filled with tears. "You don't understand. If I don't end the engagement, Aunt Pike will reveal everything about my birth. Henry will be humiliated, his family disgraced by association."

"Listen, Venetia! I have information that changes everything!" Caroline insisted. "I know you're frightened—"

"Terrified," Venetia corrected. "She means to force me away with Windermere, just as she did at the masquerade. Only this time, there will be no escape." A shudder ran through her slender frame. "Can you imagine being trapped in a balloon basket with that man? Hundreds of feet above the ground with no possibility of escape?" She sighed, and it was as if she deflated. "Well, I'm not going, so at least I won't be trapped in the basket of a hot-air balloon. That's one small mercy."

Caroline leaned closer to put her cheek against her friend's. "That won't happen, whether you go or not, I promise you. Your aunt has not done well by you, Venetia. She has been—" Caroline hesitated. Should she reveal the information divulged by Mr. Rothbury?

No, far better that the fine young gentleman who had admired Venetia from afar do it himself; that way, he'd paint himself in the light of Venetia's savior.

So she simply said, "Henry and I have made arrangements."

Hope flickered briefly in Venetia's eyes. "What sort of arrangements?"

"The fewer details you know, the better. But trust me when I say that you will not be eloping with Lord Windermere today." Caroline straightened, adopting a more casual tone. "Tell me, what do you think of Mr. Rothbury?" Now would be the time to ascertain if, perhaps, Venetia secretly harbored some kind of *tendre* for the kind, handsome gentleman.

Venetia blinked at the sudden change of subject. "Mr. Rothbury? I believe I might have been introduced. It is possible I may have danced with the gentleman. I do not remember."

This was deflating, thought Caroline, her spirits momentarily dampened.

But, injecting enthusiasm into her tone, she went on, "Truly? How extraordinary because—" Caroline rose, adjusting a ribbon on Venetia's dressing gown, keeping her expression neutral as she went on, "he's often at the same gatherings as ourselves. A tall gentleman with rather serious brown eyes and a kind expression. Surely you must remember him? He knows *you* for his father was financial steward to the Playford estates for many years, I believe."

"Heavens! Are you talking about Edward Rothbury?" Suddenly animated, Venetia smiled. "I last saw him when he was fourteen. Before he went to sea."

"Well, he's back in London and quite the young man. I can't believe you did not recognize him."

Venetia's brow furrowed before she blinked in surprise. "Yes, now I remember! After we were introduced, I believe I we performed the same quadrille. But he did not illuminate me. How was I to know this was the youth I'd followed about when I was only eight years old?"

"You did?"

"Yes, I thought him quite wonderful. For some reason, he had some tin soldiers and when our parents were engaged in some business, my dolls and his tin soldiers went into battle." Venetia paused, as she appeared to recall the details before she gave a delighted little laugh. "I remember telling him my doll, Bertha, was very timid, and that she wasn't sure she was brave enough to go into battle."

"What did he say?" Caroline prompted, for it seemed Venetia had drifted off into her own thoughts.

"He said that if the battle was worth fighting, then Bertha would find the courage." Venetia nibbled at her thumbnail. "He said that even the most timid can exhibit the greatest courage if the goal is important enough. And if the goal is freedom…"

Caroline gripped her friend's hands. "Oh Venetia, he really

said that? How prophetic! And to think that his words are coming back to you now after all these years. And that they're so true. Yes! You have to fight for it, Venetia. You have to fight for your freedom."

"You mean… not allow my aunt to coerce me into marrying Lord Windermere—?"

"Yes!"

"So I really must marry Henry instead—?"

"No!" Caroline shook her head fiercely, dropping Venetia's hands as she began to pace. "No, no, you do not love Henry, do you?"

Venetia shook her head. "But what else can I do but marry Henry… if I don't marry Lord Windermere, that is?"

Caroline tried to temper her disordered feelings, running her hands over her face in distraction as she said, "Marry someone who loves you. I mean, who *truly* loves you. Henry holds you in high regard, but he does not love you."

She had to say it. And she had to say it gently. She was afraid Venetia would take issue, but her friend merely looked sad.

"That is the worst of it." Venetia fiddled with her hairbrush and sighed. "If I knew Henry loved another, I could not bear to go through with it. But he says he doesn't—"

"What!? When did he say that?"

"When he was pressured by the Gascoynes to do the honorable thing and I asked him the question."

"Really? What were his exact words, Venetia?" Caroline tried not to sound as anxious and invested in the answer as she knew she did. But Venetia seemed not to notice.

"He just shook his head. And then we didn't really talk about it anymore. But—" Venetia looked up at Caroline, her expression appealing, "He would have said something if he loved another, would he not? He surely would not be so noble as to marry me if his heart was engaged to another?"

Caroline stilled. How could she answer this? If she confessed, right now, that she and Henry loved each other more than anyone else in the world, then Venetia would simply crumple before passively allowing herself to be married off to Windermere.

"You must marry the man who really *does* love you," she said again.

Venetia looked perplexed. "But there is no one, Caroline. And I am penniless. I have very few choices, you know."

"Then you must make the best of what choices you do have," Caroline said stoutly as she prepared to leave. "You simply *must* attend Lady Townsend's Comet Viewing Gala. Please promise? Tell your aunt that Lady Townsend, who is organizing the event, has specifically requested it. I'm sure it will not be as dreadful as you imagine."

Chapter Thirty

AN HOUR LATER, Henry couldn't decide between disbelief and hope as he paced the length of his study, Caroline watching him anxiously from her perch near the window. Her mama was out visiting and she had an hour at best before she needed to return home before her absence would be noticed.

"This is madness," he said finally, running a hand through his already disheveled hair. "Complete and utter madness."

"It's our only chance," Caroline insisted. "Think about it, Henry. Rothbury is perfect—he has connections to Venetia's family, a sterling reputation, and from everything I can tell, he's been secretly enamored with her for over a year." She decided to leave out the fact that Mr. Rothbury had actually been quite adamant about having no intention of offering for Venetia based on some apparently noble motive.

But what motive was that? Because she was currently betrothed to Henry? Well, tomorrow Venetia would *not* be betrothed to Henry. Not to please her aunt, though. She'd need to break her engagement at just the right time to deflect any danger of Mrs. Pike sailing in to push her into Windermere's evil clutches.

Henry shook his head. "Based on servants' gossip? And you expect me to trust the future of not only Venetia but ourselves to this scheme?"

"It's more than gossip," Caroline insisted. "Based on what I observed when Amelia and I saw him yesterday. And as for Venetia, you should have seen how her face lit up when she remembered him from childhood. When Mary told me he has her portrait, I didn't believe it. But in fact it's a portrait of Venetia's mother and he had it right there, to hand, among his papers. Nor did he want to give it up unless it was to Venetia directly."

Henry tried not to sound as glum as he felt. "Even if he does harbor feelings for her, it's rather unlikely he'd act on them. You say he's a man of integrity? Well, he knows Venetia is betrothed to me," he repeated.

"Then we must create a situation where they are unable to escape one another... directly after she breaks off her betrothal to you." Caroline moved to his side. "Two people, suspended hundreds of feet above London with nowhere to escape... Lady Townsend told mama there was no greater feeling."

Henry gave a short laugh. "How would you possibly mastermind such an event: first getting Venetia to break off our betrothal and then, within minutes, getting her to climb into the basket of a hot-air balloon with Mr. Rothbury? Alone. Besides, you have no reason to believe she has—or could develop—any feeling for Rothbury."

"I believe she could. You should have seen her face when she recalled him telling her that 'even the most timid can exhibit the greatest courage if the goal is important enough.'"

"But, I repeat—practically speaking? How do you propose to get Rothbury and Venetia into that basket together, when Mrs. Pike is determined to force Windermere upon her?"

Caroline smiled with more confidence than she felt. "I'll coordinate with Lady Townsend. At the appointed time, I will create a distraction for Mrs. Pike—"

"While I intercept Windermere," Henry finished, still skeptical. "And it'll all go to plan as it did when you threw those missiles through the window of Lord Windermere's hunting lodge?"

"Exactly." Caroline was not going to be deflected by his cynical rejoinder. "Meanwhile, Lady Townsend will guide Venetia to the balloon under the pretense of showing her how it works. You recall how persuasive she can be. And, you know, I'm quite sure she has a soft spot for Venetia and wants only the best for her, so I'm sure if I speak to her—"

"And Rothbury?"

"I'll say what needs to be said. Maybe I could ask him to verify some documents or matters regarding the Playford estate while the festivities are underway—documents that would show Venetia, clearly, that her aunt was telling lies when she told Venetia her parents had married after—" She blushed, before mumbling "—after her birth."

Henry swung round. "What?"

"They're lies, Mr. Rothbury says," Caroline soothed him. "Besides, you're not going to marry Venetia, so it wouldn't matter to you either way." Caroline hesitated. "In fact, this is what Venetia was intending to tell you tonight as a reason to break off your betrothal. Except that it won't happen in the way she or her aunt expect."

Henry stared at her, frozen to the spot. Then he let out a low whistle, and didn't even apologize. "My, my, Caro, what a clever, cunning mind you have inside that beautiful head of yours," he said, admiringly, if not poetically, before his brow furrowed. "Not that this will work, but Rothbury would be furious to be duped into the basket with Venetia. Alone. Meaning that... perhaps propriety would require that *he* married her rather than... me?" Despite himself, he grinned before letting out a long sigh. "Oh, Caro, this is all so masterful, and it would be so wonderful if there were even the slightest possibility that things could run to plan as you seem to imagine they might."

A moment of silence stretched between them. Then Caroline whispered, "I truly believe Mr. Rothbury harbors strong feelings for Venetia. And that being alone in the basket of a hot-air balloon would give him the opportunity to tell her this."

Almost wonderingly, Henry shook his head. "Just imagine if, by some miracle, Rothbury declared himself and Venetia accepted?"

Caroline stepped closer, raising her hand to gently brush his cheek. "Then we would be free."

"Free," Henry echoed, the word hanging between them like a precious, fragile thing.

"To follow our hearts," Caroline whispered, pressing herself against him and resting her hand against his chest. She felt his soft sigh as his arm went about her. "To be together, as we have longed to be."

His grip tightened. "It seems impossible."

"No more impossible than arranging for two unsuspecting people to fall in love in a balloon basket," she replied, smiling.

"When you put it that way…"

With a regretful sigh, Henry set her away from him as they heard footsteps in the passage. "I just fear that Mrs. Pike really will put enough pressure on Venetia to break off the engagement for no other reason than that I am still persona non grata. People look askance at me when I'm at White's. A mere sniff of scandal is enough to have one blackballed and each time I enter its hallowed precincts I'm in dread of being turned away."

Caroline put a comforting hand on his shoulder. "The reason they don't—and they can't—is that all this *is* merely gossip. Sir Frederick has done his best to put the word about that his mysterious lady in blue, this foreign Hungarian princess or whatever she was supposed to be, was actually a paid actress. I hear some wonder if it was a practical joke."

"Some might wonder that, but others don't. According to them, I transgressed during my time on the Continent and they are fully expectant that Venetia will withdraw from our arrange-ment at the final hour. And Mrs. Pike is fanning the flames."

Caroline sighed. "I wish Barnaby was called to account. The

lies have all but been proved. It's time for him to say it was just a jest or a cruel joke. Because Amelia heard the truth from the woman *he* hired to ruin your reputation. And yet Barnaby now studiously avoids you every time you want to challenge him. Does he think he can get away with this? To think he was once your friend."

Henry shrugged. "I had thought him so. And I'd thought Charlotte would believe in me. But she is quite under Barnaby's influence."

Caroline began to pace while she tried to mull over the conundrum. "Clearly Barnaby is in Lord Windermere's power. I don't know how or why, but he is playing to what Windermere and Mrs. Pike want. *Why* would he sully your name? Well, so that Venetia will break off your engagement, leaving the path clear for Windermere. We've essentially established that. But...what is Barnaby's role in this?"

Henry looked helpless and Caroline ran to him and put her arms about his waist. "Goodness and honor will prevail, my darling Henry!" she cried. "There must be a way of making Barnaby reveal his duplicity." Raising her head, she said, "I shall make Charlotte trick him into confessing the truth! Yes, that is what I'll do. And then, tomorrow, at the Celestial Comet Viewing, not only will we push Rothbury and Venetia together so that their attraction is undeniable, your name will be cleared by Charlotte revealing that her betrothed set up it all up as a joke or a wager. That way, Barnaby will not be embarrassed and perhaps lash out. I really don't trust him and am so very sorry Charlotte seems to be so taken in."

"So, now we have Venetia and Rothbury conveniently married off, and my name cleared." Henry shook his head in mock amazement. "You've thought of everything, haven't you?"

"Not everything," Caroline admitted. "I haven't yet decided what I shall wear to our wedding."

Chapter Thirty-One

T HE OAK-PANELED WALLS of Brooks's muted the murmured conversations of London's gentlemen seeking refuge from home and business. Henry, who had retreated there for a short respite after Caroline's visit, sat back in a wingback chair, ostensibly reading *The Times*.

But he was distracted and worried.

He hadn't realized how much his conversation with Caroline had rallied his hopes. Despite his skepticism at the time, he now had reason to believe all was not lost. Caroline had a wonderful ability to make him feel anything was possible.

But now, with the balloon ride fast approaching, and so much invested in the almost maniacal maneuvering required to somehow get Mr. Rothbury and Venetia into the basket alone— well, one minute it all seemed like reaching for the stars…

The next, anything felt possible.

Normally, a whisky and reading the newspaper calmed him, but right now, his nerves were on edge. He'd chosen a leather armchair away from the bow window where the greatest gossips gathered, in constant fear of being tapped on the shoulder and politely asked to leave.

The whispers of financial wrongdoing had not gone away, even though there was absolutely no proof.

Just as he was trying to force the worry from his mind, he spied the very man responsible for his tenuous grip on acceptance.

His very own future brother-in-law.

Henry lowered his newspaper slightly, careful to remain unobtrusive as he watched Barnaby enter and look around before his gaze settled on a solitary figure by the window—Edward Rothbury.

For a moment, Henry studied the man. Serious-featured, handsome in a traditional way, with dark hair and a coat from the best tailor. Could this man be Henry's salvation? Could Venetia suddenly form a *tendre* for him in less than twenty-four hours when she barely knew him?

With a sigh, he took a sip of whisky. Was Caroline's infectious enthusiasm nothing more than a pipe dream?

"Rothbury, isn't it?" Barnaby's voice carried just enough to reach Henry's ears. What business could Barnaby have with Rothbury?

Henry raised his newspaper to conceal his watching.

"James Barnaby. Forgive the intrusion and my ill manners for introducing myself."

Rothbury looked up, his face betraying mild surprise before settling into polite acknowledgment. "Mr. Barnaby. I know you by reputation, of course."

"Only good, I hope." Barnaby laughed, though there was a strained quality to it.

"My father was acquainted with yours, I believe," Rothbury replied neutrally.

Henry shifted slightly, angling himself to better observe. There was something calculated in Barnaby's approach that set his instincts on alert. And a frostiness in Rothbury's tone that Henry wouldn't have expected.

"Might I join you? There's a matter with which I believe you can assist me."

Without waiting for a response, Barnaby settled into the chair opposite. "I understand your father was steward to the Playford family for some years."

Rothbury's expression remained unchanged, but there was a curious stillness that conveyed his reluctance for this company.

"He was."

The reserve, which bordered on hostility, did not escape Henry.

"For decades, in fact!" Barnaby spoke with forced bonhomie. "What a remarkable friendship must have been built up between your father and that of my intended's dear friend." He paused to accept a whisky from a footman.

When Rothbury didn't reply, Barnaby continued, "I am to be married to Miss Charlotte Ashworth, if you did not know." After a slight pause, during which congratulations were clearly expected but not forthcoming, he went on, "And that is the reason I have accosted you like this."

Rothbury looked as if he were patiently waiting for Barnaby to get to the point.

"You see, my dear Charlotte is concerned for her friend, Miss Playford, and asked me if I could reassure her as to Miss Playford's..." he hesitated, clearly for effect, "future safety. I am sure your late father would have been just as concerned to be reassured that Miss Playford's future was not being... manipulated... by the wrong parties."

Rothbury toyed with his empty glass, the crystal catching the light. "Please speak plainly, Mr. Barnaby. I have no idea what you are insinuating."

Barnaby did not take this well but retained his easy manner. "My apologies. I merely wished not to cast public aspersions since we are in a public place. But if you are happy for me to speak plainly, then there are two reasons for Charlotte—and consequently myself—to have grave fears for Miss Playford's future."

Rothbury did not prompt him, clearly making this as awkward a conversation as possible.

"Mr. Henry Ashworth."

Henry nearly dropped his glass to hear his name spoken so clearly. Barnaby had done a poor job scanning for prying ears. He brought his newspaper up higher and hunched lower in his chair.

"A worthy bridegroom," Rothbury said, betraying nothing.

"A man mired in scandal," Barnaby countered to Henry's disgust. "Charlotte is distraught that her friend is too frightened to break off the engagement for fear of reprisals from Mr. Ashworth."

Henry tried not to let his anger draw attention to himself.

"I think your betrothed must be of a somewhat nervous nature." Rothbury's tone dripped scorn.

"It is not the womanizing I refer to. Rather, it is the financial irregularities. Charlotte fears this will all come to light too late as the marriage is planned for five days' time."

"I do not think the fears harbored by your betrothed have any grounds in reality."

Barnaby leaned forward, lowering his voice to a confidential murmur that nonetheless carried to Henry. "Perhaps you've not heard of the wager in White's betting book? A rather substantial sum placed against young Ashworth's financial ruin before the month is out. The names in that book would astonish you—men who don't make such bets lightly."

Rothbury's posture stiffened visibly. "Such wagers are the province of idle men with too much money and too little sense."

"Yet one whisper becomes truth when enough important men believe it so." Barnaby waited for a response. "It is well known that Miss Playford has no dowry. This is her third season out, and as she does not wish to reside permanently as some lowly companion to her Aunt Pike, she's prepared to marry against her natural inclinations."

Rothbury shifted uncomfortably. "I think we should not speak of Miss Playford's personal matters in public."

But Barnaby was just getting into his stride. "If Miss Playford were to find herself irrevocably tied to a husband she does not love, only to then discover she's the recipient of an enormous inheritance, would that not be a travesty of justice?"

What?

Henry nearly dropped his paper. What was Barnaby alluding to? Venetia had no relatives other than her Aunt Pike.

He waited for Rothbury to knock down Barnaby's argument with contempt and was surprised when instead he said, "I cannot respond to such speculations, Mr. Barnaby, and I am surprised you would think I would."

Henry carefully lowered the paper to view their expressions. Barnaby looked almost smug and expectant. Rothbury, for all his containment, looked wary, almost cornered. He made moves to rise, but Barnaby hurried on.

"You do know what I'm talking about, then, Rothbury. You are saying nothing."

"It is not my place to offer any thoughts on Miss Playford or her future prospects."

"But you know more than you're saying." Barnaby tried to detain him. Almost desperately, he continued, "My dear Charlotte is sick with worry that Miss Playford will become an heiress and free to do as she pleases... but only when it is too late."

"Then why does your betrothed not communicate her fears directly to Miss Playford?" Rothbury asked reasonably. "I have no idea why you think I can throw any light on the matter."

"Because you know the truth and you are doing Miss Playford a disservice by not revealing it—"

"I do not deal in speculation, Mr. Barnaby." There was a glint of something dangerous in Rothbury's eye. "Though perhaps I will, in view of what you've told me."

"No! No, you must not do so!" Barnaby responded with the first hint of real urgency. "I merely wished to understand where Miss Playford's future was placed. I asked out of concern, but I realize now that her hopes or fears should not be aroused."

Henry's heart thundered as Rothbury curtly excused himself and left the club while Barnaby followed at a distance, his intentions clearly foiled.

Dropping *The Times*, his whisky forgotten, a cold realization settled over him. This was no mere social maneuvering. Whatever inheritance Barnaby had alluded to was clearly real enough to cause genuine panic—not just in Barnaby, who wanted his suspicions confirmed, but in Rothbury too, who clearly knew the truth of it.

Chapter Thirty-Two

CAROLINE STARED AT Henry, open-mouthed. "Are you telling me that Barnaby insinuated that Venetia may be in line for an inheritance?" This was not something she had expected or even considered. But when she reflected upon the interview with Mr. Rothbury, it was plausible.

"Barnaby was certainly trying to pry information from Rothbury that, I must say, was not forthcoming," Henry replied, his brow furrowed. "Mr. Rothbury showed himself to be a man of few words and a great deal of caution. Barnaby simply showed himself up as a bully and a thug."

"That is exactly what he is, and I am distraught that Charlotte does not see it." Caroline fidgeted with the end of her shawl and sent a nervous glance at the entrance to the park. Mary, her maid, hovered nearby, her attention divided between her charge and a flower seller crying her wares at the gate. But as Mary was watching them, Caroline refrained from reaching out her hand to stroke Henry's arm.

The moment she'd received word from Henry, she'd slipped out of the house and across the street. Everyone, it seemed, was so involved with the competing events that night—with Lady Townsend's Comet Viewing Gala the most noteworthy—she felt confident her truancy would not be noticed.

Henry shrugged. "The sister who was once my greatest ally has been bewitched by Barnaby. And when he tells the world that I'm guilty of some foul felony, she will look at me sadly and agree with Barnaby."

"Then there is no time to lose in order to counter Barnaby's threat. He is working for Windermere, so it stands to reason that both men suspect Venetia is in line for an inheritance."

"And that is obviously the reason Windermere wishes to marry her."

"And perhaps Barnaby got wind of the information. Yet he is already in collusion with Windermere, is he not? Oh, Henry, there is much to discover and the sooner we speak to Rothbury, the sooner we will have answers," Caroline declared. "Clearly he knows everything."

"Yet is saying nothing."

"Well, of course he wouldn't, in public, to Barnaby. But time is running out, so I am going to petition him for the truth." Caroline swung round, her bonnet ribbons dancing in the breeze.

"Don't I even get a kiss?"

Caroline turned at Henry's plaintive tone and sent him an arch smile, her heart softening despite her urgency. "You will get a kiss after we get Venetia and Mr. Rothbury in that basket beneath Lady Townsend's balloon tomorrow afternoon. Come, Mary!"

And without waiting for a reply, Caroline hurried back home, quickly changed her clothing, and then made for her brother's house. She was relieved to find he was away, but her sister-in-law Amelia was at home.

Amelia, who was looking larger than Caroline remembered, even in the space of such a short time since she had last seen her, looked up with a smile when her sister-in-law was announced. She reclined on a blue damask sofa, her embroidery abandoned on a nearby table.

Caroline came straight to the point. After all, there was no time to lose. Lady Townsend's Comet Viewing Gala would be tomorrow, and there was much to do before then. Like find the reason behind Windermere's villainy and prevent Venetia from having to wed Henry so that Henry could marry Caroline.

"Please come with me this last time to Mr. Rothbury's townhouse. I promise I won't misbehave as I did the other day," she begged, clasping her hands before her. "I have found information that he will have to either endorse or deny, and Venetia's happiness depends upon it."

Amelia put her hand to her belly and glanced up with a regretful smile. "I really am not feeling at all the thing today, Caroline. And nor am I sure that it is wise to go rushing back to a gentleman's residence when you got into such a state last time. You really said some most inappropriate things. I don't know if he will even receive you."

Caroline didn't know what to say after such a rebuke. She could hardly venture out alone and unchaperoned, and she didn't know who else would accompany her to a gentleman's townhouse. Her mother would have a fit and outright forbid it.

Amelia sighed placatingly and then patted the sofa beside her. "I know you have taken a great deal of interest in the happiness of your friend, and for that I applaud you. But surely whatever information you have found can wait one more day. Besides, I am not convinced that Henry and Venetia would not make a very happy pairing. Do you really think it is right to meddle so?"

Caroline swallowed. She clenched her hands at her sides and closed her eyes as she felt the emotion bubbling close to the surface of her skin. She had the information that would make everything right. At least, she was almost certain that Mr. Rothbury had the information that would make everything right.

All that was needed was for Caroline to pry it out of him so he could announce the truth to the world, thus freeing Venetia and giving Caroline and Henry their chance at happiness.

Tears stung her eyes, and she had to grip the back of the sofa to stop her knees from giving way. The room's warmth suddenly felt oppressive, the scent of Amelia's roses cloying. She took a deep breath, hoping to gather her self-control, but instead exhaled on a sob.

"Darling Caroline, it's not all that bad, surely?" Amelia asked, sounding suddenly doubtful and concerned. She leaned forward, wincing slightly at the movement. "You are overwrought. Yes, Frederick has told me that as a child, you sometimes let your emotions get the better of you. And I know life can be disappointing, but we have to accept there are some things we cannot change. However, I'm not saying I won't help you because I am the first to agree that there is something very wrong about the situation regarding Lord Windermere, and the information Mr. Rothbury insinuated he had about Venetia's financial situation. On the one hand, I am wary about meddling; however, I do absolutely agree that it is important your young friend knows all the facts before she is committed in marriage. All I am saying is that surely waiting another day will not be detrimental to the cause in view of my feeling a little more delicate than usual today. Please don't cry, Caroline. You are very selfless to be so concerned about Venetia. It is very admirable."

"It is not admirable at all!" Caroline countered as she wept into her arms, supporting herself on the back of the sofa. The gilded clock on the mantel ticked relentlessly, each second carrying them closer to disaster. "Yes, Venetia is my friend, but she is also marrying the man I love. Henry and I have loved each other all our lives, but we only realized it too late, it seems. He was forced to do the honorable thing when he rescued Venetia from Windermere." Caroline raised her head, her cheeks flushed with emotion. "And now it seems he's going to marry Venetia after all—when neither of them love each other—because Venetia will only hear too late that she will inherit a fortune that will enable her to do as she pleases—"

"Caroline, Caroline, please calm yourself." With a frown, Amelia turned awkwardly on the sofa to pat her sister-in-law's arm, clearly surprised at Caroline's unexpected declaration. "You and Henry? Why, that is a surprise." She swallowed, her thoughts clearly in some tumult before she added, "But… there are still days before the wedding—"

"Amelia! There is no time to wait! Mrs. Pike is planning something evil this evening at Lady Townsend's Comet Viewing Gala." Caroline raised her head, wiping furiously at her tears. "I don't know exactly what she has in mind, but she is exerting all her power to make Venetia renege on marrying Henry so that she'll somehow submit to Windermere's pressure to marry him because Mrs. Pike says if she does not, she'll reveal to the world that Venetia's parents were not married before she was born and that Venetia is penniless when we know she's not. Yes, I want to marry Henry, and having this information confirmed by Mr. Rothbury would enable me to do so—but not if Henry's reputation is so compromised by whatever Mrs. Pike and Windermere have in mind, or if Venetia has already been spirited away by Windermere."

Caroline hadn't finished speaking before Amelia was on her feet and ringing the bell, her face set with newfound resolve.

"You've convinced me, Caroline," she said with a sigh. "It was not all smooth sailing when I married your brother and, yes, you could have bowled me over with a feather to learn that you and Henry are in love… but I am now well persuaded of the need to move with urgency." She pressed a hand to her lower back as she straightened. "Ah, Millie—" She put her hand to her belly, closing her eyes briefly as she apparently suffered a pang. "Please fetch my gray pelisse, bonnet, and gloves. Caroline and I are going to pay a call."

Chapter Thirty-Three

CAROLINE GAZED WITH barely suppressed excitement at the maritime maps that adorned the walls to the entrance of Mr. Rothbury's townhouse in Bloomsbury.

Soon, all the answers to her burning questions would be revealed.

Mr. Rothbury would announce that Venetia was an heiress and then confess his undying love for her. He would agree to a romantic proposal in a hot-air balloon at Lady Townsend's Celestial Comet Viewing Gala…

And all would be well!

She was just deciding whether to wear white for her wedding to Henry—since Princess Charlotte had made white so fashionable for wedding gowns—or if a more practical pale pink or blue would be wiser, when they were greeted by the butler who'd been summoned by the housemaid who'd answered the door.

"Lady Weston, Miss Weston, my apologies, but Mr. Rothbury is not at home," said the elderly butler, who carried himself with the disciplined bearing of one who might have served at sea.

Stricken, Caroline glanced at her sister-in-law. "I apologize for our unexpected visit, but we do not mind waiting."

The butler shook his head. "Mr. Rothbury left half an hour ago and is not expected back until the day after tomorrow."

"The day after tomorrow!" gasped Caroline, turning to Amelia with a look of entreaty. "But tonight is the Celestial Comet Viewing. He can't possibly miss that!"

"Did he say where he was going?" Amelia asked. She hesitated before disclosing, "My sister-in-law and I have a rather important matter to discuss with him, and I fear tomorrow might be too late."

"It will definitely be too late!" Caroline cried with an unladylike lack of restraint.

"That sounds rather dire," came an unknown masculine voice from the darkened corridor and Caroline turned to see a lanky, copper-headed gentleman emerge from the shadows. He bowed before sending Amelia a quizzical look. "Lady Weston, delighted to see you again, most unexpected." Then, appearing to register that she did not recognize him, he introduced himself. "I am Mr. Rothbury's cousin, Mr. Arthur Bowman, here in London on business. Business which, in fact, precipitated Mr. Rothbury's departure." He gestured for the ladies to follow him into the drawing room, saying, as he indicated a blue silk settee for them to sit, "Perhaps, if you tell me what business you have with my cousin, I can assist?"

Caroline felt close to tears. What possible help could an unknown cousin of Mr. Rothbury's provide?

Until Amelia, clearly remembering their connection, said, "Why, you are Mr. Maximilian Bowman's son—Your father was the late Mr. Playford's solicitor. Mr. Rothbury mentioned that was the case, and I do recall now that we have met."

"At the Pump Room in Harrogate three years ago. Yes, my cousin told me of your interest in the Playford family, so I am not surprised to see you," he said, crossing his lanky legs and offering them a smile. "And it was my dashing, post haste, from Winchester to inform Edward of developments that precipitated Edward's unexpected journey. Alas, I know he was greatly looking forward to tonight's entertainment."

"Mr. Rothbury is going to Winchester?" exclaimed Caroline.

"Why, that is—"

"Ten hours on the road," Mr. Bowman supplied. "But fear not, he is not going to where I have come from, and his journey is only half that time."

"Still!" cried Caroline, with no less desperation. "That means he will not be back in time to prevent a catastrophe at Lady Townsend's Comet Viewing Gala."

Mr. Bowman raised an eyebrow. "That sounds rather… dramatic. How could my cousin have helped prevent a catastrophe?"

Caroline hesitated, then at a nod from Amelia, said with as great an economy of words as she was able, "Mr. Rothbury indicated he had information that would belie the claim of my friend Venetia Playford's aunt that she is penniless. Tomorrow—I very much fear—Miss Playford will be pressured into agreeing to a marriage she might not otherwise have made had Mr. Rothbury been able to provide proof of his claims she is not… the pauper her aunt makes out."

"I am sure she can stall for a little more time before making any binding promises," Mr. Bowman said reasonably. He contemplated the matter a moment, then added, "Of course, it's easy to verify that Miss Playford was more than adequately provisioned when her father died. And the business which sent my cousin across the county will make her even better provisioned if matters proceed as I believe they will." He smiled. "So I am sure your friend, Miss Playford, has nothing to worry about it. All will be revealed with my cousin's return. More tea?"

Caroline's heart was galloping as she shook her head at the offer. Clearly, Mr. Bownman did not grasp the urgency. "Miss Playford's Aunt Pike maintains—and has done for ten years—that Venetia is quite penniless. Are you telling me that your father, who was Mr. Playford's solicitor, has proof that this is not the case?"

"Miss Playford, while not exactly an heiress, had a very substantial sum apportioned to her upon her father's death, and I believe it will not be too long before she, in fact, will *be* a considerable heiress."

"An heiress!" Caroline gasped, raising her eyes at Amelia's startled look. So, Barnaby's hunch had been correct. Carefully, she asked, "How can that be when her aunt has maintained for years that she has nothing?"

Mr. Bowman shrugged. "Mrs. Pike has been receiving Miss Playford's quarterly allowance since the death of her parents—a not inconsiderable sum that should have provided handsomely for her niece's comfort and education. The proof can be provided, if it is requested. That is all I can tell you."

This was shocking news in itself, but Caroline asked, "And you say she is to inherit *more*?"

"Miss Playford's paternal great-uncle, Mr. Leonard Harrington, is in failing health. Having no direct heirs, he indicated some months ago the possibility that he may change his will and instead of leaving his estate to his closest male relative—a distant second cousin—he'd leave it to his great-niece, whom he has never met though he has followed her progress." He hesitated. "On occasion, this has been on the basis of reports from myself."

"He asked you to spy on Venetia?"

Mr. Bowman smiled. "Mr. Harrington merely asked for a quarterly report on the general conduct of Miss Playford—which naturally was beyond reproach—as well as the conduct of his second cousin, James Barnaby, which, unfortunately, he found... disappointing."

"James Barnaby?" cried Caroline, nearly dropping her teacup. "You know him?"

"Why, he was involved in trying to... to abduct my friend Venetia in order to force her to marry Lord Windermere against her will. The two men were working in collusion." So *this* was the reason for Barnaby's involvement. With a shaking hand, Caroline carefully put down her teacup. "It appears James Barnaby has a... a motive to see Miss Playford wed to Windermere if the men had an arrangement!" She burst out, "Perhaps he didn't just intend to see her forcibly married to Windermere, perhaps he intended to… to harm her if she stood between him and his inheritance."

"Caroline!" Amelia's sharp tone brought her back to earth. "You are making some very serious allegations which can never be proven—though… it is astonishing to learn of Barnaby's involvement and… yes, the fact Miss Playford might pose a threat to his future inheritance explains a great deal."

"And Lord Windermere…" Mr. Bowman said thoughtfully. "Despite appearances, the gentleman *is* in financial difficulties. I can well imagine he would be in search of an heiress to wed."

"But Venetia is not yet an heiress," Amelia pointed out. "And might never be."

"No, but maybe Windermere intended to kidnap her and simply wait… considering Mr. Harrington was so ill and likely to die soon," said Caroline. "And her aunt was going to make some excuse while she was locked away in his hunting lodge. For money, of course!"

A small kernel of satisfaction lodged in her breast at the look exchanged between Amelia and Mr. Bowman. They did not think her logic far-fetched.

"We shall just have to be patient, Caroline," said Amelia, rising. "There is nothing more we can do until Mr. Rothbury returns."

"But what about the comet viewing?" Caroline cried. "Mrs. Pike has threatened Venetia that if she doesn't break her betrothal to Henry and agree to marry Lord Windermere, she'll tell the world she's—" she swallowed, then, blushing, added, "illegitimate."

Mr. Bowman gave an incredulous laugh. "Why, that's preposterous! There's no question of her legitimacy."

"You have her birth certificate, then? The records of her parents' marriage?" asked Amelia.

"No, but Mr. Harrington, a stickler for such things, would not consider leaving his estate to a bastard—forgive my language," said Mr. Bowman, reddening.

Caroline said quickly, "If Mr. Rothbury cannot return in time to reveal the truth about Venetia's circumstances, then we must find another way to prevent her from being manipulated into Windermere's clutches."

"That should be easy," said Amelia. "She just needs to know of her changed circumstances."

But Mr. Bowman shook his head. "Mr. Harrington is a man of fair-weather temperament. He may well change his mind at the last minute once again. I would not get the young lady's hopes up."

Caroline fisted her gloved hands. "Then it's up to us to stop Venetia from succumbing to her aunt or Lord Windermere's machinations. We'll set a trap. One that will expose Mrs. Pike's deception before all of society." She nearly stamped her foot. "Tomorrow night, all will be revealed!"

Mr. Bowman regarded her with a smile. "You are quite formidable, Miss Weston. What kind of trap did you have in mind?"

Caroline drew in a lungful of air while her mind worked furiously. "One that exposes Mrs. Pike's greed to the whole world," she said, though in truth she didn't really know what could be done.

Rising abruptly, she said, "I must speak to Lady Townsend to arrange some important matters with her. I suspect she wants Henry and Venetia go up in that balloon… and there is much she needs to know—"

"But it is late, Caroline, and your mama will expect you home," said Amelia with a regretful smile. "And I suspect you know how unlikely it is that Mrs. Pike will allow Venetia any contact. A note to your friend to caution her not to break off her engagement is the best that can be done under the circumstances."

But Caroline could tell by Amelia's look that her sister-in-law feared, as much as she did, that Mrs. Pike had too much to lose to allow the possibility of any such correspondence reaching her niece before her plans were fully realized the following day.

Chapter Thirty-Four

EUGENIA WAS IN her element. If there was one thing she excelled at beyond matchmaking, it was organization, and today required a masterful application of both. The bright morning had dawned clear and crisp—perfect weather for a balloon ascent, with its gentle southerly breeze and high visibility that aeronauts prized above all else—and now, as noon approached, the riverbank hummed with the excitement of London's finest, all gathered for Lady Townsend's Comet Viewing Gala.

"The champagne must be placed in the basket at the very last moment," Eugenia instructed the footman. "And ensure the blankets are of the finest wool. The air grows quite chilly at altitude, especially as we'll be ascending in the late afternoon when the air currents are most stable."

Oh, didn't she know everything about balloon rides?!

She consulted her list, checking items off with brisk efficiency. The large blue-and-gold balloon dominated the clearing, its enormous silk envelope partially inflated and undulating gently in the light breeze. Nearby, the aeronaut tended to the brazier that would soon heat the air to fill the balloon completely, occasionally glancing skyward to assess the cloud formations with an expert's eye.

"You appear to have thought of everything," Lord Thornton remarked, materializing at her side. "One might think you were planning a royal procession rather than a simple balloon ride."

Eugenia's heart gave a traitorous little leap at his voice. "There is nothing simple about a balloon ascent, Thornton. Particularly when so much depends upon its success. Mr. Beaumont assures me these are the most favorable conditions he's seen this season—clear skies, steady winds under eight miles per hour, and no sign of thermal turbulence."

"Indeed, nothing is more serious than your grand plan to rekindle the flame between Miss Playford and young Ashworth." His eyes twinkled with amusement. "Though I confess I'm curious how you intend to ensure they—and only they—are the ones who ascend when it really does appear that Mrs. Pike and Lord Windermere consider it in their interests that they do not."

"I have made certain arrangements with Mr. Beaumont," she replied, flicking a glance at the aeronaut who was now carefully checking the wicker basket's moorings and the strength of the hemp ropes that secured the envelope. "He understands exactly which passengers are to be permitted into the basket."

"And what of Mrs. Pike? I observed her in animated conversation with the aeronaut not half an hour ago."

Eugenia's smile turned triumphant. "I anticipated that maneuver, Lord Thornton. Mr. Beaumont has been generously compensated for his loyalty to my instructions. He knows to delay if conditions aren't perfect for our... purposes." Eugenia sent him a meaningful look.

"More generously than Mrs. Pike might compensate him for the opposite?" This came from Lady Pendleton, who had approached with silent stealth. She smiled as she positioned herself rather deliberately between Eugenia and Lord Thornton.

"Lady Pendleton! How delightful you could join us." Eugenia's greeting was sincere, if somewhat distracted, as she noted another item on her list. "I wasn't certain if the other entertainments tonight would trump my modest little gathering." How strange was this confidence and ability to speak to Lady Pendleton without self-censoring in case she should offend or speak out of turn.

"I wouldn't miss it. An opportunity to witness either triumph or catastrophe is always worth attending." Lady Pendleton studied the balloon, then turned back to her friend. "Though I must say, dear Eugenia, your optimism borders on the delusional. Mrs. Pike has been plotting Miss Playford's match with Windermere for months. Do you really believe she'll allow her plans to be thwarted by something as trivial as your instructions to an aeronaut?"

"Not trivial at all," Eugenia corrected, watching as Mr. Beaumont adjusted the cords that controlled the balloon's crown valve. "Carefully considered and well-executed. Just like Mr. Beaumont's preparations. Late afternoon is the most auspicious time for a successful ascent—the ground has warmed all day, creating gentle thermals that will carry them aloft with minimal turbulence."

Oh, she'd recited those lines and learned them by heart, just to win Thornton's admiration.

"But what if something goes amiss?" that gentleman now asked, his tone gentler than Lady Pendleton's but no less concerned. "What if Windermere or Mrs. Pike somehow intervenes at the crucial moment, putting Miss Playford's reputation into jeopardy? Have we not seen the signs?"

"Or what if your perfect match is not so perfect after all?" Lady Pendleton added. She hesitated, and when Eugenia looked up, her friend was frowning as if she truly were concerned. "I told you I believe this is not a love match and that I've heard rumors that in fact it is a match made through honor; that young Henry's heart is, in fact, engaged by another."

Eugenia waved away these objections, despite her niggling doubt. "Idle gossip, nothing more. Henry and Venetia are ideally suited. They simply need to be reminded of that fact, away from the poisonous influence of Mrs. Pike and Lord Windermere."

"And a balloon ascent will accomplish this reminder?" Lady Pendleton raised a skeptical eyebrow. "As I recall, you and Lord Thornton shared such an experience two years ago, and it led to his sudden departure for diplomatic service abroad. Hardly an auspicious precedent."

Eugenia felt her cheeks burn as she carefully avoided Lord Thornton's gaze. "Different circumstances entirely."

"Really?" Lady Pendleton's eyes darted between them.

Eugenia busied herself adjusting an already perfectly positioned basket of refreshments as a crew member tossed another bundle of straw into the brazier, sending a plume of hot air into the expanding envelope. "The situations are not remotely comparable. Henry and Venetia are young, in love, and perfectly matched in temperament and interests."

"Yet I barely see them speak to one another," Lord Thornton pointed out. "And Miss Playford looks increasingly like a prisoner being led to execution rather than a bride approaching her wedding day."

"Precisely why this intervention is necessary!" Eugenia turned to face them both. "Don't you see? Two years ago, that balloon ride showed me the world from a different perspective. For a few precious moments, floating above London, with nothing but the occasional gentle creaking of the wicker and the soft roar of the fire, the petty concerns of society fell away. Only what truly mattered remained."

She couldn't help the softening of her voice as she added, "It was… transformative."

"Transformative or not," Lady Pendleton interjected, "your plan depends on Miss Playford and Mr. Ashworth actually entering the balloon together. Yet right now Mrs. Pike is marching her niece toward Lord Windermere, and the girl looks positively ill with dread."

Eugenia quickly scanned the growing crowd. Indeed, there was Venetia, paler than her white gown, being practically dragged by her aunt toward Windermere, who stood conversing with Mr. Barnaby near the refreshment tent.

"Fear not," Eugenia said with more confidence than she felt. "I have contingencies in place."

"Such as?" Lord Thornton prompted.

"Caroline Weston will distract Mrs. Pike at the crucial moment. I shall speak to her as soon as she arrives. Meanwhile, I will instruct Henry to approach from the opposite direction. Mr. Beaumont has instructions to effect the release the instant both are aboard." She nodded decisively, watching as the aeronaut checked his pocket watch. "All perfectly timed. By four o'clock, when the afternoon air is most stable and the light most golden, they'll be aloft."

"And if Windermere physically prevents Henry from approaching? The man is not known for his restraint when thwarted." Lady Pendleton's question held genuine concern beneath the acerbic tone.

"Or if Miss Playford herself refuses to participate?" added Lord Thornton. "She appears to be under considerable duress."

Eugenia faltered for the first time. "She wouldn't. She couldn't possibly prefer Windermere to Henry."

"I am sure she does not," Lord Thornton said gently. "But fear is a powerful motivator. And Mrs. Pike has had days to work upon her niece's fears, whatever they may be. Remember," he added, "Miss Playford does not have the choices afforded to her had she been an heiress."

A cold finger of doubt trailed down Eugenia's spine, but she squared her shoulders resolutely as she watched Mr. Beaumont signal that the envelope was nearly fully inflated, the silk now straining against its moorings in the perfect afternoon conditions. "Then we shall simply have to ensure that fear does not triumph today. Excuse me."

Moving purposefully towards the balloon, she heard Lady Pendleton murmur to Lord Thornton, "She's either the most brilliant strategist or the most spectacular meddler in London."

"Perhaps both," came his amused reply, followed by what

sounded suspiciously like, "It's rather magnificent, isn't it?"

Eugenia wasn't sure whether to be bolstered by the suggestion of praise, or concerned at Lady Pendleton and Thornton's familiarity.

Chapter Thirty-Five

HENRY WAS IMPRESSED as he wove his way through the throng of London's elite gathered for Lady Townsend's spectacle.

The afternoon sun reflected off the enormous blue-and-gold balloon that dominated the clearing, its silk envelope fully inflated, straining against the ropes that tethered it to earth. Temporary pavilions with fluttering pennants had been erected along the riverbank, while liveried footmen hurried through the crowd bearing silver trays of refreshments.

What a magnificent setting to put right all wrongs!

Henry spotted Venetia immediately, standing near the balloon basket in her white gown, looking as delicate as porcelain against the robust chaos of the scene.

"Ladies, let me procure you refreshment," he said, his genial tone belying the churning in his belly. In the next few hours, he and Caroline required a great deal of luck to ensure Venetia would neither succumb to pressure nor suffer crushing disappointment if they revealed the possibility of a liberation that might not be forthcoming. Only Mr. Rothbury knew the answer to that—and he wasn't here.

Still, Henry was not going to allow his optimism to be diluted.

"Please don't leave me, Henry."

Henry had been about to procure Venetia a glass of lemonade when her plaintive request made him turn to see Lord Windermere advancing towards them. There was a malevolent gleam in the older man's eye, and unconsciously, Henry balled his fists.

"Windermere," he said, his tone barely polite. "And Barnaby," he added, not bothering to keep the acid from his words. "What an extraordinary afternoon our hostess has laid on for us."

"She has indeed," Lord Windermere said, glancing about. A knot of finely dressed revelers stood just feet away—Lord Liverpool was speaking with Lady Ponsonby and Sir William Elford.

"And look who else I happened to come upon," said Windermere with an undisguised sneer. "Why, it is the Princess Katarina von Esterházy. Otherwise known as the mysterious lady in blue."

Dear Lord—there she was! The same young woman who'd destroyed Henry's reputation at Lady Henderson's ball.

For the first time, his optimism faltered. Where were his supporters? Caroline's sister-in-law had discovered proof the young woman was an actress who'd been paid. Yet clearly, the rumors had not been sufficiently quashed.

"Henry Ashworth, where is your honor?" Barnaby taunted him. "The princess has been waiting for redress, but yet again you have let her down." He raised his voice just loud enough for their neighbors to hear.

Several heads turned in their direction. Lady Ponsonby, never one to miss potential gossip, nudged Sir William and inclined her head towards the brewing confrontation. Lord Liverpool frowned but remained watching with ill-concealed interest.

Henry felt Venetia's hand grip his arm. He sensed rather than saw her panic. Indeed, his own panic was rising. He saw Caroline in the distance—she had stopped in her progress across the lawn, perhaps sensing that drama was about to unfold.

The sight of her sent a familiar pang through his heart. Her golden hair caught the sunlight, and he could see her blue eyes were wide with concern even from this distance. In another life, he would be at her side now, planning their future together. Instead, he stood here, trapped by duty and honor, about to be publicly humiliated.

"I told you," said Henry, "I have—with all due respect, madam—never met the Princess Katarina."

"Then it is a great mystery as to why her brother has been receiving payments from you and now claims that you have reneged on a financial arrangement made to compensate the princess for certain oversights on your part. Is that not right, Barnaby?" Windermere turned to his companion.

A little to one side, Mrs. Pike looked on, her beady eyes gleaming with malevolence.

"You know I have nothing to hide and that this is pure fabrication." Henry turned his head, hoping to see understanding in the eyes of the cluster of onlookers that had grown as Windermere's voice carried across the lawn.

Instead, he saw only the avid interest of those who enjoy a scandal, and the growing disapproval of those whose good opinion he had always valued. Sir William was shaking his head, while Lady Ponsonby whispered behind her fan to the Countess of Lieven.

"Fabrication?" Windermere laughed, the sound cold and triumphant. "I have here"—he withdrew a folded paper from his waistcoat—"a draft drawn on your father's bank, made out to Count von Esterházy, dated merely three weeks ago. It bears your signature, sir. Do you deny it?"

Henry stared at the paper, confusion washing over him before it was replaced by anger. "It is a forgery! I have signed no such thing and you know it!"

"Yet here it is," Windermere thrust the paper forward, "for all to see. And when questioned about this payment, the count revealed the most distressing story about his sister's honor and your broken promises."

Barnaby stepped forward, his expression grave. "I'm afraid it's true, Henry. The princess has been quite forthcoming about your… association."

Henry's head swam. The forgery was excellent, but forgery it must be. He had never met this princess. Amelia's investigative work had proved she was an actress, paid by Barnaby to play the part.

But neither Amelia nor Sir Frederick were here to back him up.

"This is unconscionable," Mrs. Pike suddenly declared, her voice cutting through the murmurs of the growing crowd. "To think that my niece would be married to a man of such low character! A man who trifles with a lady's affections, only to cast her aside and deny all knowledge when confronted!"

She turned to Venetia, whose face had gone bone white. "My dear child, you cannot possibly continue with this engagement. Not when Mr. Ashworth has so clearly demonstrated his unworthiness."

"I have done no such thing," Henry protested, but his voice lacked the conviction it needed. Too many eyes were upon him, too many ears eager to hear his downfall. "This is a conspiracy, designed to—"

"Designed to what?" Windermere interrupted smoothly. "To protect an innocent young woman from a fortune hunter and a libertine? Yes, I suppose it is."

Mrs. Pike stepped forward, her face a mask of righteous indignation. "Mr. Ashworth, I insist that you do the honorable thing and release my niece from this engagement immediately. Surely even you must see that continuing with this charade would only cause her further pain and humiliation."

Henry looked desperately at Venetia, who stood trembling beside him, her eyes downcast. He reached for her hand, but she withdrew it slightly, whether from her own doubt or fear of her aunt, he couldn't tell.

"Venetia," he began, his voice low, "you cannot believe—"

"I think we have heard quite enough," Mrs. Pike interjected, taking Venetia's arm firmly. "Come away, my dear. Lord Windermere has kindly offered to escort us to the supper table."

Chapter Thirty-Six

B URNING WITH SHAME, Henry watched her leave. He was
aware of the opprobrium on the expressions of those who
had witnessed the spectacle. No one came to offer support;
clearly no one believed Henry.

In the distance he saw Caroline hurrying towards him, a
dainty figure in white muslin, her pink sash trailing behind her.
She looked distressed and his heart cleaved with longing for the
girl who would always support him.

Well, he thought, there is nothing I can do if Mrs. Pike is so
determined to discredit me. But if I am free to marry the woman I
really love, then surely no public shaming is too great a price to
pay.

But as Caroline neared, her mother stepped into her path,
gripping her daughter's arm. A short, intense tussle followed, but
soon Lady Weston was joined by Lady Hartfield, and Caroline
was forcibly led towards one of the crowded supper tables. And
though the sight of her desperation as she looked over her
shoulder was some compensation, it was not enough to raise
Henry from the depths of despair.

Feeling the greatest pariah, Henry took an awkward step
towards the balloon.

The aeronaut, a wiry man whose name he learned was

Beaumont, was making final preparations for the ascent. His face was tanned and leathery and Henry noticed his powerful hands, stained with coal dust and callused from handling ropes, as he checked the moorings. His practical attire of dark trousers and a worn leather waistcoat over a serviceable linen shirt made him look more like a sailor and worlds apart from the genteel society surrounding him.

Beaumont was currently adjusting the wicker basket that hung beneath the magnificent envelope, checking the secure attachment of several mysterious canvas bags tied to its interior. The brazier that would heat the air was already lit, its gentle roar occasionally punctuated by a louder whoosh as the flames caught a new supply of fuel.

The aeronaut glanced up as Henry neared, touching his cap in a rough salute. There was a simple, trusting air about him as he said proudly, "Evening, sir. Come for a closer look at the apparatus?"

"Something like that," Henry replied, his voice hollow. "Quite an impressive contrivance."

"That she is, sir. Finest balloon in London, if I do say so myself." Beaumont patted the basket with pride. "Been flying her for nigh on five years now, and she's never let me down."

Henry nodded absently, watching as the man checked a compass that was securely fastened to the rim of the basket.

"You're preparing for a lengthy journey," Henry observed, noting the provisions stored within.

Beaumont hesitated, giving Henry a shrewd look. "You know something of ballooning, sir?"

"Not really. I just wondered."

The aeronaut straightened, wiping his hands on his trousers. "Well, since you ask… more than usual lengthy. Most unusual."

"Oh?" Henry tried to sound merely curious as he hoped the aeronaut was as forthcoming as he had started out being. Perhaps he could be gently prodded into revealing more than he intended if Henry asked the right questions.

"But, of course, the balloon today will be up in the air and back down within the hour, since there will be a few guests eager to ascend."

"Lady Townsend has arranged for a lottery to take just two."

"Just two on a lengthy ascent?" Henry offered a colluding smile. "Lady Townsend is known for her outlandish matchmaking schemes. This sounds like the most outlandish of all. Why, I'd almost believe she thought she could whisk her chosen likely pair to—"

He stopped, the wind suddenly whooshing from his lips as he finished, "Gretna Green."

No, surely not, he thought, however the aeronaut's eyes had widened in surprise. "Got it in one, young man," he said, snapping his fingers. "Well, I should say that her ladyship had planned a short ascent of less than an hour. But no sooner had she walked away than I had a visit from another party, offering a handsome sum to alter the arrangements."

"Good lord! What sort of alterations?"

Beaumont lowered his voice, glancing around to ensure they weren't overheard. "I'm to take the balloon free of its tethers once the passengers are aboard and fly north. As far as the winds will carry us, though the gentleman was most specific about wanting to reach Scotland."

"Scotland?" Henry's brows rose. "So, this gentleman specifically wants to go to Gretna Green?"

"The very place mentioned." Beaumont nodded. "Though how he expects me to steer a balloon with such precision, I can't say. We go where the winds take us, and that's the truth of it. Still… anything to make a body happy."

"But those aren't Lady Townsend's instructions, are they?"

"No, and nor do I have the wind to take us all the way to Scotland for they are beyond my control."

"Then what will you do?"

The aeronaut shrugged as he turned back to tightening a rope. "I aim to please both parties. It's the winds that will carry whoever hops in that basket when the conditions are right for the ascent."

"And that's what you told the gentleman?"

The aeronaut smiled. "I told the gentleman what he wanted to hear, o' course."

Henry looked about him, spying Venetia in the distance, flanked by her aunt and Lord Windermere.

"And the passengers? Did he specify who would be joining you?"

"A gentleman and a lady, that's all I was told. Though I gathered the lady might be… reluctant." Beaumont looked uncomfortable at this admission. "I don't hold with forcing anyone, sir, but the payment was substantial. My wife's been ailing, and the doctor's bills… But, like I said," he added, more comfortably, "I made no promises. It all depends on the winds."

"Of course," Henry murmured, his mind working furiously. Windermere had already succeeded in the first part of his evil plan: discrediting Henry.

Now he intended to force Venetia into an elopement—but instead of conveying her to Scotland in a carriage which could be waylaid, he planned to fly her there.

With her engagement to Henry broken and Henry's reputation in tatters, Venetia would have no defender.

"When are you scheduled to depart?" Henry asked.

"Maybe an hour. Maybe three. Though I've orders to be ready when the signal comes." Beaumont pointed to a red flag planted near the balloon's tethers. "When that's waved, I'm to prepare for immediate departure."

Henry sent another glance across the lawn, where he could see Windermere deep in conversation with Mrs. Pike. They'd risen and were part way down the grassy slope. Venetia stood at her aunt's side, looking pale and distressed. Caroline was nowhere to be seen, likely still under her mama's watchful eyes at the supper table.

Desperately, Henry fought for inspiration. Dependable Caroline was not here. And Rothbury had decided to leave at the most crucial moment? And Amelia, with her quiet good sense, was not here to state publicly what she'd learned regarding the so-called princess.

Maybe the best way to protect Venetia in the short term was simply to ensure there was not an equipage available that could whisk her so effectively out of reach as a hot-air balloon.

"Mr. Beaumont," Henry said, "what would you say to another change of plans? One that might spare you any moral qualms about unwilling passengers, and would still provide for your wife's care?"

The aeronaut regarded him thoughtfully. "I'd say I'm listening, sir."

"The gentleman who approached you—Lord Windermere—is not someone whose orders should be followed. He intends harm to the lady in question."

Beaumont's simple face hardened. "I've no stomach for that sort of business."

"Nor I. Which is why I propose that when the time comes, you and I ensure that the balloon carries a different pair of passengers altogether."

"And who might that be, sir?"

Henry took a deep breath, hardly believing what he was about to suggest. "Myself and... someone else. Someone who deserves the chance to escape as much as I do."

He thought of Caroline, of her desperate look as she was dragged away. Of all the pain and longing they had endured while trying to do the honorable thing for Venetia's sake. Perhaps now, with his reputation already destroyed and the engagement effectively ended, they could seize this one chance at happiness.

"I'll need your help, Mr. Beaumont. And I promise you'll be *very* well compensated for any inconvenience."

Chapter Thirty-Seven

"EUGENIA, PLEASE DON'T do anything rash."

Thornton's hand on her arm might have made her stay. Any touch from him would have, under different circumstances. But now, Eugenia pulled away—not because she wanted distance, but because she needed to ensure nothing stood in the way of a more permanent kind of touch.

Yes, the wager.

Despite her wavering conscience over promoting a match between Miss Playford and Henry Ashworth, she had to win the wager if she were to enjoy Thornton's continued company.

But that altercation she'd just witnessed didn't bode well. Miss Playford, pale and frightened, was being led away by her aunt and Lord Windermere—the most dangerous threat of all.

The girl's future could not lie with that man.

Eugenia quickened her pace, but as she drew closer, it was clear she couldn't intervene. Mrs. Pike's expression was grim, Lord Windermere had Miss Playford's hand firmly clasped to his arm, and on his other side loomed the lout, Mr. Barnaby. Really, what Miss Charlotte Ashworth saw in that dull-eyed bully was beyond her. Not that it mattered now.

What mattered was preserving the tenuous balance that had existed ten minutes ago—before Windermere began closing in.

She overheard Mrs. Pike say, "Take her to the tent over there. Yes, she needs to recover after the great shock of Mr. Ashworth's perfidy." Clearly staged for any bystanders.

Eugenia, just feet away, could do nothing but step back.

Perhaps it was best to remain near the balloon. She turned toward the aeronaut, who was feeding coal into the brazier, its flames licking upward.

"Mr. Beaumont," she said, trying to keep her voice steady, "there's been a slight upset. May I remind you of your instructions? I trust you remember them?"

He gave her a bland, questioning look. "Of course, m'lady. I'm to take up the young lady and gentleman you pointed out earlier."

"And *no one else,* Mr. Beaumont. That is vital."

He looked hesitant. But she was paying him handsomely. There wasn't much more she could do.

Still, she couldn't linger by the balloon as hostess of such a grand gathering. She returned to Thornton and Lady Pendleton, seated in cane chairs with glasses of champagne in hand.

Their looks were pitying.

"All is not fair in love and war," said Thornton. "Poor Miss Playford is completely at the mercy of that menacing aunt." He sighed. "And Henry Ashworth has been the center of the most dreadful scene. Yes," he said at Eugenia's enquiring look. "The lady in blue returned, and Mr. Barnaby outright accused the young man of all manner of fiendish dealings."

Lady Pendleton twirled her glass. "And I think Mrs. Pike just ended the betrothal for both of them."

Eugenia let out a gasp! "No! That cannot be allowed." She tried to see triumph in Lady Pendleton's tone, but could not.

"And you must accept that there's nothing to be done, Eugenia," Lady Pendleton went on. "For a moment, I thought you were about to throw down your glove at Lord Windermere's feet. Pistols at dawn, and all that."

"I wouldn't put it past you," said Thornton. "Your boldness

of late has been… unexpected." Admiration colored his tone.

"I saw you speaking to the aeronaut," Lady Pendleton added. "Trying to meddle in the course of true love again, I suspect? It won't work. If Windermere has the aunt's blessing, there's little anyone can do. I think it's all over for your wager." She sighed. "Poor Miss Playford. A young lady is so vulnerable."

"Not if she has independent means," muttered Eugenia, rubbing her temples. "Poor Venetia is being bartered like a token. Lord Windermere is obsessed—with her beauty, and perhaps her compliant nature. Why else pursue her if she has no dowry? At least *I* was provided for," she added. "Poor Miss Playford… to have her papa gamble everything away. So out of character!"

"Very out of character," remarked Thornton. "Didn't know much about the family but I heard nothing of financial or gambling problems. Strange."

"Well, he did tarnish his reputation by jilting Elizabeth Pike for her younger sister," said Lady Pendleton. "Perhaps that explains the aunt's spite."

"I didn't know that," Eugenia said, looking up. "Why, that explains a great deal! No kind relative would force her niece into marriage against her will—which is clearly what's happening—unless she had a good reason." She straightened. "If this is due to spite—or anything else, for that matter—I won't allow it!"

Thornton chuckled. "You're a matchmaker to be reckoned with."

"Indeed," said Eugenia, with a faint smile. "You say she's not in love with Ashworth? That may be. But with no other options, the least I can do is ensure she *doesn't* marry that scoundrel, Lord Windermere." She exhaled. "Matchmaking is not for the faint-hearted."

Lady Pendleton's eyes gleamed. "And your wager with Lord Thornton? That has *nothing* to do with your concern?"

Eugenia felt her cheeks grow warm. "The wager is now… incidental. What matters is doing what's right."

"Of course," Lady Pendleton said dryly. "And what if your

aeronaut's instructions have already been countermanded? I saw Windermere with him not half an hour ago. A purse exchanged hands."

"What?" Eugenia sat bolt upright. "He wouldn't dare!"

"I think he would," Thornton said quietly. "Men like Windermere don't stop when they want something. And he clearly wants Miss Playford—or whatever fortune she might possess."

"But the girl has no fortune." Eugenia worried at her lip as her mind raced. "We all know that—"

Thornton's eyes were fixed on Miss Playford, now seated between her aunt and Lord Windermere across the lawn.

"Yes, that's what we were meant to believe," he murmured. "But I'm beginning to wonder if there's more to her story than meets the eye."

Chapter Thirty-Eight

"YOU'RE TO GO and bear your friend, Miss Playford, company," Barnaby said, his hand heavy on Charlotte's shoulder as he gestured towards the supper table. His fingers pressed through her silk gown—a physical reminder of his control. "She's too jittery for Windermere's liking, and we don't want a repeat of that nasty business from a few weeks ago."

Around them, lanterns strung between the trees cast golden, flickering light, throwing dappled shadows across the manicured lawns.

Charlotte swallowed and tried to steady her voice. Barnaby had taken to speaking to her in this curt, bullying tone more often, and she felt powerless to stand up to him. The last time she'd objected—even mildly—he'd gripped her wrist so tightly the bruises had lingered for a week, dark beneath her lace gloves.

And now he wanted her to sit with Venetia and Windermere? The very idea made her skin crawl.

Still, she summoned a modicum of courage. "I'm not sure Venetia really wants to marry Lord Windermere." Her voice was soft but steady, barely audible above the string quartet playing nearby under the canvas pavilion.

Barnaby's head whipped around. His voice snapped like a whip. "Windermere is wealthy and powerful. Venetia will want for nothing. And she can't marry your brother—not after his disgraceful behavior. It's a lucky escape, I'd say."

His eyes glittered with a familiar hardness, his cheeks flushed with champagne.

Charlotte swallowed again, resisting the truth that threatened to spill from her lips. "I still can't believe you really found evidence against Henry—my own brother."

"You saw it yourself," Barnaby said, squeezing her shoulder. "The letter. The signed draft. Now go and sit beside Venetia. Keep her at the table. Windermere can't afford for her to faint or make a scene." His fingers dug deeper.

"She'd have every reason to faint, after what she's endured," Charlotte said quietly, then moved off at the warning in his eyes.

It wasn't far to the supper table, but she took a detour towards the balloon, fascinated. The massive silk envelope strained against its moorings, billowing gently in the evening breeze. The wicker basket beneath looked absurdly small—fragile, even—for something meant to carry people into the sky.

Could it truly float into the heavens and away from all this?

She imagined herself drifting high above the garden party, all her troubles shrinking into nothing. When had her life become so entangled with fear and compromise? Barnaby had seemed charming once—her parents had approved. When had that charm turned cruel? And how had she let him twist her into someone so afraid, so unsure, so silent?

"Can I help you, miss?"

Charlotte startled. The aeronaut stood beside the balloon, a weathered man with kind eyes and a face browned from the sun.

"Lost your way? Or are you one of the young people I'm meant to take up tonight? Miss Playford, perhaps?"

Charlotte stared. "Miss Playford? Is she one of the people going to the moon?"

The aeronaut laughed warmly. "Not quite. The moon's a long way off. But we might reach Gretna Green—that's only a few hours' plain sailing, by my reckoning. Are you excited? Once your young man arrives, I'll cut the rope, and off you'll go." He gestured to the basket, neatly outfitted with blankets and what looked like a small hamper.

Charlotte's heart pounded. "There's something I must do first," she said, and turned quickly, slippers sinking into the damp grass as she hurried towards Venetia.

At the supper table, Venetia sat like a porcelain doll—still, pale, unreadable. Lord Windermere loomed beside her, casting a shadow despite the dozens of flickering candles. Mrs. Pike sat across from them, ever watchful.

"Barnaby sent me to see if you were feeling better," Charlotte said, approaching with a bright smile that felt painfully false. "Perhaps a little air would help?"

Venetia began to rise, but Windermere's voice slithered across the table. "Venetia has all the air she needs. Soon, she'll have even more." The silky menace in his tone sent goosebumps across Charlotte's arms.

"Then perhaps she'll accompany me to the retiring room," Charlotte said smoothly. A perfectly acceptable pretext.

She extended her hand. Venetia's fingers trembled as they closed around hers.

"Don't be long," Mrs. Pike snapped.

Once they were out of earshot, Charlotte hooked her arm through Venetia's and leaned close. "The aeronaut mistook me for you. He's been instructed to take you and a gentleman to Gretna Green. Venetia—Windermere *is* planning to abduct you, and your aunt is helping him. Barnaby too. He's lied about Henry, forged evidence—I know it now. But if you don't escape tonight, you'll be Lady Windermere by morning."

Venetia said nothing. She only stared up at the stars.

Charlotte gave her a shake. "You *don't* want to marry Windermere. I know you don't."

"I don't," Venetia said, her voice flat. "But what choice do I have?"

"You have *us*. Henry will help you escape. I'll take you to the balloon right now. You can fly away to safety. To freedom!"

Venetia's expression remained unchanged. "But I won't go to Gretna Green with Henry."

Charlotte recoiled. "You *believe* the lies about him?"

"No. I know they're lies. And I know he's a good man. But he doesn't love me. I think he never did."

"He'd marry you in a heartbeat if you met him at the balloon and said you would."

"Yes. Because he's honorable. But he's in love with someone else, Charlotte."

Charlotte blinked. "That's not true. I'd know. He's my brother."

Venetia tilted her head. "Have you not seen how he looks at Caroline?"

Charlotte frowned. "They grew up like siblings. You're imagining things."

"I thought so too. Until I intercepted a look between them." She drew in a shuddering breath and shook her head as she murmured, as if to herself, "How did I miss it before? And yet, it was so... revealing. The tenderness in their expressions—Charlotte, it was as if the world melted away. I saw it in their eyes. True love. And how did I know? Because that is how I have always wanted the man I love to look at me. And that certainly isn't Henry." She drew herself up and her look was sharper this time as she added, "Because Henry is in love with Caroline."

Charlotte was silent, her mind racing. Could it be true? She pictured Henry with Caroline and remembered the way his voice softened when he spoke to her, the way Caroline lit up in his presence.

"But then... why did he propose to you? Why did you accept?"

"You know why. Because society expected it after the Gascoynes all but demanded it. He saved me from Windermere, and it was the gentlemanly thing to do. And I accepted, because I was grateful. But neither of us loved the other."

"You never loved him?" Charlotte whispered.

"I admired him. I still do. But my heart has always wanted someone to love me for myself. And I knew Henry's love was based on something... different. Even if I haven't admitted it."

Charlotte reeled. Everything she'd believed—about Henry, about Barnaby—crumbled.

"All this time," she said slowly, "Barnaby's been lying. About everything."

Venetia sent her an enquiring look. "Lying about Henry? Well, I was sure Barnaby was making things sound worse than they were but... I don't know anything about such matters. Charlotte...? What is it?"

"I'm thinking I've been a coward. Henry's reputation is in tatters because I was too afraid to stand up to Barnaby. But no more."

She seized Venetia's hand. "We're going to find Henry. We're going to that balloon. You'll be safe tonight—and tomorrow, I'll reveal the truth."

Venetia's eyes widened. "But what about Windermere? My aunt? They'll come after me."

"All the more reason to hurry." Charlotte's voice brimmed with determination. "It's time someone told the truth. And it has to be me."

She pulled Venetia through the throng of laughing guests, hearts pounding, skirts catching on the grass. Windermere was still at the table, but—

"Charlotte!"

Too late.

She turned—Barnaby was there. His hand clamped onto her shoulder, yanking her back, while his other seized Venetia's wrist.

"No, Barnaby!" she cried, struggling as never before.

But she knew he would not be persuaded to let her go. Not now.

Chapter Thirty-Nine

ORLORN, CAROLINE STOOD a short distance from her mama and friends, gazing up the hill as she watched Venetia from afar.

It had been no good. Her attempts to protect her friend from Windermere had ultimately come to nothing. There was the young girl, once so vibrant and full of life, now a shell of herself as, once more, she sat imprisoned between Windermere and her Aunt Pike.

Caroline watched as Windermere raised a glass of champagne in unison with Mrs. Pike, who dug her niece in the ribs with her elbow, whereupon Venetia dutifully raised her own glass in what was clearly a toast to the success of the evil plans of those who would control her life. The crystal flutes caught the golden light of the sun, sparkling like tiny beacons across the distance.

"Caroline! What are you doing? Come back this moment!" It was her own mama's strident voice instructing her to obey. But unlike Mrs. Pike, Caroline's mama wanted only the best for her, even if "the best" ran counter to what Caroline believed was best for herself.

Dutifully, Caroline returned to her mother's side.

"Why so glum, my girl? This is a magnificent occasion, and you will not attract a husband with a turned-down mouth. You look as if you have swallowed a lemon." Slanting a glance at the hill, Lady Weston added, "It looks like you are no longer in the running as a potential wife for Lord Windermere. I can see Venetia looking mighty pleased with herself for dodging an inconvenient pairing with Henry—for all I've always liked the boy. Clearly, though, we have no idea what someone is really like, and who would have guessed that the lad we have known all our lives was a forger and a philanderer?"

Caroline took some comfort from the fact that her mama truly did appear sad and disappointed as she snapped her fan open and closed with agitation.

"A forger, Mama?" Caroline's fingers twisted nervously in the soft fabric of her white muslin gown as she prepared to do battle and stand up for the man she loved.

"He forged his father's signature to pay off the brother who objected to his sister, the princess's ill treatment."

"And where did you come by this gossip, Mama?"

"Why, it is being spouted in every salon and drawing room. His sister, Charlotte, even testified to seeing the incriminating evidence." Lady Weston lowered her voice as a group of ladies walked by, nodding politely.

"I find that hard to believe." Caroline summoned all the energy at her disposal to respond to the scurrilous and patently untrue gossip her mother had picked up. "Henry has been maligned. Amelia discovered the truth herself. Alas, she does not go about much these days, so cannot counter the gossip. And Sir Frederick has been away. But it's Lord Windermere who is the monster." She gazed across the lawn, where clusters of elegantly dressed guests gathered beneath white canopies, the men's dark coats stark against the colorful gowns of the ladies.

"Watch what you say, Caroline." Lady Weston sent a scandalized glance about her as if afraid her daughter may have been overheard speaking so ill of a man whose reputation was, believe it or not, pristine.

And it looked like it would stay that way.

While Henry, poor Henry, was likely to have to live with the stain upon his character unless Amelia could disseminate the truth or Charlotte could be prevailed upon to speak the truth. She'd seemed so motivated to do so earlier...

Until Barnaby had arrived.

It seemed the forces of evil really were stronger than truth and justice.

A string quartet played a soft melody in the distance, the music floating across the party like a delicate veil.

Finally, Caroline was roused from her reverie by Lord Windermere arising together with Mrs. Pike and Barnaby. Venetia, of course, was in their fold, and together they wandered down the hill towards the balloon. The enormous silk creation strained against its ropes, its vibrant blue and gold panels billowing gently against the darkening sky. The wicker basket swayed invitingly, adorned with ribbons and flowers for the special occasion.

"Mama, they have not announced who is going up. Lady Townsend said the winners would be announced after supper. Have you heard anything?" Everything was happening too soon and suddenly Caroline was more afraid than she had ever been.

"I am sure it will not be you, Caroline, unless you and I are the lucky pair, for you need a chaperone. But I don't want to go up in that dreadful contraption, exciting though it is to many others." Her mother's tone was peevish before finally displaying a modicum of sympathy. "I know you are agitated about your friend, but really, there is nothing you can do. I am not the only one who thinks Venetia has done better than could be expected to win the high regard of Lord Windermere."

Caroline ignored her as she took in the scene. The first stars were appearing in the lavender-tinged sky, and servants moved among the guests, lighting paper lanterns that glowed like fireflies in the gathering dusk.

And then whatever equilibrium she'd managed to conserve was shattered.

"No, no, no," she said under her breath as she moved towards the balloon.

"Caroline! What do you think you are doing?" her mother snapped, hurrying after her daughter, who was heading towards the balloon. "Come back this moment and stop interfering. You always did want to poke your nose into business that wasn't yours. And no, I do not want you speaking to Henry."

For Caroline had spied Henry across the expansive lawn, and as their gazes locked, she saw he shared her concern. His chestnut hair was slightly disheveled, as though he had been running his hands through it in frustration, and his green eyes blazed with determination even across the distance.

Windermere and Mrs. Pike were most definitely leading Venetia with purpose towards the basket where the aeronaut was waiting expectantly, his hands upon the thick rope that tethered the balloon to the ground, ready to unleash it at a command. Windermere's silver embroidered waistcoat glinted in the torchlight, while Mrs. Pike's distinctive feathered bonnet bobbed nearby.

Where was Lady Townsend? Surely she did not condone this? Lady Townsend had all but sponsored Venetia with Henry, so Caroline had heard. It had given her comfort that what appeared to be happening in front of her eyes—another kidnapping— would not come to pass.

But when she looked around, she saw Lady Townsend far in the distance and could not make out whether that lady had observed what was happening. The hostess's ruby red gown was visible among a crowd of admirers, but she seemed thoroughly distracted by her duties.

The aeronaut, his weathered face beaming with excitement, was gesturing animatedly to Windermere. "Just step in carefully, m'lord—that's the way—and offer the lady your hand. Mind the edge there, it's a bit unsteady." His voice carried on the evening breeze as he continued, "Never you worry about a thing. The winds are favorable tonight, and you'll have the most magnificent view of the comet. Might even see all the way to Scotland, if the night stays clear. Some say it's good luck to kiss your ladylove when you're closer to heaven than earth."

Caroline heard all this as she hurried closer, Henry closing the distance from the other side, but they were going to be too late. And, besides, what could a young girl do in the face of such adversaries? The sweet smell of the balloon's burning coal made her feel ill.

"Henry, stop them!" she called out, but of course he could do nothing, though he tried.

Lunging forward, his face flushed with exertion and indignation, he cried, "Windermere! You cannot do this!" But Barnaby stepped smoothly into his path.

Mrs. Pike—with help—had already all but lifted Venetia into the basket, the girl's face a mask of resignation as Windermere prepared to join her. The aeronaut, sensing tension but bound by his payment—for Caroline had observed another purse changing hands—continued his preparations, glancing uncertainly between the parties.

And then Caroline heard another sound—

Or, rather, was aware of something else momentous happening.

For suddenly, attention transferred from what was happening at the balloon to what was happening at the crest of the hill.

The crowd fell silent. Even the music seemed to pause, and all faces turned toward the unexpected arrival.

"Oh my goodness," Caroline murmured as she clutched her hands to her breast. "I don't believe it." The cool evening air suddenly felt charged, raising gooseflesh on her bare arms.

For there was a man on horseback galloping towards them.

The most unlikely man she would have thought to have thrown Lady Townsend's Comet Viewing Gala into such disarray. His black stallion's hooves thundered on the ground, sending clods of earth flying as they charged down the hill.

"Miss Weston?" She heard her name being called. And then, "Where is Miss Playford?" The deep voice carried across the lawn, silencing the buzzing conversations.

"I truly think someone has come to save the day," said Henry, using the opportunity when everyone's attention was elsewhere to take Caroline's hand. His warm fingers closed around hers, giving her an unexpected surge of courage.

"It's Mr. Rothbury." Caroline whispered his name like a prayer, watching as the last rays of sunlight caught the brass buttons on his riding coat, making them shine like gold against the darkening sky.

Chapter Forty

"STOP!" MR. ROTHBURY'S voice rang across the lawn, commanding and urgent, silencing the murmur of conversation as effectively as a thunderclap.

Caroline's heart did a leap of joy, it seemed, as the gentleman galloped directly towards the balloon, his riding coat, breeches, and stock flecked with mud. The stallion beneath him was lathered with sweat, nostrils flaring.

It must have been a hard and desperate ride.

Gasps of shock rippled through the assembled guests. Lady Polkinghorne's fan fluttered frantically as she whispered behind it to the Countess of Lieven. Several gentlemen stepped forward as if to intercept this wild intrusion, while others merely gaped at such an unprecedented breach of decorum. Even Mrs. Pike had frozen in place, her hand still gripping Venetia's arm at the edge of the basket.

As Mr. Rothbury reined his horse to a dramatic halt mere yards from the balloon, Caroline could see he clutched a leather portfolio in one hand. Documents spilled precariously from its edge, and carefully he ordered them, retaining his mount, high above the crowd, his eyes never leaving Venetia's bewildered face.

"Miss Playford," he called, his voice carrying clearly across the suddenly silent gathering, "I am here to speak urgently with you. For you have been the victim of a grave injustice and at last I have the proof."

"Henry, can you believe it?" Caroline turned towards Henry, gripping his hand even tighter as her heart filled with joy.

They stepped back to the periphery of the crowd. They knew what was going to happen, and it was more important for more people to hear with their own ears the proof that Caroline had feared would never be verified.

"What is the meaning of this and who are you?" Windermere demanded, putting his hands on Venetia's shoulders in a show of ownership. By this stage, he and Venetia were both standing in the basket, the aeronaut with his meaty fists gripping the thick rope ready to cast off.

The magnificent blue-and-gold balloon strained against its tethers like a living thing eager for freedom, the silk rustling in the evening breeze. Golden flames from the brazier beneath cast flickering shadows across the faces of the assembled crowd, who had drawn into a tight circle around the scene. The ladies' bright gowns formed a colorful backdrop against the darkening sky, while gentlemen in evening black pressed forward, expressions ranging from scandalized to delighted at this unexpected entertainment. Even the servants had paused in their duties, champagne trays forgotten as they watched the drama unfold.

"I am Edward Rothbury, but it was my father with whom you would be more familiar, I believe." He slanted a steely look towards Mrs. Pike. "Yes, Mrs. Pike, my father was financial steward to Mr. Richard Playford—Miss Venetia Playford's father. After his death, I went through his correspondence and discovered some anomalies with what appears to be the current status of Miss Venetia's financial situation."

Mrs. Pike's face contorted with rage, her complexion changing from alabaster white to mottled crimson in an instant. "This is a private family matter!" She turned to the aeronaut. "Captain Beaumont, I insist you release the tether immediately!" she shrieked.

Around them, guests pressed closer, necks craning and ears straining. The Dowager Duchess of Richmond clutched at her companion's arm in shock, while Sir William Elford adjusted his spectacles with trembling fingers. Young debutantes exchanged wide-eyed glances of delicious scandal, while their mamas fluttered fans vigorously, torn between propriety and the irresistible pull of emerging gossip.

"For God's sake, cut the rope!" Lord Windermere demanded, his voice hoarse. "We need to depart immediately. And certainly before the ravings of a lunatic threaten the happiness of my bride-to-be."

"Unwilling bride-to-be!" Parting the crowd, Henry stepped forward. "You have tried once already to spirit Miss Playford away against her will, and it was because I intervened to prevent it that your abduction plans were thwarted."

There was a collective gasp. All eyes were on Henry now. He stood tall and proud, his shoulders squared and chin lifted in defiance. Caroline saw the Gascoynes huddled together near the edge of the crowd, Mrs. Gascoyne's face a picture of confusion while her husband nodded slowly, as if pieces of a puzzle were falling into place.

Proudly, Caroline watched Henry finally make his mark in the way destiny ought to have engineered matters: as a noble, honest, brave young man; not the philandering forger he'd been wrongly painted.

And Mr. Rothbury let him speak for now; to fill in the gaps, because he clearly recognized that this was a story that had many sides.

And because, at last, there was an audience ready to hear the truth.

"Yes, honor demanded that I make Miss Playford an offer of marriage because we were caught in what others deemed to be a compromising position. Let me reassure everyone else that our predicament was only due to the fact that I had chased after the carriage in which you, Windermere, had forced Miss Playford in order to abduct her, and that when I tried to wrest her back to safety, you threatened me with a pistol."

The crowd erupted in exclamations of shock and disbelief. Caroline looked about her with wonder.

Barnaby's face had gone ashen, his eyes darting about like a cornered animal seeking escape. The Gascoynes' expressions shifted from doubt to dawning comprehension. Windermere snarled like a wounded beast, his handsome features twisted into something almost unrecognizable. Mrs. Pike's thin fingers curled into claws at her sides.

On the other side of the balloon, Caroline saw Lady Townsend watching with undisguised fascination, her head tilted toward Lord Thornton as if sharing observations, while Lady Pendleton's eyes gleamed with a satisfaction that surprised Caroline.

"What utter nonsense!" shrieked Mrs. Pike, turning to appeal to the crowd. "The man who stands before you is the very man who was publicly shamed for forgery and philandering. Like a dog, he is unable to bear seeing Lord Windermere winning the hand of the young woman he loves. So he spouts lies and slander. Who would you believe?" She sent an inquiring look around the onlookers, her arms spread wide in theatrical appeal. "Would you believe an upstanding man of integrity, a man of vast fortune who wishes only to benefit my penniless niece? Or would you believe the discredited Mr. Ashworth, who is in collaboration with Mr. Rothbury? What do you know of Mr. Rothbury, who has only now arrived in London after years doing who knows what on the Continent? Perhaps he is a fortune hunter himself, or worse, someone bent on revenge for some imagined slight!"

"With all due respect, Mrs. Pike, I think the facts will speak for themselves." Mr. Rothbury, still astride his horse, tapped the leather satchel for effect. "When I made plans to leave yesterday afternoon, it was to procure the evidence needed to support the fact that you, Mrs. Pike, were given a substantial sum of money for the care of your niece, Miss Venetia Playford."

Mrs. Pike drew herself up, her face a mask of righteous indignation, eyes flashing dangerously in the fading light. "That money from Richard Playford, Venetia's father, was to compensate me for reneging on his marriage offer to me."

A ripple of scandalized whispers went through the crowd. "Yes, breach of promise," Mrs. Pike went on triumphantly. "Richard Playford was to marry *me* before my younger sister Cassandra enticed him. Yes, she brought the family name into disrepute and was forced to run away to save her shameful condition being made public. Is it any wonder I have felt nothing but pain and resentment at having to bring up her child?" She indicated Venetia, who looked as if she were about to faint as she gripped the basket, which was suspended a foot from the ground.

The crowd shifted uneasily, murmurs of uncertainty passing among them. Some nodded in sympathy with Mrs. Pike's tale, their expressions hardening as they glanced accusingly at Rothbury. Others exchanged skeptical glances, eyes narrowing as they perhaps recalled past instances of Mrs. Pike's less-than-honest dealings. The Dowager Duchess of Richmond pressed her lips together in a thin line of suspicion, while young Lord Darcy whispered something to his companion that made the latter's eyebrows rise in surprise.

"No, Mrs. Pike, you were never formally engaged to Miss Playford's father. While I understand that certain letters between the two of you have been read by Miss Playford which certainly attest to the fact that you were once sweethearts, the correspondence I discovered amongst my father's papers indicate that the relationship was severed by Richard Playford after you were discovered stealing money from his desk. You then attempted to blackmail him with falsehoods about his family's business dealings."

"Lies, lies, lies!" cried Mrs. Pike, but her demeanor lacked the conviction of someone truly blameless, Caroline saw with a thrill as Henry gripped her hand tighter.

And as the attention of everyone was so firmly upon the

drama being played out before them, Caroline boldly raised her hand to cup his cheek. The look he slanted down at her was filled with such love she thought she would melt in a puddle on the spot.

"Caroline," he whispered, putting his cheek to hers. "This is your doing, you realize." His breath was warm and sweet. His words of admiration, even sweeter. "You are the real heroine this evening."

And suddenly Caroline felt that the future she had dreamed of really might come to be.

But the combat was not over. Lord Windermere stood his ground, his hand resting in a savage and proprietorial manner upon Venetia's shoulder.

Meanwhile, Mrs. Pike was still shrieking her defense to the crowd.

Lies, which Mr. Rothbury countered at every turn.

"Everything I claim can be substantiated." He tapped the leather satchel on the pommel in front of him. "You are the one who has been telling lies, Mrs. Pike. Yes, telling the world that Venetia Playford was penniless, that she had no dowry, that you cared for her out of charity, out of the goodness of your heart. But there was no goodness in your heart. In fact, that was the very reason Richard Playford switched his allegiance to your younger sister, to Cassandra Pike, who, I hasten to assure everyone, married him on the Continent well before the birth of their only child whom you see before you." He indicated Venetia with a sweep of his hand. Silent and in obvious shock, she stood trembling in the basket, her face drained of color yet somehow luminous with hope, while Windermere's features had hardened into a mask of fury, his eyes darting between Rothbury and the rope tethering the balloon as if weighing his chances of escape.

"All of this has no bearing on the fact that Miss Playford has consented to be my wife," Lord Windermere now said, his voice cutting through the murmur of the crowd. He took her hand and raised it to the sky, turning slightly to smile menacingly at the aeronaut. "I said, for God's sake, untether this balloon."

"Do not obey, sir, for I have not yet finished."

Caroline had to admit that Mr. Rothbury was rather impressive when push came to shove. He had seemed such a mild-mannered man, unwilling to intervene when she and Amelia had first approached him, but clearly, he had worked tirelessly to secure the information that would prevent Venetia's future being placed into unscrupulous hands.

He raised his voice but the crowd was already quiet.

He had promised them more, after all. As if what had played out was not exciting enough.

"I have news to impart, that as of this very evening—"

"News that pales into insignificance when compared with the joyful fact that tonight Miss Playford consented to be my wife!" Lord Windermere interrupted to a volley of gasps.

"Might I remind everyone that while Miss Playford may have been provided for in her earlier years," Windermere went on, almost shouting to be heard, "I have nevertheless been prepared to wed a young lady who has no dowry." He nodded at the quieting crowd. "Yes, her father's funds were exhausted after her schooling, but I care nothing for that, as I feel only the greatest love for such an admirable paragon of virtue."

"Not true!"

Caroline put her hand to her mouth in shock as her brother, Sir Frederick, materialized amongst the crowd. When had he arrived back from his country estates? He'd all but dismissed Caroline's assertions as the ravings of a lunatic.

But now he was here and adding his weight to Mr. Rothbury's claims.

"For reasons unknown, Windermere was determined to wed Miss Playford," Frederick went on. "And he was, in fact, so determined that he used every means possible to tarnish the reputation of my old friend and neighbor, Mr. Henry Ashworth, in order to sever his betrothal to Miss Playford."

"Good Lord," Caroline heard Lady Townsend murmur to her

friend Lady Pendleton, who nodded with undisguised satisfaction, her eyes gleaming with the vindication of long-held suspicions. "Even Sir Frederick says it true."

"My good wife," Sir Frederick continued, "who is unable to be here this evening for very happy reasons, went herself to quiz the mysterious so-called 'princess' who apparently was wronged by Mr. Ashworth. And who do you suppose this supposed princess was? Why, it was an actress James Barnaby paid to create the impression that Henry was a philanderer." Frederick's voice rang with righteous indignation. "And when further scurrilous methods were needed to discredit poor Henry, Mr. Barnaby forged bank records, which he then claimed were in Henry's hand and at his request. All these efforts were to discredit Henry Ashworth so that Miss Playford would be *forced* to call off her marriage to him so that Lord Windermere could then take control of the fortune he hoped she might one day inherit."

Clenching his fist and shaking it at Mr. Rothbury, Lord Windermere's eyes were dark as flint. "None of it is true!"

"It's all true!" Charlotte's voice cut through the murmurs, clear and resolute as she stepped forward, her face pale, her expression frightened but determined. "I overheard Barnaby speak about this plot to discredit Henry by paying an actress to pretend she was a maligned Hungarian princess whose broken heart she laid at my brother's door. At the time, I believed everything, because Barnaby made life unpleasant if I did not." She narrowed her eyes as she raked him with her disgust. "Then he threatened that my brother would face worse if I spoke a word. I was a coward, and for that, I can never fully atone, but I speak the truth now." Her voice broke and Caroline shivered in Henry's arms.

Finally, Charlotte had proven herself.

Barnaby's defamation was complete, his face a picture of thwarted fury as guests drew back from him as if his shame were contagious.

"Why go to such trouble if Miss Playford were penniless and

may not have inherited a penny?"

Someone had to ask the obvious question, and Caroline craned her head to see that Lord Thornton had spoken. He stood tall beside Lady Townsend, his hand resting lightly on her arm in a gesture of solidarity.

Mr. Rothbury's horse snorted and shifted restlessly, but it was his words that cut through the most.

"Ah, yes, for therein lies the very heart of the entire evil plan hatched between Mrs. Pike, Mr. Barnaby, and Lord Windermere."

Caroline heard Henry's breath hitch in his throat as he tensed. Yes, this was at the very heart of it. Caroline could scarcely breathe. Mr. Rothbury had raced hell for leather for news that would determine Venetia's future. News that would hopefully prevent Venetia from being whisked away by Lord Windermere or forced to remain with her aunt.

What had been the outcome?

"I am here to impart the very happy news that Miss Venetia Playford is now an heiress upon the death last night of her great-uncle, Mr. Leonard Harrington."

A gasp rippled through the crowd, followed by a wave of exclamations. Ladies clutched their companions' arms in shock, while gentlemen exchanged shocked glances. Even the normally impassive servants reacted, eyes widening as they absorbed the significance of such an announcement. Harrington was one of the wealthiest landowners in Bedfordshire, his fortune second only to that of John Russel, the 6th Duke of Bedford; and Harrington's home, Harrington Hall, second only to the Duke of Bedford's Woburn Abbey.

"No!" shrieked Mrs. Pike. "You lie!"

"Yes, lies! Nothing but an elaborate fabrication!" Lord Windermere snapped, pushing the aeronaut out of his way and leaning out of the basket to untie the rope.

But it was Barnaby's reaction that elicited the greatest shock amongst the onlookers as he lunged for the rope, his hands grasping for Venetia, his rage, for the moment unchecked as he howled, "You stole my inheritance, you Jezebel! I was his closest male relative! That money is mine!"

"Not so fast!" Henry cried, dropping Caroline's hand to rush forward. He lunged for Barnaby, pulling him back from the rope just as Windermere was about to sever it.

Mr. Rothbury, however, was faster. He leaped from his horse to deal with Barnaby, the two men struggling on the ground, while Henry battled to dislodge the knife from Windermere's hand.

The basket swayed precariously, causing Venetia to cry out in alarm. Then finally, with one powerful movement, Henry wrenched the knife from Windermere's grasp and flung it away, before bodily pulling the man from the basket.

Guests screamed as the two adversaries tumbled onto the grass in an undignified heap. The aeronaut, meanwhile, recovering from his surprise, quickly helped Venetia to safety, lifting her from the swaying basket and setting her gently on solid ground.

Caroline didn't know where to look: at Mr. Rothbury, who'd just dealt Barnaby an uppercut to the jaw before standing, as if shocked at his actions, while the other man cowered on his knees.

Or Henry in mortal combat with Windermere… before that man, too, seemed to realize his aesthetic physique was no match for Henry, clearly ready to fight to the death, and raised his hands in silent surrender.

The crowd was suddenly silent. Caroline could understand why. She was just as shocked. She glanced about her and saw their expressions: as if they had just witnessed a public execution. Some looked genuinely upset—perhaps those who counted Mrs. Pike, Lord Windermere, or James Barnaby amongst their friends. Others bit their lips, their eyes gleaming as if they had just been treated to the most wickedly delicious scandal of their lives.

Nobody, it seemed, knew how to respond.

Until Lady Townsend stepped forward, balancing herself upon a small step beside the balloon, its basket now empty.

"Ladies and gentlemen!" She clapped her hands to gain their attention. "I promised that this evening would culminate in the ascent of a lucky pair whose names would be drawn from my purple toque." With a grand gesture, she extended her hand holding the feathered headdress, from which she withdrew a piece of vellum and read in ringing tones, "Mr. Henry Ashworth and Miss Venetia Playford."

A murmur of surprise rippled through the crowd at this unexpected return to the planned festivities after such dramatic revelations. Some applauded uncertainly, while others exchanged confused glances, unsure if the announcement was in earnest or merely a ploy to restore order to the chaotic scene.

With a gasp, Caroline put her hands to her mouth. She couldn't believe it. Henry was actually stepping forward and climbing into the basket while half the crowd turned to look for Venetia, who stood frozen beside Mr. Rothbury, her face a study in conflicting emotions.

So… it had come to this? Lady Townsend really was determined to back her original pair?

Caroline's heart constricted painfully, a hollow sensation spreading through her chest. After all that had happened, after the truth had finally come to light, was she still about to lose Henry to duty and circumstance? She blinked rapidly, determined not to display her distress before the assembled company, though she felt as if the ground might open beneath her feet at any moment.

"Lady Townsend—" Henry, who was now slightly elevated, smiled at their hostess, who looked enormously pleased with herself. "Good fortune has favored me twice tonight, and I feel presumptuous in making this small request, but I truly think that if I at least ask, then I will make Miss Playford very happy, but someone else even happier." He glanced at Caroline and it was as if he communicated all the love and reassurance with which he'd bolstered her. Closing her eyes briefly, she allowed in hope once more.

Lady Townsend frowned. "Mr. Ashworth, this is a lottery.

Your names have been called, and of course, a chaperone will naturally accompany you." Her smile, however, trembled slightly. "It is the most wonderful opportunity for Miss Playford to see the world from above and to enjoy it in the company of the young man who has proved himself her real hero tonight."

A ripple of applause greeted her words, and Caroline felt the pain of loss pierce her heart like a physical wound, sharp and sudden, replacing her burst of hope, stealing her breath and clouding her vision with unshed tears.

There was no way out, it seemed.

Still addressing the crowd from the slightly elevated basket of the balloon, Henry went on, "While I am honored to escort Miss Playford—Oh!"

For suddenly, Lady Townsend's position at the top of the small ladder was being usurped by Venetia, who'd burst across the clearing and was standing on tiptoe to whisper something in Henry's ear.

Caroline gripped her pearls, frowning to make sense of the scene.

Was the vibrant, determined Venetia of earlier days suddenly back?

"Ladies and gentlemen!" Henry clapped his hands for silence and immediately it was granted. The whole crowd wanted to understand what Henry's former fiancée—who had now been restored to him—would wish him to convey.

"It is my great pleasure to inform you all that I have just received blessings from London's most notable heiress to take my future wife, Miss Caroline Weston, up in Lady Townsend's balloon tonight." With a deep bow towards his hostess, he raised his eyebrows and enquired, "Provided the new pairing meets with her approval."

"Good Lord!" came Caroline's mother's outraged tones as Caroline stepped forward, joy spreading through her body as she took in the first smile from her friend Venetia that she had seen in many a long month.

Venetia's voice wavered but the truth was clear to all as silence descended upon the crowd and she said from her elevated position, "Caroline is the one who deserves to be with Henry. For so long I have been caught up in the misery of trying to avoid the plan my aunt had hatched with Lord Windermere to force me to marry him that I did not see what was under my very nose: that Caroline and Henry have always loved each other. Please, Lady Townsend, may I rescind this very great honor and would you allow my dearest, dearest friend Caroline enjoy the trip of a lifetime, floating in a balloon with, as we must all surely call him, one of tonight's real heroes—Henry?" She glanced at Mr. Rothbury, before adding, "While I convey my thanks to Mr. Rothbury."

Caroline didn't know she was holding her breath until Lady Townsend, with a rather dazed look, first at Henry, then at Lord Thornton beside her, slowly smiled, then nodded.

"I organized this evening to play matchmaker," she said quietly but clearly, looking, Caroline noticed, at Lord Thornton. "After all, it was due to my success in matching Caroline's brother with his lovely wife, Miss Amelia Fairchild, that I was emboldened to try my hand again. No two brighter, deserving, and well-matched souls could I imagine uniting in matrimony than the delightful Miss Playford, whom I was charmed to meet several years ago at Lady Pendleton's Ghostly Gathering, and Mr. Henry Ashworth." She paused, her gaze sweeping the crowd with the confidence of a natural performer commanding her audience's attention.

"But matchmaking is not a frivolous undertaking. And it is certainly not for the faint-hearted," she went on. "I take the responsibility extremely seriously, for though I have never married, I believe that the greatest joy two people of like minds can share is to be united in the bonds of holy matrimony."

Caroline was by the basket now. Lady Townsend had all but given her approbation, but her words were important. They were important for the crowd to understand that true love was a serious business. It was important for her mother to understand that while society had its rules, matters of the heart were not frivolous matters.

The gathered company had fallen into a respectful silence, sensing the gravity beneath Lady Townsend's light tone. Even the most hardened cynics among them seemed moved by the unexpected turn of events, by the triumph of truth and love over deception and greed. In the fading light, with the even brighter stars appearing in the sky, there was a sense of rightness, of balance restored.

"And so it gives me great pleasure to announce that the two winners of tonight's celestial comet viewing are Mr. Henry Ashworth and Miss Caroline Weston, with naturally a chaperone. Lady Weston, please step forward," finished Lady Townsend to loud applause.

"No, no, I wouldn't go near that contraption if you paid me!" objected Lady Weston, fanning herself and beckoning to her son. She seemed too dazed to comment any further, and certainly not on the public declaration of Henry's reciprocal love for Caroline.

Sir Frederick stepped forward with a smile, but just as he reached the basket, Henry gave the rope a sudden, decisive tug. The heavy hemp slipped through the aeronaut's startled fingers, and with a gentle lurch, the balloon began to rise, already beyond the reach of anyone on the ground. The basket swayed gracefully as it ascended, bearing only Henry and Caroline aloft—and the dazed aeronaut—into the deepening twilight, while a collective gasp rose from the crowd, followed by laughter and cheers as the young couple's daring escape—no, elopement, perhaps— registered.

"I believe we've been outmaneuvered," Sir Frederick called up good-naturedly as the balloon continued its stately ascent.

Caroline leaned over the edge of the basket, her face illumi- nated by joy as she waved to the diminishing figures below. Henry's arm circled her waist, drawing her close as they rose higher, the lights of London spreading out beneath them like stars fallen to earth. In the eastern sky, the promised comet had appeared, its silver trail blazing across the heavens—a celestial blessing on new beginnings, on truth revealed, and love triumphant.

"I scarcely dared believe such joy would come to pass," Caroline whispered, as she tilted her head to smile up at Henry, whose hand upon the small of her back gave her all the grounding she needed—for now and the future. "All my life I've been chided for being a hoyden, a frivolous child who'd never grow up. But I've never felt more grown up, Henry."

"Don't grow up too much, Caroline, because I like you just the way you are," murmured Henry. "When you're my wife, promise me you won't change and become serious? Because—" touching his lips gently to hers, he added, "—didn't I once tell you that fortune favors the frivolous?"

Caroline drew in a quavering breath. "Oh, Henry," she whispered, on a half laugh. "That horse just bolted. You could have had your fortune, but you let Bedfordshire's most notable heiress slip through your fingers." She closed her eyes and put her cheek to his, sighing in pure pleasure as he held her tighter. "So, since I can't offer you a fortune," she went on, "as compensation, I promise you a lifetime of frivolity."

Chapter Forty-One

LADY EUGENIA TOWNSEND sipped her tea slowly, savoring the delicate Darjeeling as she gazed out over her garden. From her favorite spot in the morning room, she could see the rosebushes beginning to bloom, their vibrant colors a stark contrast to the pale blue of the spring sky beyond.

"I must say, Eugenia, you appear remarkably composed for a woman who is about to lose a valuable painting," Lady Pendleton remarked, settling her spindly frame more comfortably in the armchair opposite.

"Do I?" Eugenia responded with a smile. "I suppose I find it difficult to be entirely displeased when the outcome has brought such happiness to Miss Playford."

Lady Pendleton looked thoughtful. "Quite a transformation from the penniless girl we once knew to one of the wealthiest heiresses in the county!"

Eugenia allowed herself a small smile. "Fortune is indeed a capricious mistress. Who could have imagined that quiet little Venetia would emerge not only wealthy beyond measure but as the heroine of the most dramatic scene ever to grace a comet viewing party?"

"Not I," admitted Lady Pendleton, dabbing at the corner of her mouth with a lace-trimmed napkin. "And certainly not Mrs.

Pike, who I understand has retreated to Bath to escape the scandal. Though how one escapes such notoriety when Bath is the very epicenter of gossip is beyond my comprehension."

The butler appeared at the doorway to announce, "Lord Thornton, my lady."

Eugenia felt that familiar flutter beneath her bodice—the one she had battled for more than thirty years whenever Thornton entered a room. She watched him stride in, resplendent in a bottle-green coat that accentuated his broad shoulders. The silver in his hair caught the morning light, and Eugenia found herself quite unable to look away.

"Ladies," he said with a bow, his eyes lingering on Eugenia's face. "I trust I find you well?"

"Very well, thank you, Thornton." Lady Pendleton gestured to the settee. "We were just discussing the most extraordinary developments regarding Miss Playford."

"Ah yes," Thornton accepted the cup of tea Eugenia poured for him, their fingers brushing momentarily in the exchange. "A most fortunate young lady in more ways than one. It's not every day one not only comes into a substantial inheritance, but is spared marriage to a villainous kidnapper who is now—I came to tell you specially—ensconced in the Marshals debtors' prison."

"And all thanks to Mr. Rothbury's timely intervention," Eugenia added, clapping her hands. "I confess, I did not take proper notice of that gentleman before. So unassuming, yet so decisive when the moment demanded action."

Lady Pendleton sniffed. "I always thought him a sensible sort. Not given to the excessive displays one sees in younger men these days, but steady. Precisely the sort of man a young heiress might need to guide her through the pitfalls of her new station."

Eugenia caught the gleam in Thornton's eye and knew he, too, had detected Lady Pendleton's shift. How quickly the good lady had adjusted her assessment now that Venetia's circumstances had changed!

"I wonder," said Eugenia, setting down her teacup, "if Mr.

Rothbury will present himself as a suitor now that Miss Harrington's circumstances have so dramatically altered."

Thornton leaned back, crossing one leg over the other. "That, my dear Eugenia, is the very question I came to discuss with you today. For I have it on good authority that Mr. Rothbury has withdrawn from London society entirely. One rumor has it that he plans to go to sea again. Another, that he intends to take up a post in Italy translating a nobleman's library of Sir Walter Scott novels."

"Withdrawn from society?" Lady Pendleton echoed. "But why would he do such a thing when every door would now be open to him as the hero of the hour?"

"I believe," Thornton said slowly, his eyes never leaving Eugenia's face, "that the gentleman fears his motives would be misconstrued should he express any interest in Miss Playford now. Having performed such a service for her, he is acutely aware that any attention might be perceived as fortune hunting."

"How absurd!" Lady Pendleton exclaimed. "The man saved her from ruination. One would argue that it was at great personal risk, even given the black eye he sported for some time following that unseemly tussle with Mr. Barnaby. Surely no one would question his honor?"

"Society can be cruel," Eugenia murmured, thinking of the many times she herself had been the subject of speculation. How many seasons had she endured whispers behind fans about why the wealthy Lady Townsend remained unwed? How many pointed comments had she weathered about her advancing years making her an object of pity rather than pursuit?

"And Miss Playford?" she asked, forcing herself to focus on the present. "How is she enjoying her newfound independence?"

"Like a bird unexpectedly freed from its cage," Thornton replied. "She has taken up residence at Harrington Hall and, by all accounts, is reveling in her liberty. I hear she has even spoken of establishing a salon for intellectual discussion, much in the manner you once did, Eugenia. She is very changed from the vivacious debutante I remember from your famed Ghostly Gathering, Lady Pendleton."

"Changed, indeed?" Eugenia couldn't help but feel a surge of pride. "How delightful to think of Harrington Hall filled with lively minds rather than dusty traditions."

"Perhaps another bluestocking in the making," Lady Pendleton observed, though her tone lacked its usual disapproval. "Still, a woman needs a husband, especially with such extensive properties to manage."

"Does she?" Eugenia challenged gently. "I have managed quite well without one."

"I dare say," Lady Pendleton said, dubiously.

Thornton cleared his throat. "Which brings me to the matter of our wager, Lady Townsend."

Ah, here it was at last. Eugenia straightened. "Yes, Lord Thornton. I hope you are prepared to honor our agreement. Miss Playford did not, after all, wed Lord Windermere."

"Indeed, she did not," Thornton agreed, his eyes twinkling with an expression Eugenia couldn't quite decipher. "Though you cannot claim full victory, as she has not wed Mr. Henry Ashworth either."

"A technicality," Lady Pendleton interjected. "The young man clearly had eyes only for Miss Caroline Weston all along."

"Precisely why I propose an amendment to our settlement," Thornton continued. "The terms of our wager stated that if Miss Playford wed Lord Windermere, the Persephone painting would be mine. However, as neither of us correctly predicted the ultimate outcome, I suggest a compromise."

Eugenia leaned forward, her curiosity piqued. "Compromise, my lord?"

Thornton reached into his coat and withdrew a folded document, placing it on the table between them. "This, my dear Eugenia, is my proposal."

With slightly trembling fingers, Eugenia unfolded the paper. As she read, her eyes widened, and she looked up at Thornton in astonishment. "You cannot be serious."

"I assure you, I am entirely serious," he replied, his expression now earnest. "I have secured passage for two on the *Neptune's Folly*, departing for Venice next month. The journey includes stops at several Mediterranean ports, with ample opportunity to explore ancient ruins and historical sites."

"Venice!" Eugenia breathed, her heart quickening at the thought. "I have long wished to see the floating city."

"I know," Thornton said simply. "You spoke of it that day in the balloon."

"What exactly are you proposing, Thornton?" Lady Pendleton asked.

"I propose that instead of enjoying Eugenia's Persephone on my wall, that I enjoy Eugenia's company on this voyage. The painting can remain where it has always been—where it can be appreciated by both of us… on my visits here."

Eugenia felt heat rise to her cheeks at the curious tone of his voice.

But it was Lady Pendleton who interjected. "Such an undertaking would be quite improper without—"

"A chaperone? I have thought of that," Thornton assured her. "My sister-in-law has expressed interest in the journey and would be delighted to accompany us. You remember Catherine, I believe?"

Catherine. The cousin of Elizabeth, the woman who had married Thornton while Eugenia nursed her secret love in silence. Never having married, she was to chaperone them on an adventure that promised everything Eugenia had ever longed for?

But no doubt Catherine would be a constant reminder of Thornton's late wife, for Catherine and Elizabeth had grown up in the same household as sisters rather than cousins.

"I remember her well," Eugenia managed, her composure strained but intact.

Lady Pendleton leaned back. "Well, Eugenia? Will you accept this most unusual settlement? I'm not sure you would do well in rough swells. Are you not prone to being seasick?"

"Why should you think that when I've never been seasick in my life?" Eugenia challenged, looking down at the itinerary again, her heart racing at the possibilities it presented. Then she raised her eyes to meet Thornton's, seeing in them not merely the offer of an adventure, but something deeper—a second chance at what might have been.

And something unfurled within her—a hope she had long ago buried beneath layers of pragmatism and independence. She had built a life for herself, a good life filled with intellectual pursuits and the freedom to follow her own path. But how much richer might that life be with a companion who valued that independence rather than seeking to curtail it?

"What say you, Eugenia?" Thornton pressed gently. "Will you accept my terms?"

Lady Pendleton fidgeted impatiently. "For heaven's sake, Eugenia, you never could make up your mind."

Eugenia laughed, the tension of the moment broken by her friend's characteristic bluntness. "Oh, I think I have at least improved since my own experience of floating above London helped me see life through a different lens. And to realize that life is too short not to seize it with both hands."

Eugenia thought of Venetia, now mistress of her own destiny, free to chart her course just as Eugenia herself had done. She thought of Mr. Rothbury, withdrawing from society rather than risk being seen as pursuing Venetia's fortune, despite having saved her from a terrible fate.

Perhaps, she mused, they too needed someone to show them that love and independence need not be mutually exclusive—that the greatest adventure of all might be finding someone who cherished both one's strength *and* vulnerability.

"My lord," she said finally, extending her hand to Thornton, "I accept your terms. Though I warn you, I intend to sketch every ruin and marvel we encounter, no matter how long it delays our progress."

"Bravo!" Thornton's face lit with delight as he took her hand, pressing it warmly between both of his. "I would expect nothing less, my dear Eugenia. Nothing less."

Lady Pendleton sighed dramatically. "She will drive you mad, Thornton," she predicted. "Why, sketch every ruin when a quick glance would be good enough for me." With a harrumph, she added, "Anyway, I think the matter of your next matchmaking project is settled, Eugenia. When you return to England, Miss Playford and Mr. Rothbury will require someone with your particular talents to overcome their current impasse."

"Indeed," Eugenia agreed, her mind already spinning with possibilities as she gazed at Thornton. "Though perhaps I shall pursue my matchmaking from a gondola in Venice rather than a drawing room in London."

"A novel approach," Thornton agreed, seeming to realize suddenly that he was still holding her hand. He dropped it quickly, adding, "But then, you have always taken a novel approach towards life, Eugenia, which augurs well when it comes to being a travel companion."

Eugenia felt her heart soar like a balloon cut free from its tethers, rising towards limitless skies. Yes, she thought, she would help Venetia find her way to happiness with Mr. Rothbury. But first, she would embrace her own adventure—one that had been thirty years in the making.

Thornton had not proposed. He'd been careful to ensure the proprieties and to couch his suggestion in terms that preserved the friendship between them rather than hinting too greatly at romantic overtures.

But the possibilities were there, she thought, her heart missing a beat.

"To Venice, then," she said, raising her teacup in a toast.

"To Venice," Thornton echoed, and Eugenia couldn't be sure, but she did wonder if the expression in his eyes promised more than merely a journey across the sea.

Outside, spring sunlight danced across the garden, illuminating the roses in a warm, golden glow. Just as the balloon had lifted Caroline and Henry towards their future together, so too would a ship soon carry Eugenia and Thornton towards theirs.

And somewhere in Bedfordshire, a newly minted heiress was discovering the freedom that comes with independence, even as she perhaps wondered about the gentleman who had championed her cause and then disappeared from view.

THE END

Beverley Oakley is an Australian author of more than 30 Regency romps, and Victorian and Georgian-set romances laced with mystery and intrigue.

Under her other pen names—Beverley Eikli and B.G. Nettelton—she writes Africa-set romantic suspense and Women's Fiction.

Born in the African mountain kingdom of Lesotho, Beverley married the handsome Norwegian bush pilot she met in Botswana's beautiful Okavango Delta while managing a safari lodge.

She began her writing career as a journalist, but it was during long aerial survey contracts around the world—typically as the sole woman among the crew—that she in effect launched her romance novels, finding in them an escape from the isolation.

Beverley also adores making historical costumes, knitting, and travelling, usually to Norway to visit her older daughter.

She lives just north of Melbourne with the same wonderful husband she whisked away from Botswana thirty years ago, together with their youngest daughter, and a gorgeous, dopey Rhodesian Ridgeback who weighs more than she does.

When she's not writing, she runs a bed & breakfast & Farmstay business (called *Wuthering Heights*) in South Australia's beautiful wine growing Clare Valley with her two sisters.

You can visit her websites at:
www.beverleyoakley.com or www.beverleysbooks.com

You can also find her at:
facebook.com/AuthorBeverleyOakley
instagram.com/Beverley.Oakley
TikTok: @beverleyoakley